GOODBYE, RUDY KAZOODY

AA FREDA

WESTPOINT
PRINT AND MEDIA

CHAPTER 1

A Sleepwalker

Dunk the pail, fill it up, pass it on. Dunk the pail, fill it up, pass it on. The grueling task of bailing water out of the ship's bottom takes on a rhythmic, musical quality. One of the boys on the bucket brigade must have similar thoughts, because he begins singing an old, familiar pirate song. The others in the queue chime in, increasing the pace of their work to match the song's beat.

We're making progress. The water level at the bottom of the boat, which was up to my knees, is only ankle high. The repair of the bilge pump helped. Without the pump, our line could never have kept up with the water gushing through the hole in the hull of the old vessel. Someone nailed a tarp over the gap in a futile attempt to block the incoming water, but it isn't much help. Water still pours into the galley through the sides of the tarp. The bobbing motion of the craft, which made me sick earlier, is almost bearable now. I feel a tug on my shirt. I look behind, and it's Betty, water streaming down her face from the hood of her poncho.

"Anthony wants to see you atop!" she yells into my ear, wiping the water from her face with the back of her hand.

"What for?"

"I don't know. He asked me to come get you. You'll need this."

She hands me a poncho.

1

I turn to one of the boys on break. "Aldo, take my place in line! I have to go with Betty!"

Betty scurries up the wet metal steps the instant Aldo relieves me, so sure-footed she doesn't bother holding onto the banister. Having no such skills, I clutch the guardrail with each step. The moment my head lifts above the hatch, the driving rain hits me in the face, compelling me to pull the face cord of my poncho tighter.

As I climb on deck, the ship lurches to one side, knocking me into the ship's rail. I reach for the railing, but my hand slips off the wet surface. At that moment, a wave lifts the boat into the air, knocking me off my feet and sending me sliding down the deck on my back. Luckily, my right foot jams into a scupper, ending my trip down the boat. Before I can get to my feet, another wave engulfs the boat. Completely submerged, I lose my bearings. A hand grasps my collar and yanks me to my feet.

"Hold on to the lifeline along the side and follow me!" Betty shouts before releasing her grip.

Clutching the precious rope, I inch forward behind Betty, tilting my head down to shield my eyes from the driving rain, which appears to be coming sideways. I can't believe the change in weather. A half hour earlier, the sun was shining. The squall came out of nowhere, catching us by surprise. Finally, I reach the stairway leading to the bridge.

Gripping both guardrails, I make my way upstairs. Another wave slams into the boat, and my feet slide out from under me. Clutching the rails, I regain my footing and scurry up the steps. Once atop, Betty holds the pilothouse door open. Inside, Spike is at the helm. Judy is sitting on the floor in the corner with her head resting against the wall. She looks awful, all the color has drained from her face. Betty hands me a towel as I knock back the hood of my poncho.

"What's the matter with you?" I ask Judy.

"Ooh, I'm so sick," she moans.

"Leave her alone, and come here; she's just seasick," Spike says. "Are you all right?"

"I've been better," I reply as I dry myself. "How are we doing?"

"Not good. Going against the current is a slow process."

"Why don't you turn the boat about and head down river?"

"The current is so strong. I'd have no control of the ship. I'm afraid we'd crash into the riverbank."

I look out the window. "Do you think the storm will blow over soon?"

Spike shrugs. "It's hard to say. Sometimes these squalls pass as quickly as they come. It doesn't matter, though. The river will continue rising for hours after the storm ends."

At that moment, a wave lifts the ship and heaves her to the side, causing the wheel to spin out of Spike's hands. The vessel's beam broaches the wave, putting the ship in danger of capsizing. When the boat comes to rest, it's heading toward the shoreline. Spike grabs the wheel and swings the craft around, narrowly missing the riverbank.

"Whew, that was close!" I exclaim once Spike regains control. "I thought we were done for!"

"Let the stupid boat sink!" Judy yells from the corner. "Drowning can't possibly be worse than how I feel."

"Listen, I have an assignment for you," Spike says to me, ignoring Judy's outburst. "It's kind of dangerous, but it's important. We're coming to a spot on the river where the riverbank rises almost to the height of the ship. The water near the shore is very deep. I'm getting the boat as close to the bank as possible, say within five or ten feet. When we pass by that spot, I want you to jump and land ashore. There's a bridge spanning the river just north of that spot. That's the main road to a small town. I need you to go to that town and get help."

"Why can't we just ride out the storm?" I ask. "I'd rather ride it out with you, Betty, Judy, and the guys."

Spike looks over at Betty. "You see what I mean, Betty? Make one mistake, and everybody second guesses you." He turns back to me. "I'm sorry I screwed up. I thought I could outrun the storm. The weather turned faster than I anticipated, but now I need your help. There's a hairline crack in the hull, port side. It begins where the hole is in the bow and heads astern. The ship won't last long. One more good wave, and it'll come apart."

He nods out the window. "Soon, we'll reach a small island just past that bridge I told you about. The island has a sheltered cove with a sandy beach. My plan is to run the ship aground there. We'll disembark and try to ride out the storm on the island until you get back with help. Try not to take long. The way the river is rising, the island could be under water soon."

Spike looks me straight in the eyes. "Are you going to help, or are you going to be your usual self, on the sidelines looking in?"

I pause for a moment before nodding. "I'll do it. Which side will I be jumping from? Did you say port side?"

"No, starboard. Betty will go down with you and show you the way. You better get going; we're almost there."

I reach into a locker and pull out a life jacket. As I'm strapping it on, I notice a big grin on Spike's face.

"What's so funny?" I ask.

He shrugs. "Nothing." His smile is noticeably wider.

I pull the hood of my poncho over my head, tie it in place, and follow Betty out. She leads me down the steps amidships, unhinges the rail of the gangway, and turns to me.

"Move back a little so you can get a running start. I'll signal when it's time to jump. Try to jump as far as you can. I'll try to time my signal so you leap when the ship is at the crest of the wave. Good luck!"

She kisses me on the cheek. Her lips are ice cold. Moving back about ten feet, I crouch down to await Betty's signal. I make the sign of the cross and pray my jump will reach land. The raging water sends shivers down my spine. Suddenly, Spike's joke comes to me. The life jacket will do nothing if I don't clear the river. If I don't make land, staying afloat will be the least of my problems. With that realization, I remove the cumbersome jacket and drop it to the deck. It will only hamper my jump anyway.

"Now," Betty screams!

Startled by her shout, I run and leap into the darkness. Unbelievably, I land on shore, face down into the mud. It takes a moment to gather myself. Wiping the muck from my eyes, I look upriver for the boat, but it's already out of sight. I pray for their safety. It's up to Spike to bring them through; it's totally under his control. I pause to take stock of my whereabouts.

I'm on a small piece of land that juts out into the river like a peninsula, surrounded by water on three sides. If I had landed a few feet to my right or left, I would have fallen into the icy water. An embankment about eight feet high is in front of me. The outline of the bridge, some two hundred yards to my left, is barely visible.

Leaping to my feet, I climb up the embankment, not getting more than a couple of feet up the muddy slope before I slide back down. The riverbank is so slippery it's impossible to get a hold. I try again, this time reaching within inches of the top before sliding back down. Moving back to the edge of the shoreline to get a running start, I make a mad dash up the cliff, only to fall a few inches short once again. If only I were a little taller.

As I pick myself up and wipe the mud off my hands and face, I gaze up at the summit and see a bizarre sight that takes me aback. A man is standing at the top dressed in black, a large Stetson on his head. How can he keep that hat on his head in such a storm? He kneels down and, without saying a word, stretches his arm toward me.

Hesitating, I gaze at the stranger to get a better gauge of him. Should I trust him? His face seems curiously familiar. From a distance, I hear banging, like someone is knocking at a door. A muffed sound of a boy screaming follows the noise. Has something happened to the boat?

"Come on, give me your hand," the stranger says in a deep southern drawl. "I'll help you up."

I can't afford to waste any more time. Grabbing his outstretched hand, he yanks me toward him. Digging my foot into the side of the cliff and giving a final heave, I land on top, face down in the mud once again. A faint sound is coming from the distance, like someone is singing, it's accompanied by garbled shouts. Again, I wipe the mud from my eyes.

The stranger is staring, smiling, his tanned face somewhat familiar, and then it hits me: It's the buckaroo, Buck Owens!

Abruptly, I wake up from my nightmare, gasping for air. Despite the coolness of the night, I'm soaked in my own sweat. I decide that's the last time I'm eating a whole bag of Chips Ahoy cookies with a quart of milk before going to bed. A moment passes before I become aware of the loud music coming through my bedroom window from downstairs. It's a Buck Owens record.

People are shouting out their apartment windows. "Turn the damn music off! Don't you know what time it is?"

The clock on my end table shows 4:10 a.m. Who could be playing music so loud at this hour? There's banging at my front door.

"Uncle Sal! Uncle Sal! Wake up, we need you downstairs," my cousin Vito yells for my father. "Please, Uncle Sal, wake up. We need you!"

Now fully awake and alert, I leap out of bed and run out of my room to see what's wrong. My parents and sister are already in the hall.

"What's the matter?" my father asks Vito when he opens the door.

"It's Spike. He's sleepwalking. He's locked himself in the clubhouse and is blasting music," Vito explains, rushing to get the words out. "Mom needs you to come downstairs right away!"

"Just give me a second to get my coat, and I'll come down with you," my father says.

I run back in my room for my jacket, throw it over my pajamas, to follow my dad and Vito downstairs.

"Where in the world do you think you're going?" my mother cries.

"With them!"

"Oh no, you're not. It's four in the morning, and you've got school tomorrow. Go back to sleep!"

Just then, my dad comes out of his room and heads out of the apartment, followed by Vito. I bolt after them before my mother has a chance to protest any further. When we reach the courtyard, Aunt Lucy and several of the neighbors are standing in front of the clubhouse door. Inside, Spike has the phonograph volume cranked. The song is the same country tune I heard earlier.

"What happened?" my father asks Aunt Lucy when we get there.

"I don't know!" she shouts over the music. "I was sleeping when I heard the music coming from downstairs. When I looked into Anthony's room, I noticed he wasn't there. That's when I realized he must be the one in the clubhouse playing the record. When I got down here, the door was locked, and Anthony wouldn't answer."

"Does anybody have a key?" my father yells at the people in the courtyard.

"It's bolted from the other side," one of the onlookers replies. "And the metal door is too heavy to break down."

I run over to the other side of the building where a window affords a view into the clubhouse. Pulling a garbage can under the window, I climb on top to get a look. Spike is standing on top of the coffee table wearing his pajama bottoms and nothing else. He's holding a broom, strumming the handle as if he's playing a guitar, singing along with the music playing on the phonograph.

Spike is oblivious to anything going on around him, singing that same self-deprecating Buck Owens song over and over again. Watching Spike sing that song is somewhat of a surprise. Spike isn't much of a music fan; he's one of the few kids who doesn't own a record player.

"What's he doing?" my father asks when he gets to me, followed by Aunt Lucy. After I tell him, he turns to Aunt Lucy.

"At least he's not doing anything to hurt himself."

"That doesn't mean he won't try. Remember the last time?" she replies, not swayed by his reassurance. "Sal, we need to get in there right away!"

By now, more tenants of the building have made their way into the courtyard. Many others are looking out of their apartment windows. Despite the hour, it looks like everybody in both buildings is awake. They are discussing the event no differently than if it were two in the afternoon instead of four in the morning.

"We should call the fire department," one of the neighbors suggests. "They can break down the door."

"Someone, please call the fire department!" another yells up at the people looking out their windows.

"I'll do it!" a man on the third-floor volunteers.

Within minutes, the firefighters are here. Betty's father, Mister Sargent, is one of the men who answers the alarm.

"What's the matter?" the big, bulky fireman asks as he comes into the courtyard.

"It's Anthony," my aunt informs him. "He's locked himself inside and won't open the door. I think he's sleepwalking."

With that, one of the other firemen runs back to the truck and returns with a sledgehammer. The sledgehammer does the trick. After two blows, the lock splits, and the door bursts open.

The disturbance of smashing open the door does nothing to dissuade Spike's singing. It's only when Mr. Sargent turns off the record player that he finally stops. As the music ends, Spike turns to stare at the man, a blank expression is on his face. He doesn't appear to recognize Betty's father. Mr. Sargent takes Spike's hand and helps him off the table. Mr. Sargent takes off his rubberized jacket and drapes it around Spike's shoulders. With his arm around Spike, he escorts him out of the clubhouse.

As they walk out of the courtyard, I hop off the garbage can and follow them out into the street. Attracted by all of the emergency vehicles, the street outside is even more crowded with bystanders than the courtyard. Fat Augie is part of the throng, wearing a blue robe and smoking one of his huge cigars. Our neighbor, Mrs. Maderno, peeks her head from behind Augie to get a look.

"Is he, all right?" Augie asks Mr. Sargent as they walk by.

"Yes, I think he's fine."

None of my friends are around except for Twitchy, who never sleeps.

"Did you get the priest?" Augie asks, when he notices Twitchy.

"Father Diritto is on his way; he's just getting dressed," Twitchy replies, his eyes blinking wildly. "He'll be here soon."

"*La faccia del diavolo*!" Mrs. Maderno shouts as Spike walks by.

"What did you say?" Aunt Lucy demands, having heard Mrs. Maderno's statement from behind Spike.

"Don't pay her any mind," Dad says.

"Did she just call my son 'the devil'?" Aunt Lucy asks.

"Ignore the old fool," Dad advises. "You need to take care of Anthony."

Aunt Lucy points a finger at Maderno. "I'll talk to you later!"

In the street, two fire trucks and three police cars are parked in front of the building. An ambulance has just pulled up. The red bubble lights flashing atop of all of the emergency vehicles reflect off the walls of the apartment buildings and provide a strange, carnival-like atmosphere.

The entire avenue appears to be out of bed. Hundreds of people on both sides of the street look out their windows.

Two medics come out of the ambulance, and one of them takes the firefighter's jacket off Spike and wraps him in a blanket instead. He bends down and puts a pair of slippers on Spike's bare feet. Spike stands there listless, not acknowledging anybody, offering neither help nor resistance.

"I think we should take Anthony to the hospital overnight just as a precaution," Betty's father suggests to my aunt.

"But he's fine," Aunt Lucy insists. "Anthony was just sleepwalking. He's probably very tired. All he needs is to go back to bed and get some rest." It's more of an appeal than a statement.

Father Diritto arrives just as my aunt is finishing her remark. "Look, Lucy, I'm sure Anthony is fine; it's just a precaution. They'll check him out and make absolutely certain nothing is wrong. I'll go to the hospital with him and stay by his side until you arrive later in the day. I won't leave him alone, not even for a minute. I promise."

"Listen to the man, Lucy. He makes sense," my father urges.

"But he's fine," she insists meekly, her lips quivering, her hands fidgeting.

"I'm sure you're right," Father Diritto answers, "but don't you think it's better to play it safe?"

With that, she relents. "I just need to get some information," one of the medics says to Aunt Lucy while the other escorts Spike into the ambulance. While the attendant takes the information from Aunt Lucy, Twitchy and I approach the back of the ambulance. Spike is sitting on one of the side benches, his head back, eyes closed, legs outstretched, hands clasped over his stomach.

"Is he asleep?" Twitch asks me, his irrepressible eyes still opening and shutting uncontrollably.

"Spike, are you all right?" I ask.

He opens his eyes slowly and turns to look at me, but he doesn't say a thing. He gives no indication of recognition as he closes his eyes again.

"Hey Spike, it's me, Twitchy. Are you okay?"

Spike's eyes open ever so slightly, the movement of his eyeballs in Twitch's direction barely discernible beneath his eyelids. His lips contort into a faint smile. "Hey, Twitch. How's it going? You seen Rudy Kazoody?"

"No, Spike. I haven't seen him," Twitchy replies, his ever-blinking eyes still opening and shutting incessantly.

"Well, I saw him tonight," Spike says, turning his head to look straight ahead once more, staring blankly at the side of the ambulance.

"You saw Rudy Kazoody?" Twitch asks, the oppressive blinking stopping momentarily.

Before Spike can respond, the paramedic and Diritto come over and get inside the ambulance.

Just as the attendant is about to shut the door, Twitchy grabs ahold of it. "Spike, I'll come see you at the hospital later. Take care of yourself. Remember what you always told me."

"Hold on tight and fight as hard as you can," Twitch and Spike utter in unison. Twitch releases the door, and the paramedic slams it shut. Twitchy and I stand motionless as we watch the ambulance pull away.

"Who broke the window in the clubhouse?" I ask Twitchy.

"What?" Twitch stares at me without blinking. "What the hell are you talking about?"

"The other day, I noticed the window to the clubhouse was cracked. I thought you might know how it broke."

"Who cares about that stupid window?" Twitch's eyes blink wildly once again. "I think it's always been cracked. Spike is being hauled away in an ambulance, and you're worried about a stupid, damn window?"

"Spike's going to be all right," I reply. "Father Diritto said he's coming home tomorrow. He's just going to the hospital to be checked out."

Twitch glares at me and gives an incredulous shrug. The blinking stops long enough to allow me to notice the moisture accumulating in his eyes. "You're such a jerk. Spike's not coming home tomorrow."

With that, Twitch turns and heads home.

"Joey, you better get upstairs," Dad, says. "Tell your mother I'll come up in a little while. I'm staying a few minutes with your aunt."

Curiously, when I arrive upstairs, my normally inquisitive mother doesn't bother to ask what happened. She simply tells me to go to bed, goes into the kitchen, and sits at the table to wait for my father. With Twitch's revelation about Spike not coming home reverberating in my head, I walk to my room and slump back into bed.

There'll be no more sleep tonight.

CHAPTER 2

The Bell

The particulars that led to that strange night are actually set in motion years earlier, on a Friday morning when I'm in the eighth grade. That morning begins with the familiar knot in the pit of my stomach and the dreaded, anxious, scared feeling I always experienced before going to school, ever since the fourth grade, all of which was the result of one childhood incident.

I'm still trying to come to terms with how a single, seemingly harmless event in fourth grade could have such an impact on my childhood. It was all so innocent and unintentional. Who could have foreseen that it would lead to such catastrophic consequences? If given another chance, I would have gladly given the ball to my classmate, Rodney Bell, that day.

The episode happened three weeks after my family moved to Orange, New Jersey, from a small farming village in the Apennine Mountains of Southern Italy. After arriving in Orange, my first days are uneventful. The Orange community is a typical suburban town some twenty minutes from New York City. The area features mostly single-family houses with neatly trimmed lawns.

We lived in rented rooms on the bottom floor of a house owned by relatives who moved to America years earlier. Our street was quiet and, unfortunately for me, no children my age lived on the block, so, naturally,

I looked forward to the beginning of the school year and making some friends.

That first school day, however, could not have been more disappointing. None of the kids spoke Italian, making it virtually impossible to talk to anyone. Since I couldn't speak English, I couldn't understand the teacher, most of the morning passed quietly as I sat in my chair and stared dreamily out the window.

At lunch, I happen upon a basketball lying in the schoolyard. Walking away from the other kids, I sat alone, bouncing the basketball against the schoolhouse wall. A group of boys notice and come over to ask for the ball. I am not about to surrender my only friend so easily. When I refuse to hand it over, one of them, Rodney Bell, tries to snatch it from me.

A brief shoving match ensued, but the precious ball remained in my possession. Embarrassed by his failure to dislodge the ball from me, Rodney spends the next four months telling anyone who would listen that I'm a freak. By the time I learn enough English to defend myself, it's too late. Rodney has convinced all of my classmates I'm some sort of weirdo.

None of my classmates would have anything to do with me, except for Lenny and Pauly, two of Rodney's other targets. As a result of our common desperation, Lenny, Pauly, and I become close. Things wouldn't have been so bad if Lenny and Pauly lived nearby instead of on the other side of town, except for school, I didn't see them much.

Even the prospect of seeing my only friends didn't take the edge of going to school. I dreaded the trip each day, as did my two lonely friends. Lenny swore that someday, he'd blow up the place.

My home life wasn't much better during those early years in New Jersey. Only one kid my age lived on my block, and he was one of Rodney's friends. So, I whiled away my time at home watching television. In that fantasy world, I lost myself and did not face my woeful existence.

Families called Nelson, Anderson, and Cleaver became my reality. Guys like Bud, Ricky, Wally, and, of course, the Beaver, were my pals. No matter how many dumb mistakes they made, invariably, they came out fine, their friends always willing to forgive. Years passed without me ever having to face the real world, until one day, the real world came calling for me.

Lenny, Pauly, and I are playing in an empty lot one afternoon after school. Rodney and some of the boys walk by, and someone from his group called Lenny a douche bag. Lenny flicks him the bird in response. The boys run toward us, and we tear ass out of there. Lenny and Pauly scatter for their homes while I cut across the lot in the opposite direction toward mine. It's a block before I turn and realize that nobody is chasing me, so I walk home.

After dinner, I'm watching television with my mother and Josephine when the news reporter cuts in with a bulletin.

"This is John Reed with ABC News reporting live at a construction site in Orange, New Jersey. A young boy has fallen into a dry well and is trapped deep inside. A rescue crew is working feverishly to extricate the young man, who is wedged some twenty feet below. Although injured, the boy is conscious and talking to the rescue crew. His name is Paul Fontana, and it's believed he was playing at the lot this afternoon."

Upon hearing the name, my mother turned to me. "Joey, isn't that your friend?"

Before I can answer, the doorbell rang.

Josephine answers and lets two policemen inside. Startled, my mother jumps up to greet them.

"We're sorry to bother you, ma'am," one of the policemen says, "but we were hoping to have a word with your son."

"My son? Why?" Mom looks at me. "Joey, what did you do?"

Tears stream down my face as I recount the afternoon's events to the policemen. "I never saw Pauly fall in the hole; otherwise, I would've never left," I conclude.

"Well, that's all for now," one of the policemen says. "Please don't go into the lot anymore. If we need any further information, I'll be in touch."

"Joey, why were those boys teasing you?" My mother asked the minute the police leave.

I shrug her off. "They're always teasing."

"What do you mean they're always teasing? Why are they teasing you? How long has this been going on?"

Once again, I burst into tears, this time uncontrollably.

Josephine answers in my stead. "Oh, Mom, stop acting so innocent! Don't tell me you don't know the kids are always picking on Joey! Can't you see that Joey and I have no friends? We haven't had any friends since we left Italy. Why do you think we sit here every night watching television? Don't you ever wonder why none of the other children call or visit? You act like it's a big surprise. We've been here for years and never had company! Haven't you ever wondered why?"

At first, my mother simply stared at us.

"Children, I'm so sorry," she says after a moment. She turns and goes into her bedroom.

"My God, she really didn't know," Josephine says to me after Mom leaves.

Dad comes home just as they're pulling Pauly safely out of the hole. Pauly had some minor cuts, bruises, and a twisted ankle, but he is otherwise unhurt.

My father is tired after finishing a double shift at the park. He's looking forward to taking a bath, eating his dinner, and going to bed early. Mom had other plans. My parents hardly ever fight, but this one was a doozy. To Mom, it's simple: we are leaving Orange and moving to the Bronx near my Aunt Lucy, case closed.

My dad is unflinching. He has a good job at the parks department and refuses to move. My mother is equally steadfast. Surely, he can find a decent job in the Bronx. Besides, the rent in my aunt's building is half what we're paying in Orange. Mom's argument doesn't sway my dad in the least. He refuses to move unless he's absolutely certain of a job in the Bronx. The battle ended in a stalemate.

With my father so determined my sister and I are convinced we're doomed to spend our entire lives in Orange. There is no way my father could ever find a job in the Bronx. Heck, he doesn't even have a driver's license, and he barely speaks English. How can he fill out applications?

Josephine is convinced there is no hope. In my loneliness, I never realized how much she hates this place. She wants to move more than I do. Although two years older than me, her social life is no better. She goes to school, works in a department store until seven, comes home to eat, does her homework, and watches television. The Bronx can't possibly be worse.

Days passed, and nothing happened. Then one night as our family sits down for dinner, my mother turns to my dad.

"Giuseppe Marzoti called. The furniture store where he works in the South Bronx is looking for a receiving supervisor. The job pays more than you make in the park. I called the owner and told him about you. He said the job is yours if you want it."

"But I don't know anything about furniture or receiving," my father protests.

"You didn't know anything about working in the park, but you learned," my mother counters. "Besides, the owner says he's willing to teach you. All he needs is someone who is loyal, honest, and hardworking. You certainly have what he's looking for.

"You can use some of your vacation time you've built up so we can stay with my sister during the Easter break to check it out. While you look in on your new job, I can look into the apartment my sister found for us in her building. We can also use the time to enroll the children at their new school. If everything goes as planned, we can leave in June, right after the kids get out of school."

"Are you sure you want to do this?" It's a final, futile question as resignation sets in. "You know, the city is not as good as you think. It's crowded, dirty, and unsafe. Most people are leaving the place."

"I'm sure I want to go, and I know the children agree. Now it's up to you to decide."

◆ ◆ ◆ ◆ ◆

Nine people, in a five-room apartment in the Bronx is not exactly a vacation. The hardest is sharing one bathroom. Somehow, we survive the Easter week at my Aunt Lucy's place on Arthur Avenue in the Bronx and are still talking to each other. Best of all, we are still moving to the Bronx in June.

I'm in the kitchen having lunch with Mom and Aunt Lucy on Saturday when my cousin Spike gets off work.

"How's everybody doing?" he asks when he comes in.

"There's a sandwich for you in the Frigidaire," Aunt Lucy informs him.

Spike opens the refrigerator and takes out the dish containing his sandwich. He places it on the table and takes a bite.

"I'll eat it later," he says, his mouth full. "I've got something to do, and I'm running late."

"Sit and eat, it'll only take a minute," Aunt Lucy protests.

"I don't have time," he replies while taking another bite.

"How about the halls? When are you going to mop the halls?"

"I'll do it tomorrow." He takes one more bite of the sandwich and places the uneaten portion back on the dish. "I don't have time to do it today."

"Take Joey with you," Aunt Lucy suggests. "He's been cooped up all day with nothing to do."

"Why can't he go with Vito?"

"Vito is at baseball practice and won't be home 'til late."

"Get your jacket, and let's go!" Spike barks. "I'm in a hurry."

I dart into my room and grab my jacket. Spike is already out the door, and I have to rush to catch up.

"Where are we going?" I ask when I get to him out in the street.

"You'll see," is all he'll reveal.

We turn into a hallway at a building at the end of the street and climb up a flight of stairs. At the top of the stairs is a boxing gym. Spike walks past the ring where two boxers are sparring. He goes to an area where some metal lockers are located and begins working on one of the combination locks. A tall, lean, dark-haired, freckle-faced kid comes over.

"What are you doing here?" the kid asks. "Aren't you supposed to be fighting right now?"

"Hey, Sean," Spike says. "I had to work, and I'm running a little late." He pulls a duffel bag out of the locker and closes the door.

"You better hurry," Sean warns. "You don't want to lose by disqualification."

"Don't worry, I'm on my way," Spike assures him. "When's your fight?"

"Tomorrow. Good luck!" he yells as Spike, and I dash out.

"Where are we going?" I ask Spike again when we get outside. "Downtown."

The revelation stops me cold. "Spike, I don't have any money for the train."

"Neither do I," he says as we walk toward the Third Avenue El.

We hear the shrieking of the metal wheels making contact with the tracks as the train approaches the 183rd Street station.

"Come on!" Spike yells as he runs toward the station. Spike bolts up the steps to the El. When he gets to the turnstiles, he throws his duffel bag to the other side and jumps over. Snatching the bag, he lunges for the doors of one of the cars, grabbing hold just as they're about to close. The door opening isn't wide enough for Spike to get through, but the train can't pull away as long as he keeps the doors partially open. Finally, the conductor reopens the doors to let him in.

"Come on," he urges as I crawl under the turnstile, Spike maintaining his hold on the door until I get in. Spike and I take two seats side by side. This being a weekend, the car is virtually empty, no more than four or five people in addition to us.

"Aren't you afraid of getting arrested?" I ask after catching my breath.

"Arrested for beating a ten-cent fare? Not likely," he replies as the train pulls out of the station. "A slap in the back of the head, a kick in the ass, maybe, but no cop is going to waste his time writing an arrest report for fare beating. Besides, didn't you say you had no money?"

"Where are we going?"

"Madison Square Garden," Spike says, finally letting me in on the secret.

"Wow, really? Why are you going there?"

His slight smile expands further. "To box!"

"What?" I nearly jump out of my seat.

The smile spreads across his entire face. "I'm in the Golden Gloves."

"The Golden Gloves? How long have you been doing this?"

"About two weeks. I've won three fights."

"That's incredible! Really, really great!"

This is unbelievable! Not only is my cousin boxing in the Golden Gloves, but he's also won three bouts. I contemplate this silently for a few minutes and then turn to him.

"Spike, what's it like to box at Madison Square Garden?"

"I don't know; this is my first time," he answers. "Up to now, all my fights were at Saint Nick's. Listen, Joey, do me a favor: Don't tell my mother. She doesn't know I'm boxing."

"Sure, Spike. You don't have to worry." When the train pulls into the next station, two more passengers get on board. I watch them take a seat and turn to my cousin. "Spike, do you know Betty Palm?"

"Who?" The question and change of subject catches him by surprise. "Sure, I know Betty. What about her? Let me guess. You like her?"

"No, I'm just wondering if you know her, that's all. I just met her yesterday."

"Liar." A slight smile creases his face. "You met lots of the girls this week, but haven't asked me about any of them."

"I'm just curious if you know what's her problem?"

"What problem?"

"I mean, is she a little slow?"

"Huh? Slow? What makes you think she's slow?"

"Well, yesterday when we were all together, she appeared out of it, hardly saying a word. It's almost as if she doesn't understand what the kids are talking about."

"Listen, Joey, I'll let you in on a secret. There's nobody in the neighborhood smarter than Betty. I don't know what happened yesterday to give you the idea she's slow, but you got the wrong impression. You are way, way, off!"

"Why do they call her Betty Palm?"

"Because they're jerks. Listen, Joey, if you want to get close to Betty, I suggest you don't call her by that name."

"The kids were all calling her Palm yesterday, and she didn't seem to mind. She didn't say a word."

"She wants to be called Betty!" he says. "How hard is that? Just call her Betty! Got that? Betty!"

The train pulls into the 149th Street station, the last stop on the El, and we get off to walk down the two fights to catch the subway. Two more trains and we reach 50th Street, where the Garden is located. We don't say another word to each other for the rest of the trip. We walk past the front arcade to a back entrance, where a guard is sitting on a folding chair reading a newspaper.

"Where do you think you're going?" he asks as we walk through the door.

"I'm scheduled to box," Spike says.

The guard holds out his hand. "Where's your pass?"

Spike puts down his gym bag and unzips it.

"Never mind, I don't need to see it." The guard nods at me. "What about him? He's not old enough to get in. He looks like he's ten years old."

"That's my cousin. He came from New Jersey just to see me fight. Can't you make an exception?"

The guard looks around. "All right, but if he gets caught, you snuck in through another door, you hear?"

"Sure thing," Spike replies.

We walk down a long corridor with a blue concrete floor and gray cinder-block walls, but the most distinguishing feature is the overpowering smell of sweat. So distinct is the smell that it permeates the halls. Even with nobody around, I can smell it. The stench appears to have attached itself to the walls of the old brick building. We arrive at an area where some men are milling about in the hall.

"Do you know where I can find Doogie O'Neil?" Spike asks one of the men.

"Around the corner, third door on the left," the man replies. "No, wait, make that fourth door on the left," he corrects as we walk away.

A huge, bald elderly black man is standing outside that door when we arrive. He greets us with a big smile. "He's not in a good mood," he warns Spike.

"What else is new?" Spike replies, "Thanks for the heads-up, Satch."

Inside the room, a white-haired, pudgy middle-aged man is waiting.

"Where the fuck have you been? You're due to fight in fifteen minutes! I've been looking all over for you!"

"I had to work!"

"Work? Didn't I tell you not to work during the tournament? You'll be too tired to fight!"

"You also told me not to go to school. Anyway, I need the money, and I won't get tired." Spike takes of his clothes and changes into his gear.

"You see how far I've sunk, Satch?" Doogie says, turning to address the other man. "Other trainers have boxers on their roster. I'm left with a school kid and a worthless Irishman. Get him ready!" He barges out.

Spike finishes putting on his trunks and sits on the table as Satch begins taping his hands.

"What's his problem?" Spike asks.

"He's pissed because Mad Dog lost today," Satch reveals. "Out of the eight fighters we had when we started the tournament, we're down to just you and Sean."

"Mad Dog lost?" Spike appears stunned by the news. "Out of all of us, I was convinced he'd be the most likely to win. What happened?"

"He got his clock cleaned. That's the best way I can describe it. Mad Dog had nothing for the guy he was fighting. Every judge had him losing."

"There's going to be a twenty-minute delay," Doogie says as he walks back in the room. By then, Satch is finished taping Spike's hands.

"Sugar Ray and Rocky just came in and are signing autographs," Doogie reveals. "Do you have to go to the boy's room?" he asks Spike.

"No, I'm fine. Are Sugar Ray and Rocky really in the audience?"

"Yeah. Just make sure the only thing they see is not the bottom of your boots. Go take a leak anyway. I don't want you thinking about taking a piss during the fight."

Doogie turns and finally notices me. "Who are you?"

"I'm Spike's cousin."

"How old are you? How'd you get in?"

"Leave the boy alone," Satch says. "He's harmless."

"Just stay out of the way," Doogie warns. He turns to Satch. "Well, what do you think? Does the kid have a chance?"

"You don't have to worry about Spike; he'll come through. I've never seen a smarter fighter."

"He's got some right, too. Three fights so far, three knockouts," Doogie agrees. "Do you think he'll go pro?"

"I don't think so."

"Then why's he doing it?"

"I asked him that a few days ago. He said it'll look good on his college application."

"College? Why the fuck does he want to go to college? With his talent, he can have a great career in the ring."

"That boy doesn't have to worry about a boxing career. He's got a good head on his shoulders," Satch replies. "Spike can do anything he sets his mind to. He doesn't have to waste his life on this crap."

"I'm going back outside to fish around and see what I can learn about this guy, Torres, he's fighting," Doogie says and walks back out of the room.

Satch turns to me. "What's your name?"

"Joey."

"Can you box like Spike, Joey?"

"No, I'm not much of a fighter. Besides, I'm too small."

"Spike wasn't any bigger than you when he first came to the gym a little more than a year ago," Satch says. "He wanted me to teach him how to fight so he could defend himself. Some kids at school were picking on him. I'd like to see those guys try something with him now." Satch smiles. "Spike would deck them."

Spike returns from the restroom and sits on the table.

Satch grabs a head protector and hands it to him. "Here, put it on."

Doogie comes in a few minutes later. "Listen, pay attention," he says to Spike. "I did some snooping around on this Jorge Torres guy you're fighting. Turns out he's not twenty-one like it says on the sheet. He's twenty-six. The grapevine says his name is really Manuel Peres, and he's a pro in Puerto Rico with some twenty fights under his belt.

"You got a lot of work in front of you, but he can be beat. Torres has won all his fights by decision. He's not much of a puncher, so you don't have to worry about one punch taking you out. Do you remember what I've always told you?"

"Don't get into a boxing match," Spike responds. "Look for the knockout."

"And what's the best way to knock a guy out?"

"Counterpunch."

"It's even more important with Torres," Doogie says. "If you try to out-finesse him, you'll lose. Torres is a southpaw, and southpaws make their opponents look bad. Torres being a lefty is perfect for you, though. A lefty jabs with his right and leaves his left side open, vulnerable to an overhead right. Here, let me show you what I mean."

Doogie gets into a fighting position and throws Spike a right jab. "See how my left arm drops down when I throw the jab, leaving my left side exposed, wide open for one of your patented overhead rights?" Doogie smiles at Spike. "Just wait for the jab, and look for the opening."

Spike salutes with his taped fist. "Got it, boss."

"Don't get smart," Doogie growls. Someone opens the door. "Time!"

Satch throws the boxing gloves over his shoulders.

"It's show time, put on your robe!" Doogie hollers at Spike. He turns to me. "You stay here."

"Just wait 'til we get down the hall," Satch says to me after Doogie leaves. "Then you can sneak out and take a seat in the back."

As soon as the coast is clear, I steal out of the dressing room and make my way into the arena. The Garden is so crowded that I struggle to find an empty seat. Finally, I notice a chair in the middle of a row in the rear that will do just fine. Spike is in the ring with Doogie and Satch, his robe is still on. Satch is lacing Spike's gloves over his hands. Doogie is saying something in Spike's ear. From where I'm sitting, it's impossible to tell if Spike is paying attention.

The announcer introduces the fighters, and when I hear Spike's name, a sudden rush of pride runs through me. I want to shout to the guy next to me, "Hey, that's my cousin up there!"

The bell sounds, and it's a good thing I'm paying attention, because the bout is over in an instant. Spike and Torres come out to the center of the ring and circle each other for a few seconds, each boxer sizing up the other.

Torres throws a harmless jab with his right. Spike ducks under it, preventing the blow from making contact. Spike moves to Torres' left, and Torres leads again with his right. Suddenly, Spike counters with an overhead, just as Doogie instructed.

The punch catches Torres square on the jaw and drops him to the mat. The crowd leaps to its feet, screaming. The ref motions for Spike to go into a neutral corner. By the time the ref turns to begin his count, Torres is on his feet. The ref gets in front of the flagging fighter and asks him something. I see Torres nod.

The ref motions for the fight to continue, but as Spike comes toward his opponent, Torres takes a misstep as his legs begin to wobble. Noticing Torres' buckling legs, the ref steps between the two fighters and stops the fight before either of them can throw another punch.

Twelve seconds, that's all it takes. Spike never breaks a sweat. I rush back into the dressing room to wait for him. It isn't long before they come bursting into the room.

"Unbelievable!" Doogie yells as he walks in.

"Did you see it?" Satch asks me, Spike's gloves tied over his shoulders.

"Yes! Spike, you were great!"

"Thanks." He turns to Doogie as he removes his headgear. "I told you I wouldn't be tired."

Doogie smiles and rubs Spike's head. "You're the best. Are you sure you don't want to turn pro?"

"Just two more fights, and my boxing career will come to an end," Spike replies. "I'm going out undefeated."

A commotion in the hall interrupts our talk. A couple of burly men, one black and one white, burst into the room.

"That's some fighter you got here, Doogie," the black man says.

"Get out there and do it again," the white guy says. "I turned to say something to somebody and missed the fight."

Spike laughs. "Only if you'll take the ring against me, Rocky."

"He won't stand a chance against you," his sidekick says. "You got some right, kid. I'd like to see the rest of your punches. When are you scheduled to box again?"

"Thanks, Sugar Ray. My next fight is Wednesday."

"Maybe I'll come see you. But don't get too cocky. Not all of your fights will be that easy. Anyway, good luck the rest of the way, not that you need any luck with that punch."

I can't stop yapping on the train ride home. I'm so excited I don't let Spike get in more than a couple of words. We go back to the gym to drop of Spike's gear. It's well past dinnertime. Sean is still there, and when he learns of Spike's victory, he's thrilled. Spike and I don't stay long; we need to get home for supper. In front of the building, Fat Augie and two of his henchmen are standing around talking. Augie is the head of the local crime family. When he notices Spike, he comes toward us immediately.

"How'd you do?"

"I won!" Spike yells, his arms raised high.

"All right!" Augie yells.

"By a knockout, twelve seconds into the first round!" I add for good measure.

"Is that right?" Augie asks, impressed.

"You're almost good enough to take me on," one of the men with Augie says as he feigns throwing a punch. "A little more and you'll equal my record in the Golden Gloves."

"Where do you get the nerve to compare yourself to Spike?" Augie growls at the guy. "You can't hold his gloves, much less fight with him, you fucking blabbermouth. I should let Spike loose and have him get into the ring with you. You won't last any longer than that guy Spike fought today."

He turns to Spike. "Don't pay attention to him. He didn't get past the first fight when he fought in the Golden Gloves." Augie puts his arm around Spike's shoulders and pulls him to the side. "Listen, Spike, you have a problem. Your mother found out you're boxing in the tournament."

"Who told her?"

"She was in the bakery buying a loaf of bread, and the guy behind the counter asked her how you made out in your fight. She threw a fit, and I think she's inside waiting for you."

Three Italians sitting around a kitchen table without food or drink is a sure sign of trouble. That's how we find my parents and Aunt Lucy when we get inside.

"Where've you been?" Aunt Lucy asks.

"Don't get cute! You know where I've been," Spike responds.

"Who gave you permission to box?"

"Who says I need permission?"

"Is that what you want to do in life, become a hooligan? What kind of job will boxing get you, bouncing drunks out of a bar?"

"Stop getting so dramatic. It's only the Golden Gloves. I'm not spending my entire life boxing."

"You're not spending another minute! You're going to the gym right now and quit!"

"Oh no, I'm not!"

"Then I'll do it for you!" Aunt Lucy says, getting to her feet.

"You better not!"

"What are you going to do, beat me up? It's a nice thing you're learning, not only beating up boxers, but also your mother."

"Stop treating me like a child. I'm old enough to make my own decisions."

"I'll see what the gym thinks about that when they find out you're only fifteen."

I can feel the final nail penetrating as my aunt utters those words.

"Let's see if they agree that you're old enough to make your own decisions."

"Please, Mom, don't do it," Spike begs. "I'm in the semis. Just two more fights, and I'll win the championship."

"Really?" my father sits up, when he hears the news. An icy glare from my mother cools his excitement.

My aunt is immovable. "What happens if you get hurt? Who's going to pay the doctor bills? Have you thought about that? I'm sorry, Anthony, but I'm doing what's best for you."

"You just won't budge," Spike says, making a final stab. "You wouldn't budge with Grandpa, and you won't budge now. You just refuse to bend and see my side." He slams the door on his way out.

"Joey, will you show me where the gym is?" Aunt Lucy asks.

"Maybe it's not a good idea to get Joey involved," Dad says.

"Fine, I'll find it myself," she says defiantly. "I know it's somewhere down the street."

"Joey, take your aunt to the gym," Mom says.

At the gym, Doogie is behind the counter talking with Sean.

"Are you in charge?" Aunt Lucy asks.

"What can I do for you, ma'am?" Doogie responds.

"I want you to remove my son, Anthony, from the gym and take him out of the Golden Gloves tournament."

"You can't do that. Anthony is in the semis. He'll probably win the welterweight title," Sean cuts in.

"Quiet down, Sean," Doogie orders. "Listen, ma'am, Sean's right. Your son is a good boxer; he's probably going to win the title. Do you really want to stop him from doing that?"

"I don't care about any title; I want him out!"

"What's Spike got to say? He's old enough to make up his own mind. Have you asked him how he feels?" Doogie asks.

"Since when is a fifteen-year-old boy old enough to make his own decisions?" Aunt Lucy proclaims.

"Oh crap," Sean says.

Doogie turns to Sean. "Did you know about this?"

Sean holds up his hands to proclaim his innocence. "Not a bit."

"Unless you let my son go, I'm reporting it to the tournament commission!"

"That won't be necessary, ma'am. We'll take care of it, I promise you,"

With that assurance, Aunt Lucy heads back out of the gym. Thus, ended my cousin's boxing career, undefeated as he proclaimed but not champion, as he hoped. Spike runs away from home for about a week in protest, but in the end, he comes to terms with his mother's decision and returns.

CHAPTER 3

Liar's Club

Those last months in Orange are almost tolerable. When the kids in school discover I'm moving, they begin noticing me, and some are almost nice, but no last-minute nicety can make me forgive their treatment over the past five years.

Josephine and I are helping my mother unpack the moving boxes at our new apartment in the Bronx when we hear Spike holler from the other side of the cartons stacked in the hall.

"Is anybody home?"

"In here!" Josephine calls.

"How are you guys doing?" he asks after making his way in. With him is a girl.

"Do you need any help?"

"It's about time you came to say hello!" my mother yells as she walks into the room. "I was beginning to think you forgot us."

"Zi Zi!" Spike says. Smiling broadly, he walks over, picks her up, and swings her around. "Even in your house clothes, you look great," Spike adds as he puts her down and gives her a kiss.

My mother blushes as she rearranges the polka dot kerchief covering the curlers in her hair.

"Maria, this is my Aunt Isabella," Spike says, introducing the girl to my mother. "Isn't she gorgeous?" He doesn't wait for an answer. "All the boys are going gaga knowing you moved to the building, Zi Zi."

"Are you here to help or to chit chat?" my mother asks, ignoring his flattery.

"Maybe I came at a bad time," Spike replies. "Maria wants to introduce Josephine to some of her friends, and I thought Joey could come with me and meet some of the guys."

"Go ahead and take them," my mother says. "They're only in the way."

Josephine drops the box she's carrying and runs out with Maria. Spike helps me carry an end table to my room, and then we head out.

"Who's that girl?" I ask him as we walk down the stairs.

"Maria Alferi," he replies. "Isn't she cute? We're sort of dating!"

"Isn't she much older than you?"

"Just two years. She's Josephine's age."

"Where are we going?" I ask.

"To the clubhouse. You're joining the Black Knights."

"The who?"

"The Black Knights. It's a gang I belong to."

"Isn't it dangerous to belong to a gang?"

"Not this gang. It's absolutely harmless," he says as we emerge into the street.

"It's like being in the Bowery Boys or the Little Rascals."

To my relief, Spike is right. The Black Knights isn't much of a gang, at least not in any sense of the term. Getting into the gang is easy. Spike is the leader, but not just of the Black Knights. Spike takes me with him everywhere in the neighborhood, and for weeks, I cling to my cousin like a person clings to a lifeline. The neighborhood accepts me, and eventually, I release my hold on Spike.

There isn't a dull moment, one adventure after the next. Normally, I have an eleven o'clock curfew, but this summer, my mother hardly ever enforces the time, and I take full advantage of the freedom. From early morning until late at night, I spend my time hanging with the guys on Arthur Avenue.

And that's not all. For the first time in my life, I fall in love. I've had crushes before, but they're nothing like my feelings toward Betty Sargent. Betty's real name is Megan Elisabeth Sargent. Betty didn't like the name Megan, so she began calling herself by her middle name. Then she shortened the name further to "Betty." And that's the last time Betty had a say in her name.

Everybody calls her "Palm." She got her nickname because of an episode with Joey Cooks. Cooks is the leader of the Disciples, another gang in the neighborhood. Apparently, Betty dated him at one time, and, according to Cooks, she gave him a hand job. The imbecile went around bragging to the entire neighborhood, and one of the fellows in the Disciples labeled Betty with the dreadful moniker.

The awful appellation bonded to Betty like glue. With such a reputation, none of the fellows want anything to do with her, and no one takes her seriously. Most of the girls also join in the teasing and taunting. Spike is her savior. For some strange reason, he takes her under his wing, and it's impossible for anyone to make fun of her. Spike deals immediately with anyone who is foolish enough to refer to Betty by her nickname or to give her a hard time. Even the girls are not immune to his harsh retribution.

◆ ◆ ◆ ◆ ◆

About two weeks after arriving in the Bronx, we're all circled around Betty and Judy Four Eyes as they have a massive argument. The guys are roaring with laughter as the normally poison-mouthed Four Eyes gets a thorough tongue lashing from Betty. No matter what insult Judy hurls at Betty, Betty has the perfect comeback.

"Why don't you shut up and go do what you do best, jerk off all the guys?" Four Eyes blurts out, frustrated that she's losing the argument.

It's poor timing on her part. She's unaware that Spike just arrived and is standing directly behind her. Having heard the insult, he throws her a swift kick, which, I swear, travels right up her butt. Thrown with such force, the boot appears to raise Four Eyes off the ground about two feet.

Stunned by the kick, she turns to Spike, as tears are pouring down her face. "You're always on her side! I'm getting my father!"

With that, Judy bolts down the block.

Betty walks up to Spike. "How is that going to help?"

Spike stands there, a wry smile on his face, fingers fidgeting. He simply grimaces and shrugs in response.

"I'm going after her." Betty turns and walks after Judy, followed by the rest of the girls.

"Don't worry, Spike. Four Eyes had it coming," Aldo says. "She's the most annoying bitch in the world."

"Maybe you should leave before her father comes," Twitch advises.

"Why should he leave?" Aldo asks. "Four Eyes' father is nothing but a bag of wind, just like her."

"I'm just saying Spike should leave to avoid an ugly mess, that's all," Twitch retorts, his eyes blinking wildly.

"That's what you would do, chicken shit," Aldo taunts.

"Who you calling chicken shit?" Twitch turns beet red, his eyes opening and shutting furiously.

"You, you cockeyed, blinking douche," Aldo says, ratcheting up the noise.

"You take that back!" Twitch screams, pushing Aldo.

Distracted by the commotion, nobody notices Judy's father running up the street until he screams like a madman and charges at Spike. Spike turns and punches him square on the nose, stopping him in his tracks. A dazed look comes over his face as he drops to the ground, belly up. The man's nose lies tilted and flat to one side, blood gushes from his nostrils.

It's the first, but not the last, time I witness Spike breaking someone's nose. More blood oozes from the corner of the man's mouth, so much blood that a pool of red liquid is forming under his head. Vito the baker comes out of his store and bends over the poor stiff.

"You should watch what you're doing," he warns Spike. "Your fists are dangerous!"

Spike rubs the knuckles of his right hand. "It was just instinct; I never saw him. Vito, you know I would never hit him if I knew who it was. Is he okay?"

"I think I'll bring him to the hospital," Vito says as Judy's dad comes to and tries unsuccessfully to get up. "Run in the store, and get me a couple of towels and my car keys."

Other than the broken nose, Judy's dad recovers just fine, but after the fight, Judy is not allowed to hang with us anymore.

◆ ◆ ◆ ◆ ◆

Betty and Spike have a strange relationship. They're inseparable. For a guy and girl who aren't dating, they're always together. It's Betty who drives the process, always by his side no matter where he goes. Not that Spike suffers from the arrangement. Both Betty and Spike are in advanced academic courses in school. As you can imagine, it wouldn't look cool if a renowned gang leader and neighborhood tough guy is seen carrying textbooks of advanced algebra, biology, or literature, would it?

Therefore, Betty carries not only her own textbooks but also has the unfortunate burden of carting all of Spike's, as well. Only in class, or at Spike's home is she able to relinquish his schoolbooks. Each day, we witness Betty looking like she's going to bust a gut as she lugs the enormous satchel of books. Even when Spike isn't with her, Betty still has to transport his books back and forth from school.

Betty has no clue how many times I've fantasized about having a fling with her. She's the main attraction to my constant jerking off. My arm gets weary with her vision in my head. Betty is incredibly beautiful, some three inches taller than me, around five feet six inches. She has blondish hair, an absolutely flawless face, not rounded but a more defined, chiseled outline. Although she never wears anything to accentuate it, she has an awesome figure. Her neckline is long and narrow.

However, her most striking features are her eyes. She has eyebrows that slant downward from her brow to her cheeks. The feature gives the appearance of sadness. In contrast, her blue eyes are large and bright, appearing to sparkle. The distinction appears to say, "Here is a sad person with such joyful possibilities." She rarely laughs, but if you are lucky to be rewarded with her laughter, you will be mesmerized, so enchanting is the effect.

One night, I determine to ask her for a date. Betty probably likes Spike, but since he's never shown any interest in her romantically, I decide to take a chance. Most people would probably say I'm getting her on the rebound, but that doesn't matter to me. Unless we're dating someone who has never been dumped, we're all getting somebody on the rebound. Besides, Betty is worth it.

I decide to wait until Betty goes home and then offer to walk her. On the way to her place, I'll ask her out. Spike, however, unknowingly spoils the plan. The three of us are sitting on the steps in front of the building. Everybody has gone home except for us. Spike, who is almost always the last to turn in, stays up talking, as usual. Betty also seems reluctant to go home. Finally, worried that my mother might call me in, I tell Betty that if she wants to go home, I'll walk her.

"Thanks, Joey, but I'm in no hurry," she replies.

A few minutes later, my mother looks out the window and calls me up. After that night, I keep looking for the right opportunity.

Talking to girls isn't easy for me. I didn't get much practice in New Jersey. Talking about girls is easy for the guys of the Black Knights, going on and on constantly about how they made it with some girl or other. Strangely, no girls mentioned by the boys live in our neighborhood. All live conveniently out of the area.

On a late July night, we're hanging in front of the building, waiting for the Mount Carmel feast to begin. The conversation centers naturally on how the guys are going to pick up some girls at the feast. These feasts, the guys say, are ideal for picking up girls. Girls from all over the Bronx will be attending the week-long affair. The teenagers come from all over the city: Van Courtland, Tremont, Pelham, the South Bronx, even Manhattan.

The boys are planning to take full advantage of the opportunity. This is the second feast of the season for the community. I missed the Saint Anthony feast, which occurred in June. The boys are bragging about how many girls they scored with at that feast. Coincidentally, all the girls live in another part of the Bronx, far from Arthur Avenue.

When this type of talk is going on, I don't say much. I don't have much to say, and my imagination is not as good as some of the guys'. Spike is also quiet, just listening to the boys ramble on.

"Let's get started," he says just after eight, ending the pretensions.

The stands for the Mount Carmel feast are set up along five blocks of 187th Street, about two blocks from my building. The feasts are carnival-type affairs. Neighborhood religious societies sponsor the occasions. The events honor the patron saints of the hometowns back in Italy from whence the members of these societies originate. Four of these celebrations occur annually. The two largest are the feasts of Saint

Anthony and the festival honoring Our Lady of Mount Carmel, which also happens to be the name of the local church.

To attract spectators from all over the borough, great care is devoted to providing the proper atmosphere. Decorations adorn the arched streetlights along the cavalcade route, generally along 187th Street, between Beaumont and Arthur Avenues. The associations construct a platform at the plaza on Crescent Avenue. Entertainers and musicians, hired to amuse the throng of festival-goers utilize the stage for performances. Stands assembled along the route to provide food and games for the pedestrians. Amusement rides are available for the kids. Thousands of people come from all over the Bronx to attend the weeklong affair.

Although it's still early, about a quarter past eight on a weeknight, the feast is crowded. The pleasant summer weather may be the reason, but an unusually large crowd is attending tonight's affair. Aldo is at one of the stands trying to win a goldfish for his kid brother, but is having no luck tossing the ping pong ball into the fishbowl.

"You can buy a goldfish cheaper than the amount of money you're wasting trying to win one," Rafaelo taunts.

"Hey, Spike, those girls are eyeing us," Reject says.

"Where?" Spike asks as we all turn to look.

"Over there." Reject points at five girls in front of the cotton candy stand.

Sure enough, the girls are looking. In fact, they're pointing at us. Spike walks over immediately, and we hustle after him.

"Hello girls from section four, Orchard Beach," he says when he reaches them. "What brings you all the way up here from the South Bronx?"

"Well, at Orchard Beach you said you'd show us a good time if we came up to the neighborhood," one of the girls answers.

"That I did," Spike agrees.

She smiles. "So here we are."

Spike introduces the guys, and we walk through the feast with girls.

After spending the entire night with them, we walk the girls to the bus stop on Crotona for their return trip home. One, in particular, has caught my eye, a cute, petite redhead. She has vibrant red hair and the prettiest, rounded, freckled face. She hasn't talked much, and I'm convinced that none of the guys has noticed her. As the two of us walk in front of the rest of the group, I try to work up the courage to strike up a conversation.

"How come you've been so quiet?" Spike walks up just as I'm about to speak. "Aren't you enjoying yourself?"

Startled by the question, she pauses. "It's not that I'm not enjoying myself. I'm just not comfortable talking in a crowd. I'm more of a one-on one person."

"Is that right? Well, maybe you'll have more to say next Saturday when we go out," Spike suggests, "I'll pick you up at eight, if that's all right with you?"

"S-suuure," she stammers. "I'd love to go out with you!" She almost faints, caught completely by surprise, as am I. Spike hasn't said two words to her the whole night.

"Where do you live?" Spike asks.

"Five hundred Southern Boulevard, section four, apartment three D," she answers, grinning from ear to ear. She's ecstatic. Unexplainably, she's nabbed the biggest catch of the night.

After we drop of the girls and I'm alone with Spike back on the block, I ask him about his choice.

"Why did you pick that particular girl to ask out? She wasn't the prettiest. I don't even think she puts out."

"Puts out? What difference does that make? And where do you get off talking about girls like that?"

"Well, all the guys are always looking for a girl who'll put out."

"They're jerk offs." That's Spike's favorite expression when someone ticks him off. "I thought you were smarter."

"Then why?"

"You just gotta love that rounded, freckled face and that carrot top," he says. "I could just eat her up."

That's exactly what I could have done if he hadn't interfered. Honestly, though, I don't think I would have summoned the courage to ask her out. That night, I lie in bed still moping about how easily Spike took the girl from me. How does he get so many girls? It's all so easy; girls are always flirting with him.

Granted, he's got looks, but other boys are good looking and aren't nearly as popular. Being a gang leader helps, too, but the Knights are a nothing gang. Other boys are leaders of tougher gangs, and girls aren't after them. His tough guy reputation could be a reason, but again, there's plenty of tougher guys, and that does nothing for their social life with women. No, Spike has something special, that's clear.

If I can solve the mystery, I'll definitely get better with the girls.

A week later, I'm sitting outside my building late one night, waiting for my apartment to cool off from the scorching summer heat. The temperature hit ninety-eight earlier in the day, and at night, it isn't much cooler. The guys have gone home. With me are my mother, Aunt Lucy, and Mrs. Maderno, a widower who lives on my floor. The women are talking, but I'm not paying attention. Looking down the street, I notice Spike, my sister Josephine, and Maria approaching.

"How's everybody doing?" Spike asks when he reaches us. Mrs. Maderno turns her chair and her back to Spike.

"Trying to keep cool," Aunt Lucy answers. "This heat is awful."

"Maria, let's go up to my place and listen to my new record," Josephine says.

"Don't make too much noise; your father is sleeping," my mother says as the girls run into the building.

Mom pulls Spike aside. "I want to thank you for all you've done for your cousins."

Spike grabs her in a hug. "Talk is cheap. How about giving me a big kiss as my reward?"

My mother gives him a shove. "You're awful," she says, blushing visibly.

"It's disgusting the way you talk to your aunt," Aunt Lucy declares.

"Do I detect a bit of jealousy?" Spike asks as he pulls his mom toward him and kisses her neck.

Aunt Lucy breaks the embrace and shoves him away. "You're sick!" She throws him a smack, hitting him on the shoulder.

Spike bursts out laughing. "Well, I'm going in to take a cold shower, since I can't get any action from the women out here."

"Your son is not good with women," Mrs. Maderno tells my aunt after Spike leaves. "Someday, he's going to get a girl into a lot of trouble."

"Anthony will do just fine," Aunt Lucy snaps and then walks into the building to turn in.

The next day, a heavy rain breaks the heat spell. It's one of the few times I'm at home watching television with nothing to do. I was downstairs earlier, but none of the guys were around.

"Joey, please take out the garbage," my mother asks as the nightly news is about to come on. I go into the kitchen, grab the brown paper bag containing the trash, and head downstairs to toss it out. As I go out the back door, which leads to the courtyard where the trash cans are located, I notice the clubhouse lights are on. From my vantage point outside the rear doorway, I can see right through the small rear window of the clubroom.

Two people are on the couch. When I realize what they're doing, I nearly pass out. The girl is naked and on her knees, and the boy, also naked, is thrusting at her from behind. It takes a few seconds to recognize who they are: Spike and Maria. By then, I have an erection and can't take my eyes of the couple. The whole thing is so unbelievable. Some of the guys say they've done it, but I know they're lying. Here Spike is, really doing it. Christ, he's only fifteen! Suddenly, his thrusts get harder, and everything stops. Spike is motionless in that position for a few moments, and then he pulls out. The bag of trash is still in my hands as they get dressed.

I go down the steps and place the bag in one of the empty metal containers. I give a final look as I reenter the building to go upstairs, and they're sitting fully dressed on the sofa talking. The hardness in my groin hasn't subsided. There's only one way to bring it to a halt. I hope nobody is in the bathroom when I get upstairs.

Between the constant imaginative discussion among the boys of the liars' club and looking in on Spike in the clubhouse that summer, I learn a lot about sex. Spike, in particular, is extremely helpful. In addition to his regular jaunts with Maria, he has four other girls in the clubroom that summer alone. Not all of the girls are teenagers. Olga, who lives two buildings down from us, is married with four children.

Yes, sir, that secret viewing spot in the back of the building provides quite a show.

CHAPTER 4

Oh No, Not Again

The glorious first summer in the Bronx goes by quickly, and September is here, my freshman year, first day of school. The familiar dread makes its appearance the night before. I'm so restive I barely sleep, glancing at the clock every half hour. For the umpteenth time, I sneak a peek at the clock, five thirty. The time has barely moved since the last time I looked over.

A noise comes from the kitchen. There's no mistaking the distinct sound of the espresso percolating on the stove. The sound signals my dad is up and making breakfast. The brewing coffee provides only a minor distraction to my fear as my thoughts turn again to my upcoming day. The Rodney Bell episode creeps back into my mind and sends quivers down my spine. One more look at the clock, five forty-five. Christ, it's been only fifteen minutes. Daylight seeps through the blinds. Might as well get up. No way I'll fall asleep now. My father stops making his lunch as I walk through the kitchen.

"What are you doing up so early?"

"I couldn't sleep," I respond, heading for the bathroom.

By the time I come out, my dad has left for work. I glance at the clock on the wall over the stove: six twenty. I go back to my room and get dressed. With plenty of time to kill, I turn on the television in the living room and flip through the dial. At this hour, there isn't much worth watching, and I finally settle on some Farmer Gray cartoons, not that I pay any attention. My thoughts are solely on the upcoming day.

The usual panic has taken hold completely. I'm working myself into quite a state. Despite the fantastic summer, I still fear this day, convinced that something will go wrong. My pensiveness is interrupted by someone heading to the bathroom. I go into the kitchen to check the time: five after seven. Maybe Spike is up. I decide to get my jacket and head down to his place. Aunt Lucy answers the door holding a loaf of sliced white bread.

"Hi, Joey. You're all dressed and ready to go. What are you doing up so early today?" I follow her into the kitchen.

Sitting around the table eating their breakfast cereal are Spike's brother, Vito, and his two sisters, Eva and Angela.

"Would you like some breakfast, Joey?" my aunt asks.

"No thanks, Aunt Lucy. I'm not hungry," I reply, "I just came down to see if Anthony is up."

"He's still sleeping," she informs me. "He was up until four thirty in the morning reading some stupid book. You can go wake him if you want; it's almost time for him to get up anyway."

Spike reading until dawn doesn't surprise me. He's a voracious reader. Every month, he goes to the West Farms public library and checks out seven books. You're not supposed to take out so many books at once, but the librarian always makes an exception for him. Sometimes he reads an entire book in a single night.

For some reason, Spike requires little sleep, sleeping no more than about four hours each night. He's usually one of the last of the guys to turn in. There's no logical explanation for his behavior; he just doesn't seem to need a lot of rest. From time to time, when he's feeling really tired, I might see him take a twenty-minute nap in the clubhouse, usually waking up refreshed and ready to go.

In his room, Spike is sleeping on one of the twin beds closest to the window. As always, he's wearing his pajama bottoms and nothing else.

I shake him. "Spike, wake up, it's time to get up."

He peers at me through the corner of one eye. "What are you doing here? What time is it?"

"It's almost seven thirty."

"Seven thirty? You've got to be kidding! What the hell are you doing up so early?" He puts one of the pillows over his head to block me out.

I wait patiently, knowing that, once awake, Spike won't be able to go back to sleep. It's not long before he stirs and sits up.

"I hope you're not making this a regular routine," he says.

"No, I'm just wound up because it's the first day of school. What book did you read last night?""

Just some poems by Milton, you probably wouldn't be interested."

He's right; I'm not interested. "The book must have been pretty good for you to spend the entire night reading."

"It was good, but that's not why I spent the night reading. It's due back at the library tomorrow, and I wanted to make sure I got it finished."

He gets out of bed, walks out of the room, and goes into the kitchen. On the kitchen table is a large bowl of his favorite cereal, Raisin Bran. After slicing a banana to add to the cereal, he pours in some milk and begins eating.

"How'd you make out sparring with Murphy at the gym yesterday?" Vito asks.

Aunt Lucy's eyes widen. "Anthony! You promised you weren't going to box any longer. Why are you still going to the gym?"

"I go to the gym to work out and get some exercise, not to box," he explains. "I never promised not to go to the gym; I just said I wouldn't box anymore."

Satisfied with his explanation, she goes back to preparing her children's school lunches. As her back turns, Spike, reaches over and slaps

Vito on the back of the head. When he finishes his cereal, Spike jumps up and grabs his sister Eva just as she's about to go into the bathroom.

"Oh no you don't. I'm first!" He pushes her aside and runs in.

"Mom! He'll be there all day," Eva moans, looking for help from my aunt, who refuses to intervene.

Twenty minutes later, Spike comes out of the bathroom, hair wet from the shower, a towel wrapped around his waist, and goes into his room to get dressed.

"It's about time!" Eva exclaims, running into the bathroom just ahead of Vito.

Ten minutes later, Spike comes back out, dressed and ready to go. "That jacket isn't warm enough. It's cold out! Look at the heavy jacket Joey is wearing," his mother says after seeing Spike wearing a lightweight leather jacket.

"I'll be fine," Spike insists, shrugging her of.

"Take your lunch," Aunt Lucy reminds him as she puts the brown paper bag on the table.

"I'm not bringing my lunch," Spike declares.

"Why not? There's nothing wrong with it! It's capicolla and provolone. I even added the eggplants marinated in olive oil you like. What's wrong with that?"

"There's nothing wrong with the sandwiches. I just don't want to bring my lunch."

"The food will go to waste."

"Just put it in the fridge. I'll eat the sandwiches when I get home from school this afternoon; it won't go to waste."

"I'm not bringing my lunch either!" Vito chimes in.

"See what you started?" Aunt Lucy says. She points at Vito. "Don't get smart! You're bringing your lunch!"

"How come Anthony doesn't have to bring his lunch, but I do?" Vito moans.

"When you get as old as Anthony, you can make your own decisions. Until then, you're bringing your lunch!"

The truth is, Vito will never have the same rights as Spike in this family, even if he lives to be a hundred. Spike is not only the eldest son, but, since his father's departure, is now the *capo de famiglia*, the head of the family. Vito will never achieve that status. All the bitching and complaining will never change my aunt's resolve. In their clan, Spike is the alpha, and Vito is the beta, and that's that!

Not to give you the wrong impression; my aunt's sandwiches are great. Eggplant parmigiana, mushroom frittatas, veal, and peppers are only some of her choices. Aunt Lucy gets up early to make sure she cooks everything fresh. No, the reason for the protest is a matter of convenience, not taste. No one wants to look like a doofus carrying a brown paper bag all day. Not that Spike would have carried the unseemly lunch sack anyway. That duty would have fallen on poor, old, reliable Betty.

As Spike and I leave the building, the sun is shining so brightly we can barely see Betty waiting outside, leaning against a parked car. The sky is cloudless. It's one of those late summer mornings where the night temperature dropped dramatically, making it unseasonably cold. Hit with the cold air, Spike snaps his jacket closed while I put on my jacket but didn't zipper it, as is the custom. With the sun-drenched skies beaming on the city, it's unlikely I'll be wearing the jacket on my return from school this afternoon.

Crabby is there talking to Betty. Crabby doesn't go to school. School wouldn't have helped Crabby much; even though he's some fifteen years older than we are, his mental capacity is closer to a fifth grader. You can't miss lanky Crabby. He's more than a foot taller than any of the guys.

"Crabby, are you putting the moves on Betty?" Spike yells as we come out.

"Just saying hello, Spike," Crabby replies and then scurries down the street.

Betty scowls. "Why did you have to do that?"

"Oh, Betty, you know I didn't mean anything by it; I was only kidding. Crabby takes everything I say so seriously," Spike replies as we begin walking to school.

My senses are peculiarly acute this morning. I become aware of things I usually take for granted. As we walk down the avenue, I notice the street is full of merchants who are beginning to set up their wares and constructing the stands outside their stores. The street cleaners are sweeping the refuse from the previous day's activity, and people are rushing off to their jobs. The avenue is normally a crowded, bustling boulevard, but due to the early hour, it's a relatively quiet, tranquil place. The air smells unusually clean and fresh. The wind is blowing away from the live chicken market across the street. I peer over at Spike and Betty to see if they're also experiencing a keen sense of their surroundings. They're busy fighting over who can kick a soda bottle cap farthest down the sidewalk without causing it to roll into the street.

"Hey, Harve!" Spike yells at one of the kids walking down 187th Street as we approach the corner. It's Harvey and a group of his friends, walking to school from their homes on Southern Boulevard. Southern Boulevard is about six blocks from where I live and is the eastern boundary of our neighborhood. Harvey is a friend of Spike's and a teammate on his baseball team.

"Hi, Harve. Hi, Janice," Spike says as we meet up with the group. "What brings you guys this way? Don't you usually take the bus to school?"

"We haven't had a chance to buy our bus passes yet, so we decided to walk," Harvey explains. The two groups mingle and walk to school together. Spike walks alongside Janice while I tag along with Beth, Harvey's younger sister, who, like me, is an incoming freshman. As we pass a candy store, Spike notices Aldo inside and goes in. Betty follows.

At that point, the groups separate once more, but I decide to continue with Harvey and his friends, leaving Spike and the others from my group behind. As we come alongside the schoolyard of Junior High School 45, close to where I'm to meet the rest of my friends, I notice a bunch of guys standing on the corner.

A queasy feeling comes over me as I recognize the boys. It's Joey Cooks and his gang, the Disciples. At our current direction, we're sure to cross their path. Cooks is a neighborhood bully and loves taking advantage of weaker kids. He picks his targets carefully, making certain he can't lose. Even Spike was a victim of Cooks' abuse several years earlier. Unlike Cooks' other targets, Spike fought back and, although Cooks won, Spike fought so fiercely Cooks never picked him on again. The victory over my popular cousin, however, raised Cooks' standing in the neighborhood.

We're heading directly toward this tormenter, and our group is exactly the type he loves to abuse. Oh, no, not again, I think as panic sets in. Will history repeat itself? Am I going to have another confrontation on the first day of school? How is this possible? I had planned things so carefully. As we get closer, I notice Vinnie Beast and Johnny Reject across the street, two of my friends and fellow members of the Black Knights.

This is my opportunity to avoid the possible unpleasant situation. Without saying a word, I leave Harvey and his group and sneak of across the street to join Beast and Reject. As I reach my friends, I glance back. Harvey and his crowd have reached Cooks and the Disciples. Just as I feared, the bully begins picking on them. Harvey appears to be Cooks' primary target.

"Should we do something?" Reject asks Beast when he realizes what's taking place. "Harvey is Spike's friend."

"It's none of our business," Beast says. "We have a pact with the Disciples not to interfere with each other."

Attempting to get away, Harvey and his friends cross the street toward us. Cooks and his cronies follow close behind. Whether we like it or not, we're going to be in the middle of this mess. As they get closer, Cooks puts his arm around Beth. When they get to where we're standing, Beth pushes Cooks' arm off her. Cooks puts his arm right back and squeezes even tighter.

"Harvey, make him stop," Beth pleads to her brother.

That's exactly what Cooks is aiming for, since Harvey is his real target. Cooks smiles and looks at Harvey, waiting for a reaction. Harvey is panic stricken. He just freezes and stands there helpless, saying nothing. He doesn't know what to do.

"Yeah, Harvey, make him stop," one of the Disciples urges, trying to incite a reaction.

Immobilized with fear, Harvey still doesn't budge. Another of the Disciples grabs the yarmulke off Harvey's head. As Harvey attempts to retrieve the cap, the boy tosses it to another boy in the group. Harvey tries to snatch it back, but the boy hurls it to another Disciple. This time, the boy misses the catch, and the yarmulke falls to the ground—right next to Spike's feet.

"Get your filthy hands off her!" Spike barks at Cooks.

Startled, Cooks turns and releases Beth. "This is none of your business, Spike! Just move on and don't get involved."

"It is my business when you pick on one of my fellow gang members. Remember, we have a neighborhood pact against that kind of thing."

"Who's the gang member?" Cooks asks, confused and suspicious.

"Harvey, Harvey the Yarmulke," Spike says, with a big grin on his face. He looks so calm, as if he's enjoying breaking Cooks' chops. The possibility of a fight doesn't concern him at all. "He's a new member of the gang; he just joined a few days ago."

This is obviously a lie, since I hadn't seen Harvey for nearly two weeks, and he wasn't a member at that time.

"Now pick up the yarmulke, dick weed, and give it back to him!" Spike demands, turning to address the boy who was tossing Harvey's cap around. Stunned and confused by Spike's orders, the boy turns to Cooks for instructions.

"Tell him to pick it up, Joey!" Spike says, shifting the responsibility back to Cooks.

By now, the crowd is beginning to swell as passing kids realize what's happening. Everybody is hoping for trouble between Cooks and Spike. A fight on the first day of school is an unexpected but a welcome treat, especially one between two rivals like Spike and Cooks.

Cooks stares at Spike expressionlessly, but he must realize his predicament. The simple teasing of some geeks has backfired, and now he's facing a much more serious opponent. If he fights Spike, he's sure to get his ass kicked. On the other hand, backing down will brand him a coward. Regardless of which option he selects, his reputation is lost. Cooks is obviously aware Spike lied about Harvey's gang membership; however, proving Spike a liar is the least important thing on his mind at the moment.

The truth is, no one, except maybe the members of Cooks' gang, has any sympathy for Cooks. He's a nasty creep, and everybody is hoping Spike will hand his head to him. Cooks is an equal-opportunity abuser, and most of the spectators have been victims of his abuse at one time or another.

Finally, Cooks turns to Harvey. "Lucky for you there's a neighborhood pact, Harvey." Cooks turns and yells at the other boy in his gang. "Give him his stupid hat!" Without looking back at Spike, he walks away, followed by the remainder of the Disciples.

"I knew Cooks would punk out!" one of the onlookers yells as Cooks walks away.

Disappointed that there's no fight, the crowd begins to disperse. Like the guy who yelled out from the crowd, I had also concluded there wouldn't be a fight. Spike never took of his jacket. If he had expected trouble, he would have removed it before he arrived. No way would Spike risk damaging his jacket. Spike knew Cooks would back down.

While putting on his yarmulke, Harvey turns to Spike. "Thanks, Spike, I really don't know what I would've done if you hadn't showed."

"Cooks is harmless; you've got nothing to worry about," Spike says. "He's just breaking your balls, because you're on the same baseball team as me. After a while, he would have given up and let you go. He really wasn't looking for a fight. He just wanted to make a statement for the benefit of the crowd. You and your friends just happened to come along at the wrong time."

"Are you all right, Beth?" Spike asks Harvey's sister.

"I'm okay, thanks," she replies. "That guy gives me the creeps." She turns to her brother. "Thanks for coming to my rescue!"

"Never mind," Spike says. "Harvey did exactly the right thing. Cooks would have loved to intimidate your brother into a fight that Cooks couldn't lose. You weren't his real concern."

Spike spends a few more minutes talking with Harvey and Janice, and then Harvey and his friends continue on their way to school.

"Now that Cooks knows you're a member of the Black Knights, he's not likely to pick on you any longer. Don't forget, there's a gang meeting at the clubhouse this afternoon at three thirty. I think you know the place. Make sure you're there on time."

Once Harvey and his friends are gone, we settle in and concentrate on our own group. By now, some sixty kids have joined our crowd. Although I've been in the community for only a few months, I'm delighted that so many of the kids recognize me. Most of them greet me by my new nickname. I don't like my moniker, but you don't get to choose.

Reject tried to choose. A few years earlier, he slipped and fell from the second floor of an empty building. The fall impaled him on the spike of a metal fence, requiring forty-two stitches. When he came out of the hospital, he began referring to himself as Scar, hoping the name would catch on. It didn't. Three weeks later, his mother ran off and left Reject's family. Soon after that, Reject and Aldo had a massive argument, and Aldo called Reject a complete waste.

"Nobody likes you!" Aldo shouted at Reject. "Even your own mother rejected you and took off."

With my first name so prevalent in the neighborhood, I knew it was only a matter of time before the guys gave me a nickname to differentiate me from other boys named "Joey." However, I was determined that if I was branded with a nickname, it should be a sterling name similar to my cousin, Spike, not like the stupid nicknames of some of the other guys, such as Reject, Bowlegs, Cumquat, Twitchy, Slinky, Gaga, Mousy, and Casper.

When we first arrived in the neighborhood, my sister advised me that the knack for getting a good name is to avoid saying or doing something stupid, at least not acting like a moron until after I got a good nickname. Her suggestion sounded reasonable. To follow her advice and accomplish my mission of getting a great name, I came up with the following plan.

Throughout the summer, whenever I was in a crowd, I barely spoke, determined not to give the guys an opening. They couldn't label me if I didn't say anything stupid, I reasoned. Unfortunately, even the best-laid plans can go begging. Despite the enormous amount of energy, I expended on this effort, Vinnie Beast still managed to tag me with an unseemly moniker.

One hot summer night, all of the guys were hanging out aimlessly and ranking on each other to pass the boredom. Taking my usual stoic stance, I barely said a word. Noticing my lack of participation in the revelry of insults, Beast pointed at me and turned to the rest of the group.

"Look at him, he never speaks. He's like a priest taking confession." And the name stuck, Joey Priest!

Upon hearing the school bell, we leave the corner and head out for our first period. But the entire group isn't going to school. Part of the crowd, all boys, dropped out of school when they turned sixteen. That bunch starts back for the clubhouse.

CHAPTER 5

The Clubhouse

Theodore Roosevelt High, like most schools in New York City, is a massive, ugly, gray structure. All it needs are metal bars on the windows, and it could just as easily be mistaken for a prison. It's a mystery why they build schools that look so ugly. Do they want us to think we were in prison during school hours? It certainly doesn't foster a learning environment. Nearly half of the incoming freshmen class drops out before they reach their junior year. I'm not saying the ugly building is the only reason for the dropout rate, but it doesn't help.

Despite the high rate of kids quitting, the school still has an enormous body of students, numbering well over two thousand. It's so massive that, once inside, I barely catch a glimpse of my friends. The fact that I'm a freshman and most of my crowd are sophomores also contributes to the lack of contact. Although a sophomore, Spike isn't in any classes with the guys, either. He attends mostly advanced academic classes. The only person from our crowd in his classes is Betty. Most of his classmates are Harvey, Janice, and the rest of the kids whom he rescued so valiantly this morning.

Spike's classes, however, aren't on my mind. I have my own subjects to which to look forward. The next time my schedule allows me to meet up with my friends is at lunchtime. Because of the large student body,

Roosevelt spreads its lunch break over three periods. Even though I'm in a different grade level than my friends, our lunch break takes place at the same time. Earlier this morning, we designated a certain area in the cafeteria as our appointed meeting place. The first of us to arrive is to garner the tables and save them for the remainder of the group.

When I get to the lunchroom, I go and purchase my lunch. Tray in hand, I head for the designated meeting place. When I get to the spot, none of my friends are there. A different bunch of kids occupies the tables. Confused, I walk through the cafeteria searching for my friends. After a while, I spot the group sitting in a long row of tables on the opposite end of the dining hall from where we were supposed to meet.

On one side of the row are Spike, Harvey, and his friends, while my gang occupies the remainder of the tables. Due to my lateness, no seats are available next to my friends. The only free spot is next to Harvey, Spike, and Janice. Although I would have preferred to sit with my own crowd, I sit next to the three of them.

"Hi, Spike. Hi, Harve," I say as I sit down.

"Hey, Priest," Spike answers. "How's your day going?"

"Nothing eventful," I reply smugly.

Spike turns his attention back to Janice, the same Janice who was with Harvey this morning. From the tone of the discussion, it's clear that Spike is putting the move on her. Janice is his next target. Now it's clear why we're sitting across from our appointed spot. Spike changed the tables to be with Janice, and the rest of the guys followed. Not wanting to listen in on their conversation, I turn to speak to Harvey. After about ten minutes, Spike leaves and goes to join my friends at the other end of the table. Miraculously, all the kids manage to squeeze together and make room for him.

"When did you become a member of the Black Knights?" Janice asks Harvey.

"I didn't," he says.

Janice frowns. "I don't understand. This morning Spike said you're a member."

"He made a mistake!"

"Aren't you supposed to go to a meeting this afternoon?" she asks, sounding disappointed that Harvey, in fact, is not a member of the Black Knights.

"No, I'm not!"

"Listen, Harve," I chime in. "I don't want to tell you what to do, but if you don't show up at the meeting, you're going to piss off Spike."

"That's just too damn bad!" Harvey says. "He'll just have to be pissed off! I'm not going to the meeting!"

"All right, smart guy," I say, annoyed by his attitude, "even if you don't care about Spike, what are you going to do when Cooks finds out you're not a member of the gang?"

With this disclosure, Harvey looks worried. Detecting the change that comes over Harvey, a big smile spreads across Janice's face. "I hope I'm there when that happens."

We're silent for a few minutes as the situation sinks in for Harvey.

"Look, Harve," I say finally, "just come to the meeting this afternoon. Spike is your friend; you've known him for a long time. You have nothing to worry about. Just see what he has to say. If you don't want to join, you can still change your mind. Don't embarrass him by not showing up. You owe him an explanation."

Harvey doesn't answer. The bell goes off, signaling the end of lunch break. As we're leaving, I turn to Harvey. "Think about what I told you, and try to come to the meeting."

My entire community is probably no bigger than three square miles. An area no bigger than a nice size Kansas farm. In that small space are over fifty thousand people. The area starts around 180th Street, running north some ten blocks to Fordham Road. The eastern boundary of the community is Southern Boulevard. The Bronx Zoo parallels that street for the most part. From Southern Boulevard, you head west, once again about ten blocks, to Webster Avenue, the western limit of my neighborhood.

Almost directly in the middle of the area are two adjoining apartment buildings, one of which is where I live. Between those two buildings is a stairwell leading to a courtyard. To the left of the courtyard, just at the bottom of the steps, is a utility room in which they used to store tools. Spike convinced the landlord to rent the room to him for ten dollars a month and converted it into our clubhouse.

Although small, the clubhouse can fit as many as forty people. Inside, we have some used furniture, including a sofa, two armchairs, a side table with a lamp on it, a coffee table, and a small bookcase containing a phonograph. We also have a folding table and some folding chairs, which we use for card games, but most of the time they're stacked against the wall. Even though the room has a window, a large ceiling bulb provides most of the light. The sun never hits the window.

The walls are bare except for two banners—one from the Yankees and the other from the Mets—and a painting of a farm scene that hangs directly across from the couch. We don't spend much time inside the clubhouse. Most of the guys prefer to hang out on the sidewalk. That's because the clubhouse is off limits to the girls who hang with us—their folks don't appreciate it when the girls are out of view. Whenever the girls are around, the boys naturally stay outdoors to keep them company. Besides, even when the girls aren't around, something is always happening on Arthur Avenue, and nobody wants to miss out on the action.

Mostly, the clubhouse is crowded when the weather is lousy or there's a meeting, like today. To allot for the large crowd attending the meeting, we push the furniture against the walls and open the folding table. Sitting behind the table is Spike. To his right sits Vinnie Beast. Beast is second in command, in charge when Spike isn't around. To Spike's left sits Betty, the club's secretary and its only female member.

It's so crowded we have to leave the door open to allow the kids in the courtyard to see the proceedings. After a few minutes, Spike calls the meeting to order.

"All right, quiet down and listen up! I'd like all of you to say hello and welcome a new member, Harvey the Yarmulke," he says looking at Harvey standing in the doorway. "Hey, where's your yarmulke, Harve?" he asks, noticing that Harvey isn't wearing his skullcap.

We all look in Harvey's direction.

"It itches sometimes," Harvey says, "so I take it off."

"Well, I hope you don't feel you have to remove it for our sakes," Spike says. "Whether you wear it or not, your nickname is still Yarmulke." Everyone laughs.

"Listen up!" Spike shouts over the noise. "The dues this year are seventy-five cents per month. Last year, a lot of you cheapskates were late in paying, so this year, to make sure you pay on time, there's a twenty-five-cent penalty for late payers. You don't pay, you can't play! The punishment is getting kicked out of the Black Knights, but before that, Vinnie Beast will kick your ass!"

Nobody laughs at Spike's attempt at humor. Most of the boys have experienced Vinnie's storm trooper-style enforcement tactics.

"For those of you who are new and for the benefit of the freaking morons who probably have forgotten, Beast will repeat the club rules."

Spike gets up and turns the meeting over to Vinnie, who begins reciting a litany of regulations, such as no spitting, dump your cigarette butts outside, remove any liquor bottles or beer cans, and so on. When the meeting ends, as usual, the kids gather on the sidewalk outside the building. Because it's approaching the dinner hour, the avenue is crowded with pedestrians doing some last-minute shopping. As we gather outside, I see that Harvey is trying to get Spike's attention. Finally, he manages to collar him and pull him aside.

"Listen, Anthony, would you be terribly upset if I didn't join the gang?"

"Why don't you want to join?" Spike asks.

"It's just that I feel my parents wouldn't be very happy knowing I belonged to a gang. Besides, Jewish kids just don't belong in gangs."

"First of all, you're mistaken about Jewish kids not belonging in gangs," Spike counters. "It may surprise you to learn that many of your Hebrew brethren are already in gangs. Louie the Jew is a member of the Baldies. Mark Cohen is part of the Daggers. Marty Moscowitz is in the Disciples. Besides, what type of gang do you assume the Black Knights are? There's nothing dangerous or threatening about our group. We don't wear leather jackets or have a gang insignia. You know most of the guys. Have you ever known us to get into any kind of serious trouble?"

"No, I haven't, but I still don't think my folks would appreciate me joining a gang, even one as harmless as the Knights."

"Do you always listen to what your parents tell you?" Spike asks. "Listen," he says in a gentler tone, "just make an effort for a month or two. If you still don't want to belong, you can quit. I won't hassle you any further. But do me a favor and just give it a chance."

With that compromise, Harvey agrees to join, and the matter is settled.

The clubhouse also serves a few other important functions. It is a place to hang out for the guys who have turned sixteen and dropped out of school. Since they quit school, their parents expect them to find a job, and their parents hassle the boys if they stay home and sleep late. The clubroom is an excellent hiding place where the boys can stay without anybody's knowledge.

The guys usually stay at the club every weekday morning until noon, when Cicci's poolroom, located right down the street, opens for business. At that time, they switch to the billiard hall, where other guys from the neighborhood, in similar unemployed circumstances, gather.

Since there are few employment opportunities and so many people out of work, the pool hall is usually crowded.

Ironically, the poolroom is the only place in the community that can provide the guys with any possible job leads. Should somebody or some company be hiring, Cicci's is the first place that will know the information. Usually, the boys return home at around dinner time, relating to their parents how hard they searched but, unfortunately, were unable to find work.

Another significant role of the clubhouse is that it serves as sort of a motel room. Whenever a guy needs some privacy, he can utilize it. Everybody defers and shows consideration for the rights of a couple to exploit the clubhouse in that manner. Except for Spike, though, none of the boys take advantage of this rule. Practically all the guys are pathetic virgins like me.

Finally, the club is the site of our weekly Saturday night poker game. The card game is an important source of revenue for Spike. He generally wins; it's just a matter of how much. No wild parties or raucous activity occur in the clubhouse, making the landlord and the tenants of the apartment building happy. Not that the tenant immediately above the club would complain much. It's Spike's apartment. In fact, his room is directly above the place.

CHAPTER 6

The Flow

The first week of school is survived without a problem. It couldn't have gone better, not that I achieve instant popularity, but I do make some friends. We all dream of being popular, but in reality, we'd all settle for being allowed to hang with the in-crowd. As time passes, our aspirations become tepid. Eventually, we're just happy not to be on the bottom of the rung, content that someone is in a worst stead than we are.

The bottom of the heap is a role I know well. I wasted many years making others feel good. My turn to shine has finally arrived, and under no circumstance am I heading back to the boy I was in Orange. I've been given another chance, and I'm going to make it work.

It's not long before we get into a predictable routine—school, hanging out in front of the club, dinner, homework, and more hanging out. After dinner that first Friday, I go downstairs to begin a nice, easy weekend. It's raining, and none of the guys are outside. I head downstairs to the clubhouse, where the boys hole up in bad weather. Spike, Twitchy, Casper, Reject, and Crabby are sitting around the folding table.

"But what's his name? How can I call him if I don't know his name?" Crabby asks Spike.

"His name is Rootie Kazootie," Spike responds.

"Come on, Spike, don't bring that up," Twitchy pleads.

"Don't worry, Twitch, I'm not going down that road," Spike says.

"Rudy Kazoody?" Crabby repeats.

"No, not Rudy Kazoody," Spike corrects. "Rootie—never mind, Rudy Kazoody it is."

"Hey, Spike, who's Rudy Kazoody?" I ask.

"Don't tell him, Spike; he's not one of us," Casper says.

"That's right, Spike, don't tell him," Crabby seconds.

Spike laughs. "Sorry, Priest. You heard the guys. You're out of the loop."

"Come on, Twitch, let's walk Crabby home," Reject says to Twitchy. "We'll see you guys later."

As they leave, Nick Bonaparte walks in. Bonaparte isn't his real name, but the nickname attached to Nick because of his fascination with dictators like Castro, Stalin, Hitler, Caesar, Napoleon, and so on. When you consider the other names, Nick is fortunate he got Bonaparte and not one of the other possibilities.

"Well, are we in or what?" Bonaparte asks Spike.

"Our first game is Sunday; we have to be at the field at eight," Spike replies.

"All right!" Bonaparte says, raising his clenched fist in the air.

They are talking about touch football, which is due to start on Sunday. An organized league is running the games. The association takes its work seriously, and all players are required to have uniforms. Even the referees wear striped zebra shirts, emulating the professional gridiron sport. Any guy age fifteen to fifty who can make a team can play.

Well, that's not really true. There are no tryouts. There's only two ways of getting on. You either know someone on a team, who lets you on, or you're such a good athlete that they ask you to play. Not being very good at football and not knowing anybody on a team that can get me on, I didn't even make an attempt to join the league.

Spike reaches into a bag beside him, takes out two blue jersey shirts, and hands one each to Casper and Bonaparte. Bonaparte unfurls the shirt, exposing the word Giants and the number seventeen on the shirt's back.

"Giants? I thought we were playing for the Baldies or the Ravens."

"There was a change of plans," Spike says.

Bonaparte sits down, his shoulders slump. "The Giants? They stink. Christ, they're the worst team in the league."

"Not anymore," Spike says. "With you, me, and Casper on the squad, we're going to the championship."

Bonaparte is unaware of the negotiations that had gone on behind the scenes. It's Spike the teams want, not Bonaparte or Casper. Every team in both divisions tried to recruit him. Since his success in the Golden Gloves, Spike is almost a god in the neighborhood. It's amazing how those four fights affected his reputation. Not that winning those fights isn't quite a feat, but to rise to the level of reverence with which the community bestows him is incredible.

To his credit, Spike stays loyal to his buddies in the Black Knights. He could have chosen to hang out with any crowd, but he sticks with our peculiar group on Arthur. Heading the list of teams wooing Spike are the Ravens and Baldies. The Ravens consist mostly of gang members from the Daggers. Since the head of the association running the football league is a Roman Catholic brother, they had to change to a more respectable name. The brother found Daggers too offensive.

The Baldies, although also consisting of gang members, don't have to alter their identity, an ironic twist when you take into account that the Baldies is one of the most violent gangs in the city, much worse than the Daggers. I guess the name 'Baldies' is more benign and acceptable to the priest than 'Daggers.'

The two teams aren't interested in Spike's athletic qualities, but rather his tough guy reputation after his performance in the Golden

Gloves. Spike's fighting skills are becoming legendary in the community. He'd fit in perfectly with the image the two teams were trying to portray. So impressed with his reputation they would have taken Spike even if he couldn't play football. His being good was an added bonus.

The Baldies and the Daggers aren't just arch-rival gangs. Last year, they played against each other in the league championship game. Rumor had it that, although the Baldies lost the championship, they won the brawl that followed the game.

Unfortunately, Spike made one demand too many. He insisted that any team that wanted him also had to take Casper and Bonaparte. Adding a colored kid, Casper, to the mix, removed Spike from the recruitment lists of all the teams except the Giants and the Webster Wolves, a predominantly black team.

The Wolves would have taken Casper and Spike, but adding another white guy, Bonaparte, was too much. The Giants, although consisting of all white players, were willing to overlook the color of Casper's skin. Moreover, with the worst record in the league, they were in no position to be selective. Wanting my cousin badly enough, they agreed to his demands, and now all three are rookies for the Giants.

As it worked out, the Giants got a great deal. Of the three, Spike is probably the worst player—not that I'm saying he isn't good. It's just that, in my opinion, both Bonaparte and Casper are much better. The Giants may have had inklings as to how good Casper is, but no one but Spike knew about Bonaparte's football talent.

Bonaparte stands a lumbering six feet three inches. His long arms reach unnaturally down to his knees, appearing to droop even lower due to his rounded shoulders. His hands are enormous, nearly twice the size of anyone in the neighborhood. A natural athlete, Bonaparte can hurl a football on top of a five-story building. Bonaparte is a shy, introverted kid who doesn't participate in any organized neighborhood sports. He plays his sports at Salesian, where he goes to school.

Although Casper doesn't possess all of Bonaparte's natural attributes, he does have lightning speed. One time he beat me in a race while he was running backward and I was going forward. No sir, the Giants don't have a clue just what a favor Spike did for them by insisting both Casper and Bonaparte become part of the team.

Sunday arrives, and, as usual, the touch football schedule calls for two games. The Giants are to play the earlier of the two games at the field of Junior High School 45. I use the word "field" loosely. Basically, it's a fenced-in concrete schoolyard. Their opponents are the division champion Baldies. The Giants are going to be tested early, and soon they'll know whether the new recruits are going to make a difference to their stinking team.

I get to the schoolyard about half an hour before the game. Most of the guys from the Black Knights are already there and waiting on the sidelines. Few of the girls ever attend the games. The only girl present is good, old, reliable Betty. She never misses a match when Spike is playing. She's standing there on the sidelines by herself, some twenty feet from the guys, minding Spike's jacket.

Spike, Casper, and Bonaparte are on the field, loosening up and practicing some last-minute plays. After saying hello to the guys, I walk over to keep Betty company. There's no way I'd pass up an opportunity to be alone with her.

"Hi, Betty," I say when I reach her.

"Hello, Joey."

Having such an unseemly moniker, Betty never addresses anybody by anything other than his or her proper name.

"How was your first week of school?"

"Just fine. How about you?" she replies cheerfully.

"Really great. I think I'm going to like Roosevelt." My dream girl always makes me nervous when I'm alone with her. This day is no different as I struggle for the words to start a conversation. It seems like an eternity before I can come up with something to say.

"Don't you hate the word 'keen'?" I blurt out finally.

"What?" She looks at me, confused.

"You know, 'keen,' like when people say 'peachy keen.'"

"I haven't thought about it that much," she responds indifferently. "Besides, I don't know many kids who use that phrase."

"That's just my point! Who comes up with these sayings? I'm sure it's not kids. Otherwise, we'd hear it more often. It's got to be some stupid grown-up who wishes we would use the phrase. I mean, what kind of phrase is 'peachy keen' anyway? What in the world does it mean?"

"I guess you're right," she answers, unimpressed, and looks across the football field at Spike, who is milling around, talking to five men.

What a jerk! My great moment to have a meaningful conversation with Betty, and all I can come up with is how I hate "peachy keen." She must think I'm the biggest free-hole in the world.

Completely depressed, I join Betty in staring at Spike as he talks to the men across the field.

Spike would have no problem coming up with the right lines. He's so smooth; he can talk with anyone, even with the bunch of guys he's talking to now. The group is a who's who of neighborhood thugs. Everyone at the field recognizes them. They're some of the toughest, meanest fighters in the community. They built their reputation by beating the crap out of some unfortunate people.

Now they're standing around waiting for the game to begin. The gathering is an extremely exclusive club; not many other guys in the neighborhood have their notoriety. No sane person would dare confront them or challenge those bruisers to a fight, so fearsome is their reputation. Spike, however, is cool and collected, completely in his element. Even though he's only recently acquired his standing, the men know they can't take Spike lightly.

Spike knows there's little chance of any one of this group instigating trouble with him or each other. Having worked so hard to achieve their lofty status, they wouldn't jeopardize losing their position with a foolish fight with one of their equals. Each gives his contemporaries the deference he deserves. Never in a million years would it ever cross my mind to join the group and cut in on their conversation. In fact, the majority of the people at the field is of the same opinion and wouldn't dare interrupt that congregation.

Despite his reputation, the elite group still gives Spike a good going over. Not only is Spike a newcomer to this crowd, but he's also a rookie to the football league. These two things make him a target of some friendly digs. Not that Spike needs anybody to defend him. Spike can take care of himself, even around that bunch. He's a master of allowing someone just the right amount of leeway before firing back an appropriately well timed comeback. Since all of the guys in the group are older than him, they would expect—and Spike would give—a certain amount of respect. Any reciprocity by Spike cannot be malicious or overdone.

Cooks, who is also present at the field, does not merit the same regard Spike is getting from these fellows. Understanding this, Cooks, like most of the schoolyard crowd, steers clear of that crew. No, Cooks is not in the same league as Spike, that is clear. After a few more minutes, the teams gather at their respective sides and wait for the game to begin.

The ref blows the whistle, and the teams take the field. Good thing. Thinking about Spike is beginning to make me puke!

The Giants win the coin toss and elect to receive. Spike and another one of his teammates are back awaiting the kickoff. It's not really a kickoff. The opposing team tosses the football instead. The Baldies start the game by intentionally throwing the ball short of the two receivers. The maneuver seems to confuse Spike's teammate. This is the exact reaction the Baldies hoped to achieve by throwing the ball short. Create confusion and get the receiver to fumble, allowing them time to get downfield to cover the kick.

Spike is not fooled. Expecting such a ploy, he runs downfield, catches the ball on the first bounce, and, without breaking stride, rushes down the middle of the field. Just as the opposing players get close, he feigns to his right. The move is designed to get the players off balance. The minute the other team moves to cover the gambit, he darts back in the opposite direction, running in for a touchdown. We all cheer wildly as Spike crosses into the end zone.

The new recruits from the Black Knights acquit themselves superbly. Casper, on defense, intercepts two passes, and Bonaparte, playing wide receiver, catches a dozen passes, four of the receptions snared with one hand. The Baldies have no defense for Bonaparte, who has total command of the field. They even try to intimidate him by pushing him around, and at one point, one of the Baldies slaps Bonaparte on the back of his head. Bonaparte, however, is oblivious to the abuse and just goes about his business, catching passes.

The final score is 42–7 for the Giants, a complete rout. The Giants go on to have their best season ever, winning the Eastern division crown. Due primarily to the efforts of Spike, Casper, and Bonaparte, they go from the worst to the best team in their conference. The championship game at the end of the season was close, but the Ravens prevailed in double overtime, taking the title from the upstart Giants.

Because of the lopsided score, most of the guys, except for Betty and me, went home. After the game, Spike, Betty, Bonaparte, Casper, and I walk home together. Casper and Bonaparte, basking in their glory, excitedly relive and recount the highlights of the game. We head towards a bakery on 187th Street, where Spike purchases a dozen glazed cinnamon buns. The bakery stop is a regular Sunday ritual of his. He buys the cinnamon rolls each week for his family's breakfast. I'm a regular guest of this weekly tradition. Today, Spike also invites our three other companions. Bonaparte begs off, saying he has to go to Mass. Betty and Casper agree to join us.

The next stop on our journey is the candy store for newspapers. Spike purchases the Sunday Times and the Daily News. I buy Il Progresso, the Italian newspaper, for my father. Betty gets stuck carrying Spike's papers. No way is anyone going to catch Spike with the Times under his arm. On our way out of the candy store, we bump into Fat Augie and one of his cronies. Fat Augie and Spike go way back, even if their relationship got off to a rocky start.

A few months after Spike arrived in the Bronx from Italy, he had a run-in with Fat Augie. Spike was playing slap ball with a few friends in front of his building. He turned to spit and had the unfortunate luck of hitting Fat Augie on his pant leg as he walked by. Augie must have been having a bad day, because he grabbed Spike by the neck and slapped him behind his head.

Speaking in Italian—Spike didn't speak English at the time—Augie pointed at the loogie on his slacks. "Now clean it up, you *strunzo e` merde*!" (lump of shit)

Spike looked at the man for a second as if he was confused. Then he hauled off and kicked the mobster in the shins.

"*Tu si un strunzo e` merde*!" And tore ass!

When my aunt discovered what Spike had done, she dragged him kicking and screaming to the social club, where the mobster hung out, to apologize. Standing in front of Augie, his mother ordered Spike to say he was sorry.

Spike looked up at the mobster for a second, then lowered his head in shame. "I was wrong, sir, you're not a lump."

"So, you no longer think I'm a *strunzo*," Augie said, grinning from ear to ear, reveling in Spike's humiliation.

"No, I no longer think you're a *strunzo*," Spike repeated meekly. He looked up. "I think you're a *strunzo e` mezzo!*" (a lump and a half).

Aunt Lucy was mortified and began slapping the crap out of Spike. Augie, however, laughed hysterically and grabbed her hand.

"That's enough, Lucy, don't hit him anymore. I don't think it would do much good anyway. The boy is more stubborn than a mule, but I've got to admit, he's got balls."

He turned to Spike. "Come inside, I'll buy you a soda. I don't know why, but I like you." He put his arm around Spike's shoulders as they walked into the social club for a drink. "But you're going to have to learn how to treat people with some respect, or you won't last long in America. What are you drinking?"

"Yoo-hoo," Spike replied.

Since that day, the two of them have been the best of friends, and Augie is sort of a mentor to my cousin. The families got so close they started referring to him as Uncle Augie, out of respect. To this date, all of our relatives treat him like an uncle, inviting Augie to every family affair.

"What have you troublemakers been up to?" Augie asks when we bump into him.

"Just got done playing football at the field," Spike says as he goes over and kisses the man on the cheek.

"Really, what team are you on?"

"The Giants," Spike boasts.

"The Giants? They stink!" The fellow with Augie interjects. Spike doesn't even bother to look at the guy.

"They're a lot better this year with us on the team, Uncle Augie. We already won our first game."

"Is that right, who'd you beat?" Augie asks. "The Baldies, forty-two to seven," Spike reveals happily.

"The Baldies? You must be pretty good; they're a good team. And how's my beautiful princess?" he asks, turning his attention to Betty.

"Just fine, Uncle Augie," Betty replies as she goes over dutifully to give him a kiss.

"Isn't she beautiful?" Augie says to his friend as he holds Betty in his arms.

"She's gorgeous," his associate agrees quickly.

"So, tell me, sweetheart, when are you and Spike going to run off and get married?" he asks, still holding Betty in his arms.

Betty's face turns beet red.

"I'm sorry, dear," the big man adds quickly, seeing the change in her demeanor. "I didn't mean to embarrass you. I just think you and Spike would be perfect for each other."

"Come on, Uncle Augie, can you give us a break?" Spike says, trying to put an end to the direction the conversation is heading.

"Never mind, wise guy, you won't do better than Betty," Augie says. "I wish I was thirty years younger." He gives Betty a kiss and releases her.

As he's leaving, Augie turns back to Spike. "Do me a favor, Spike. Please tell your mother not to cook anything for me today. I'm eating out."

When we get to our building, I run upstairs to give my dad his newspaper and rush back downstairs to join the group at Spike's place. Aunt Lucy has already started to cook her sauce for the Sunday dinner. The fragrant aroma of the gravy simmering on the stove permeates the apartment.

Spike's younger brother, Vito, is very upset at seeing such a large contingent of guests. He's annoyed that Spike hasn't bought more than the usual dozen cinnamon buns. Vito carries on so much that Betty feigns not being hungry and relinquishes her roll. Spike gets so angry he calls Vito, Nerone, which means a person who is a bigger glutton than Emperor Nero.

Spike takes one bite from his bun and hands it to Betty. "Here, take my roll, I'm not in the mood."

"Are you sure, you don't want it?" Betty asks.

"Absolutely," Spike replies. "Playing the football game left me famished but not for sweets. I'm in the mood for something more substantial. I'll just wait for Mom's meatballs to cook and pick some out of the pot."

Satisfied with Spike's explanation, Betty digs into the bun. Aunt Lucy whispers something to Vito, and, based on his expression, the glutton seems annoyed by her remarks. After the buns, we go into the living room and divvy up the different sections of the newspapers.

After a while, my aunt comes in with a dish containing several meatballs for Spike. She turns to Casper. "Will you be joining us for dinner?"

"No, I'm sorry, Aunt Lucy, I can't. Mom and I are going to visit some people, and we'll be eating with them. Thanks just the same."

"Betty, you're certainly staying, aren't you?" The inquiry is more of a command than a question.

"Sure, Aunt Lucy," Betty replies. "I'd love to."

Both Betty and Casper are frequent guests at my aunt's Sunday dinners. You really didn't need an invitation, you merely needed to be present at mealtime, and my aunt expects you to dine with the family. Resistance is futile. Aunt Lucy unleashes such a harangue of prodding that any effort to contest her is useless.

Every two minutes, she'll ask you to eat something. "Just a small dish," she'll say. "How about a meatball or a small piece of sausage?" Her prodding is unending, and eventually, you eat a morsel just to shut her up. Unfortunately, this capitulation encourages her into even more prodding. The alternative is to make sure you're gone well before dinner.

"How about you, Joey?" she asks.

"No, Mom is expecting me. It's better I eat with my family."

"Oh Mom, Uncle Augie said you shouldn't make him a dish," Spike says. "He's going to eat out."

Like my mother, Aunt Lucy also makes a few extra dishes for people in the building who live alone.

"I'll put his dish aside, just in case he gets hungry later tonight," Aunt Lucy says, never giving up.

"Hey, Mom, Uncle Augie said that Betty and I should elope," Spike says, trying to needle his mother.

"You won't get better than Betty, that's for sure," Aunt Lucy fires back as she leaves the room.

Spike looks at Betty. "What are you smiling about?"

She responds by sticking out her tongue. He crunches a sheet of the newspaper into a ball and flings it at her. Thirty minutes later, Casper says he's leaving, and I make my exit at the same moment. With little variation, this is the typical Sunday routine during the autumn football season.

CHAPTER 7

Girls in Turmoil

The next afternoon, we're all hanging out in front of the clubhouse shooting the breeze. Spike just finished working at the vegetable store, where he has a part-time job. As we talk, Janice and two of her friends, Rachel and Miriam, walk up and pay us a visit. Well, not really us, but Spike. It's apparent the attention my cousin devoted to Janice is paying off. She wouldn't be stopping if she weren't interested in him.

All the other fellows are enthusiastic fans of Spike's amorous exploits. When he pursues some teenager outside our normal group, it always means that a few of her friends will be available for the remaining guys. Just like today. Janice is here to meet Spike, not wanting to come alone, her two girlfriends accompany her. While Janice and Spike divert their attention to each other, the remainder of the fellows pursue her friends. For most of the boys, this is an important avenue of social contact with the opposite sex. All that's required is clinging to Spike and waiting until girls show up with their friends.

Aldo, in particular, has perfected this technique. He always seems to be in the vicinity whenever girls appear for a rendezvous with Spike, and with my cousin, there appears to be an inexhaustible bevy of opportunities. Girls are always coming by to pay him a visit. Arthur Avenue teen gangs have a notorious reputation among teenagers throughout the Bronx.

This is a really cool thing. Spike, a gang leader, is a natural attraction for the girls.

Of course, if they did any kind of checking into the Black Knights, they would discover that the Knights isn't much of a gang. However, if they delve into Spike's standing in the community, they won't be disappointed. Most of the girls living outside our area hardly ever venture into our neighborhood unescorted. To outsiders, our community can be a frightening place, and most girls always come accompanied by friends.

Looking over, I see Spike and Janice talking intently some twenty feet from where we're standing. His arms are on Janice's shoulders as she leans back against the wall. Aldo and Reject, apparently, are the victors for Rachel and Miriam. The rest of us congregate in a larger group apart from all the romantic activity.

Betty has a strange look about her. She's preoccupied, staring at Spike and Janice. From what I can figure, she isn't pleased with the turn of events. For some reason, Betty doesn't like Janice. I mean, Spike has gone out with other girls, and Betty hardly gives it a thought. Janice, however, appears to be another matter.

After a while, Spike whispers something to Beast as he and Janice go down the stairs into the courtyard and disappear into the clubhouse. Beast takes up his customary sentinel position at the top of the stairwell, a pose he always takes when Spike is with a girl in the clubhouse, making absolutely sure that the couple is not disturbed.

Recognizing what's about to unfold, I wait about twenty minutes and then excuse myself and head for the back door. Upon reaching my secret peephole location, I look in to see what progress Spike is making with Janice. I'm not disappointed. The rascal has made considerable advancement. Already, Spike and Janice are in a passionate embrace. Janice's blouse is open, and Spike has removed her bra, exposing her beautiful, bountiful breasts. They're sitting alongside each other, one of his hands stroking one of her firm mounds, the other between her legs and up her skirt. They shift slightly, and then Janice's back turns towards me. She's above Spike, opening his shirt. All the while, their lips never part. As his shirt comes open, she kisses his chest, working her way down to his stomach.

With her body blocking my view, it's difficult to take in what she's doing. There appears to be some fumbling movement, and then her head disappears on his lap. I struggle to make sense of what's happening. He caresses the back of her head as it moves up and down in his lap. It takes a few minutes to realize what's transpiring, and then it hits me. That lucky son of a bitch!

Much to Betty's dismay, Janice becomes a regular with Spike. Not only is she around most afternoons during the week, she and Spike date on the weekends. He's with her constantly—at school and throughout the day as well as during almost all of his available free time. Since Janice shares most of her classes with Betty and Spike, there's seemingly no end to Janice's presence.

Unfortunately, there's little Betty can do. She's a third wheel now and has no choice but to sink deeper into Spike's shadow and ride out the affair. I look in on Spike and Janice a few more times when they have their jaunts in the clubhouse. Their sexual activities have a similar refrain to the first day I spied on them. Not that they always need the clubhouse for their trysts. Apparently, the couple has plenty of other locations to carry on their relationship.

Unlike Betty, the boys of the Black Knights are thrilled with the current turn of events. As well as Rachel and Miriam, who came along with Janice that first afternoon, Janice brings many of her other girlfriends to the block. The steady flow of young women from Southern Boulevard creates a constant stream of possibilities for the fellows. As more girls arrive, they bring even more of their girlfriends, creating a never-ending cycle of opportunities. Most of the guys take full advantage.

Like Betty, the remainder of the regular girls aren't exactly thrilled with the invasion of teenagers from Southern Boulevard. Unfortunately, they, too, are helpless, they have no alternative but to wait for this fling to end. I don't get involved in trying to hook up with any of the girls from the boulevard. Instead, I consider it an opportunity to get close to Betty. With Betty so worked up about Spike and Janice, it might be the perfect time for me. It appears to be working, too. Betty allows me to walk her home regularly.

Finally, one night in front of her building, I dig deep and ask the important question. "Betty, will you go to the movies with me Saturday?" My palms are sweating, my stomach turning.

"Oh, Joey, I really don't think that's such a good idea," she answers quickly.

"Why not? Is it Spike?" I ask, my hopes sinking and my heart breaking.

"No, it's not Anthony," Betty explains. "Anthony doesn't look at me like he looks at the other girls. Anthony thinks I'm his best friend, you know, one of the guys."

"Then what is it? Don't you like me?"

"No, I like you," she says. "It's my nickname and my reputation. I think the other kids would make fun of us."

"I don't care about the other kids!" I insist. "What they say doesn't bother me!"

"Listen, Joey, it may not bother you, but it bothers me. You have no idea how cruel the kids can be. That awful name they call me, but worst of all is that hand gesture they make every time I pass by. Things are just beginning to get better. When the kids realize, we're going out, the teasing will start all over again, and they'll be unmerciful. I'm not in the mood for any more of their hassling."

For an instant, I'm about to tell Betty about my days in Orange, the years of being an outcast, how I understand what she's going through, but I decide against it. "Aren't you ever going to go out with anybody? How long are you going to let this one thing affect you?"

"You probably don't understand, but this type of thing is hard on a girl. I'm not letting it bother me forever; I just need more time!"

Then, seeing how disappointed I am, she smiles. "Listen, Joey, I promise, the minute I'm ready to begin socializing, you'll be the first boy to take me out."

Although I'm not completely happy with the outcome, her last remark does make me feel a lot better.

"You swear?" I ask pathetically, looking for more assurance.

"I swear," Betty says without hesitation before she goes upstairs.

CHAPTER 8

Charla

Things appear to be getting back to normal again. Spike breaks things off with Janice, and the girls from Southern Boulevard vanish as quickly as they came. Betty and the rest of the girls are all happier and begin to come around more often.

My best friend is Casper, the only black boy in our group. Casper's real name is Elridge. You might be wondering about his nickname. After all, Casper is a milky-white ghost, and Casper is a black kid. Did the moniker have some sort of racial connotation? The truth is much simpler.

Last year, the boys decided to explore an old, abandoned house in the neighborhood. The rumor had it that the house was haunted. One evening, the guys set out to find out for themselves. As they walked through the place, the guys huddled together for safety. None of the boys noticed that Casper had broken off from the group. He hid behind a closet door in what appeared to be the living room. By then it was nightfall, and the place was pitch dark.

When the boys opened the door where Casper was hiding, he jumped out and howled, "Boo!"

The guys tore ass out of the house. They ran about three blocks before they realized it was Casper. The boys got the last laugh when they branded him with his nickname.

Today, Casper and I are walking home from school. He's on his way to rehearse with his band, and I agree to go along and watch. We're going to my place first to drop of my books and then onto his place on Belmont to pick up his sax. When we get to his place, his mother, Charla, is on the stoop in front of his building looking up at a bag on the fire escape on the second floor.

A word about Casper's mom: Aside from Betty, she is the most featured woman in my sexual fantasies. She is absolutely gorgeous with probably the most beautiful set of breasts I have ever seen—a fact I would confirm shortly that very day.

Every Sunday afternoon, someone in the neighborhood places phonograph speakers on his fire escape and blares opera music aloud throughout the community. One of the operas is Giuseppe Verdi's Aida, an opera about a tragic affair between an Egyptian prince and an Ethiopian princess. I would like to think that Verdi had someone like Charla in mind when he wrote the opera. It's a plain and simple truth that in my dream world, Betty is my goddess and Charla is my princess.

"What's up, Mom?" Casper asks when we get to her.

"I need to get that bag of clothes that's on the fire escape, but there's nobody home," Charla explains.

The fire escape ladder is some twelve feet of the ground from where we're standing.

"I'll go up the ladder and get it for you," Casper volunteers. With that, he climbs onto the railing on the side of the stoop.

"Are you sure? I don't want you to fall and get hurt," Charla says, but it's too late, as Casper has already jumped from the rail and gotten hold of the bottom rung of the ladder. He pulls himself up and climbs to the second floor, throwing down the bag of clothes when he gets there. After he scoots down, he goes inside to drop of his books and get his sax.

While Casper is inside, I climb up the rail to see if I can make the jump to the ladder. I look up and realize that I probably can't. Just then, Casper comes out.

"What are you doing?" he yells, "Get off of there before you kill yourself."

"I think I can make it!"

"You're too small!"

With that dare, there's no turning back. I leap for the ladder. My right hand latches onto the bottom rung, but my left slips off. I'm dangling from the ladder clutching it with one hand.

"Let go and drop down," Casper advises.

Instead, I decide to swing like a monkey and try to grab the ladder with my left hand. Unfortunately, at the top of the swing, my right hand slips off, and I come crashing down head first, knocking myself out.

Minutes later, I awaken to Charla clutching my head against her chest, my eyes staring directly into her partially open blouse, giving me a great view of her ample, braless right breast right down to her large, pink nipple. Even in my suffering, I can appreciate this great vision.

"Are you all right?" she asks, stroking my face and looking at the top of my head. "That's quite a bump you got growing there." She turns to Casper. "Elridge, run inside and get some ice out of the icebox and put it into a towel and bring it to me."

She's still stroking my face, and I'm still enjoying the view, when Casper returns. She places the ice on the bump on top of my head, and I lose my stunning view of that beautiful breast.

"How do you feel?" she asks. "Any better?"

"My head hurts; otherwise, I'm okay."

"Go inside and lie on the couch for a bit," she says.

"Hold the ice bag on your head."

"I want to go with Elridge and watch him rehearse," I respond.

"That's not such a good idea, sweetie. Maybe some other time," she says. "Let's see if the bump on your head goes down. That's quite a fall you took. I'll check on you in a few minutes."

With that, Casper leaves for rehearsal, and Charla and I go inside the house. I'm still lying on the couch of Charla's apartment a bit later when I hear a knock on the door. It's Spike bringing Charla two bags full of vegetables and fruit. They are the fully ripened vegetables and fruits that are about to be thrown out of the fruit store where Spike works.

"What's the matter with him?" Spike asks Charla when he sees me.

Charla tells him the story, and they both walk over to me.

"How do you feel, sweetie?" she asks, peering at the top of my head. "The bump has gone down," she adds before I can answer.

Spike dropping in on Charla is nothing new. He always stops by to bring her fruits and vegetables and to help Charla with chores. Sometimes the two sit on the front stoop and talk for hours. Aside from Spike, I don't think Charla has any friends. She devotes all her energy to taking care of Casper.

"A little better," I inform her, trying to get up. "My head still hurts a bit, but I think I'm okay. I think I'll head home."

"Are you sure you're up to it?" Charla asks.

"Yes, I'll be fine. Thanks for everything. I'm sorry for all the trouble."

"No trouble at all," she says, "just take care of yourself. You gave me quite a scare."

With that, I leave her and Spike and walk home. The bump on my head is still throbbing about an hour after dinner when I decide to go downstairs. Spike is leaning against the car by himself.

"How do you feel, Tarzan?" he asks when he sees me, a huge grin is on his face.

"Very funny."

Just then we notice Casper coming up the street. Spike's smile disappears immediately.

"You're a no-good motherfucker!" Casper screams, taking a wild swing at Spike's face.

Spike pulls back, and the punch misses, so wide that Casper loses his balance and almost falls down. What the hell is going on? I wonder, pulling myself back from the action. What's got Casper so mad that he wants to fight one of his closest friends?

Casper regains his balance and goes at Spike again, swinging with both arms. Spike simply ducks, bobbing and weaving and avoiding all of the punches. I don't think he wants to fight or hurt Casper.

"Are you going to fight, or are you going to run, you chicken shit?" Casper shouts.

If the words are meant to intimidate Spike into fighting, it doesn't work as he continues to evade Casper's attack. Suddenly, Spike makes a mistake, and Casper catches him with a clean haymaker right under his right eye. The punch hits him with such force that his head whips back. As Spike tries to move, I notice his knees wobbling. Unbelievable, I think, somebody is actually going to take down my cousin. Encouraged by the turn of events, Casper comes at him once more, hauling another haymaker at him, which, if it landed, would surely bring the fight to a close.

Spike has enough strength left to evade Casper, and the punch flies harmlessly by his chin. The miss causes Casper to lose his balance and exposes his kidney area to Spike. Spike hits Casper with a right cross, directly at the exposed weak spot. The punch does the damage, and Casper drops to the ground, coming to rest on one knee, gasping for air. At this point, the fight goes out of Casper, but Spike, probably still brooding about the cherry forming on his cheek, hits Casper with a left-right combination that seals his fate.

Charla arrives and looks at Spike and he at her. Without saying a word, he turns and goes back into the building down the steps to the clubhouse. Casper is stirring and struggling to get to his feet. Blood trickles from his nose. Charla goes over to help, but he pushes her off. Only after he falls once again does he submit to her assistance. The two walk home arm and arm.

I stand there staring incredulously at the two of them as they walk away. What the hell just happened? I run down to the clubhouse. Spike is in there looking at the cherry on his face.

"I hope this doesn't turn black and blue," he says," I'm going upstairs to put some Vaseline on it."

"What's going on?" I ask when he returns. "Why did you and Casper have a fight?"

Before he can answer, there's a knock on the door, and Charla walks in.

"Joey would you mind leaving us alone for a few minutes?" she asks.

I'm out in the street for about twenty minutes before Charla comes out. "Good night, Joey," she says as she heads home.

Once again, I bolt downstairs into the clubhouse. Spike is sitting on the couch, his legs outstretched on the coffee table, his hands folded behind his head as he stares at the ceiling.

"Are you going to tell me what happened?"

He looks at me and rubs his cheek where the cherry is barely visible. "All right, I'll tell you, but if I ever find out that you repeated this story to anyone, you're history. Do you hear?"

"I hear, you got my word."

"Right after you left this afternoon," Spike begins, "Charla asked me to fix one of the legs of her bed. It was just loose, so it didn't take long to repair. After the job was done, I asked her if there was anything else she needed me to do.

"She stood right in front of me and said, 'You're so good to me, bringing fruits and vegetables, working around the house. I wish there were some way I could do something for you.' She was looking right into my eyes when she said it, and I tell you, Priest, there was no doubt in my mind as to what she was referring to."

Spike takes a breath. "Still, I tried to avoid the subject, so I said, 'Your smile is my reward.' Without moving and looking directly into my eyes, she said, 'Are you sure? Isn't there anything else that you might find more rewarding?' Without waiting for a response, she proceeded to kiss me. I was about to pull back when I felt her hand rubbing my groin."

I'm dumbfounded as Spike relates his story and can barely say a word. Spike stops talking and stares silently at the painting on the wall.

"Then what happened?" I ask, knowing the answer but hoping for a different end to the story.

"It was the point of no return," Spike continues, "either I remove her hand, which felt so good rubbing my groin, and run out the door, or proceeded with the inevitable. The truth is, Priest, I've always had a crush on Charla."

You, me, and the rest of the world, I think.

"So I grabbed her in a strong embrace, and I could feel her yielding to me. I slid my hand up her blouse and caressed her firm breast. She began unzipping my pants. I unbuttoned her blouse to get a look. Once her blouse was open, I bent down and saw her breasts pointing straight at me, begging for attention, and, of course, I obliged.

"We fell onto the bed, and she tugged at my pants to get them off. I stood up and removed my clothes and looked down at the bed. By then, Charla was completely naked. I stopped for a moment and just stared at her, taking it all in.

"'What's the matter?' she asked.

I lay on top of her and responded, 'You're beautiful.' She smiled, and her hands and lips began exploring every part of my body. It wasn't long before I penetrated her.

"Within moments after I was inside of her, Charla began trembling all over in that unmistakable quiver. A slight gasp from her, and then she laid there, motionless. I pull off her and simply stared at her naked, motionless body. Her eyes were closed, but there was a blissful look on her face. She opened her eyes and looked at me. 'I'm sorry, Anthony, for the suddenness, but you don't know how long I've longed for this moment to be with you.'

"We lay silently next to each other without speaking. Then she began to snuggle closer to me and kiss me once again. It wasn't long before we were wildly passionate and furiously stroking each other again. This time, she jumped on top and inserted me into her. Her thrusts were so strong I could barely move. It seemed as if all of me was inside her, but Charla shoved harder, trying to get every last decimal. Finally, the climactic moment arrived, this time in unison, and she fell onto the bed, breathless.

"'How was that?' she gasped. "'Absolutely magnificent,' I responded, and she gave me a huge smile, thoroughly satisfied by her accomplishment.

"We were so excited we made love two more times, and we were so preoccupied that we lost track of the time. We had just completed our final lovemaking when Charla noticed Casper in the doorway. He bolted out of the apartment, slamming the door on the way out."

Spike looks at me. "Well, you know the rest of the story."

I stare at him, astounded. He has made love to my princess, and it was better than I could have ever imagined. Never before has he told me of his exploits in the detail as he has today. Did he do it to punish me? Does he know of my love for Charla, and he is rubbing it in my face? Or is he reliving the moment for his own benefit?

"What did Charla say to you earlier?" I ask after I collect myself enough to speak.

"She told me it's over, that we're not doing it again. She apologized for seducing me. Apparently, she had planned it for a long time. Priest, I know she's probably right and that it couldn't go on, but it would have been nice if it had gone on a little longer. It would have been great getting to know Charla on a more intimate level."

He clasps his hands behind his head and stares at the ceiling, probably dreaming of what could have been. I hope he isn't waiting for my sympathy. The dirty bastard has soiled my princess. I will never be able to dream about Charla again without him coming into the picture. With that in mind, I leave the clubhouse, abandoning the dismayed lover to envisage what could have been.

CHAPTER 9

A Smooth Move

My house is in an uproar. My mother, sister, aunt, and dad are in the kitchen shouting. I'm in my room trying to ignore the fray, which is impossible to do with the level of yelling. Every once in a while, my mom asks my dad to keep his voice down—not that he's the only one shouting. My mom caught my sister and a boy in a compromising situation earlier. I guess the screaming is to get it across to my sister how bad her actions were.

Finally, my dad yells a final insult, "*Putana!*" and storms out of the apartment.

With that affront, Josephine begins crying and runs to her room. Of all the slurs that you can yell at an Italian woman, that is the lowest. For my normally mild-natured dad, this is unbelievable. I cannot imagine the hurt he's feeling for him to haul of such an insult at his daughter. A few minutes later, my dad comes back, and Aunt Lucy and my mom are still sitting in the kitchen. Josephine has locked herself in her room.

"Get her back out here," he orders my mom, speaking in Italian, as he always does when he doesn't want to be misunderstood.

"What are you going to do?" Mom asks. She's worried that the normally mild-mannered Italian has taken leave of his senses.

"I just want to talk to her. Get her out here!"

Despite her trepidation, my mother goes to get Josephine. It takes a little persuasion, but eventually, Josephine comes back into the kitchen.

"Don't lie to me," Dad says, still in Italian. "I want to know the truth. Did you have sexual intercourse with that boy? Are you still a virgin?"

"No, I didn't have sex with him, and I'm still a virgin," Josephine says, sobbing, and runs back to her room.

Her response appears to calm the situation, and the conversation returns to a quieter tone. It all centers around what they are going to do to keep this from happening again. Finally, they hit upon one of the most harebrained schemes imaginable. They are going to ask Spike to have a talk with Josephine.

I almost pass out when I overhear their plan. Are these people crazy? What the hell is Spike going to advise Josephine to do? Use condoms? Be more careful? Don't get caught? Beyond that, I can't imagine he'll have any worthwhile advice to offer.

Doesn't my family know Spike? Don't they know his reputation? He's the biggest philanderer in the neighborhood. Probably the biggest deflowerer of young girls of all time. He couldn't care less about the sanctity of virginity. I'm so disgusted with their plan, I get my jacket and head downstairs.

Speaking of the devil, Don Juan himself is out there. So are Aldo and Gaga. They're talking to two girls I've never seen before. Gaga steals the hat off one of the girls, and she chases him to get it back. Laughing as he runs around parked cars to avoid her pursuit, he hides behind Spike. Spike pulls the hat away from Gaga and hands it back to the girl.

"Cut it out," Spike says.

Gaga ignores the warning and snatches the hat off her head once more. Spike cuts in and grabs it back. This time, he slaps Gaga in the back of the head. As Gaga recoils from the slap, Spike puts his leg behind Gaga and shoves him causing Gaga to fall backward to the ground.

Anticipating the likely reaction from Gaga, Spike stomps on his back with his right leg, pushing Gaga back on the ground before he can get up. By then, Gaga has the message not to try anything stupid and gets up slowly. He looks at Spike, moisture accumulating in his eyes, he turns and heads home.

Gaga shouldn't be embarrassed. I'd seen the move dozens of time, so smooth and efficient that nobody sees it coming. Dozens of boys have fallen victim to the ploy, and there is nothing anybody can do about it.

Spike and Aldo turn their attention to the two girls, a tall blonde and a petite brunette with jet-black hair. Not wanting to be a third wheel, I stand away about ten feet from where they are, but I can still hear their conversation. Apparently, the petite girl just moved to the neighborhood and lives right down the block. She comes from Manhattan, a neighborhood called Washington Square. Her friend, the tall blonde, is visiting her.

Spike pays particular attention to the petite teenager. Nine out of ten guys would be wooing the blonde, but I know Spike, he is attracted to the brunette. Aldo will settle for Spike's leavings no matter which girl Spike chooses. However, this time, Aldo will be pleasantly surprised it's the blonde.

In addition to her jet-black hair, the young teen has smooth, milky white skin and puffy red lips. No way will Spike be able to resist that combination. A few minutes later, Spike calls me over.

"Priest, I want you to meet Lois," he says, pointing to the shorter girl, "and her friend Janet. They're new to the neighborhood. Aldo and I have to go to Beaumont Avenue to take care of something. Do us a favor and introduce the girls to some of the guys when they show up. We should be back in about an hour."

"We'll see you later," Spike says to the girls as heads out with Aldo.

Following Spike's instructions, I begin chatting with the girls. They're friendly and interesting, and we have a nice conversation. As some of the boys begin to show, I introduce the girls. Quite a crowd of boys has formed around the newcomers when Betty and a bunch of the usual girls show up.

Strangely, they don't come up to us but congregate some thirty feet away. It isn't long before the boys walk off to hang with the usual girls, leaving the newcomers and me alone. Trying to make sense of the awkward arrangement, I tell Lois and Janet I'll be right back and walk off to confront my crew.

"What's the matter with you guys?" I ask when I reach them. "Why are you snubbing these girls?"

"Because they're tramps," Betty responds for the group. "Joey, you have to tell them to leave! Those girls' reputations will mar all of us girls."

"How do you know they're tramps?" I ask.

"We just do!" Nancy replies.

"Are you going to tell them to leave?" Betty asks.

"Let's not do anything hasty," Beast cuts in. "Let's wait for Spike and see what he has to say."

"Yeah, Spike will be back soon," Rafaelo says, seconding Beast's suggestion.

"Why do we always wait on Anthony?" Betty asks. "Can't we make any decisions without him? Joey, are you afraid to tell them?"

This is the first time my goddess has ever relied on me. Isn't she right? Who the hell is Spike, anyway? Who died and made him boss? Don't we have a say in who can hang with us? This is exactly the kind of challenge I need to impress Betty and win her over.

"I'll tell them to leave," I say.

As I'm about to walk over, Twitch grabs my arm, eyes blinking wildly. "Don't do it!" he says.

When I walk over, I don't have to say anything; the girls have heard everything.

"We'll leave," Lois says.

As they're walking through the crowd to go home, Matilda can't leave well enough alone.

"Tramp!" she hollers and shoves Lois.

Janet comes to Lois' defense and pushes Matilda back. "Who are you calling a tramp?"

Betty hauls off and hurls a haymaker at the tall blonde, knocking her to the ground. Beast jumps in front of Betty, blocking her from doing any more harm to Janet. Janet jumps up, and the two girls bolt for home some two blocks down the street.

The rest of the afternoon, I'm feeling pretty good about myself. All the girls are talking to me as if I'm somebody important. Betty, in particular, lavishes a lot of attention on me. Yes, sir, this worked out pretty good! About an hour later, though, the wind changes direction. Everybody has gone home except for Beast, Rafael, and Twitchy.

"There's Spike," Twitchy says.

I look down the block at Aldo and Spike coming down the street. For the first time, a nervousness runs through me.

"You're fuckin' screwed," Rafael informs me gleefully.

"What happened to Lois and Janet?" Spike asks when he reaches me.

"We told them to leave and that they couldn't hang out with us," I reply.

"What the hell is he talking about?" Spike asks Beast. "Why can't Lois and Janet hang out with us?"

Beast holds up his hands. "Don't ask me, I had nothing to do with it."

"We told Priest to wait until you got back!" Rafael adds.

Spike turns to me, "Can you please explain what's going on?"

"Well…er, Betty and the girls said the girls are tramps, and that if we allow them to hang with us, it will ruin all of the girl's reputations."

I fumble to explain and shift the blame somewhere else, now completely aware of the trouble that I'm in.

"What reputations? Who the fuck died and put Betty in charge? And why didn't you stop her?"

Spike's beady eyes are stone cold, the beating of a vein in his right temple clearly visible. My refusal to answer makes him angrier.

He shakes his head. "I can't believe you're that fucking stupid!"

He's so upset he's having a hard time getting the words out to sustain his arguments. He's so incredulous that somebody could be so dumb that he can barely collect himself to make his point. His fingers twitch in an attempt to calm himself.

"Okay, Priest," he says, finally gathering himself. "Let's say, for the sake of argument, that the girls are right and Lois and Janet are tramps, even though they're not. Why wouldn't you want them hanging around? Can you please explain? If the girls are as loose as you say they are, doesn't it stand to reason that even a loser like you might get lucky? Or do you like pulling on your pecker alone in your bathroom every fucking day, you fucking douche bag?"

Suddenly, he slaps me in the back of the head, puts his leg behind mine, and heaves me to the ground. I try to jump up to retaliate, but he stomps on my back with his right foot. That last stomp makes me furious, and I leap up to hit back. I'm halfway up when he hits me with an uppercut just below my chest, causing me to fall back to the ground on my knees, and my head slumps over between my legs. I must have passed out, because the next thing I feel is Twitch tugging my arm.

"Are you all right?" he asks.

I'm in such pain that I can't respond, only nod. I don't know how long I was out. I never knew that anybody could be knocked out by a body blow—I can't catch my breath. It feels like my chest has been pushed to the back of my body and there's no room for air—I kneel there gasping and praying that the pain will stop.

"When you collect yourself, you're coming with me to apologize to Lois and Janet," Spike says.

In no position to argue, I merely nod. I don't know how long I'm kneeling there, but it seems a lifetime. Eventually, I make it to my feet.

"Let's go!" Spike says when he sees me up.

Spike, Aldo, and I walk down the block to Lois' apartment building. When we arrive, the girls are leaning on a car parked directly across from Lois' place. When Lois and Janet see us coming, they head towards the door of their building.

"Lois, don't leave!" Spike yells. "Don't be afraid; we won't hurt you!"

With that assurance, the girls stop

"Lois, I'm so sorry for what happened today," Spike says when he reaches them. "I can't believe how badly you were treated."

"The girls were horrible," Lois replies. "Why did they say those awful things about us? They don't even know us."

"They're just a bunch of jerks," Spike says. "I can promise you this, though: It won't happen again."

"I hope not," she answers.

"My cousin, Joey, is here to apologize for the entire crew and for letting everything get out of control."

He looks at me and nods. "You're up."

I bow my head and look at my feet. "I'm sorry for everything that happened today."

With that, I walk home, leaving Spike and Aldo with Lois and Janet. That night as I lie in bed, I reflect on the day's events. Realization sets in. Instead of being a hero to Betty, I was duped into one of her schemes. Spike had warned me that she is a lot smarter than she lets on. She knew nothing about Lois and Janet. She just didn't want them around.

Betty didn't want a repeat of what happened with Janice and the girls from Southern Boulevard. Betty is in no mood for a new influx of girls from Greenwich Village. She just needed a sap like me to help carry out her conniving plan, and in me, Betty found the biggest sucker of all time.

Later, I learn that as I was admiring the huge red mass on my chest, Aldo and Spike were getting blowjobs in Lois's hallway. Yeah, that was a real smooth move on my part. Thanks, Betty!

Lois never does hang with us. I guess the trauma of that affair was too much for her. Instead, she decides to continue hanging out with her old friends in Greenwich Village. Spike goes with her sometimes. Other times they sit on her stoop and talk. He gets pretty close to Lois. Not as close as he is with Betty, but close. It's more than physical; he genuinely considers Lois a friend.

My sister's punishment is to dump the teen with whom she had the fling. She also has to be home from school by three thirty, or my mom will go out looking for her. She can't go anywhere unless my parents know exactly where she is. I guess they forget that the whole episode transpired in the apartment right under their noses. I don't know if Spike ever had a talk with her. Frankly, I believe Josephine has learned a lesson and will make better decisions.

CHAPTER 10

Two Sisters

The fellows observe a custom every Saturday morning. By around ten, most of the guys gather in front of my apartment building. At this choice viewing locale, they await the neighborhood girls, who accompany their mothers on the weekly shopping trip. As the girls pass by, the guys utter a wisecrack or some flirtatious remark, hoping for a reaction from the girls. Since Arthur Avenue is the busiest commercial boulevard in the area, my building is an ideal vantage point to conduct these voyeuristic activities.

The Italian people are keen on the freshness and quality of their food products. Food is an important part of Italian daily life and culture. To appease these consumers' wants, the community has a large, diverse variety of specialty retail outlets. Not only do we have butchers selling meats, but they are also divided into smaller specialty stores. Should a customer require pork, for example, he or she can purchase the meat in a butcher store dealing only in that product, appropriately named a pork store. In the mood for live chicken or rabbit? There's a market whose sole concern is the sale of these foodstuffs.

Other stores specialize in the distribution of fresh eggs or ground coffee. Bakeries marketing fresh bread and rolls are abundant throughout the vicinity, as are pastry shops selling cakes, cookies, and other sweet delicacies. Seafood and produce markets are too numerous to count. Then there are the grocers, whose specialty is homemade pasta and macaroni, and cheese establishments that make their own ricotta and mozzarella. I'm probably omitting something, but the point is that a routine Saturday shopping trip is not your typical one-stop supermarket jaunt. It requires visits to several different establishments.

Located strategically between the city market and the live chicken markets, the front of my building is ideally situated to observe the shoppers on their trip. In addition to those two popular shopping destinations, to the left of the apartment complex are several butcher and pork stores. To the right of our locale are seafood shops and grocers. Next to my residence is a popular bakery. It's extremely unlikely that anyone can complete their entire shopping excursion without passing our position at least once.

Since most of the neighborhood has Saturday off from work, it's the busiest shopping day. The boulevard bursts with pedestrian traffic. Although the street can normally handle two lanes of traffic, the vehicles need to proceed in single file because of the many double-parked cars loading their groceries. The sidewalks are thick with consumers heading towards their destinations. The crowds are so heavy that pedestrian traffic advances at a snail's pace.

Because he works on Saturdays, Spike isn't with us; however, I expect him to stop by on his break, around half past ten, the approximate time the DeFavio twins are due to stroll by our vicinity. There's no way Spike will miss a chance to see the twins.

Concetta and Rosa DeFavio are non-identical twin sisters who moved to our neighborhood from Sicily some six months earlier. Their parents are extremely strict, and outside of school, we hardly ever run into the girls. Although the twins are not identical, they're both gorgeous. We refer to them as the "Sicilian Beauties." All the guys lament that such beauty is kept sheltered from the outside world. Every Saturday, the twins accompany their mother on their weekly shopping trip, pulling their two-wheeled shopping cart behind them.

The first time the sisters appeared six months earlier, all the fellows were falling all over themselves, competing with each other for the cleverest line to attract the girls' attention. Unbeknownst to everyone, the girls didn't speak or understand a word of English, having just arrived in America. Annoyed by our flirting, their mother attempted to stop our pestering by yelling insults in her Sicilian dialect. Although many of the guys, including me, can speak Italian, none could understand the old woman's regional dialect.

The only one among us who understood the woman was Patsy Bowlegs, also a native of Sicily. Bowlegs made the unwise decision of responding to the lady in her regional tongue. When the woman realized that Bowlegs knew what she was saying, she directed all her curses and insults at him. Recognizing some of the Sicilian curse words that she was hurling at Patsy, the rest of us howled with laughter. Our laughter made the woman even angrier, and she lunged for poor Bowlegs.

Patsy wisely backed off to avoid the enraged mother. Undeterred, she chased after him. In an attempt to evade her, he ran around the parked cars. Tired of the pursuit, the woman broke of the chase and continued on her journey, yelling a final disparaging curse at Patsy as she walked away. The twin daughters followed dutifully behind. Since that episode, whenever the woman walks by, she sneers at Bowlegs. Instinctively, and wisely, he keeps a safe distance between her and himself. That episode, however, does not stop the rest of us. By now, the girls speak English, and we can talk with the twins without their mother understanding what we're saying.

Something weird always seems to happen to hapless Bowlegs. On another occasion, Bowlegs and Aldo were atop a flatbed truck parked in the street in front of our building shooting paper clips at passing girls. An Amazonian-sized girl named Maryann happened to stroll by.

Approximately six feet tall, Maryann is a tall, muscular blonde who is a member of the high school track team. As Maryann approached the truck, Bowlegs took careful aim and fired a clip, hitting her in the ass. Furious, she turned and rushed towards Patsy, leaping onto the truck without breaking stride.

Terrified, Bowlegs jumped of the truck and tore ass down the avenue, Maryann in pursuit. In an effort to shake her, Patsy started a serpentine motion as he ran. The evasive action had no effect on Maryann, who gained on him. Desperate, Bowlegs darted around parked cars. The guys lost sight of the duo when the chase led them around the corner. Some twenty minutes later, he emerged from the alleyway that adjoins the apartment buildings.

"God, it took me forever to ditch her," he said, perspiring profusely and breathless from exertion.

Suddenly, Maryann burst out of the alley and grabbed Bowlegs in a headlock. As she held him in her vice-like grip, she rained down punches on his head. It took four guys to pull her off.

Spike finally makes his appearance. As usual, his timing is impeccable; we just spotted the Sicilian Beauties approaching. The girls are deliberately trailing some twenty feet behind their mother, an adequate buffer that allows them to flirt with the boys without their mother's intervention. As the mother passes by, she directs her usual disparaging leer at Bowlegs.

Finally, the twins stroll by. Spike engages the girls in a conversation and walks with them for a bit. The mother notices her daughters dallying behind, turns and yells a few words in Sicilian, motioning for the girls to increase their gait. Upon hearing their mother's voice, the twins scurry off. We don't set sight on the duo, outside of school, for another week. His break over, Spike walks across the street and returns to work. The next visitation from him will occur around eleven-thirty when Antoinette Bruceta, a.k.a. "Toni Boobs," makes her appearance.

Toni Boobs is an attractive, young teenager, about my height (five foot three) and weighs approximately a hundred pounds. Half of that mass is located on her chest. Those bazookas are so large the fellows swear it takes Toni twenty minutes to complete her journey past us. The girls insist that Boobs wears falsies and that the huge mounds aren't real. None of the guys subscribe to that possibility. My God, Toni would need to stuff a gross of toilet paper in her bra to simulate those giant mammary glands.

Toni doesn't go to our high school; she goes to Mother Butler, an all-girl Catholic school on Pelham Parkway. Since Boobs doesn't socialize with the girls in our group, we rarely catch sight of her. Saturday is our best chance. Should you succeed in being able to set aside the huge protrusions sticking out from her chest, you might be pleasantly surprised to learn that Toni is an extremely attractive young woman. Apparently, Toni has a crush on Spike, because whenever she passes by, she makes it a point to stop and talk with him.

As the appointed Boobs time grows near, the gathering gets larger. Nobody would dare miss the upcoming event. Toni's breasts will be the topic of conversation the remainder of the day. As predicted, Spike schedules another break and joins the gawking boys. The anticipation growing, the boys direct their conversation exclusively at the expected occurrence.

I turn to say something to Spike when I notice a strange look come over his face. His whole demeanor changes, and his jaw clenches. He's glaring at a man walking across the street and heading in our direction. Vito, Spike's younger brother, must have also recognized the fellow. He tugs on Spike's shirt to call his attention to the man.

"Look," Vito says, pointing.

However, the heads-up isn't necessary. Spike has already detected his father, my Uncle Vito. At that moment, the younger Vito runs inside to break the news to his mother. I haven't seen my uncle in nearly three years. He looks precisely like he did back then; he hasn't changed a bit.

"Hello, Anthony," his father says to Spike in broken English when he arrives.

By now, the entire gathering is aware of the situation, and an anxious silence befalls on the group. They all know of the tension between Spike and his dad.

"What do you want?" Spike asks.

"I just need to talk to your mother about something," his father answers in his thick Italian accent.

"She's in no mood to discuss anything with you," Spike says, "so just scram!"

"Is that the way you talk to your father?" My uncle, asks Spike, annoyed at his son's harsh words.

"My father died years ago," Spike replies. "He doesn't exist any longer."

"Look, I no have time to discuss with you. I need to talk to your mama, so I'm going in!"

"You're the one who doesn't understand. You're not getting past me!" Spike cautions, blocking his father's path.

"Is that what you going to do, Anthony? Beat up your father?" Vito asks rhetorically. "Is this the way you being brought up?"

The two stare at each other for a few seconds, and I worry that they really will come to blows.

"The way I'm raising my children is not your concern, Vito," Aunt Lucy says from the doorway, just in time to avert the ugly confrontation. "You gave up all rights to their upbringing when you disappeared several years ago. Stand aside and let him through, Anthony. I'll listen to what he has to say."

She turns to her ex-husband. "Come inside, Vito."

Spike steps aside and clears the way for his dad's passage, his face is red with rage. As his father and mother go into his apartment, he leans back against the wall, staring into space. At that point, Toni Boobs and her mother arrive. Toni directs her customary flirtatious smile at Spike, but he fails to respond, continuing his pensive stare into nothingness.

Incredibly, nobody takes notice of the vixen, all of us preoccupied with the recent encounter. A puzzled look comes over Toni's face as she strolls by and Spike doesn't even acknowledge her existence. After Toni passes, Vinnie Beast finally breaks the silence.

"Are you going to be all right, Spike?"

"If she thinks I'm going to sit by while she reconciles with that asshole, she's deeply mistaken! She takes back that son of a bitch, I'm out of here! I'm sick and tired of their games!"

With that, Spike goes back to work. Spike usually works until two in the afternoon on Saturdays. When his shift ends, his parents are still in the apartment, locked in conversation. After his work at the vegetable stand is over, Spike and Vito routinely sweep and wash the hallways of the two apartment buildings. Having nothing to do, I offer to help, as I do quite often. The three of us go into the basement utility room to get the janitorial supplies. Spike pulls out a long whiskbroom and hands it to Vito.

"Start at the fourth floor of the north building," he says.

Then he removes the wringer and bucket from the shelf and starts filling it with water. Grabbing the mops, he hands one to me. "The floors appear pretty clean, so we'll just rinse them with water; we won't need to use a cleanser."

"What are you going to do?" I ask.

"I'll help you mop the floors," he replies.

"No, I meant about your parents."

"I've been thinking about that during work. There's a building on Crescent Avenue looking for a super. The landlord is desperate.

In addition to free rent, he's willing to throw in the utilities to attract someone. It's even less work for me. If my mother takes back that jerk off, I'm taking the job.

"I earn thirty dollars a week at the produce store, and I believe I can live on that salary. Even if I'm wrong and I need some extra money, I can always wash a few cars on Sundays to make up the shortfall."

Just then, the basement door swings open, and Aunt Lucy comes in. My heart beats faster in anticipation of what Spike's parents may have decided.

"Your father's gone," she divulges.

"I can't understand why you bothered," Spike replies.

"He won't be giving us any problems," Aunt Lucy continues, ignoring his sarcasm. "Apparently, his *cummara* dumped him in California for a younger man. He's moved back to the Bronx, someplace on Buhre Avenue."

His curiosity piqued, Spike stares at his mother, waiting for the remainder of the story.

She pauses for a moment before continuing. "Listen, Anthony, I know you didn't agree with me, but I had to speak to your father. He could have caused some problems for our family. I needed to be sure he wasn't aiming to start trouble. I made it quite clear to Vito that we're managing just fine without him and that he's not wanted."

A relieved look comes over Spike.

"I don't think he will be any trouble," my aunt concludes. Spike walks up to his mother and, in a rare show of affection, gives her a hug, just as tears begin to form in her eyes.

My Aunt Lucy is my mother's older sister. They emigrated from Italy to the United States for economic reasons. They have a younger sister, my Aunt Anna, who stayed behind in Italy. Anna is married to a *carabinieri*, an officer for the Italian national police. Unfortunately, my family and Spike's weren't as well off. Our fathers didn't have a good job and struggled to eke out a measly existence.

After the Second World War ended, Italy lay in ruins. Our region was particularly hard hit. Southern Italy was the scene of some of the more horrific battles of the war. In the immediate aftermath of the conflict, the economy actually experienced a slight upturn due to the cleanup of the war debris. However, as daily life returned to a more predictable pattern, employment opportunities disappeared.

The victorious Americans tried to restore Italy's economic structure by pouring huge amounts of money into the national coffers. Regrettably, the politicians diverted the funds to the northern provinces, such as the Piedmont and Lombard regions, which had the most political influence. The southern districts, which needed the aid most, received little in reconstruction remuneration.

That's why most of the Italian immigrants who come to America are from southern Italy. The northerners scoffed at their countrymen's plight in the south. Thumbing their noses at their brethren, calling their fellow citizens in the south lazy and shiftless, they neglected the real reason for their affluence, the pirating of the American reconstruction proceeds.

Desperate for political change, my father became a member of the communist party. The political winds, however, were not quick to change direction. In desperation, our families decided to leave the land their families had inhabited for centuries for the greener pastures of American soil. Not that emigrating from Italy to America would guarantee them financial stability. Nearly one-half of all their countrymen who made the trip to America returned to their homeland heartbroken and no better off than when they departed, learning the hard way that the streets of America are not really paved with gold.

Still, the odds were more to our families' liking than those facing them at home. With the decision arrived at, the families borrowed the proceeds for the tickets of the sea voyage from some relatives and set out for America. Spike's family was the first to immigrate to the United States, relocating to the Bronx. My family followed approximately a year later, moving to Orange, New Jersey, where we were guests of some relations. My Uncle Vito managed to find decent employment and became a member of the carpenters' union guild. Life for Spike and his family prospered until one day my Aunt Lucy awoke to discover that her husband had abandoned them and had run off to California with another woman.

To make matters worse, Uncle Vito had cleaned out their bank account, absconding with the family's entire life savings. Destitute and penniless, Aunt Lucy and her children were facing a penurious and uncertain future. At first, Spike blamed himself. He had a major fight with his father the week before he ran off. When he realized, it wasn't his fault, he became angry. When the rage subsided, he went into action.

To help the family, he took a position as the super of the apartment complex in which they now live. The free rent, provided by the landlord as compensation for the janitorial services, assured that the family would at least have a roof over their heads. Spike also got a part-time job at the vegetable store, where he continues to work. Through his neighborhood contacts, he found a job for his mother as a seamstress sewing blouses in a local sweatshop. The position paid based on the number of pieces sewn. At first, my aunt earned little, not being a very good sewing machine operator. Eventually, she improved and saved enough money to purchase her own sewing machine, which she keeps at home.

The extra machine allows my aunt to bring some work home to sew in her spare time, supplementing her regular salary. My Aunt Lucy is a tough taskmaster, strict and not afraid to use her hands, belt, or any other object she finds necessary to dole out punishment to assure discipline in her household. Even I am not immune to her retribution, the few times I am out of line.

Despite Spike's contribution to the family's welfare and his status as a surrogate father, she's not bashful about appearing at a location where my cousin's behavior is in question. One time, a coworker told Aunt Lucy that she had seen Spike playing hooky from school and going over to some girl's house. My aunt asked her boss for time off and crashed into the girl's apartment, dragging Spike all the way back to school. My cousin took this behavior in good cheer and, except for once, never rebelled, understanding the fragile nature of his mother's psyche.

My mother, Isabella, is of a different disposition, not that I got into much trouble. She barely ever metes out any punishment to me or to Josephine. Heck, she rarely raises her voice. She's one of those women who has people eating out of her hand, especially men. All the boys are always helping her with her packages or, if they see her doing some chore, they go over immediately to help. One look of disappointment from those beautiful motherly eyes corrects any bad attitude problems.

Our family is also more fortunate than Spike's, as my dad, a dedicated and devoted family man, found gainful employment immediately upon his arrival in America. Even when my mother wanted to relocate to New York to be near her sister, he managed to get a good-paying position at a company that manufactures furniture. Other than my D in algebra, that one problem when Pauli fell down that hole, and the recent incident with my sister, Mom has never faced any serious crisis since landing in the States.

On Sunday, the day after the encounter with Uncle Vito, our two families attend a wedding reception. Some relative, whom I hardly recognize, is getting married. It's weird, but everybody from my old town in Italy appears related to our family. The village where we come from has a population of less than three thousand people. When I lived there, I barely remember any kin. However, since arriving in America, all the kinfolk has popped out of the woodwork. Not a weekend passes without some distant uncle, cousin, or other relative dropping in or our family visiting them.

The truth is, I hate weddings. You need to make small talk, or some fat lady pinches your cheeks. The most-asked question of the night is, "Do you remember me?" I usually don't! The entire evening can't end fast enough to suit me.

Josephine isn't allowed to come—further payback for her sexual escapade. It's not much of a punishment, if you ask me. Instead, Josephine is babysitting Spike's younger brother and sisters. Spike's youngest sister, Angela, has a high fever. Not wanting to leave her daughter in such a state, Aunt Lucy decides not to attend the reception.

Spike asks his mother if Betty can take her place, and my aunt agrees. Despite the short notice, Betty is delighted to go to the wedding. The reception is at the Alex & Henry catering hall, located in the South Bronx, not too far from Yankee Stadium. Many Italian weddings are held there, and I'm thoroughly familiar with the evening fare. Aside from the delicious Italian wedding soup offered by the restaurant, there's not much to which I look forward.

Betty meets us in front of the building, and we walk to the El to take the train to 161st Street. From there, it's a short walk to Courtland Avenue, where the restaurant is located. Arriving at the restaurant, we check our coats. When Betty removes her overcoat, we stare at her in amazement. She's wearing a low-cut, strapless, powder-blue dress. It fits her perfectly, and she looks gorgeous. The low cut reveals her beautiful, firm breasts, and I have to use all my willpower to keep my eyes off her.

"Betty, you look like a movie star," my mother exclaims, staring at Betty in astonishment.

"You look fantastic," Spike adds quickly.

Betty blushes at the compliments.

"Where did you get such a lovely gown on such short notice?" my mother asks.

"It was my mother's," Betty explains.

"Why, it fits you perfectly," Mom gushes. "It looks beautiful on you!"

"Your mother must have been beautiful," I add.

"Yes, she was," Betty replies, going no further than that simple explanation.

I really didn't know much about Betty's mother, other than she passed away a few years earlier. You can't really ask a person how their mother died. I mean, what difference does it make? There's a rumor that she committed suicide. Spike knows the cause, but he's never told me.

The rest of the evening, all the men keep ogling Betty; that's how striking she is. I expend my usual amount of energy trying to evade most of my distant relatives. The band, a typical three-piece Italian orchestra consisting of a mandolin, accordion, and guitar, is quite decent. Most of the tunes are Neapolitan folk songs, which I happen to like. The dance of the night is the tarantella. Aside from the music, the evening is a complete disaster, as far as I'm concerned.

Some supposed cousin visits our table to say hello, but mostly to flirt with Betty. Apparently, the word through our family is that he's some sort of gangster. Spike has no use for him; he hates mobsters. Spike loathes the stereotype Americans have of Italians, that we're mostly racketeers. Whenever an Italian succeeds in politics or business, people attribute the achievement to a mob connection. However, what really infuriates Spike is when fellow Italians idolize these crooks. To my cousin, these gangsters are the scum of the earth, a black eye on all of the Italian people living in America.

The irony is that all these gangsters whom Spike despises would gladly welcome him into their fold. With Spike's popularity throughout the community, he'd make a great addition to their circle. They have made overtures to him, which he always respectfully declines. With his family financially strapped, however, the mob remains vigilant, ready to seize any opportunity where he might weaken and change his mind.

The truth is, if it weren't for Fat Augie, the only mobster for whom Spike has any respect, he may have been tempted. But the big man, who has taken a shining to Spike, makes sure he steers clear. Fat Augie was actually invited to this evening's affair, but when he couldn't make it, his nephew, the guy putting the moves on Betty, took his place.

Now this fellow is putting the moves on Betty right in front of Spike. I can tell by the look on my cousin's face that he's not pleased. This guy's mob connections will not stop Spike from punching his lights out if the mood suits him. I'm pretty sure that if Spike had his way, the thug wouldn't get within twenty feet of Betty. Still, this guy is Fat Augie's acquaintance, and Spike tries to be somewhat respectful.

The hoodlum puts his arm around Betty. "Would you like to dance?"

"No, she would not!" Spike answers immediately on Betty's behalf.

The mobster looks at Spike and smiles. "What? Are you jealous?"

"Yes, I'm jealous!" Spike retorts. "I don't know what's the matter with you? I'm sitting here with her, and you cut right in as if I'm part of the furniture. If you want to dance with her, you could at least ask my permission. Now you ask me if I'm jealous. So what if I'm the jealous type? Why don't you just get lost?"

The guy takes Spike's harangue in good form as he turns to Betty. "You're a lucky girl; your man obviously likes you a lot, doll."

He slaps Spike slightly in the back of his head. "Lighten up! Don't be so uptight. I can't really blame you though; she's very beautiful."

When the mobster leaves to acknowledge other people, Betty turns and looks at Spike. Spike is staring straight ahead, avoiding her gaze.

"What was that?" she asks finally.

Spike turns to her. "Why? You wanted to dance with that crumb bum?"

"I think it should have been my decision," she says. "I believe I should be allowed to decide who I can dance with."

Spike stands up and throws his napkin on the table. "Fine! In the future, I'll keep my mouth shut!" He turns and heads for the restroom.

Betty looks at him walking away, shakes her head, and then a big smile develops on her face. Strangely, despite this incident, Betty is in a great mood the rest of the night. When we get back to the neighborhood, Spike walks Betty home. The last I see of them is when they are walking arm and arm with Betty leaning on his shoulder on their way to her house.

My Aunt Lucy comes up to my apartment to ask my mother about the wedding reception. To my aunt's delight, my mother fills her in on all the minuscule details of the affair. When she relates the episode of Spike's confrontation with the gangster, Aunt Lucy becomes concerned.

"I must have a talk with Anthony," she states. "It's not good to embarrass those people; he must go and apologize."

She rushes downstairs to have a talk with my cousin. Spike ignores her advice and never does apologize.

CHAPTER 11

Our First Car

I'm leaning on a parked car watching a scrawny, dried-up old man sitting on a milk crate and staring at the back of his hand. Slowly, he pulls on his skin until it can go no farther and releases his hold. His skin appears to take forever before it shrinks back into its original shape. Again, the old timer tests the elasticity of his skin by stretching the back of his hand as far as he can pull. Once more, the skin folds back slowly into shape. Fixated, he repeats the process, with the same results. Finally, he notices me watching and smiles, exposing his greenish-yellow teeth.

"*La vecchia!*" he says, commenting at what age is doing to his body.

Bored by these activities, I go downstairs into the clubhouse. For some reason, the clubhouse is almost always empty on Monday nights. Maybe the kids have just done too much partying during the weekend and need to get back to reality. At any rate, as I walk into the clubhouse, the only guy around is Ralph Mouse, who is stretched out on the couch, fast asleep. I pick up the newspaper and sit across from Mousy, reading the sports section.

Mousy is snoring loudly. Mousy is not one of the popular kids in our crowd. Like me, he's a smallish kid who has a head shaped like a mouse, hence his nickname. Slightly older than most of the guys, Mousy dropped out of school six months ago, just before his senior year. The oldest of five kids, his father was extremely upset when Mousy quit. The old man tried to have Spike intervene and talk to his boy, but it had no effect.

You see, Mousy has a plan. Mouse's plan is simple: Drop out of school and go work with his father as a bricklayer. The money he saves during his seventeenth year is to be set aside for a down payment on a new Chevy. Ownership of a car will be an instant ticket to popularity. Girls, who up to now have ignored the hideous boy, will overlook his features and find him acceptable. No girl can resist being in a new Chevy.

Even the guys will view him differently, hoping they might be among the select few whom Mousy might let ride in his car when he's out cruising. Nothing anyone can say will assuage Mouse's resolve. Quitting school and working in construction is a small sacrifice compared to the rewards he anticipates. Unfortunately, like other boys in the neighborhood, Mousy can't look far into the future. All he needs is to go into the social club around the corner on Crescent Avenue, where Spike spends some of his afternoons, to learn what happens to men who get too old to work in their chosen trade. Retirement pensions are small and their life savings nonexistent. The only pleasure left in the old men's pathetic lives is playing cards at the club. Most can't afford cars any longer. Their social life is no more exciting than Mouse's.

Spike spends time at the club, a habit I can't quite understand. Why waste time playing cards with the Old Italian geezers? Many a day, I find him sitting at a table playing games like pinochle, rummy, brisk, and scopa. The reason for Spike's fascination is a mystery to me. The men barely speak English, smoke smelly cigars called stogies, and have nasty dispositions. They're always yelling at Spike.

Whenever they play cards, if Spike happens to win, they call him lucky, unable to admit he may just be better at cards than they are. The stakes of the card games are insignificant, no more than a nickel or dime, but to listen to these old men's complaints, you'd imagine they lost a small fortune. Had any of the younger guys levied the insults these old fogies hurl at Spike, he'd certainly deck them, yet he takes all their crap without a whimper.

My opinion is that these old geezers are ingrates. Instead of admonishing my cousin with abuse, they should be worshiping the ground on which he walks. Not only does Spike devote his valuable time entertaining the men in these meaningless card games, but he also assists them in reviewing or filling out forms, which the men can't do, because they're not literate in the English language, nor would they understand the forms, even if they could read English.

Annually, and without any pay, Spike also prepares the men's income tax returns. Should any of the seniors have a problem with the Social Security administration or their union pension, Spike goes with them on the visit. Despite all these noteworthy deeds, if Spike beats them for a crummy nickel, they unleash a barrage of laments. Still, if Spike doesn't show for several days, all the men ask about his welfare.

Whenever Spike has some free days, he grabs the City Island bus, which stops on Fordham Road. Once at the island, he purchases a ticket and boards a party boat. The name "party" refers to a ship that handles a multitude of customers, not to a festive activity. Once on board, Spike spends the day fishing. I've never heard him ask anyone to accompany him on those trips, preferring instead to pass the hours in solitary contemplation. If Spike is lucky enough to snare any fish, he usually donates the catch to the retirees at the social club.

One of Spike's favorite charities is the old bachelor, Rosario Scalva. Old Scalva devoted his life to the upkeep and caregiving of his mother. Because of his passion for the woman, he would not marry until she passed away. Unfortunately for the dutiful Rosario, the matriarch lived to a ripe, old age, and the bachelor missed any opportunity at matrimony.

Not that finding a mate would have been any easy task for old man Scalva. He's one of the scariest, most foreboding men I've ever seen.

Anthropologists are seeking the missing link that connects the humanoids to their ancestors, the apes. To solve their riddle, all they need to do is study old Scalva. Scalva is a short, stocky man, a bull-like figure, more than obese. His body always tilts to the right, the result of an arthritic hip. Because of an industrial accident, his left arm hangs motionless and curves at the elbow. He's got practically no neck and an unusually large head, disproportionate to his small body. His facial characteristics include a protruding forehead, dark, bushy eyebrows, sunken eyes (more from the effect from his brow than anything else), and a long hook nose, which features a pronounced wart on the tip. He has bushy, gray hair, with no diminishing hairline, despite his advanced age. His teeth are yellow from the constant smoking of cheap, smelly cigars.

The sum of the package is a scary, creepy-looking old man. Scalva always appears to have a scowl on his face. The grimace seems more pronounced when he's looking my way. I'm so frightened of him that I'll go out of my way to avoid the guy. If he's standing in front of the building, I sneak out the back door. Should he be walking down one side of the street, I walk on the opposite side. Anything to avoid the encounter. Whenever our paths cross, I always make believe I haven't noticed him and never give him a glance or a greeting.

One day, Scalva has the audacity to stop me on the street in front of my friends and ask why I won't give him my regards or salutation. I shrug and don't offer an explanation. Sometimes my mother, taking pity on the old bachelor, sends down a plate of our supper. I always make an excuse for why I can't go, leaving the unseemly assignment to my sister. On the rare occurrence when Josephine isn't around, and I get stuck bringing the meal to Scalva, I knock at his door and leave the dish at his doorstep, making my escape before he answers.

One afternoon, Scalva asks me to go with him to the basement to get a box of nuts and bolts off a shelf. Apparently, the box is too heavy or too high on a shelf where he can't retrieve it with his injured arm. Caught by surprise at the request, I can't come up with an excuse fast enough to avoid the chore. Despite the thought of being alone in the cellar with the old fart sends chills up my spine, I relent and agree to help.

When we get to the dark basement, Scalva tells me the box is on the top shelf of one of the rooms in the basement. There's no light in the room, and it's even darker than the rest of the basement. My imagination runs wild. I'm absolutely certain Scalva is planning to do me in and bury my body somewhere in the cellar.

"Where is it?" I ask, hoping to get it over with as soon as possible and get the hell out of the basement.

"Inside on the top shelf," Scalva says. "You have to stand on a milk box to reach it. Here, use this one."

In a hurry to get it over with, I slide the milk crate next to the shelves, climb on top, and slide the carton with the hardware towards me. The heaviness of the carton catches me by surprise. I lose my grip, and the box crashes to the ground, spilling all the nuts and bolts across the dark basement floor.

Scalva is beside himself in rage. Italian curse words emanate from him. "*Stu gatz*," the most prevalent of his curses, appears to be attached to every sentence the man utters. He's so beet-red with anger I begin to wonder if he's going to have a stroke. Terrified, I decide to get the hell out of the cellar, leaving the old man the unenviable chore of gathering the fallen pieces by himself. That night, my father gets an earful from Scalva. After a lengthy tirade on what a useless, lazy, shiftless vagabond I am, Scalva sums it all up.

"He's nothing like his *cugino*, Antonio," he concludes, comparing me to my more venerable cousin.

Spike and Scalva's relationship goes far back. Scalva has lived in our apartment complex almost his entire life. He produces wine, which he manufactures for his own use and sells to the public. By offering the landlord a complimentary gallon of wine each week, Scalva receives permission to conduct his wine-making activities in our basement. Due to his infirmities, it's nearly impossible for the old man to produce the beverage by himself. When Spike's father saw the hardships of Scalva's endeavors, he volunteered his son.

As payment for his son's labor, Scalva rewarded Spike's dad with a free gallon of wine each week. Since his father abandoned the family and nobody in Spike's household drinks, Spike gives the gallon to my dad, who is only too happy to receive liquid.

In reality, Scalva is cheating my cousin. Due to Scalva's handicap, Spike does most of the physical labor. There is little in the form of exertion that the old spinster performs. As payment, Spike gets the free weekly gallon of wine, and every once in a while, Scalva throws him a few bucks. One day, I warn Spike that Scalva is cheating him of the proceeds.

"How do you figure?" he asks.

"I overheard Scalva telling some guy that this year the two of you have produced eleven hundred gallons of wine," I say, beginning my careful, methodical calculation. I've given this matter a lot of thought. "If you deduct the fifty gallons my Dad drinks, the fifty Scalva gives to the landlord, and the fifty he keeps for himself, you're left with over nine hundred gallons for sale. At three dollars per gallon, the take is at least two thousand, seven hundred dollars.

"You once told me the cases of grapes needed for production cost approximately seven hundred dollars. Even if Scalva spends another two hundred on miscellaneous expenses, it still leaves a healthy profit of over one thousand eight hundred dollars. He gives you no more than a measly hundred bucks, pocketing the rest for himself."

Satisfied that I proved my point, I smile smugly.

Spike gives me a knowing grin. "You've been a busy little man. You know, Priest, intelligence is a good trait, but shrewdness is not."

I look at him, bewildered. What the heck is he talking about? I wait for him to clarify his statement, but Spike doesn't offer any. Frustrated at his inability to grasp what I'm trying to show him, I try to restate my point.

"Don't you understand? He can't do it without you. All you have to do is play hardball, and he'll give you more money!"

"You don't understand, Priest. I'm satisfied with my pay; I don't want any more money," Spike replies, putting an end to the issue.

The wine-making business nearly crapped out several years earlier. The vintners had bad luck, and the production for that year turned to vinegar. Trying every trick known in the business, they could not prevent the bitter result. Scalva despaired; he had invested almost all his life savings in that year's vintage. Without the sale of the current crop, he wouldn't have enough money to bankroll the following year's grapes.

Selling the vinegar for salad dressing was an option, but how much salad dressing would the public buy? There wasn't enough of a market for the sour beverage.

Spike came to the rescue once again. He talked to every customer and explained Scalva's plight. He asked if they would mind buying some of the vinegary wine this year and pouring it down the sink. He would give them an equivalent quantity of next year's vintage free and a ten-percent discount on any additional purchases. Not all the regulars took advantage of the proposition; however, enough did to fund the next year's purchase of grapes, saving the enterprise.

Scalva always has a stogie dangling from his mouth. He lights a fresh Palombo each morning, takes a few drags, and then extinguishes the cigar, relighting it later in the day. The process continues the entire day until the cigar is completely smoked and finished at night. He never seems to put the partially smoked cigar in his pocket or away; it's always dangling from his mouth.

Recently, as a result of deteriorating health, they admitted Scalva into Union Hospital, just off the Grand Concourse. Although the hospital is almost a one-mile walk from the neighborhood, Spike and Betty visit him each day. On each visit, Spike brings Scalva a copy of Il Progresso, the Italian newspaper, a fresh Palombo, a flask of wine and sits with Scalva, going over the tally from the proceeds of the wine sales.

Rosario has been diagnosed with cancer, and the hospital does not give him long to live. Despite the prognosis, Spike maintains his daily ritual. I accompany Spike to the hospital one day when Betty can't make it. Mrs. Maderno is coming out as we enter the room. She barely glances at Spike but says hello to me. Scalva is lying on one of the twin beds near the window looking at a television monitor. A golf match is on the television, and I feel sorry for the old geezer. Not only is he stuck in the hospital, but he's also forced to watch a sporting event he knows nothing about.

"Hey Rosario, you having one last fling with old lady Maderno?" Spike asks when he enters the room.

Scalva waves him of with the back of his hand. "You be nice to her. You know she's a witch, and I think she's got a curse on you."

"I'm not worried," Spike says nonchalantly. He looks up at the television. "Hey, your old friend is on the telly."

"*Schifoso!*" Scalva says.

"Look at that, he's tied for the lead," Spike says when they show the scoreboard.

The golfer on the television is standing and getting ready to putt.

"He'll choke!" Scalva predicts. Sure enough, the golfer misses the putt, bringing a smile to Scalva's face.

"I didn't know you liked golf?" I remark.

"This might come as a surprise to you, Priest," Spike answers, "but Rosario once caddied for that same man you see on the screen this very moment."

"Really, is that true?" I ask in amazement. Once again Spike answers on his behalf.

"Absolutely! They even won the US and British Open together."

I look over at Scalva. "Then what happened? Why did you stop caddying for him?"

"*Schifoso*," is all Scalva will say, looking up at the television monitor.

Spike, however, tells the story. "The golfer on the television is Paul Abner, also known as 'the Earl.' Abner isn't really his name. His original name is Paolo Abbruzzese. After he won the Open, an agent advised Abbruzzese that if he changed his name to something English-sounding, he could get him a lot of money in endorsements. Abbruzzese saw the logic of what the agent was proposing and quickly changed his name."

"What's that got to do with Rosario?" I ask.

"With a caddy named Rosario Scalva, people might have remembered that Abbruzzese was Italian, so Abbruzzese asked Rosario to change his name, too."

"Change his name, to what?" I ask.

Spike is already grinning from ear to ear. "Are you ready? Ross Scanlon."

"Ross Scanlon?" I repeat in amazement. "I can't picture you as a Ross Scanlon," I tell Scalva.

"Neither could Rosario," Spike adds, "so when he refused to change his name, Abbruzzese fired him."

By now the television shows the leader board, and Abner has fallen three strokes behind the front runner.

Spike looks up at the screen, "I guess you're right, Rosario, he did choke."

"*Schifoso*," is all Scalva says.

Several weeks after my visit at the hospital, Scalva passes away. No more than eleven old men from his social club and Spike attend his funeral.

"After a few years have passed, nobody will even know old Scalva ever existed," Spike laments to me at the clubhouse afterward.

Spike is heir to Rosario's estate. I'm with him when he goes to the bank to withdraw the man's life savings of around two thousand two hundred dollars.

"What are you going to do with all that money?" I ask, marveling at the huge sum.

"Add it to my other savings. With this money, I should have nearly four thousand dollars," he reveals.

"Four thousand dollars? Where did you get that much money?" I'm stunned that Spike has such a fortune stashed away. It's more money than most people in the community have saved up.

"I've been saving some extra cash," Spike explains.

"What are you going to do with all that money?"

"It'll help pay for my college tuition," he replies.

"Does your mother know about your savings?"

"No, she doesn't!" He says and looks straight at me. "And you're not going to tell her!"

"Doesn't you mother need the money?" I persist.

"I'm sure she could use the money. In fact, there's no doubt if she had this money she'd put it to use."

"If you know she needs the money, why don't you give it to her?"

"Because I need it more."

"But your mother has to provide for the whole family."

"That's my point. While she's providing for the family, who's going to provide for my schooling?"

"But your mother has always supported your schooling. She's very committed to making sure you graduate."

"Listen, Joey, my mother's goals for me are not necessarily the same as I've set out for myself. Already I've gone further in school than anyone else in my family. I'm sure my mother wants me to graduate high school, get a good job, and help support my family, but that's not what I want. What I want is to go to college, go on to law school, become a lawyer, and, ultimately, go on to public service. I want to start making a difference in this world. I want to help the political process in this city.

"To do that, I have to graduate college and law school. These goals conflict with what my mother wants, but that's the way it has to be. In the end, I have to do what's right for me. I'm not going to end up like Scalva."

"Even with your savings, you won't have enough for college. How will you come up with the rest of the dough?" I ask.

"ROTC," he responds.

"ROTC? What the hell is that?"

"The Army will pay for part of your tuition if you agree to join the officer's reserve program. All you need to do is two years of active duty, which we're required to do anyway under the draft. At least I'll be an officer. Doing the two-year stint will feel like a vacation."

"Aren't you afraid of war?"

"After the Korean conflict debacle, there's little chance the politicians will go to war anytime soon," he answers assuredly.

Rosario Scalva did toss a final parting salvo at me after he died. Not wanting to continue his winemaking, Spike offers the enterprise to my father. He simply wants reimbursement for the value of the equipment, which my father can pay him from future proceeds. My dad tells me that I'm to be his assistant in the project. If I thought Scalva underpaid Spike for his toils, what I'll receive in compensation from my dad will pale in comparison. Compared to my parsimonious father, the miser Scalva will look like a philanthropist. Years of unpaid labor are in my future, and I know that Rosario Scalva is the cause.

Spike's association with the social club leads to one interesting prospect: it gets us our first car. A few days after Scalva's funeral, Spike returns to the clubhouse all excited. In the room with me is Vinnie Beast.

"Listen," he says. "Tony Beans just offered to give me his car. It doesn't run anymore, and he said I could have it."

"If it doesn't work, why in the world would you want it?" I ask.

"Tony said the clutch is gone, and it doesn't have first gear. As for the car not running, Beans thinks that with a tune up and maybe a new battery, I can get it moving again. There's a big, unpaved parking lot behind Artuso's Pastry Shop, right between Beaumont and Cambrelling Avenue. I know the super, and for five dollars a month, I'm sure he'll rent us a space."

He looks at the two of us for a moment to see if we understand where he's heading. Still seeing a confused look on our faces, he continues to explain.

"The three of us can chip in, fix the car, and practice driving in the parking lot when everybody is working and the garage is empty." He looks at Beast and me. "How about it, in or out?"

Beast agrees quickly. I think about the proposition for a moment and then nod. "All right, count me in!"

We hurry over to the social club and find Beans playing cards. Spike tells him we'll take the car, and Beans hands him the keys.

"It's all yours," Beans says happy to be rid of the piece of junk. "It's parked right down the street, a blue Ford Fairlane."

We find the auto parked exactly where Beans said it would be. The 1954 Ford Fairlane doesn't look bad. The exterior has almost no dents, and the upholstery, except for some wear, is in its original shape. On a hunch, Spike tries to start the car, but, as Beans predicted, the engine wouldn't fire.

"Let's go find the super, rent the parking space, and get the key to the lot. After that, we'll come back and push the car," Spike suggests.

Once we locate the super, he is happy to rent us the space, seeing as there are lots of empty spots available. He hands Spike the key to the gate. We return to the Fairlane and start pushing the lifeless vehicle. The trip to the parking lot is only three and a half blocks. We accomplish the first part of the journey easily. The streets are flat and slope downhill. However, the last segment is another story. Although only a half block, it rises up a steep hill, and we struggle to push the car. Fortunately, a few boys spot us and run over to help. With their aid, we manage to push the Ford the remainder of the journey without really exerting ourselves.

Over the next several days, all our efforts go towards repairing the automobile. Beast, in particular, has a natural aptitude for car repair. We change the points and plugs, replace the oil and air filters, change the oil, clean the carburetor, and install a new battery. I learn more about the workings of cars that month than I have the remainder of my life. Our service of the Ford complete, we cross our fingers as Spike attempts to fire the engine.

Without a sputter, the car roars to life. Delighted and relieved, Beast and I jump in and join Spike in a lap around the parking lot. The car has a manual, three-speed shifter mounted on the steering column. Spike places the car in first and releases the clutch. The Ford shakes, buckles, and stalls. Without first gear, driving in the small parking lot won't be easy.

After several attempts, Spike finally gets the knack. The trick is putting the car in second and flooring it while riding the clutch, never completely releasing it. We take turns driving the car, and for the next month, we visit the lot daily. After the first month, driving around the lot gets monotonous.

Spike suggests we borrow some license plates from another parked vehicle and install them on ours. With the plates on the car, we can drive the Ford out of the lot and around the neighborhood. After a tour of the community, we return our car to the garage, reinstalling the borrowed plates on the car from which we snatched them. So that the other car owner won't discover the missing plates, we make certain to remove the tags from an automobile that is hardly ever used. The newfound car routine reinvigorates our desire for driving, and we head to the garage enthusiastically once more.

One afternoon, Casper comes with me to the lot. Showing off and trying to impress my friend with my driving ability, I remove the plates from a Buick parked next to ours and place the tags on our car.

"Should you do this without Spike? Do you know what you're doing?" Casper asks.

"Sure!" I reply adamantly. "Get in!" I add, after installing the tags on the Ford.

Once inside, I start the car, place the shifter in reverse to back out of the parking space, and shove the gas pedal to the floor, flooding the engine to avoid the car stalling, just like we usually do. I release the clutch slowly, but this time, something goes horribly wrong. The car jumps backward violently, speeding toward the wall of the building abutting the lot. Instinctively, I release the gas and stomp on the brake, to no avail as the vehicle continues speeding in reverse. The car flies across the lot, smacking into the brick wall of the apartment building.

Casper and I jump out of the car, which, thankfully, has stalled. The crash has done considerable damage. The trunk lid is up in the air, and the entire rear end is folded in like an accordion. A liquid is flowing beneath the car, and by the smell of it, I can only assume it's gasoline. That means there's also damage to the gas tank.

"Spike's going to kill you!" Casper says and runs off to get him.

When Spike arrives, he surveys the accident and turns to me, puts his arm on my shoulder. "Are you all right?"

"I'm fine," I assure him. "Spike, I'm sorry, but I couldn't help it."

"What happened?"

"The gas pedal stuck," I explain, "the car just wouldn't stop."

"You don't fool around, when you wreck, you really wreck," he observes as he walks around and inspects the car. "I don't think we can ever get it running again. Let's push it back into our parking spot." I wait for his scolding, but it never comes. Spike studies the damage a little longer.

"Take the plates off and put them back on the Buick. Then let's go to A&R Body and see if they'll buy the car for parts."

We get fifty dollars, just about what we spent fixing the car. Spike never mentions the fiasco again.

CHAPTER 12

'Tis the Season

Christmas, although observed on December 25, is not a holiday celebrated in a single day; it's really a month-long affair. The minute Thanksgiving ends, Christmas festivities begin. Installing of decorations and lights, the purchase of a tree, the mailing of Christmas cards, and Christmas shopping are all part and parcel of the holiday. People are always in a happier, more generous mood during this period. However, something always happens during this time that takes the gloss off my holiday.

The season starts out on a high note. Spike begins a car-washing business, and along with Beast, I'm one of the partners. Every Sunday afternoon, the three of us set up in front of the building and wash cars. The fees are two dollars for a full wash of both the inside and outside. Waxing the car costs an additional two dollars, as does compounding. Thanks to Augie, business is good, and the three of us split forty dollars for each Sunday afternoon's work. The big man makes sure we get plenty of business. All the wise guys have to get their cars washed by Spike, and all give good tips, too.

Not that Spike would have told Augie if someone was a bad tipper. Still, it's better to play it safe. Nothing is worse than having Augie think you're a cheapskate. Most of the girls avoid hanging out in front of the building when we're washing cars. Spike always turns the hose on them, especially Betty. Betty does strike back once. We're washing a car when we leave the hose unattended in the street. Betty sneaks up and turns the hose on Spike. Not wanting Betty to get the last laugh, Spike chases after her and nabs the laughing girl about a block away. He throws her over his shoulders and carries her back, hosing her down until she's completely soaked.

Later in the season, Spike comes up with a new venture. With the help of his boss at the produce store, we begin selling Christmas trees. There's an empty lot around the corner on Crescent Avenue, where we store and sell the trees. The owner of the property lets us have it rent free. Nobody can dump garbage on the lot while we're in business, the lot owner reasons.

Spike's boss puts up the money to buy the three hundred trees, and it's our responsibility to care for and sell them. That means two of us are to be on duty every day between three in the afternoon and ten in the evening. We also need to be available on the weekends. For our efforts, Spike's boss pays us two dollars for every tree sold. We also get to keep the tips from customers when we help tie the trees to their car or deliver them to their apartment.

Spike figures that, with people being in the Christmas spirit, we could average as much as a dollar tip for each tree. So that it won't interfere with the car-washing service, Spike takes on Reject as an additional partner. Spike estimates that, after expenses, the four of us should average two hundred dollars apiece for the month's work. With all the money generated from the activities, it looks like it's going to be a great Christmas.

To help attract customers and sell the trees, Spike says the lot needs to have the proper holiday atmosphere. We need a bright, cheery place to make people feel comfortable and in a festive mood. To accomplish this effect, Beast and Spike run a string of Christmas lights around the perimeter of the lot. Spike gives twenty-five dollars to a super in a nearby building so we can plug them in. To keep warm, Spike puts two metal garbage cans in front, and we burn the trimmings from the trees inside the cans.

Spike is worried that someone might steal some of the trees when we're off duty. To secure the place, he borrows some barbed wire from a used car dealer in the area and runs it around the top of the fence where the trees are stored. He also borrows a neighbor's German shepherd and locks the dog inside the lot at night with the trees. These security measures do the trick, and we don't lose a single tree to theft the entire season. Much to our delight, Spike's estimate on our take is off. We actually earn two hundred fifty dollars apiece. Better yet, my parents don't ask me for a dime.

One of the traditions of our group and most of the community is attending midnight Mass on Christmas Eve. It's amazing that most of the guys who never go to church all year, never miss the Christmas Eve midnight Mass. I attend Mass every Sunday, but most of the guys do not. I don't understand their hypocritical religious beliefs. All year, no Mass, but on Christmas Eve, they make an appearance. I'm not saying that God came down and said we should go to Mass every Sunday, but if you believe that somebody created you, why wouldn't you devote an hour each week to give him his due?

The Church makes it so easy; you can even go on Saturday afternoons if you can't make it on Sunday. I like to attend the early morning mass. That leaves the rest of the day free. The priests are kind of boring, so I don't pay much attention to them, but I do spend some of my time reflecting on God.

◆ ◆ ◆ ◆ ◆

The most interesting religious discussion, however, happened the past summer among Spike, Betty, and me. The three of us were sitting around in front of my building late one night when Spike began telling us about the fight he had with his father just before the old man ran off to California. Spike was helping one of the old men from the social club carry some boxes home one Sunday when he was thirteen.

It was the time of year that kids his age were making their Confirmation. A priest recognized Spike, and, noticing he wasn't dressed to receive the sacrament, stopped him and asked why he wasn't making his Confirmation. Spike told the preacher that he believed getting confirmed was a waste of time.

"I haven't received Holy Communion either," Spike adds.

Spike's revelation stunned the priest, especially since he knew that Spike's mother was devout. Next day, the priest went over to Spike's house around dinnertime and chastised Spike's mom for allowing her son to miss getting two of the required sacraments. The preacher told my aunt she wasn't following Catholic customs and was committing a mortal sin by allowing that type of insolence to permeate her family.

Aunt Lucy took the admonishment to heart and got into a huge argument with Spike. My cousin was his usual stubborn self and gave her a tough time. His father intervened, and, apparently, the two of them came to blows. That night, Spike's father threw him out of the house. Spike began living in the utility room, which is our clubhouse now. Aunt Lucy, feeling guilty that she caused the fight, let Spike sneak into the apartment during the day when Uncle Vito was at work. The next week, my uncle took off for California with another woman, and Spike was allowed back home.

"I didn't know you didn't believe there's a God," Betty said to Spike that night.

"That's not quite right, Betty. I believe there's a God. I just choose not to worship him."

"Why not?"

"Because God is worthless, and believing in him is for suckers."

"What makes you say such a horrible thing?" Betty retorts. "How could you say that about the Almighty?"

"Well, if you really must know, I'll tell you," Spike responds. "When I was seven years old, my grandfather, Papa Nonno, was hurt in a hunting accident. I loved that old guy more than anyone in the world. Suffering from serious injuries, Grandpa was brought to the hospital at the provincial capital. Unfortunately, since the hospital was so far away, I couldn't visit him. Still, I looked for some way to be of help.

"Across the street from where I lived, there was an old lady who I used to see sitting and praying in front of her house every day with a rosary in her hands. So, I got this idea that if I said a rosary each day, maybe God would make Papa Nonno better. I walked over and asked the lady if she'd show me how to say the rosary.

"She gave me these old rosary beads she had tucked away in the pocket of her apron and explained how to use them in saying the prayers. Every morning, I'd go to the small church at the center of town, carrying the old lady's rosary beads, and, kneeling in a pew, say my prayers. I'd start with the Apostle's Creed and continue with the Glory Be's, Hail Marys, and Our Fathers until the entire rosary was finished, just like the woman told me. At the end, I'd always ask for God's help and to please have Papa Nonno get better and come home.

"My prayers seemed to be working; my grandfather was getting better. By the end of the week, Papa Nonno had recovered to the point where the hospital was going to release him. He was to come home the next day."

James looks away for a moment. "The next morning, I went to church to say my prayers once again. Uncle Sal and my father left for the hospital to pick up Papa Nonno. After my prayers, I thanked God for all his help and told him that I would continue to say my rosary, every night before bed in appreciation for all he had done.

"That afternoon, my father and uncle came home without my grandfather. They told me that Papa Nonno died unexpectedly during the night, some sort of blood clot. I gave the old lady her worthless rosary beads back and told God to go screw!"

When Spike finished his story, Betty had a conniption! Not being a Catholic, she never knew Spike had abandoned his religion. She had just assumed he was indifferent like the other boys in our group.

"How dare you question God's will?" she asked. "Who are you to demand God's services? What gives you the right to question God's judgment?"

"Look, Betty, it's got nothing to do with questioning God," Spike explained. "It's a question of leadership. God is supposed to be the Supreme Being, the leader. What kind of leader would I be if one of the guys in the Knights asked me to do a simple favor and I ignored him? If God is everywhere, then he was in the church when I made my request. If he is all knowing, he knew what I needed. If he's all-powerful, he could have granted my wish. It's obvious he refused and chose not to help. Now I'm supposed to adore and worship him? Well, I choose not to! I'm not going to follow a leader who refuses to get into the action!"

That last statement from Spike did nothing to silence Betty. It just made matters worse. At one point, the yelling got so bad that, if Betty were a man, they would have come to blows. Spike was unflinching. He would not give any ground at all to any of the points Betty tried to make. Witnessing Spike's attitude that day, I could only imagine what the fight with his father must have been like three years earlier.

Finally, in an attempt to help Betty, I chimed in. "Aren't you afraid of going to hell?"

Spike had an answer for that, too. "I think hell is a lot of crock. If you believe the devil runs hell and that Satan is an angel who God threw out of heaven, then why would the devil do God's dirty work? Why would the devil punish anybody who didn't worship God? Why wouldn't Satan welcome me with open arms? After all, we're on the same side."

James shakes his head. "I'm sorry, Priest, I just don't believe there's a place like the hell depicted by the Church!"

The argument continued like that for about another half hour. Finally, Betty got totally frustrated.

"You are so fucked up and warped!" She turned and stormed home.

After Betty left, I assumed we had settled the issue and that we would probably never speak about it again. For the next few days, Spike doesn't bring it up. I assumed it was probably going to disappear as long as no one mentioned it again. Betty, however, had different ideas. She can be every bit a *capa tosta* as Spike and just as determined to get the last word on a subject.

The next week, right after dinner, she showed up with a Jesuit priest from Fordham University, a fellow named Father Diritto. The guys, Spike, and I were hanging out, as usual, when the priest walked up to Spike and presented himself.

"Hi, Anthony, my name is Father John Diritto. Betty has told me a lot about you. She's told me about some of the interesting observations you have about God."

"Betty should learn to keep her big mouth shut and mind her own business," Spike said, sneering in Betty's direction as he realized what she was up to.

The preacher was making the guys uncomfortable, so the fellows began slithering away. They walked down the street, happy that Spike, and not them, was the target of the sermon. I decided to stay to see how things turn out.

"Anthony, don't be angry with Betty," Father Diritto said. "It may interest you to know that I share your viewpoint, and I believe you might be right."

"What?" Spike exclaimed.

"I think you're right at being angry at God for not granting your request and coming to your grandfather's assistance. After all, what you asked for wasn't much, and he certainly could have granted your appeal, if he wanted."

"My point exactly!" Spike answered, looking in Betty's direction.

"You must have really loved you grandfather to get so angry with God," the Jesuit remarked.

"I did," Spike replied, beginning to warm up to the man.

"Did you and you grandfather do a lot together?" Diritto asked.

After a little more coaxing, Spike loosened up. It's like the priest unlocked a vault. Suddenly, he starts recounting all the adventures that he and his grandfather shared together. How they used to go hunting, fishing, or just exploring through the mountains and valleys. How his grandpa taught him how to play cards, swim, and so on.

"You have a lot of happy memories," Diritto said, smiling at Spike when he finished his narrative. "I can see why you would miss him. You and your grandfather were very close. Did you take the time to thank God when you were having all those happy adventures?"

Spike stood there, speechless, looking at the preacher.

"I mean, if we're going to blame God for things when they go wrong, shouldn't we give him some credit for the things he does right?" Diritto continued.

Once again, Spike could not come up with a response.

"I hear that you also don't believe in hell?"

Normally combative, Spike was silent and merely shrugged.

"Look, Anthony, I don't have all the answers, but you have to agree, neither do you. Nevertheless, this I can tell you: Hell is not fire and brimstone, as most people think, and you probably already figured out. No, sirree, that's not hell. I don't know why God called for your grandfather, but from what you tell me, your grandfather was a good man. I'm sure he's in heaven and sharing God's love and wisdom. He may be hunting, fishing, or exploring the mountains and valleys of heaven.

"However, at the rate you're going, you probably know you won't get to heaven. So, Anthony, every day after you die, you'll spend your time looking into Paradise and seeing your grandfather happy as he shares God's love. You, on the other hand, will never know that feeling. No matter what, throughout eternity, Anthony, you will never get into heaven.

"That will be your hell: knowing you can't ever get into heaven, join your grandfather, and share God's kingdom. That's what you and Satan will share in common. Neither one of you will be allowed into Paradise. At least Satan can say he'd been there once. You won't even get that opportunity."

Spike stood there without saying a word as the two of them stared at each other.

Finally, Diritto broke the silence. "Listen, Anthony, I'd like you to think about what I've just told you. After you've thought about it for a while, I'd like to discuss God further with you. Betty has my telephone number. If you want to learn about God, give me a call. I'd be more than happy to point you in the right direction. You're a bright young man, and I believe you're open minded. Don't form an opinion about something without doing the proper homework.

"Betty tells me you like to read. Come and see me, and I'll give you some readings of scholars and philosophers who espouse God's point of view. After you look at both sides of the issue, you can make up your mind. There are no barriers to the exits from heaven; it's the entrance that's well fortified. I hope you won't let your bitterness stand in the way of possibly learning the truth. Will you at least do that for me?"

"I'll think about it," Spike replied, probably more to get rid of the priest than anything.

Diritto must have realized Spike's intentions, but he still turned to leave. After a few steps, he turned back suddenly.

"Hey, Anthony do you think your grandfather would have come with you and the family to America had he lived?"

Spike looked at Diritto for a second as it all sank in.

"Touché!" Spike said, not adding another word, nor is another word needed as the priest had won the argument soundly.

The priest bid Spike farewell and headed out. As he disappeared down the street, Betty walked up to Spike with a big grin on her face. It was a combination victorious and an in-your-face smile. Anticipating what she might say, Spike, grimaced and, with a wry smile on his face, swallowed hard. Betty strutted by him slowly, then, with her gaze still on him, turned and went home without saying a word, nor did she have to say anything else, since she already had the final say.

Spike, to his credit, did call Father Diritto, and the priest, as he promised, gave him plenty of reading material. Sir Tomas More, Tomas of Aquinas, Saint Augustine, John Milton, and so on. Spike read everything the preacher gave him.

Diritto stopped in and visited Spike from time to time. One Sunday, he even knocked on Spike's door at dinnertime. Spike's mother opened the door and almost passed out when she saw the priest standing there asking to see her agnostic son. Spike had never told her of his reawakening.

"Good afternoon, Father. What can I do for you?" Aunt Lucy asked.

"I'm sorry to bother you, but I was wondering if Anthony is at home. I have this book I think he might find interesting and may like to read," the priest explained.

"Come in, Father. Anthony is in the kitchen. We're getting ready to sit and have dinner."

My aunt ushered Diritto into the kitchen. "Please, won't you sit and join us?" She beamed with the knowledge that her son had befriended a priest.

"No thanks, I've already had lunch," the priest replied.

This ought to be interesting, I think, my Aunt Lucy versus Father Diritto about whether or not he was going to eat with us. I believed my aunt had met her match, especially knowing how soundly the preacher had trounced Spike in their argument. It was no contest. It took my aunt only thirty seconds to convince the priest to sit and join us for dinner.

Since it was October, most of the dinner chatter centered on the Yankees and whether or not they'd beat the Giants in the World Series. Diritto, like Spike, Vito, and Betty, is a Yankees fan. I'm a Mets fan and don't share their enthusiasm.

"Why do you think the Yankees always have great teams?" Vito asked Father Diritto.

"The answer is quite simple," the priest replied.

He looked around the dinner table to see if anybody else knew the answer. When no one responded, he reveals, "God is a Yankees fan!"

The table roared with laughter. Seeing how comfortable everyone was with Diritto, and realizing that the priest had developed a bond with Spike, Aunt Lucy tried to use the preacher to her advantage.

"Father, don't you think Anthony should get his First Communion and Confirmation sacraments?"

The wily priest was too cunning to fall for her trick. "The path to the kingdom of God may have several different roads. It's not important which road a person chooses as long as he's on one of them."

◆ ◆ ◆ ◆ ◆

That was in October, but now it's Christmas Eve, and the Christmas evening starts with a traditional dinner at my house. Spike's family joins us, as does Mrs. Maderno. Mrs. Maderno doesn't like Spike much. The only time she glances at Spike is to give him a dirty look. The whole thing has to do with her late husband. Mrs. Maderno's husband was a strong, burly blacksmith. Her husband worked at some horse stables on

Pelham Parkway. He enjoyed two things most: drinking wine and using his wife's face as a punching bag.

Many nights, Mrs. Maderno would flee from her husband and run into my apartment, crying in the kitchen and telling my mother how scared she was. She was too frightened to leave him, but if she stayed, she was afraid her husband would kill her someday.

Things got so bad that one day the police were called. Four cops couldn't get control of her burly husband. Finally, Spike brought the husky blacksmith down by cracking his head open with a lug wrench. Two weeks later, her husband was killed shoeing a horse when the animal kicked him in the temple. Now she sits in my kitchen every night crying to my mother about how much she misses her beloved husband. She won't talk to Spike, because he had the audacity to crack her beloved husband's head open.

Because of the abstinence rule, Catholics don't eat meat on Christmas Eve. As a result of the rule, the evening's fare consists mostly of seafood. We call it *La Vigilia di Natale*, sometimes referred to as the "feast of the seven fishes." It's a loose canon, since often more than seven fishes are served. It's not really a feast, just a huge dinner.

Before dinner, we pick at Zeppole's, fried smelts, and a baccala salad. The salad is raw codfish chopped into small pieces, stirred in olive oil, and mixed with diced garlic cloves. It doesn't sound good, but it's very tasty. On the table is a tray of strufoli, little balls of fried dough dipped in honey with sprinkles added. We're not supposed to eat the strufolis until after dinner, but we all sneak some.

While the second course of the dinner might differentiate between holidays, the first is always my mother's linguini *con vongole*. A long tubular pasta mixed in a clam sauce. The *vongole* are little clams, which are also cooked and added to the dish. I'm not much of seafood lover, but I do enjoy this particular entrée.

After the linguini and baccala, the only other seafood that I like is fried shrimp. My mother gives me an extra helping of the shrimp, knowing I won't be participating in the remainder of the supper. The next course consists of five different dishes: baked sea bass, filet of sole oreganata, the previously mentioned shrimp, and a seafood casserole, which, having never tasted, I can't tell you its ingredients.

There's also a dish called *capitone*, a giant eel that mom bakes. Nobody but my father eats this particular course. Spike always has a morsel just to make Dad happy. After the last serving, my mother brings out the desserts. In addition to the *zeppoles* and strufoli, there's a tray of pignoli cookies and assorted Italian pastries. My favorite is the *babba*, a mushroom-shaped pound cake dipped in rum.

After dinner, Spike and I go downstairs, where the girls and guys are gathered. Midnight Mass is still two hours away, so we have plenty of time to hang out before church. It's snowing lightly, and it appears we're going to have a white Christmas after all. Just then, Patsy Bowlegs runs up.

"You won't believe what just happened!"

"What?" someone asks?

"I'm walking alone, down 187th on my way here," he begins. "Suddenly, I get this strange feeling come over me. I turn, and someone's following me. There's this guy wearing a black trench coat, and I couldn't see his head. I'm not even sure he had one."

At this point, we all realize this is going to be another classic Bowlegs escapade.

"Scared, I start walking a little faster," Bowlegs continues. "The apparition appears to walk faster to keep up. When I stop to look, the specter also stops. This stop and go action goes on several times. I decide to make a run for it, rushing into the Half Moon restaurant for safety. When I barge in, a waiter, seeing how scared I am, asks me what's the matter? I tell him about the guy who's trailing me. The waiter offers to come outside with me and check out the situation.

Outside, we notice the man has disappeared. There's footsteps in the snow leading to the restaurant, but none leaving."

We all shake our heads in disbelief, Bowlegs is a wonder. Someone passes around a bottle of whiskey. Because of its inexpensive price, the whiskey of choice for our group is a brand called Four Roses. Normally, the girls don't participate in the drinking, but tonight they make an exception and join the guys in the festivities. Margaret Salerno, in particular, dives enthusiastically into the Four Roses, taking hefty swigs from the bottle. Not liking the taste of whiskey, when it's my turn to drink, I pretend to take a sip and pass it on.

Since the entire group is drinking, it doesn't take long to polish off the liquor. The minute we sip the last drop of whiskey, Beast pulls out another fifth. Margaret is the first to take a swig. After taking a healthy dose, she passes the bottle to one of the other kids. With all the booze she's consuming, it doesn't take Margaret long to start feeling good. Her cheeks form a distinctive rosy glow.

Soon, the second bottle meets the same fate as the first and gets polished off. With the emptying of the second bottle of whiskey, I figure the drinking binge is over, but one of the boys pulls a gallon of red wine out of a bag. Once again, Margaret is the first to partake. By this time, she's obviously drunk and feeling no pain. Finding the taste of wine much more to my liking, I join in the drinking.

Determined to make up for lost time, I take some large gulps. With the speed I'm chugging the wine, it doesn't take long for me to catch up with the other kids. By the time we finish the gallon, I'm out of control. It's almost time for Midnight Mass, so the group heads for Mount Carmel Church.

On the way to church, we pass the Half Moon Restaurant and, jokingly, we ask Bowlegs to show us the footprints. The church is crowded.

Having arrived late, no seats are available, so we have to stand in the back of the cathedral, packed in with a huge crowd of other latecomers. The combination of the warm air, the tightness of the throng, and the effect of the wine makes me nauseous.

My stomach feels queasy, and I think I'm going to heave my supper. Feeling sick and woozy, I make my way through the crowd and go outside. Once out of the church, the cold, fresh air has a soothing effect, and my queasiness dissipates. Feeling better, I walk to the corner and lean on a parked car across from Nat's candy store to wait for my friends.

Suddenly, my stomach turns into a knot, and all of the evening's dinner comes hurling out. Vomiting calms my stomach but does nothing to dispel my dizziness. At that point, I decide not to wait for the guys and make my way home and call it a night. Little do I realize I'm about to miss out on something big.

The most important subject to a teenage boy is sex. No other topic comes close. Any guy who tells you otherwise is lying or is going to be a priest. That's why boys are so preoccupied with losing their virginity. It is the most sought-after activity for teenage boys. The guys from my group are no exception; they're making every effort to lose the dubious label. Most resort to lying about their sexual exploits. Those fibs, however, are exposed quickly, and the fibber is cast with the undesirable title once again, only now they're pathetic losers as well.

That holy night, Margaret Salerno unwittingly makes it her mission to remove the virgin label from most of the boys. I learn the details of the episode from Bonaparte a couple of days later.

After church let out, most of the group, except for Margaret and five guys, went home. All of the other kids had curfews. Margaret had a curfew, but her parents were visiting relatives in upstate New York for the holiday. Not wanting to miss the Christmas Eve action, Margaret feigned illness and convinced her parents to leave her at home. With her parents gone, Margaret had no fear, staying out as late as she pleased. The effect of the earlier drinking binge was beginning to wear off.

"Does anybody have any more liquor? I could use another drink!" Margaret yelled when they got back to our block.

"There may be some left in a bottle we opened last week; it should still be in the clubhouse," Vinnie Beast said.

"Let's go see," Spike suggested.

The group went into the clubhouse to find the whiskey bottle. After a brief search, they found it behind the folding table, about two-thirds of the booze still inside. Margaret snatched the Four Roses from the boy who found the whiskey and started chugging away. Bonaparte told me that she polished off most of the bottle. The boys got barely a sip.

Someone put a record on the phonograph, and when the music started, Margaret jumped on the coffee table and started dancing.

"Take your clothes off!" one of the boys yelled. To everyone's surprise and delight, Margaret started to do exactly that. Encouraged by the boys, she stripped down to her bra and panties.

"All the way!" another boy yelled.

Once again, she complied with the request.

"Come on, I'll take you all on!" she shouted as she removed her undergarments. "Who's going first?"

She spread herself naked on the sofa with her legs wide open. Spike was the first to answer the call. Margaret was fortunate only five boys were in the clubhouse, not the usual crowd; otherwise, she might still be lying on the couch with her legs up in the air.

It was that easy for four boys to lose their virginity. Spike, the fifth, had lost it a long time ago. *Too bad I can't hold my liquor, or I could have had a great Christmas present.* We didn't see Margaret for weeks after the episode, so embarrassed was she of her behavior that night.

A Christmas to Remember

Other than a slight headache, I'm not too hung over the next morning. Vito comes up and asks me to go downstairs and play catch so he can break in his new catcher's mitt he received as a present from Spike. As we toss the ball to each other, Vito notices Iggy walking across the street. Iggy lives on our block but doesn't hang with us. Rumor has it that Iggy is hooked on heroin, and Spike won't allow him in our group. Vito, foolishly, lent Iggy ten dollars, and the debt remains unpaid.

"Hey, Iggy, where you going?" Vito yells.

Iggy shrugs and begins walking a little faster.

"Where's the ten dollars you owe me?" Vito asks.

Getting no response, Vito runs across the street to confront Iggy. Fearing a fight, I rush after Vito.

"Well, when are you going to pay me the money you owe me?" Vito asks again.

"I could pay you today, if you and Priest are willing to give me a hand," Iggy suggests.

"What the hell are you talking about?" Vito fires back, losing patience.

"I've been working at an electronics store on Fordham Road. The boss said, as a Christmas bonus, I can have a stereo. He left the stereo at the store for me. He left the back door open so I can pick it up today," Iggy explains.

"What's all this got to do with me?" Vito asks.

"There's a guy on Beaumont who wants to buy it from me for his daughter. He's willing to pay me sixty dollars. I can't carry all of the boxes of stereo and speakers by myself. If you and Priest give me a hand, I'll pay you the money I owe, plus, I'll give you another five spot apiece. How about it?"

With the holiday dinner still a way off, Vito and I agree to help Iggy and garner the easy money. We rush upstairs to put away our baseball gear and accompany Iggy to Fordham Road. We arrive at a place near Kingsbridge Road called Sam's Electronics. Since it's Christmas, the shop is closed. In fact, the entire block is deserted. Without hesitating, Iggy leads us to the back of the store.

"My boss said he'd leave the back door unlatched," Iggy repeats his earlier statement to us. When Iggy tries the handle, the door is unlocked, just like he said.

"The stereo is supposed to be on a shelf to the right of the door," Iggy says.

Once again, Iggy is right on. We find the components exactly where he said they'd be. We grab a carton apiece and start back out of the store. We're returning down Fordham Road carrying our boxes when a police squad car pulls up.

"What do you boys have in the boxes?" one of the two cops in the car asks.

"It's a stereo," Iggy says.

"Where'd you get it?" the cop asks.

"It's my Christmas present," Iggy replies.

"Where are you going with it?"

"Just bringing it home."

"Do you have a receipt for the merchandise?"

Unexpectedly, Iggy drops his box and makes a run for it. Paralyzed, Vito and I stand there in confusion and stare at each other. The cops jump out of the police car, and one of them races after Iggy.

The other cop looks at Vito and me. "Don't even think about moving!" he warns.

After a few minutes, his partner returns empty handed.

"You two, get in the back of the car!" he shouts at Vito and me, still breathless from the chase.

They put the boxes in the trunk and haul us to the 46th precinct headquarters. At the station, they bring us to an interrogation room. When they ask us to explain ourselves, we proclaim our innocence and recite the story of how Iggy tricked us into going to the electronics store with him.

"What's your friend's name?" one of the police officers asks.

"We can't tell you," Vito responds.

"Why not?"

"Because we can't snitch on a friend."

"I don't understand?" The cop says. "I thought you told me you were tricked into the affair? What kind of person would do that to a friend?"

"We're no rats!" Vito answers defiantly.

The copper loses his patience, grabs Vito by the collar, and slaps him on the head. "Listen, you shit head. I don't have time for all this nonsense. You tell me his name, or I'll kick your fucking ass!"

The cop grabs Vito, raises him of the chair, and flings him against the wall. Luckily for Vito the other cop steps in and tells his partner to calm down.

"Why don't you go outside and get a cup of coffee?" he suggests.

After his partner leaves, he turns to Vito. "Listen, the truth is, I believe you boys, but if you don't reveal your friend's identity, we can't confirm your story. So, how about it?" Vito stands steadfast and does not utter a word, so the cop turns to me.

"How about you? You look more intelligent than your stupid friend over here. Will you give me the other boy's name?"

"I stand with Vito!" I reply in a show of solidarity with my cousin.

The cop walks up and slaps me with his ring hand on the back of my head. The smack almost knocks me of my chair. My head throbs where the ring impacted it.

"Listen, you little prick, stop playing with us. Give me the kid's name, or I'll make sure you spend Christmas in jail!" Although tears are forming in my eyes from the smack, I maintain my silence.

His partner returns. "Let's call their parents. Maybe they can talk some sense into the little bastards," he states.

He leaves to make the call. Vito, is about to say something to me when the other cop, the one who stayed behind, kicks the chair from under him, sending him crashing to the floor.

"You got something to say, fuck face?"

Vito doesn't answer.

"Sit there still with your mouth shut 'til your parents get here, you stupid douche bag!"

The next half hour feels like a lifetime as Vito and I wait. I dread the moment when my father will walk through the door. Never in a million years will Dad believe I'm innocent. As afraid as I am of the police, I'm terrified of facing my father. When Spike and Dad arrive at the precinct, it turns out that one of the cops knows Spike from the PAL. He fills Spike and my father in on the particulars of the arrest and our explanation of the event. Throughout the policeman's account, my father doesn't say a word; just stands silent, listening attentively to the details.

"Spike, I believe their story," the officer says, "but if they don't give me the boy's name, they leave me no choice but to book them. They don't seem to understand the seriousness of the burglary charge facing them."

When the policeman finishes speaking, my father walks up to me. "Joey, please tell the policeman the other boy's name!"

"I can't, Dad," I reply. "You see, if I ta—"

The words don't make it out of my mouth before my dad slaps me across my face.

"Tell the policeman his name!"

My face throbbing with pain from the slap, I drop a dime on Iggy. Once we cooperate, the police release us. They don't even write us up. The cop who knows Spike goes as far as to give us a lift home in the squad car. When we get home, my father stops me before we go inside.

"We'll talk about this tonight. Let's not ruin everybody's holiday dinner."

No problem there, as Vito and I gladly heed my father's request, although I dread the discussion that will take place that night with Mom. The dinner is at Spike's place. When we get there, all the guests are present and waiting for us. Fortunately for Vito and me, nobody asks where we've been. Because of the large size of the group, they're sitting at makeshift tables in the living room, the only area in the apartment that can hold such a large gathering.

As well as Spike's family and mine, the guests include Betty and her father, Charla, Casper, Crabby, his mom, and Mrs. Maderno. Crabby would have loved to sit next to Betty, but with Spike just across from her, Crabby sits as far away as possible. My Aunt Lucy is serving the cold antipasto, a dish comprised of prosciutto, provolone, capicolla, anchovies, olives, and jardinière vegetables.

Despite today's incident, my aunt appears to be in excellent spirits. She's wearing the new, pear-shaped gold locket Spike bought her for Christmas. Inside the piece, Spike inserted a picture of her four children. Spike has also been generous to his best friend, Betty, who is sporting the friendship bracelet she received from him. Seeing Spike's generosity, I'm feeling a little guilty, as I've stashed my entire take of the holiday venture safely in the bank.

"What got into you?" I ask Spike when nobody is listening.

"What do you mean?"

"How come you've been so generous this year?" I whisper. "Why aren't you stashing all the money in your secret account? Do you already have enough for college?"

"No I don't have enough," he replies, "far from it!"

"Then how come?"

"I don't know. For some reason, I felt this Christmas should be special."

When Betty's dad starts talking to Spike, I drift off and worry about today's fiasco. How will I explain to Mom what I did? Although I'm not paying attention to the talk between Betty's dad and Spike, I can sense by the ease of their mannerisms that the two of them probably get along pretty well. Spike is talking to him more like one of the guys than an adult. My father, sitting next to Spike, is trying hard to get in on the conversation. Finally, he is able to interrupt.

"Anthony," he says, "why don't you tell Mr. Sargent the story of the farm and the door?"

My dad enjoys telling the stories of life back in Italy. More particularly, he likes the way Spike recounts the tales. Always willing to please my father, Spike begins the story.

"When my grandfather died, my mother and her two sisters inherited a parcel of farmland some two miles from town. My Aunt Anna, who is married to a police officer and lives in another region, couldn't farm the land, so our two families were the direct beneficiaries of this legacy. The land is not much, about six acres, but it supplied the households with much-needed farm products. As is the custom in the region, nobody lives on the farms but walks to the farm from the village when they need to do some tilling, harvesting, or other chores.

"Since the land was over two miles away, carrying the tools back and forth was a real pain. So, Dad and uncle Sal decided to gather some mortar blocks from bombed out houses and build a small masonry shed to house their equipment, eliminating the need to carry their tools back and forth to the farm. Unfortunately, one day, somebody broke into the shanty and stole the tools.

"Disappointed by the break-in, Uncle Sal told my father that he had seen a discarded heavy iron door in a nearby town. With such a secure door, it would be impossible for thieves to steal the farm tools, Uncle Sal reasoned. Because the town where the door was located was some five miles away, they decided to leave really early one Saturday so they could both haul and install the door in the same day.

"They had the misfortune of picking a day that was unusually scorching hot and humid. The biggest obstacle was that the farm was located nearly four thousand feet above the town, and the entire journey was uphill. They caught a break when a fellow with a mule-drawn cart happened by and offered to give them a lift. Their luck ran out when they reached a fork on the road.

"One of the paths led up the mountain to the farm; the other was the cart's normal route. At the fork, the mule kept walking on its customary journey. Nothing could get the mule to turn and take the dirt road to the farm. After a half hour of trying, my father and uncle gave up and decide to make the rest of the trip on foot. No easy task, because it was the uphill, mountainous segment of the journey. However, the two of them persevered and succeeded in completing the mission, as planned.

"The next day, my uncle and father both rested, and they chose not to look in on the farm, trusting that the door had done its job and guarded the tools. However, on Monday, my Uncle Sal became curious and wanted to make sure the door had warded off the thieves. So, he asked my father to go with him to the farm and inspect the shanty. Dad, however, had taken an assignment to clear a field, for which he'd earn a piglet, so Uncle Sal asked me to go along instead.

"When we arrived at the farm, we discovered that the door had performed its purpose admirably, and all the tools were safely inside the shack. The door, however, was another matter. The robbers, being so impressed with the massive metal door, had unscrewed it from its hinges and stolen it instead of the tools."

The table breaks out in laughter at the strange twist of the tale. Although my father has heard this story thousands of times, he laughs the loudest. By now, we've finished our lasagna and are awaiting the sauce meats.

My Aunt Lucy rings in. "Anthony, please tell everybody the story of you skinny dipping."

"Oh Mom, let's not start boring these poor people with all these stories from back in Italy,"

Spike replies not wanting to tell that particular story.

"What's this?" Betty asks, perking up suddenly.

"Come on, Anthony, please tell the people the story," Aunt Lucy pleads.

Finally relenting, Spike begins the saga. "When I was eight, the guys and I were swimming in the river Sabato, about a mile from town. Since none of us owned bathing suits, we swam naked. We had placed our clothes on the riverbank where they wouldn't get wet. Just about a quarter of a mile from where we were swimming was a bend in the river. At that spot, because of the wide expanse of the river, the water becomes significantly shallower. Rocks are exposed, and the place is ideal for washing clothes.

"The women use the rocks like a washboard to scrub and rinse their laundry. That day, my mother and some of the other village women were busy washing clothes. Seeing us swimming naked, my demented mother and some of the other perverted women concocted a scheme to steal our clothes. Distracted by our activities at the swimming hole, we never noticed the women sneak up and steal our clothes."

Already the table is roaring with laughter. Ignoring the distraction, Spike continues. "When we finished swimming, we realize the clothes were missing. Naked and not knowing what to do, we arrived on a plan to sneak back to town through a back route. The path required us to cut through some cornfields.

"Huddled together, we started home, hoping not to be noticed. Luckily, it was late summer, and the corn was fully grown, allowing for adequate cover. Other than getting filthy and some minor cuts from the stalks in the cornfields, we managed to get back to town without detection.

"All of the other boys except for Pasquale and me lived in another part of town. At that point, we agreed to split up and head our separate ways. Since Pasquale lived across the street from me, we walked back together. However, going to his house required that we cross the busy main street of town, and we'd surely be spotted. So we decided to cut through a neighbor's field abutting the back of my house and try to sneak into my place through the back door.

"Unfortunately, the door was locked and so were all the windows in the rear of the house. Pasquale and I walked around to the front, and I peeked around the corner to look down the street. My mother was standing outside the front door with six ladies. Peering my head around the corner, I hollered for her to open the back door."

"'Why?'" she asked.

"I can't explain!" I yelled. "Just open the back door!"

"'Why don't you come through the front door, and I'll give you your clothes,' she said. Then she pulled my clothes out of the laundry basket and waved them in the air. 'You don't have anything I haven't seen before.'"

The entire table stops eating and laughs hysterically. Betty is beside herself, laughing uncontrollably.

"So what did you do?" Betty asks, barely able to get the words out.

"With the mystery revealed of who stole our clothes, I got really angry, but I was in no position to argue," Spike continues. "Mom was standing in front of the house with the other hysterical women waiting for me to come out naked. Pasquale came out first. Fortunately for him, he lived up the street from the women, and all they got to see was his bare ass. My path required that I walk right past the gawking women.

"Unsure of what to do, I delayed a few minutes trying to devise a plan. As I was contemplating, I peeked out once more and realized a few other women had joined the crowd. If I didn't make my move soon, every woman in the town would be witness to my problem. Slowly, I came out with my tiny hands in front, hiding my most private possession. As I walked past the women, they roared with delight.

"'Would you like your clothes now?' my mother asked as I strolled by, hoping I'd uncover my prize when I reach for the garments.

"I simply gave her a dirty look. When I managed to get to my door, one of the women shouted, 'Why don't you give us a peek at what you've got? Are you afraid?'"

"'There's nothing to see!' another of the taunting women yelled.

"My patience at an end, I turned to the women and removed my hands to expose my joy. I thrust my hips, and it, at the laughing women and screamed, *'Mangia!'*" (eat me)

We're all beside ourselves with laughter. I have heard many of Spike's stories, but this one has been mysteriously missing.

"You know, Mom, if you tried something like that in this country, they'd arrest you for child abuse!" Spike shouts at his hysterical mother.

"What I wouldn't have given to have been there," Betty says.

"I'm sure you would have enjoyed yourself, you sadistic monster," Spike fires back. "What I want to know is, why do you get such joy when I'm at the wrong end of a practical joke?"

Betty just stares at him coyly, and her grin gets even bigger. The empty lasagna dishes are removed, and the sauce meats, meatballs, sausage, braciola, and pork ribs are served.

"How did you fellows make out with your Christmas tree business?" Charla asks Spike as she puts a rib on her plate.

"We did very nicely," Spike answers. "Even better than we expected."

"How come you didn't ask Casper to play a part? We could have used the money."

"I'm sorry, Charla, I didn't think Casper had time. He appeared to be preoccupied practicing with his band. Had I known he was interested, I certainly would have offered him a place," Spike explains apologetically.

He turns to Casper. "Why didn't you speak up?"

Casper shrugs.

"Do you know anybody who would be willing to give Casper a part-time job?" Charla asks. "He's got some free time after school."

Spike thinks it over for a moment, and then an idea hits him. "I think the Epstein Brothers are looking for someone. If Casper doesn't mind the brothers' shouting, I'm sure they'd offer him a job."

"Do they care about Casper's color?" Charla asks.

"No, that won't be a problem. The biggest obstacle is whether Casper can tolerate their constant shouting. It can get on your nerves, even though the brothers are harmless."

Casper tells him he can tolerate the screaming, and the next week, Spike finds him a job with the Epstein Brothers, just like he promised. After my aunt serves the sauce meats, Betty's father informs her that he has to leave to go to work. Apparently, his shift starts that evening. My aunt, disappointed that he will miss the final two courses of the dinner, fixes him a dish of food to take with him.

"I just want to let you know what a lovely young man your son Anthony is," Betty's father says. "He is a dear friend to my daughter, and I appreciate all he's done for her. I don't know what I would have done without his help after my wife died."

Aunt Lucy thanks him for the kind words and kisses him farewell. The next course after Betty's father leaves is the rack of lamb, which Aunt Lucy bakes like a casserole with sliced potatoes, onions, and peas. Spike's stories have really loosened up the crowd, and I completely forget the morning's police incident. Noticing Mrs. Maderno at the other end of the table, her stare fixed on Spike, I decide to have a little fun at his expense.

"Hey, Spike, Maderno is giving you a dirty look," I inform him.

Spike looks down at the old spinster at the end of the table, and, sure enough, she's looking his way.

"That old bag has a curse on me," Spike utters.

"She does not," Betty chides.

"Yes, she does," Spike counters. "Old man Scalva warned me of the curse. Ever since her husband died, she prays every night, hoping something bad will happen to me. I tell you, Betty, the lady freaks me out,"

Spike ducks back on his chair to avoid Maderno's gaze. This is working out better than I anticipated. Spike looks really worried.

"Yeah, like she really has the power to put a hex on you," Betty says.

"I don't know if she does, but if I start clucking like a chicken, you know where it came from," Spike retorts.

At that point, we hear a knock on the door. It's a couple from the fourth floor. They walk in with two boxes of used clothing.

"We thought your children might need these clothes. Ours have outgrown them, but the clothes are still in pretty good shape," the couple tells Aunt Lucy when they enter the apartment.

"Thank you," she replies.

Spike starts to get up, but Aunt Lucy turns to him and points at his chair. "Anthony, sit down!"

Although his face is beet red, Spike does as he's told.

"Well, enjoy your dinner and have a Merry Christmas," the couple concludes.

"Merry Christmas to both of you and thanks again for the clothes," Aunt Lucy replies as she escorts them to the door. The minute they leave, Spike throws down his lamb chop, gets up, and goes to his room, slamming the door behind him. I don't expect to see him the rest of the evening.

Spike hates accepting clothes from people. When his father ran off, his family was penniless and began taking used clothing from the community. Spike was thirteen at the time, and with his mother unemployed, could do nothing to stem the tide of the charitable contributions from their neighbors. One day, an older boy recognized a shirt Spike was wearing as his own. Embarrassed at having been discovered wearing hand-me-downs, Spike swore he'd never accept used clothing again.

From that day onward, Spike never wears an article of clothes unless he purchases it himself. Due to his poor economic condition, however, Spike can't buy a whole lot. On one occasion, when I was living in New Jersey, Spike and his family paid us a visit. We'd been outside playing in the rain, and when we came back in, my mother told us to remove our wet shoes and leave them outside in the hallway. While removing his shoes, a piece of wet cardboard slipped out of Spike's. He grabbed it and hurried to slide it back into his shoes, hoping that I hadn't noticed. However, he couldn't do anything to conceal his wet socks, which were soaked from the water seeping through the holes in the soles of his shoes.

Part of Spike's duties, after the family became superintendents of the apartment buildings, was performing minor repair work, such as fixing leaky faucets and toilets. Most tenants in the neighborhood tipped the supers after they complete such repairs. While other janitors in the community got money, the tenants of our buildings gave Spike their discarded clothing as his reward. While his mother didn't mind, Spike would get furious. He was becoming a regular charity case! One day, Spike devised a clever strategy. Whenever someone gave him clothes at the completion of a job, Spike would say, "No disrespect, I appreciate the gesture, but I can't eat clothes."

The tenant usually got the message and gave Spike money. This strategy helped Spike's financial condition but dried up the family's supply of used clothing. Aunt Lucy, unaware of what Spike had done, couldn't understand why the clothing donations had disappeared. Spike's devices, however, were exposed one day by an unexpected turn of events. By law, the landlord of a rent-controlled apartment building in New York City is required to paint each apartment every three years. To facilitate meeting this requirement, sometimes the landlord offers the residents a monetary allowance to do the painting themselves. The tenant can accept the landlord's offer or require him to proceed with the work.

If the owner of the building had to do the painting, the landlord hired Spike to do the job. In addition to the compensation paid to him by the landlord, Spike also received tips from the residents. On one assignment, Spike completed painting an apartment of some of his mother's friends. The tenants offered him two boxes of used clothes as his reward. Spike gave his customary, "No disrespect, but I can't eat clothes" speech and turned down the reward. The tenant was stunned by his reaction.

"Well, how much do you expect as a tip?" she asked.

"The size of the tip is entirely up to you," Spike replied, "but most people give me twenty dollars."

"I'm a little short right now," she said, surprised at the size of the bounty. "I'll bring it over tomorrow, if you don't mind?"

"No problem, whenever you get a chance," Spike said.

The next day, as promised, the tenant brought the money to Spike's house. Spike, unfortunately, wasn't home, and Aunt Lucy answered the door. The neighbor gave her the twenty dollars and then proceeded to tell her how she didn't appreciate Spike's wisecrack remark. That weekend, we were in the Bronx visiting Spike and his family.

Aunt Lucy, still upset at Spike's conduct on the clothes, asked my father to intervene and have a talk with him. She believed that Spike stood a better chance at listening to a man's point of view. My father agreed and told my aunt he'd try to reason with Spike. When Spike got home, my mother and aunt feigned running an errand to allow the two of them to sit and talk in private. The men didn't know I was sitting in the living room and could hear their conversation.

"Anthony, you're making your momma very upset," my father began. "You know she tries hard to provide for you kids. You can't give her such a tough time."

"How so, Uncle Sal?" Spike asked.

"You know, she has to take the clothes from people," my dad said. "She doesn't want to, but how else can she provide for you guys?"

"Listen, Uncle Sal. I know the difficult spot my mother is in, but taking handouts from everybody in the neighborhood is not the answer. I didn't say anything when my father left and we had no money. Things have gotten better. I'm kicking in a lot of money doing odd jobs. She gets twenty-five dollars a week from me from what I earn at the fruit store. I give her another ten dollars a week from my car washing. We live here rent-free, because I'm the janitor, and I'm the one who washes all the hallways and takes out the garbage. With all due respect, I think I should have a say as to how the family is being run."

"But you make some people unhappy by what you say."

"Uncle Sal, be honest with me. How would you like it if your wife never listened to you? You're the man of the house. Don't you have a say? Mom shouldn't worry if the neighbors aren't happy. She should be concerned as to my feelings. We shouldn't live like beggars in the streets with our hands out. My mother shouldn't be so greedy. She has enough money that we don't have to rely on people's charity. She needs to manage her money more carefully. Maybe we won't have as many pants or shirts, or she might have to mend some clothes when they tear, but the family would be happier knowing the clothes were purchased by our own hard work. I don't want any more handouts. How would you feel if your wife went out begging for clothes?"

The talk with Spike had the opposite effect for which my aunt hoped. Instead of Spike seeing my father's point of view, my father came around to Spike's way of thinking. The truth is, my dad always has liked and respected Spike. In most cases, the two of them converse better than Spike ever spoke to his own father. Getting my father on his side on almost any matter is relatively easy for Spike.

That night, my dad told my aunt to stop complaining and to start listening to her son. He also advised her to stop accepting charity and to start managing her money better. If she needed extra money, she should come see him and not rely on strangers. It was time she realized her son had grown and she should thank God for what a good boy she had in Spike.

Spike has gotten good at arguing with the tenants over money. They're always trying to chew down his price or beat him out of paying altogether. He has a way of coming up with great responses in the middle of these money disputes. In one instance, a tenant felt that Spike had overcharged her for his services. "This argument is not about money, I'm just trying to make a point," she said.

Finally, when she repeated her point for around the tenth time, Spike fired back. "I know it's not about money. It's about the money!"

Another time, one of the residents complained that Spike wanted to charge him for a job that he believed Spike should do for nothing.

"Remember," Spike said, "any job that's done for nothing, can be done a lot better when it's done for money."

The last of his countless comebacks that I recall is when someone complained that Spike was asking too much to do a job. "Any man who doesn't ask to be paid what he's worth is probably not worth paying," Spike maintained.

◆　◆　◆　◆　◆

We're finishing our Christmas dinner while Spike has shut himself in his room. Finally, my father breaks the disconcerting silence.

"I thought you promised you would not take any more clothes," he says to Aunt Lucy, upset that Spike has left the table.

"It's Christmas," she replies. "How could I insult those nice people and turn them down?"

"Then you won't mind if I insult them!"

Dad gets up from the table, grabs the two boxes of clothes, and heads out of the apartment. He returns a few minutes later and sits down.

"I'm afraid they won't be bringing you any more clothes," he explains to Aunt Lucy.

We're eating our deserts, and Spike is still in his room, when the phone rings. Aunt Lucy gets up to answer, and when she returns, she's visibly upset.

"What's the matter?" my mother asks. "Is everything all right?"

"It's Vito. He's been in an automobile accident. He's at Jacobi Hospital."

The minute she hears the news, Betty jumps up and runs to get Spike. He comes out immediately and sits next to his mother

"Are you all right?" Spike asks.

"Your father has been in an automobile accident," she says.

"I know. Is he okay?"

"I don't know. He's at Jacobi Hospital," Aunt Lucy replies in a state of disbelief. Then she shrugs and turns to him. "Anthony, I don't know what to do."

"What do you want to do?"

"I think I should go to the hospital."

"Then that's what you should do," Spike says. "Get your overcoat. I'll go with you."

"What about the company?" she asks.

"Don't worry about us, Lucy," my mom answers. "We'll manage. You go to the hospital and look in on Vito."

Aunt Lucy does as she's told and goes into her room to get her coat.

"I'll go with you," Betty volunteers.

"Thanks, Betty, but that won't be necessary. Besides, we don't know how long we'll be at the hospital," Spike explains. "We could be there all night."

"I don't mind. My father has a twenty-four-hour shift at the fire station, and I'll be home alone. Please let me come, Anthony."

"All right, maybe you can be of some help."

"I'm coming, too!" I chime in. It's more of an excuse to get away from my father's lecture for my police misadventure than for any willingness to help.

"Fine, let's get our jackets and get going," Spike says.

The four of us grab the Pelham bus on Fordham Road and set out for Jacobi Hospital. In the emergency room, we learn that Uncle Vito is in intensive care and the doctors have listed his condition as critical. Spike and Aunt Lucy go in to see him while Betty and I sit in the waiting room. After about fifteen minutes, Spike comes out.

"How is he?" Betty asks.

"Pretty bad. They don't think he's going to make it. They have him in intensive care, and he's in a coma."

"How's your mother taking it?" Betty asks.

"Not well. I think she still has feelings for that slimy bastard."

"Please, Anthony, this is no time for that kind of talk," Betty says. "At a time like this, you should put your personal feelings aside. Your mother needs your support."

Spike follows Betty's counsel and doesn't make any more snide remarks. A policeman comes by and fills us in on the details of the car accident. My uncle was a passenger in a car when the driver took a sharp turn and lost control. The car jumped a barrier and went off the road into a twenty-foot ditch. The passenger door few open, and my uncle was tossed from the automobile. The driver, who managed to stay inside the car, didn't even get a scratch.

The rest of the evening, we sit in the waiting area with Spike going in and out of his father's room. After four hours pass, Spike comes out with Aunt Lucy.

"Joey, Mom is going home to put the kids to bed and get some rest. Please go home with her and keep her company," he says. He turns to Betty. "You might want to go with them, too. I'm staying here just in case something happens."

"If it's all right with you, I'd rather stay and keep you company," Betty says.

Aunt Lucy and I don't get home until around eleven. Because of their concern about my uncle, my parents forget about my debacle with the law. Their questions are directed at my uncle's medical condition and nothing else. I've dodged a bullet, at least for now. Next evening, I agree to accompany Aunt Lucy to the hospital again. Spike and Betty are waiting there when we arrive. Aside from a two-hour break to wash and eat, the two of them have spent nearly the entire time at the hospital.

It's difficult to read Spike. I can't tell if he's concerned about his father's well-being. He shows no emotion, yet he never leaves Uncle Vito's bedside. Aunt Lucy gives the two of them some sandwiches and then goes in to visit Uncle Vito. His condition has not improved, he's still in a coma, not expected to recover.

"I'm sorry, Betty, what did you want to talk to me about?" Spike asks as he starts working on his sandwich.

Betty looks my way for a second. "Joey, please don't repeat this to anyone."

I assure her that she can count on my silence.

"My dad wants to get married again," she reveals, "some woman he's been seeing the past six months."

"Really? Do I know her?" Spike asks.

Betty shakes her head. "I don't think so. She lives in Yonkers. I've met her a couple of times."

"What's she like? Do you like her?" Spike asks.

"I haven't given her much thought," Betty replies. "I didn't think it was serious. She's divorced and has two children, a boy and a girl. She's also some ten years younger than my dad."

"How do you feel about him getting married?" Spike asks.

"I don't know how to feel. I'm in sort of a shock. Dad says he won't marry her if I object."

"That's horrible!" Spike exclaims. "That's so unfair to dump all this on you. What are you going to decide?"

Betty shrugs. "If I say yes, my whole world is going to change. A stepmother, a brother, and a sister. Can you imagine that at my age? It won't be just Dad and me. Still, I know he's been so lonely since Mom died. How can I deprive him of the happiness he deserves?"

"So what will you tell him?" Spike presses.

"I'm telling him that he doesn't need my permission," Betty concludes. "I'm going to reassure him that I love him very much, and I will support him in anything that he wants to do. I will always adore him no matter what he decides, and he will never lose that love."

Spike gets up and gives Betty a hug. "Have I ever told you how wonderful you are?"

"Yes," she answers "but it's still nice to hear it again."

Later that evening, we run into some neighbors, who are visiting a relation. "Would you mind if my mother went home with you?" Spike asks.

The neighbors agree to give Aunt Lucy a lift, at which point Spike turns to me. "If you don't mind, Priest, hang out here a little while longer, and then you can escort Betty home. I'll stay and keep an eye on my father."

After Aunt Lucy departs, the three of us go into Uncle Vito's room. It's the first time I've seen him since he's been in the hospital. He's lying motionless with tubes going everywhere, and the top of his head is fully bandaged. A monitor measures his pulse, making a constant beeping noise. None of us say anything the entire time we're in the room. The air is thick with the sickening odor of medicine. Back in the waiting area once again, we sit in silence.

Finally, Betty speaks up. "What's bothering you, Anthony?" she asks, noticing that he's not himself.

"I'm just thinking of my relationship with my father."

"What about it?"

"Remember after your mother died, and you were reminiscing about some of the things the two of you did together? How you two would go ice skating, shopping, or just sit around talking? Should my dad not pull through, the only word that can sum up my relationship with him is '*meneste*.'"

Betty thinks about it for a moment and then shakes her head. "I don't understand. You're comparing the relationship with your father to an Italian vegetable soup?"

"I guess Spike means that he and his father have an awful relationship, just like how bad *meneste* tastes," I clarify on Spike's behalf.

"That doesn't make any sense," Betty retorts. "I've had your mother's *meneste*, Anthony, and it's very good."

Spike smiles. "What Priest remembers is the *meneste* we ate as kids back in Italy. You only know the soup my mother cooks now."

"What's the difference?" Betty asks.

"The *meneste* you love is generally prepared with escarole or broccoli rape. To increase the favor, my mother adds a prosciutto bone and sausages. Then she fries some garlic in olive oil and adds it to the *meneste* at the end of the process. What Priest remembers is something quite different. Since escarole or broccoli rape weren't always available, they substituted other greens, such as spinach, celery, or any other leafy object. It didn't matter how the vegetable tasted as long as it filled the plate.

"I swear there were times I suspected they picked leaves from bushes on the side of the road. Because we couldn't afford prosciutto or sausages, they substituted any other pork bone. The bone did nothing to improve the flavor, but at least the marrow supplied some meat to the evening meal. The dinner was so bad and still evokes such awful memories to Joey, that even today, he won't taste a bite.

"But that's not what I'm referring to when I compare my relationship with my father to *meneste*. When my mother was in the hospital giving birth to Angela, my father was doing the cooking for us. Not being much of a cook, he decided that *meneste* would be the simplest dish to prepare. He was wrong. The meal came out terrible, much worse even than the dish we used to eat back in Italy. Undeterred, he decided to make the same dinner the next evening, and that time, I was his assistant. Once again, the meal tasted horrible. Steadfast, we tried our hand a third time the next day, and once again, we struck out. We never did figure out what we were doing wrong."

Spike ends the story and sits in silence. Betty and I look at each other, totally bewildered.

"I still don't get it! What does this story have to do with your relationship with your father?" Betty asks finally.

"It was the only time my father and I did anything together," Spike says. "I can't think of any other instance where we spent time alone. It was the only thing we did together, and it came out bitter, as bitter as our relationship."

A few minutes later, the three of us go back to Uncle Vito's room. Spike sits next to him while Betty and I stand at the foot of the bed. Unexpectedly, my uncle opens his eyes. He stares around the room for a minute and then recognizes Spike. A painful smile crosses his face as he reaches out feebly and grabs Spike's hand.

"Anthony, I'm so sorry," Uncle Vito whispers, barely audible.

"Don't speak, Dad. Save your strength," Spike says.

Over the next few days, Uncle Vito makes a rapid recovery. By the end of the week, the hospital releases him. There's an even happier ending to the story. Uncle Vito finally decides to provide some financial support for the family. In turn, he receives visitation rights to his children, except for Spike, who still doesn't want to have anything to do with the man.

"Are you ever going to forgive him?" Betty asks Spike later that week.

"Betty, you know I'm not one to harbor a grudge. Let him keep some of the promises he made, and I'll reconsider. It's easy to make statements when you're near death. Let's see what he does when he recovers."

CHAPTER 18

Apology Accepted

The Christmas humiliation with Iggy finally catches up with me after Uncle Vito is released from the hospital. I've been locked in my apartment for three weeks now after school. As my punishment, I'm not allowed to go out except to school or church. The punishment would have lasted longer except that Spike and Betty got arrested. It happened while they were demonstrating against the construction of a housing project on 180th Street.

They chained themselves to a bulldozer in an attempt to stop the work. It took the police no more than five minutes to cut the lock and haul the two of them, kicking and screaming, into a paddy wagon along with some forty other protestors. Their archenemy, Commissioner Moses, was scheduled to attend a ribbon-cutting ceremony. When the commissioner learned of the demonstration, he opted out.

Spike and Betty never missed an opportunity to get in Moses' face. A few years earlier, they pelted his limo with tomatoes when he showed for the dedication of the Cross-Bronx expressway. I never quite understood their hatred for these projects. The city obviously needed urban renewal. There's no point arguing with them, though, especially about the Cross Bronx. They nearly take my head off when I try to make a counter point one night when we are discussing the road.

Betty, in particular, is adamant. In her mind, these projects are destroying the city. She feels Moses is constructing these projects for no other reason than to feed his massive ego. The expressway is one of his doings. According to Betty, that one road will be the ruination of the Bronx. The route cuts right through the heart of the borough. Thousands of residents have been dispossessed to make room for the highway. Hundreds of businesses have also closed—the remaining ones are barely surviving. The road does little to increase the quality of life for the citizens of the Bronx.

Then Betty rattles of a list of twenty reasons why the tenement housing programs are also killing our neighborhoods. Spike simply maintains the government has no right becoming landlords. How can bureaucrats run houses better than the owners of the buildings? Where will the powers of government end?

Mr. Sargent, Betty's father, picked them up after their arraignment. No bail needed. All the demonstrators were released on their own recognizance. Everybody is in Spike's apartment when Spike and Betty come in, except for Betty's father, who is downstairs looking for a parking spot.

"*Sfaccima*!" Aunt Lucy screeches at Spike the minute he walks through the door.

With tears streaming down her face, she lunges to slap him. Spike lifts his hand and blocks the blow.

"Cut it out!" he hollers. "I spent a whole night in jail, and I'm in no mood!"

He opens the fridge and pulls out a container of milk and takes a slug.

"You're in no mood? Well, that's too damn bad," she retorts. "Now you really did it. You're a damn criminal. *Tu si un disgraziato!*" She lunges for him again. This time, my father steps in front of her and pushes her back.

"Calm down, Lucy. What good is this?" he says, holding her aside.

She finally sits, probably more from exhaustion than anything else. She's been up all night. Holding her head over into her hands, she starts to sob.

"What am I going to do? He's ruined his whole life. My son is a criminal." She's talking more to herself than anybody in the room.

"Oh, for Pete's sake," Spike says and heads for the bathroom.

Aunt Lucy looks up at Betty. "And what's the matter with you? I thought you were a nice girl. Why would you get mixed up in this mess? My son is stubborn as a mule, but I thought you had more sense!"

"Don't pick on the girl," my dad admonishes. "Don't blame her; it isn't her fault."

"Maybe it's true what they say about you around the neighborhood," Aunt Lucy continues, ignoring my dad.

"What did you say?" Spike howls from the hall as he comes out of the bathroom.

He runs up to his mother, his finger pointing at her face. "You apologize to her!"

I'm sure the entire building can hear this latest blast.

"Anthony, please stop," Betty pleads.

"What did I say?" Aunt Lucy asks.

"If you don't apologize to her, I'm going to put you through the fucking wall!" Spike warns.

By now, everyone in the room is standing between Spike and his mother.

"Okay, I'm sorry," Aunt Lucy relents. "Are you happy? I'm sorry, Betty," she repeats, looking at Betty.

Spike walks off and goes to his room, slamming the door behind him. Right then, Mr. Sargent walks in.

"What's going on?"

"What's going on? My son has been arrested, and now he's a criminal," she fires back. "My son is going to have a criminal record. What kind of job can he get with that? Sweeping and mopping floors?"

"What they did isn't a felony, Lucy," Mr. Sargent says. "A misdemeanor isn't much. I've already spoken to somebody at Tammany Hall, and they think they can get the whole matter expunged. Nothing will show up on their record."

With that, Aunt Lucy appears to calm down. "Can you really do that?"

"Yes, I'm pretty certain," he, Mr. Sargent says. "Come on, Betty, let's go home."

Before Betty leaves, Aunt Lucy grabs her and hugs her tight. "I'm so sorry I said those things," she says through her tears. "I was just so angry. Can you please forgive me? Please don't hate me. You're family to me."

"There's nothing to forgive, Aunt Lucy. It's all forgotten," Betty assures her.

"Thank you, thank you, thank you, oh, I love you so much," Aunt Lucy wails as she kisses Betty wildly on her cheeks. Betty has to struggle to pull her off.

"I'll walk down with you," I offer.

As we're walking down the stairs, Betty's dad turns to her.

"What was that all about?"

"Just a family squabble," Betty says and continues down the steps.

Mr. Sargent stops for a second. "Why was she apologizing to you?"

"Well, I'm sort of part of the family, ain't I?" Betty responds craftily. "I do call her Aunt Lucy," she adds and hustles down the steps ahead of us.

"Where are you going in such a hurry?" Her dad yells at her.

"Over to Judy's. I've got some important news for her!"

"We need to talk about your arrest!" He says. "Don't think you're getting away with it. You haven't heard the last of this!"

"I know. We'll talk later!" Betty hollers back as she dashes out of the building.

Despite their arrest, some good comes out of their protest. While they were sitting on the floor of a holding cell that night waiting for their arraignment, Betty asked Spike if there was a way to mend things with Judy Four Eyes. Even though Betty was the target of Judy's insult, which caused the fight in the first place, she misses Judy, as do all of the other girls.

Nearly seven months have passed since Spike's fight with Judy's father. Since that date, Judy hasn't been seen on our block. Her father has forbidden her to have anything to do with us. None of the guys miss her. She's a whining, annoying bitch who has the nasty habit of opening her big mouth and putting somebody down at the most inappropriate time. Spike is the only guy who has found a way to curb her acrimonious tongue. At one time or another, all of the rest of the guys have fallen victim to her poisonous words. The situation is really awkward. The girls are torn between their loyalty to Judy and their friendship with us.

Spike also feels bad; he genuinely likes Judy. Besides, he'd never been the target of any of her untimely comments. On several occasions, Spike has had some of the girls intercede. He's asked them to talk to Judy's parents and arrive at some accommodation that would allow her back into the fold. All these efforts are to no avail. Judy's parents refuse to budge, and the banishment continues.

Personally, I didn't have any quarrel with Judy. She's never said anything to embarrass or humiliate me. Because I'm new to the neighborhood, she hasn't had a chance to get around to humiliating me, but my relationship to Spike also causes her to steer well clear of me. Whenever our paths cross in school or around the neighborhood, she never gives me a glance or says a word.

In the police cell, Betty pressed Spike to find a solution that would bring Judy back into the group. Spike finally relented and came up with the only plot that made any sense. Judy related the story to me at a later date. Judy lives on the third floor of an apartment building on Hoffman Street, around the corner from the clubhouse. One night, in early January, around dinnertime, she heard a knock on the door.

Her mother answered. "Good evening, Anthony. What can I do for you?"

Judy heard her mother say.

"Good evening, Mrs. Ascola," Spike replied, as sweet as can be. "I was hoping to have a word with Mr. Ascola, if he's available."

When Judy realized, it was Spike, she peeked out of her room. Mrs. Ascola looked into the kitchen where her husband was sitting. "Ralph, would you like to talk to Anthony?"

"Send him in," Judy's father snapped.

As Spike walked into the house, he winked at Judy and walked into the kitchen, where Judy's father was reading the paper.

"Have a seat," Judy's father said. "Why don't you take off your jacket?"

"I'm fine, sir," Spike replied. "What I have to say shouldn't take long."

Judy came out of her room and stood at the entrance to the kitchen to get a better look.

"Well, son, what can I do for you?" Mr. Ascola asks.

"You know, I've been trying to talk to you for months, but only now did I finally summon up the courage to approach you. I want to apologize to you and Judy for the way I behaved last summer." He cleared his throat and continued. "I certainly did not want to strike you. It's just that you came up on me so suddenly, and, not knowing who you were, I instinctively swung and caught you with a lucky punch. I was in shock when I realized it was you that I struck."

I can picture Spike's performance; he's a master of playing the adults. By the time he was finished, they were eating out of his hand. Spike looked straight into the man's eyes. "Lucky for me, because as angry as you were, if my punch had missed, I think you would have killed me." He gave a slight, well-timed pause as he let the last remark sink in and looked meekly at the floor before continuing. "Anyway, I know should've come sooner, but I was embarrassed and afraid." He raised his eyes and looked directly at Judy's father. "Well, that's all I have to say, sir, except, I'm really very, very sorry."

Spike turns. "And Judy, I'm glad you're here, because, I especially want to apologize to you. How I treated you that day was terrible, and I promise never to do it again. I hope you can find a way to forgive me."

Spike can be so convincing. A period of silence followed. After waiting a few moments, Spike rose to leave. As he started out of the kitchen, he looked at Judy, and without her parents noticing, gave her a thumbs up. Betty had filled Judy in on the plan earlier that afternoon. Realizing the feud had gone on too long, Mrs. Ascola stopped Spike and turned to her husband.

"Ralph, don't you have something to say to Anthony?"

Ralph looked at Spike and smiles. "Apology accepted. Now, sit and have dinner with us!"

Spike had enough sense not to refuse the offer.

Next day, Judy is back with the gang, and she acts as if she never left. This works out great, because she takes a liking to me. The fact that I'm Spike's cousin may be the reason, but she begins treating me really well. Emboldened by Judy's warmth, I decide to ask her for a date. I know I promised Betty that I'd wait and that she'd be first, but she has made no effort to overcome her fears. How long am I supposed to wait? I'm fifteen years old, and I've never been on a date. Heck, I've never even kissed a girl.

At least Betty has gone out with Joey Cooks. Should Betty change her mind and start dating, I'm still available. Until then, I need to get on with my life and have some fun. Granted, Judy is no goddess, but she's very attractive. Except for the fact she wears glasses, Judy is one of the prettiest girls in our crowd.

With my mind made up, I summon the courage to ask her for a date. Unbelievably, she says yes. We make plans to see a movie at the Lowe's Paradise on Saturday. The Paradise is a large, ornate theater, probably the largest in the Bronx. The ceiling has small lights in it to simulate looking at the night sky. The theater has statues of gods and goddesses throughout. It's the premier movie theater in the Bronx, and I really want to impress Judy.

Sitting up in bed that night, I make another monumental decision. One of my biggest concerns is my height, or, more precisely, the lack of it. Not having grown an inch in more than six months, I've been despairing that I won't be any taller than my current five-foot-three. That evening, I resolve that there isn't much I can do about my growth, but I can improve my physical appearance.

The next day, I'm going to join the bodybuilding gym that opened recently around the corner. The next day, still resolute, I join the gym as planned. Sergio, the trainer who runs the place, puts me on a weightlifting regimen, requiring me to exercise for one hour, four days per week. "Four hours a week to a completely new body," as Sergio phrases it.

That Saturday can't come soon enough. At seven, I pick up Judy. Although it's really cold, we decide to walk the nearly one mile to the theater instead of grabbing the bus. It's a decision that works out great, as it gives us an opportunity to talk and get to know each other. It's amazing how comfortable I feel talking to Judy. I had been apprehensive about our date. All the fellows told me she would probably be her nasty, whining self. However, the guys are completely wrong.

My conversation with Judy is so casual and effortless; it's as if I've known her my entire life. Our talk is so pleasant and interesting that I'm slightly disappointed when we arrive at the Lowe's Paradise, not wanting our talk to come to an end. After the movie, I take her for a sundae at Jan's Ice Cream Parlor on Kingsbridge Road, just south of Poe Park. The ice cream parlor is a popular date destination for most teenagers. At the ice cream parlor and the walk home afterward, the conversation is as delightful as when the evening began. The date with Judy runs me into some money, especially when you consider I bought her popcorn, coke, Raisinets, and a box of bonbons, but it's worth it. I'm enjoying every moment.

When we arrive at her building, Judy turns to me. "You don't have to walk me up."

"All right," I say, somewhat disappointed. "I guess I'll just say goodnight, then."

We stare awkwardly at each other for a moment, and then she kisses me on the cheek. "Joey, I had a great time, and I hope you did, too. Please, let's do this again."

"Of course, I'd love to," I reply quickly.

She smiles and runs upstairs. During the short walk back to my building, it feels like I'm walking on air. My first date ever, and it turns out better than I could have imagined. In front of my building, I see some of the guys are still about.

"Hey, look, here comes Romeo!" Vinnie Beast yells as I approach.

"Did you score, Casanova?" Aldo asks with a big grin, knowing full well the answer to the question.

"He probably didn't even cop a feel," Rafael chimes in.

"Fuck all of you and the horse you rode in on!" I shout as I head upstairs, not in the mood to put up with their crap.

My date with Judy is a new awakening. I can think of nothing else; she's always on my mind. The world around me is moving, but I seem separate from it. I barely notice or pay attention to anyone. At bedtime, I toss and turn for hours, thinking of her. Betty is completely forgotten. Nothing seems important except seeing Judy. That Sunday, I look for Judy, but she's upstate visiting relatives with her family. Disappointed, I go to the gym, and instead of my usual one hour, I work out for four. The next morning, my body is so sore I can barely get out of bed. Every one of my muscles aches.

Instead of going to school with my usual crowd of friends, I pass by Judy's place, hoping to bump into her. Once again, my efforts to see her are in vain. She's already left for school. Throughout the school day I search for her, to no avail, since she's a sophomore and isn't in any of my classes. Finally, just as I'm about to give up, I run into her before the last period.

"Hi," I say.

"Hello, Joey," she replies. "It's so nice to see you."

"Would you like to walk home together after school?" I ask. "I'll meet you at the Fordham exit."

"Oh, I'm so sorry, I'd love to, but I have to stay after classes," Judy explains. "I'm a member of the dance committee, and there's a meeting this afternoon to plan for the spring dance. I'll see you tonight," she says as she walks away.

Although I'm disappointed that I can't walk her home, I'm thrilled that I'll finally be able to spend time with her that evening. That afternoon, despite my sore muscles, I return to the gym and pump iron for another two hours. After dinner, I wait for Judy in front of my building. It's a miserable night with a cold, wintry rain hitting the city. It's a damp, bone-chilling rain that feels like it's going right through me. All the guys are in the clubhouse sheltered from the weather, but I stay in front of the building, not wanting to miss Judy should she show. She never does!

When I finally turn in and go home, my mother can't believe how wet I am. My clothes are soaked through, and I'm shivering from head to foot. Concerned that I might catch a chill, she forces me to take a hot bath. She boils some tea, which I drink after adding some honey. The tea, honey, and bath do wonders, and I start warming up and feeling better. Inside, though, I'm miserable. My insecurity manifesting, I wonder whether Judy really likes me.

Why didn't she show? What made her change her mind? Is it some other boy she met after school? With these irrational thoughts running rampant through my mind, I don't fall asleep until nearly three in the morning. The next morning, I awake, drenched once more, this time in my own perspiration. When I come out into the kitchen and my mother sees my condition, she orders me right back to bed. She takes my temperature, and it's a hundred and three. She calls Doctor Goldberg. He gives me a penicillin shot and advises my mother to keep me in bed for the remainder of the week.

That medical advice appears to seal my destiny. I won't see Judy for a week, and by then, she will have forgotten me and found a new boyfriend. This is one of the worst days of my life. I'm convinced that fate has conspired against me, and I've lost my chance with her. After dinner that night, Spike comes up and pays me a visit.

"How are you feeling, pal?" he asks.

"Lousy," I reply, more because I'm sulking over Judy than my illness.

"Your friend Judy is asking about you."

Hearing her name, I perk up.

"Really?" I ask, sitting up in bed. "I didn't think she cared for me."

"Huh? What makes you say a stupid thing like that?" He shakes his head in amazement.

"Well, yesterday in school, she said she would meet me last night, and she never showed."

Spike looks at me for a second and bursts into hysterical laughter. "So that's why you were standing out in the rain like a fucking moron!" he howls, doubled over the bed with laughter.

Finally, he regains control of himself. "Listen, you stupid, fucking jerk, maybe, unlike you, she has enough sense to stay home on such a miserable night. She probably assumed that you stayed in, too."

Although I don't like Spike's teasing, somehow, my spirits feel better. I look at him pathetically. "Do you really think she likes me?"

"I know she does."

We spend a few more minutes on other topics, and then Spike stands up.

"Listen, Priest, I gotta go. Take care of yourself. I'll give Judy your regards."

On his way out of my bedroom, he turns back. "Hey, Joey, why didn't the moron have enough sense to get out of the rain?"

I look at him in confusion.

"Because he was in love with Judy!" he howls as he heads out of the room.

Despite his teasing, Spike is just the medicine I need. Having slept most of the day, I can't fall asleep that night. I just sit stare out the window thinking of Judy. Down below, all the kids have turned in except for Spike and Betty. As usual, they are the last ones to go home. She's sitting on a parked car. Spike is standing facing her and is doing most of the talking.

He must be saying something funny, because Betty has a big smile on her face. I can't understand what she sees in Spike's humor. He isn't very funny, but Betty always laughs hysterically at his jokes. The kids think I'm a lot funnier than Spike, yet she barely cracks a smile at my jokes. Even if you dispute whether or not I'm funnier than Spike, you'd certainly agree Bowlegs is funnier. There's nobody in our entire crowd who can make people laugh faster, or better, than Bowlegs, yet Betty hardly ever laughs at his jokes either. The only person who makes her laugh is Spike.

I've often wondered as to the true nature of their relationship. Are they just good friends, or is it something more? They certainly like each other's company. They spend an inordinate amount of time together. People who are married don't spend nearly as much time together as they do. Since Betty is my secret goddess, I always conclude it's nothing but friendship. Besides, they've never given a hint of being involved romantically.

Now the two of them are downstairs by themselves, and once again, Betty appears amused at one of Spike's antics. His arms flail in the air as he does some sort of walk, which looks like he's waddling. Whatever it is, she's hysterical. Suddenly, she hops of the hood of the car, and they begin dancing cheek to cheek. It looks like they're doing a tango. They take several steps to one side, flip, and make the same maneuver the opposite way. Betty breaks the embrace and starts dancing solo, snapping her fingers over her head and stomping her feet like a flamenco dancer.

Spike raises his hands to his head and holds out his index fingers to simulate a bull's horns. Bending his head, he charges at Betty like she's a matador. She runs in circles attempting to evade him. Finally, he catches her at the car and tosses her over the hood of the vehicle, burying his horns into her stomach. Betty laughs uncontrollably and struggles to push Spike away, begging him to stop. Her pleas have no effect as Spike, encouraged by her merriment, tickles her sides. This makes her lose control, and she shakes violently with laughter.

Although I'm not happy that Spike is the cause of her happiness, I enjoy seeing Betty so content. Nobody can make her happier than Spike. I appreciate that fact. Finally beginning to get drowsy, I decide to turn in and go to sleep. By Friday, my condition has improved dramatically, and I feel good enough to go to school. Normally, I'd have begged to take the extra day off, but I'm anxious to see Judy and ask her to go out on Saturday.

In a complete role reversal, my mother insists I stay home.

"Listen, Ma, I'm struggling with math as it is. If I don't get back to school and get my assignments, I'll fall even further behind."

The well-timed remark has the desired effect, and she relents. Determined that Judy won't leave for school before I have a chance to speak to her, I get up earlier than usual and scurry down to be in front of her building before she comes out. This time, my calculations are correct. Judy comes out of her apartment and finds me leaning against a parked car opposite her doorway.

Surprised to see me, she smiles. "Joey, what a lovely surprise. How are you feeling?"

Seeing Judy genuinely happy to meet me, I heave a sigh of relief. "Much better, thank you," I reply. Then I get right to the point. "Judy, will you go out with me tomorrow?"

"Sure, Joey, I'd love to go out with you. Are you sure you're feeling up to it?"

"Yes, I'm fine! I was thinking we could go see a movie at the Dumps, since I'm a little short of money this week."

The Dumps is a local movie theater located just around the corner from the clubhouse. As its name implies, the theater is a rat hole. Half the seats are ripped with the foam sticking out of the seat bottoms. The other half don't even have cushions. Since they never clean the place, you can usually find gum and other sticky stuff on the floors. The Dumps features only movies that have already been shown at other theaters. Sometimes the flicks appear on television before they're shown at the Dumps. As a result, most of the kids don't go there.

The name "Dumps" is so common that many people in the community probably don't know that the theater's real name is the Savoy. Still, with the ticket price being less than half the cost of a regular admission at the first-run theaters, it comes in handy when we're strapped for dough.

"I've got a better idea," Judy offers, "my parents are going out to dinner tomorrow night. You can come to my house, and we'll listen to some music. Be there after eight," she advises as she rushes off to join her girlfriends.

On a cloud once again, I set out for school. The next morning, I don't even bother joining the guys in the regular Saturday flirting ritual. Instead, I head straight to the gym to get back to my workout schedule. However, I make it a point that afternoon to help Spike and Vito in their usual janitorial work, cleaning up the two apartment buildings.

"I want to thank you," I tell Spike when we're alone.

He gives me a puzzled look. "For what?"

"Because you told me about Judy. I was beginning to doubt myself."

"Don't doubt yourself," he says. "You have a lot to offer, and you're a pretty good catch. Just relax and be yourself, and you'll be just fine."

"Spike, can I ask you something, in confidence?"

"Sure, go ahead."

"Can you tell me some moves that will help me score with Judy?"

He looks at me incredulously. "Let me get this straight. You're proceeding from wondering whether or not Judy likes you to going all the way?" He shakes his head in amazement. "You're unbelievable!"

"No, I just want some techniques that will improve my chances," I clarify.

He shakes his head again, frustrated at my stupidity. "This may come as a surprise to you, bonehead, but there are no magic techniques or moves."

"Then how come you score more than any of the other guys?"

"What leads you to that conclusion?" Spike asks.

I hesitate, not wanting to reveal my peephole secret.

"Oh, come on, everybody knows that fact. Are you going to tell me you don't score?"

"All right, that may be so, but it's not the result of any mystery moves or magical lines. Girls aren't stupid; they'll only do what makes them comfortable. You can't trick them, and you certainly should not pressure Judy into doing something she doesn't want to do!"

"Then how do you account for your high rate of success?" I persist, refusing to let him of the hook.

He muses over my question for a moment before replying. "Well, you know how the boys are always yapping about some girl's reputation, how some girls are easier to score with than others?"

"Yes."

"Well, maybe girls do the same thing," Spike says with a silly grin on his face.

I shake my head. "I don't understand?"

"Maybe, among the girls, I have the reputation of someone who will go all the way," he clarifies. "You know, someone who is easy to score with."

"All the fellows would go all the way given the chance!" I reply, unable to believe his stupid reasoning. "What makes them think you're any fucking easier?"

"You're missing the point," he says. "It's not that I'm any easier; it's just that girls know that going out with me comes with certain expectations. So, if I ask a girl out, she knows if she agrees, it means she has to go further sexually than she might with the other boys. You know, because of my reputation."

"You mean all you have to do is ask?" I look at him in awe. "Then you can have any girl you want!"

"No! Plenty of young women won't go out with me," Spike says. "Not because they don't want to date me but because they don't agree with the conditions they presume I have set."

"Like who?" I ask, not believing any girl can resist my cousin's advances.

"Well, there's Toni Boobs, the DeFavio twins, and your girlfriend, Judy, for starters," Spike answers. "Look, Joey, the bottom line is that most girls have a pretty good handle on the situation, and they know just how far they're comfortable going. You're not going to score with trickery, treachery, or deception. Judy will let you proceed up to the point where she's comfortable. If you like her, you'll have to respect her wishes."

That night, I'm anxious to see Judy. I'd have gotten there early, but she specifically said not to arrive before eight. I reason that means her parents will still be home until then. I pass the time looking at the clock. Earlier, I shaved my peach fuzz and put on some cologne that I purchased especially for the occasion. That afternoon, I also stopped at the pharmacy and purchased a three pack of Trojans.

It took four attempts before I presented the condoms to the woman behind the counter. You never know, I might get lucky. Always an optimist, I insert one of the precious wrappers into my wallet. My mind is running wild. It's only my second date with Judy, and I've already concluded she will go all the way. Why isn't the clock moving? Is it broken? Concerned that I'm late, I ask my mother if the clock is working. She just gives me a dirty look. Finally, after what appears to be an eternity, the clock reaches eight, and I leave for Judy's place.

For some inexplicable reason, I'm more nervous tonight than on our first date. With my palms sweating, I knock at her door. When Judy answers, she's wearing dungarees and a tight green pullover sweater. Her hairstyle has changed. Now she's wearing her hair cropped up. She looks fantastic, and I'm thinking how lucky I am to be dating her.

"Hi," she says, "come on in. You smell nice," she adds as I enter. "I love your cologne."

After that compliment, I vow to buy a gallon of it. She leads me into her living room.

"Sit," she orders, pointing to the sofa. "Can I get you something to drink?"

"Seven and seven," I reply smartly.

She stares at me, bewildered. "Just a Coke or a Pepsi," I add quickly, realizing she doesn't get the joke.

"Oh, I get it." She laughs as she walks away, the joke finally penetrating. She returns with two Cokes.

"Are there any songs you like in particular?" she asks, moving toward the phonograph.

"No, whatever suits you; I'm easy to please."

"I'll put on an album by the Platters, Mr. Easy to Please," Judy offers. "I hope you like it. It's one of my favorites."

Her apartment has almost the identical five-room design as mine, but it feels more luxurious. All the furniture appears to be in just the right place. Her sofa and living room chairs don't have plastic covers on them like mine either—an annoying custom I don't quite understand. Why would you go to all the trouble of choosing the proper fabric for your furniture, only to cover it with polyethylene? The covers make you sweat in the summer and are cold in the winter. I'm glad Judy's parents don't ascribe to the obnoxious custom.

Her place also smells a lot better than mine. She has fresh flower petals in a box called potpourri that emit the most fragrant odor. The only potpourri in my place is the smell of my mother's dinner cooking on the stove. After putting the album on the record player, she sits next to me.

"You like?" Judy asks as the Platters begin to sing.

I nod. "I like.

We spend the next hour just shooting the breeze, talking about nothing in particular, mostly about some of the kids in our group and some about our classes and how we're doing. For some unexplained reason, the conversation turns to Spike and Betty.

"What are Spike's feelings toward Betty?" Judy asks.

"I don't understand?" I reply, confused at the sudden change of topic.

"Well, does he like her? They're always together. Don't you think there must be something going on between them? Why else would they spend so much time together?"

"No, I think they're just good friends." I reply, even though I've wondered the same thing.

"What about the bracelet he gave her for Christmas?" she persists. "Friends don't give each other jewelry."

The conversation is making me uncomfortable. Now I know what the guys mean about Judy not knowing when to keep her mouth shut. I don't understand how we got here. What's Judy driving at? Spike and Betty, a couple? Doesn't she realize that Betty is my fantasy girl? Spike has already soiled my princess, Charla. Is he going to deflower my goddess, too? Judy doesn't understand. If I can't have Betty, then nobody can. She belongs on a mountaintop untouched by mere mortals like Spike. Betty is for my dreams and certainly not for my philandering cousin.

"It's just a friendship bracelet," I explain in frustration. "He gave it to her, because he values her companionship. There are no ulterior motives. They enjoy each other's company, sometimes spending hours just talking."

"That's exactly my point," Judy presses. "They seem to spend an inordinate amount of time together. And they never disagree on anything."

"That's ridiculous," I reply. "Of course, they disagree. There's a lot of things they don't agree on."

"Like what?"

Caught by surprise, I can't think of anything. Then I remember an argument Betty and Spike had recently. "They are on opposite sides on the president."

"How so?"

"Betty loves Kennedy, but Spike hates the man."

"He hates the president?" Judy exclaims, shocked at the revelation. "Everybody likes him. Why does he hate Kennedy?"

"I know, I couldn't believe it either, but he doesn't like Kennedy."

"Why?"

"As near as I can determine, it has something to do with a highway that was built in Boston. Apparently, to build the road, the city had to dispossess the residents in the way of the route. Most of the people were of Italian descent. To make matters worse, the local government miscalculated the cost of the project and couldn't afford to pay the homeowners the fair value of their property.

"So the politicians came up with a cruel trick. They used their power of eminent domain to evict the people and paid them one dollar for their house as compensation. The politicians reasoned that even if the homeowners filed suit, the courts probably wouldn't hear the cases for years. And even if the courts forced them to pay up and give the property owners the fair value of their houses, they would be able to use the money for years, interest free.

"The problem was that most of the people didn't have money to hire attorneys. They had no choice but to move and lose their lifelong investment. Not only were the neighborhoods destroyed, so were many Italian families."

"That's a sad story, but what does it have to do with President Kennedy?"

"Spike believes that Kennedy is a big fake. Since he was of the same political power as the men who made the decisions, he must have known what was happening. Kennedy was a congressman in Boston and senator of the state. Even if you foolishly believe he was not responsible, he must have been aware, and he certainly didn't lift a finger to help. Now Kennedy is saying he's for housing for the poor. Where was he when they were robbing the Italians of house and home right in his backyard? In any event, Betty doesn't agree with Spike's reasoning."

"Well, I think there's more to their relationship than mere friendship," Judy maintains. "I think Betty has her designs on him. Mark my words, someday she'll get him. Betty is more cunning than people realize!"

Judy's last remark doesn't make me happy at all. I hope she's wrong. Thankfully, the conversation turns to other subjects, because Judy is beginning to ruin what I had hoped would be a great night. The music moves from the Platters to the Everly Brothers. Even Elvis makes an appearance. It doesn't matter what she plays, I just enjoy being with her—once the conversation gets off Spike and Betty.

She moves closer, and I reach for her. We embrace and kiss. This is not the same kiss as our first date; it's longer and more passionate. Slowly, our lips part, and she inserts her tongue into my mouth, seeking mine. I clutch her tighter. Now her tongue is deep within my mouth, twirling around my tongue.

Nothing in my fantasies has prepared me for such a kiss. I never knew anything could feel so wonderful. When the kiss ends, she falls back on the sofa, pulling me on top of her. Her mouth finds one of my ears, and she nibbles at it. Once again, her titillating tongue comes out and twirls inside my ear. My body weakens from the sensation. It feels like it's turning into gel. I have no control over the situation. This girl and her tongue are mocking all the plans I have designed.

Somehow, I manage to regain some of my composure and begin kissing her neck, and my hands stroke her ass. To my delight, Judy doesn't object to my advances. Could tonight be the time I finally get lucky? Good thing I brought the condom. Encouraged by my progress, I move my hand up to caress her breast. She grabs my hand, pushes it away from her breast, and places it on her back. "No!" she whispers.

It turns out this will not be my lucky night. She pulls my head toward her, and she begins one of her exotic tongue kisses. This time, I'm prepared, and our tongues join and twirl in unison. She moves and grinds her body beneath me in a rhythmic, sexual motion. Delighted, I respond in kind and match her tempo. The grinding maneuver lasts several minutes until I sense an explosion in my groin.

There's no mistaking what just happened as I feel the pulsating of the muscle inside my pants and the resulting release of the liquid in my underwear. I rise up, fully expecting to see that the sticky substance has permeated through to my trousers. Looking down, I'm relieved to discover that the boxer briefs have done their job and shielded my pants.

"What's the matter? Are you all right?" Judy asks, surprised by my strange behavior.

"I guess, I'm still feeling the effect of my illness," I say, too embarrassed to reveal the truth.

"Are you going to be all right?" she asks, looking concerned.

"Yes, I think so. But maybe I should turn in early and get some rest."

There's no way I can stay there with that package in my pants.

"Oh, that's too bad," she says, "but I understand."

"Will I see you tomorrow?" I ask on my way out.

"What time?"

"Around two in front of the club," I suggest.

"Okay, feel better," she says and kisses me goodnight.

When I get home, my mother must think I've totally flipped out. The minute I enter the apartment, I dash for the bathroom and take a shower. When I come out, I sneak downstairs to toss my soiled underwear into the garbage. My relationship with Judy settles into a similar routine after that date. She never allows me to go much further than that night at her apartment. The best I can get is an occasional feel and a dry hump until I come in my pants. My mother can't figure out what's happening to my diminishing supply of boxer shorts.

CHAPTER 15

A Simple Painting

The temperature drops to nearly zero. No wonder no one is around. Inside the clubhouse, Spike is sitting on a couch reading a book, his legs outstretched on the coffee table. Sitting on a chair opposite Spike, a Maryland blue crab dangling from his lips, is Crabby. It must be cold; Crabby is never in the clubhouse. Normally, he doesn't ever go in the place, especially when Spike is there. As I walk in, Crabby pulls the crab from his lips and smiles.

"How you doing, Priest?"

"Okay, Crabby. What are you doing out tonight?"

The crab falls to the floor and scurries around the room. Spike jumps up, grabs the fleeing crab, and hands it back to Crabby.

"My mother is visiting my aunt in Brooklyn, and I'm spending the night with Spike," Crabby reveals as he allows the crab to reattach itself to his lips. "I'm sleeping in his room," he adds happily.

"Isn't that just peachy keen," Spike chimes in, peering at me. He turns to Crabby. "The crab stays in the bathtub."

I put a record on the phonograph and sit across from Spike. Looking over at Spike and Crabby, I can't help but notice the contrast of friends surrounding my cousin. There's no pattern to any of his selections. I just can't figure Spike. Take Crabby, for instance. Why would Spike ever strike up a friendship with him? Nobody in the neighborhood but Spike will give Crabby the time of day. You can spend your entire life trying to analyze Spike, and you'd be no closer than when you first met him. Spike is nothing like any other guy in the neighborhood. To some extent, he's the most unlikely guy to be the leader of our group.

By now, you might have concluded Spike rose to the top by the use of his fists, but that's not really the case. I'm not even sure he's the toughest in our crowd. Certainly, Beast could give Spike a run for his money and possibly so could Bonaparte and Hervey. When Spike took over the leadership several years earlier, he definitely was not the toughest. Before turning fourteen, Spike was no taller than I am and a lot skinnier. He resembled the guy featured in the comic books as the ninety-pound weakling.

However, what he lacked in size, Spike made up in heart. Since he was such a runt, the other kids picked on him constantly. Spike, who is fearless, never backed down and got into lots of fights. His temperament is similar to a junkyard dog, and in a fight, he's tenacious. Even though he was so small and lost more fights than he won, he fought so hard and gave such a good account of himself, no guy ever wanted a rematch.

Eventually, the kids stopped picking on him. When Spike founded the Black Knights, there were only twelve boys and no more than half a dozen girls who hung with the guys. The gang grew, reaching its current size of almost fifty boys and some two dozen girls. It's probably the easiest gang to join. There are only three requirements: 1) Spike is the leader, 2) no drugs, and 3) the dues are seventy-five cents a month.

The only one of the three, and the only rule that really counts and might get you thrown out of the gang, is the one about drugs. We don't have to swear an oath to Spike's leadership. We just can't go around saying we're in charge. As for the dues, lack of payment only gets us kicked out of the clubhouse. We can still hang in front of the building, where we stay most of the time anyway.

In bad weather, Spike usually has pity on the deadbeats and lets them into the clubhouse. Spike doesn't really care about the dues as long as we have the fifteen dollars each month to pay the landlord for rent and utilities. The remainder of the money goes to buy booze, chips, White Castles, and sodas. It's no skin of his back if we don't get the extras. That's Vinnie Beast's problem as the treasurer.

Other than the three conditions, there's no other barrier to joining the gang. Someone merely has to show up and ask to join, and they're in. We attract a wide range of kids, from the very bright to, I'm sorry to say, the mentally challenged. In the category of the very bright are Spike, Betty, and Bonaparte. There's also a fellow named Oscar who goes to the high school of performing arts. But probably the smartest of all is Guantanamo, who goes to the Bronx High School of Science.

At the other end of the spectrum are people like Little Elvis, who always dresses and tries to look like the teenage idol, even though he looks nothing like him. Then there's Coop, who is obsessed with raising and flying homing pigeons on his roof. All he ever talks about is those stupid birds. Even though he's got more than a hundred birds, he can recognize each one. The conglomeration of guys includes fat kids with weight problems and boys with severe acne and pimples all over their face. There's also Stinky who never takes a bath and has horrible body odor. None of this seems to concern Spike. He's a laid-back leader and hardly gives any direct commands or instructions.

We don't really see Spike a lot; we merely feel his presence. He's too busy to spend a lot of time with us. Spike's typical day consists of waking up and going to school, working at the produce store from four to six thirty, dinner, repairs required by the tenants of the building, and his homework. At nights, when there's no repairs or any janitorial services needed in the building, he goes to the boxing gym and works out. Aside from school, if we ever see Spike at all, it's after ten or on the weekend. Most of the activity among the group occurs when Spike isn't around.

When Spike is involved, however, it always appears to be more fun and memorable. He has a knack for making things more interesting.

When Spike was fourteen, he began filling out, growing almost six inches in about a year. A natural fighter, the extra bulk made him one of the toughest kids his age in the neighborhood, and he hasn't lost a fight since turning fourteen. Spike hardly ever pushes his weight around, even when guys are hanging and ranking on each other. Spike is fair game. He enjoys the back and forth teasing and is a good sport when someone gets the best of him.

Not that it happens often, as he's quite good at the one liners. As long as it isn't malicious or vindictive, he doesn't mind being at the wrong end of a practical joke. Unless someone takes leave of their senses and picks on Betty, we have little to fear from him, not that many of us test him often. It's better to leave him be and not tempt his wrath.

Spike is always willing to help someone in need. Almost everybody in the group has been the benefactor of a favor from him. One day, after her mother died, Spike saw Betty throwing out her ice skates.

◆ ◆ ◆ ◆

"Why are you throwing out your skates?" he asked.

"I've outgrown them."

"Oh, did you get new skates? Can I see them?"

"No, I don't have new skates. I'm not going skating anymore."

Later that year, Sears was having a close-out sale on ladies' ice skates. Sears was practically giving them away. Spike decided to surprise Betty and buy her a pair.

"I told you that I don't skate anymore! Why did you buy me skates?" Betty asked when Spike gave her the present. "Don't you ever listen?"

"I'm sorry, Betty. I didn't know it would upset you," Spike said, surprised by her reaction. "I just thought we could go skating together, and you could teach me how. I'd love to learn."

"You want to go skating with me? Where are your skates?" Betty asked, calming down when she realized Spike had an interest in the activity. "Sears didn't have men's ice skates, they had only hockey skates. Not only are they no good, but they were also too expensive," he explained. "So I figured until I learn, I can rent a pair at the rink."

"Do you really want to go skating with me?" she asked.

"Yes, as long as you don't make fun of me," he assured her.

That week, they went ice skating, and Spike was terrible. He spent most of his time holding onto the rail. Whenever Betty managed to coax him off the railing, he slipped and fell immediately. Finally, he feigned twisting his ankle and sat on the sidelines and watched Betty skate. Later, he told me what a wonderful skater Betty is. She was so graceful on the ice that the entire rink stood aside and watched her skate.

After that date, and for a time, he accompanied her to the rink regularly. They traveled all over finding spots where Betty could skate. They visited any body of water that froze over: Central Park, the Botanical Gardens, Sprain Brook reservoir, and, on one occasion, they snuck into the rink at Rockefeller Center in the middle of the night.

Money for transportation was never a problem. They were quite good at sneaking into a subway station, using the exit or jumping a turnstile. If they needed to take a bus, they would crawl through the back door while people were getting off. When all else failed, they would mooch the fare money by panhandling or hitching a ride. How could anybody turn down Betty?

Their behavior might have seemed strange or unacceptable to someone with money, but to a person who was poor and had no money, paying was not an option. Spike was always a spectator, watching Betty skate around the ice. Eventually, Betty made some friends and began going to the rink without him, even going roller skating during the summer when the ice rink was closed. As she became more independent, Spike stopped going with her.

On another occasion, Spike helped Twitchy. Twitchy got his nickname because his eyes are always blinking. I can barely concentrate on what I'm saying when I talk to Twitchy. His eyes, which blink a hundred times a minute, are too distracting.

Twitch's mother is an alcoholic and likes fooling around with men. His father, a merchant marine, is hardly ever home. On nights when she's entertaining some guy, she throws Twitchy out of the house. I can't tell you how many mornings we've found Twitchy sleeping on the couch in the clubhouse. Although his dad is rarely home, Twitchy loves his father. One day, Twitchy got news his father was hurt in an accident on a ship and would be coming home. Although not life threatening, the injury is permanent, and his father would be coming home for good. Twitch was ecstatic. Finally, he would have his father home.

The unfortunate man, however, wasn't home a week when he caught a severe flu, which turned to pneumonia. A week later, he succumbed to the illness and died. Twitchy became so depressed he never went out of his apartment. His mother was annoyed that Twitch was always around.

"Stop moping; I'm not even sure he was your father."

Not long afterward, Twitchy climbed on the roof of Mount Carmel Church and stood on the ledge, threatening to jump off and kill himself.

"Where are you, Rudy Kazoody?" he cried. "Can you hear me, Rudy Kazoody? Does anybody know where I can find Rudy Kazoody? Why don't you answer me, Rudy Kazoody? Why are you ignoring me, Rudy Kazoody?"

Suddenly, Twitchy spread his arms out as if to simulate a cross. "Goodbye, Rudy Kazoody!"

He leaps off the roof. Luckily for Twitch, someone had seen him on the roof and called the police. Even more fortunate, he hesitated for a while, allowing the police time to get to him. Just as Twitchy leaped, one of the cops grabbed him by the back of his trousers. For a moment, Twitchy dangled from the roof, held precariously by the policeman. Finally, another cop arrived and helped pull Twitchy back up to the roof.

It turned out that Twitchy had taken some sort of drug, not heroin, but something hallucinatory. Spike called it "acid."

"Twitch can't seem to catch a break," I said to Spike after that episode.

"What do you mean?" Spike asked.

"I mean, his father dying right after he gets home. Twitch was so looking forward to having his dad home and improving his home life."

"What makes you think things would have been better for Twitch with his old man home? Twitch has had a father for sixteen years and was never very happy. Things will get better for Twitch when he makes them better!"

Despite the hard words, Spike asked his mother if she'd mind taking Twitch in for a few days. When his mother agreed, they moved Vito to the couch, and Twitchy slept in one of the twin beds in Spike's room. Spike took Twitchy everywhere with him—to school, to work at the fruit store, to the gym—and he even got Twitch to help him with his janitorial duties. Spike also made Twitchy the captain of the clubhouse, putting him in charge of making sure the place is kept clean.

Twitchy devised a demerit system for anybody dirtying the place. If someone gets five demerits a month, they're fined a quarter, and they always pay. Twitch haunts them until he gets his money. He does such a good job that by the end of the month, Twitch collects enough money to hold a pizza night. Twitchy, like Spike, is a bit of an insomniac and requires little sleep. Twitchy stayed up with Spike on the nights when Spike did his reading. Normally a quiet and shy kid, Twitch talked all night long while Spike read.

Whether the constant chatter bothered Spike or not, he never said or complained. I learned of Twitch's talkative habits from Vito, who was unable to sleep from the constant yapping. The change seemed to agree with Twitchy, and he looked much happier. Twitch's two-day stayed turned out to be nearly two months until Twitch's grandparents decided to take him in. Things seem to be going well for Twitchy, and he seems to have adjusted to his new life, even though he still blinks a lot.

When Spike was a boy back in Italy, he treated the farming region where we lived as if it were his personal backyard. There was no place he wouldn't explore. Mountains, rivers, streams, and caves, Spike searched for them all, his curiosity showing no boundary. He wandered for miles on end, hiking through the region, even following streams up the mountains to find their source.

New York City is no different for him. He wasn't in this country a month before he went by himself to a baseball game at Yankee Stadium. The next year, despite the fact he was only ten, he visited Coney Island, once again all by himself. He's probably been in every borough, including Staten Island. To Spike, the city is just a larger, more interesting backyard.

His favorite is going to museums—the Museum of Natural History, art museums, modern art museums, the Guggenheim, the Frick, and so on. I don't know any museums he hasn't visited. Any free time he gets, he goes, especially if there's some sort of special exhibit. Spike's next favorite place has to be Greenwich Village, especially when they have their annual art festival at Washington Square.

It was at one of those festivals that Spike bought the art piece that hangs in the clubhouse. The painting is a simple work. It features a run-down red barn, an old, broken-down tractor, and a wheat field. The wheat appears to be fully grown and swaying gently in the breeze. Other than that, it has no interesting characteristics. That night with Crabby in the clubhouse, I ask what the artist was trying to convey.

"Hope and despair," he replies.

"How do you figure?" I ask, unable to understand what an old, broken-down barn and a wheat field have to do with hope and despair.

"Well, the dilapidated barn and the broken tractor represent despair, while the bountiful harvest of wheat, growing from this squalor, is hope."

I shake my head. "To me, it just looks like a farm in a state of disrepair."

"That works, too," he says, smiling in agreement.

"Is that why you bought the painting, because of its meaning?"

"No, I bought it for another reason."

"What?"

"It's a long story," he says trying to put an end to my pestering.

"I got some time," I say, settling back into my chair. With that, Spike relents and tells me the story.

"One day, I'd been out in the countryside against my mother's orders. It was the day my grandfather was hurt in a hunting accident. Since it was very late and I wasn't home, she became worried and had the whole village looking for me. When I finally showed, around four in the morning, she was standing by herself in front of the house. I began to offer an explanation of where I'd been, but she never gave me a chance. She grabbed me by the collar and started slapping the crap out of me. One after the other, those slaps came at my head.

'Why don't you ever listen to me?' she screamed. 'Why are you so stubborn?' My head was spinning. I was worried about Grandpa, and yet I couldn't stop my mother from hitting me. What did she want, anyway?

Did she want me to say I was sorry? Did she want me to cry? Those thoughts rushed through my head, but I couldn't focus on any of them. My body was getting hotter, and it felt like I was going to explode. No matter how hard I tried, I couldn't concentrate and straighten out my confusion. In an attempt to get away, I pushed her. Because of my shove, she lost her balance and fell to the ground.

"My father had just arrived. Witnessing my shove, he thought I had pushed her to the ground on purpose. Already upset about his father and the hunting accident, he was in no mood to put up with any of, what he called, 'my nonsense.' He began punching and hitting me unmercifully. One of the blows knocked me to the ground, but even that did not appease his anger as he started kicking me while I was lying helpless on the ground. I covered up as best as I could to protect myself. Finally, Uncle Sal grabbed him, saying, 'That's enough, Vito. You're going to kill the boy.'

"The minute he stopped, I jumped to my feet and ran away to the road that led up the mountain. Out of control, I really didn't know what direction I was heading. My head was spinning, and I was still unable to concentrate. No matter how hard I tried, I couldn't gather myself and focus on anything.

"Eventually, I came upon a stream, you know, the one that has icy spring water where we used to stop to drink on the way to the farm. Since I was thirsty, I stopped and had a drink. When I bent over to drink, I realized I wasn't able to swallow. My throat had closed, making swallowing impossible. The saliva building in my mouth had nowhere to go. I kept spitting to discard it. Instead of my body feeling like it was going to explode, it was pushing into itself, as if somebody was sitting on my chest. My head made an echoing sound similar to the way you feel when you're swimming underwater. Still, I couldn't concentrate on anything for any length of time.

"Somehow, I found myself walking through the fields of the Sabariello farm. Don't ask me how I got there. The back of the farm is right at the edge of the mountain overlooking the valley. The scenery is so beautiful. Exhausted, I sat there to rest. It was so lovely; I don't know why I'd never been to that spot before.

"The rising sun began to fill the valley below with the shadow of the surrounding mountains. To my left was the river, which, at first glance, looked like a snake, as its muddy water meandered through the valley. But a longer view, with the irrigation ditches leading from the river to the surrounding fields, gave the appearance of a spider's web. The morning train was chugging down the tracks, which cut through the farmlands. People were beginning their journey to work on their lands, carrying their tools over their shoulders.

"On the right, I saw old man Sabariello's farmstead. His land was easy to recognize, because an earthquake partially destroyed the farmhouse years earlier. Next to the house was a large wagon with one of its metal wheels missing. Weeds were growing all around the wagon from the lack of use. The remainder of the valley was full of wheat, which, at that time of year, was full grown and ready for harvesting.

"The gentle winds blew over the fields, creating calming waves. The waves were unlike the ones you see near the seashore but more like the swells you see when you're farther out at sea. Those gentle waves of grain had a soothing influence on my mind, and I began to regain my thoughts.

"I sat there all day, even when the sun went down, and nightfall engulfed the valley, and I could no longer see the fields, the picture of the wheat swaying in the wind was engraved in my mind. I was so relaxed I lost track of time, and it wasn't until very late that I began to think about going home.

"Aching from the soreness of the beating, and getting quite cold, I decided to go home and face the consequences. With my head clear and resolute, I arrived at a plan. If my parents decided to beat me again, I'd run away to the provincial capital. At one time, I read somewhere that many young boys were living on the streets of the city. If they could do it, so could I.

"Since it was nearly dawn before I got back to town, the scene was identical to the previous day, with the entire town out searching for me. Uncle Sal was the first to see me and walked me home. My father had already left for the hospital to look in on Papa Nonno, and Mom was waiting for me by the front door. When I got to her, she didn't hit me but instead gave me a hug. I didn't hug her back.

"Upstairs, she took of my clothes and put me in the washtub. When she noticed the bruises on my body, she began to weep. My left cheek was swollen and gave the impression a plum was growing under my skin. My left eye was partially closed. I also had a cut on my swollen upper lip, my right ear was so swollen it looked like a cauliflower, and I had black and blue bruises all over my body from my father's kicks. Anthony, I'm so sorry,' Mom said tearfully, gazing on the devastation.

"From that day onward, and after Papa Nonno passed away, I'd get similar spells to the ones I'd experienced that day, and each time it felt like I'd lose control. The only remedy was to grab a piece of dry bread and an empty bottle, which I'd fill with water at the stream on the way to that peaceful spot on the Sabariello farm. Even after the wheat harvest, I continued to go to my secret place. Although there was no wheat in the field, I could still imagine the grain blowing in the wind, so embedded was that memory in my head. The trip was always soothing and had a healing effect on me."

"The scenery must have been fantastic," I remark. "I remember going to school some mornings, and I would look up at the mountains and think how beautiful they looked."

"No matter how great something looks from the bottom staring up, the view is always more spectacular from the top looking down," Spike says.

"How long did the spells continue before they went away?" I ask.

"They've never stopped, they just occur less often," he replies. "At first, I used to get scared when the spells occurred. Eventually, I got used to them."

"You scared? I don't believe it; I've never seen you scared of anything. You're the bravest guy I know."

He looks at me for a second before responding. "Don't be stupid, Priest. Of course, I have fears. That doesn't mean I'm not brave. It just means I'm human. Courage is measured by the ability to overcome your fears."

"I don't understand."

"Let me demonstrate. Would you say you're brave for going to school?"

"Of course not," I answer "It doesn't take any effort to go to school."

"That's right! But if you knew that tomorrow some of the boys were going to get together and beat the crap out of you at school, then that would be different. You certainly would be frightened. Now, in spite of your fear, if you went to school and faced your troubles, then that would show you had courage. On the other hand, if you played hooky and ran away from the mess, you wouldn't be very brave. Without the fear factor, you can't measure a person's courage."

"What did your mother say about the episodes?" I ask, changing the subject.

"She said I was feeling sad about Grandpa, and eventually they'd go away. But they never really have. I just don't tell her about them anymore,"

"What did you do when you came to America and couldn't go to the farm any longer?"

"That was really hard. At first, I used to sit in the hallway and stare at the wall. Then people began thinking I was weird, just sitting there staring at nothing. So I grabbed a rubber ball and bounced it off the wall over and over until I felt better. It's funny, but nobody thought I was weird once I began bouncing the ball off the wall. Somehow, a ten-year-old boy bouncing a ball against the wall for hours is not as strange as him just sitting there.

"One night, I got one of the spells at four in the morning, and some neighbor complained that the sound of the bouncing ball was keeping him up. That's when I decided to go into the utility room whenever I got an episode."

"What's this story got to do with the painting?" I ask, trying to get him back to the original subject.

"One day, I was attending an art festival at Greenwich Village when I noticed the painting. The scene looked almost identical to the view from the Sabariello farm back in Italy. It was unbelievable that somebody had that same exact image in their head. As I was standing there, mesmerized by the painting, the artist who painted the piece noticed me.

"'Do you like the painting?' he asked.

"'Yes, it's very nice,' I replied.

"'Do you want to buy it?'

"'Oh no, I can't afford it,' I replied. 'I have only a dollar and a subway token.'

"'I'll take it,' he responded immediately.

"'What?'

"'I'll take the buck! It's a deal,' he explained. 'Do you want the painting or not?'

"'I can't do that. It's worth a lot more,' I said.

"'Look, I know it's worth more than a measly dollar, but I haven't sold a single painting all morning. I'm hungry, and I don't have any money. I guess this is your lucky day; the painting is yours for a buck.'

"That's how I came to possess the painting. It reminds me of the Sabariello farm, and whenever I need to, I come down, sit on the couch, and stare at the scene."

"So that's why you bought the painting, for the memory."

"Exactly," he responds. "Luckily, I don't get these spells too often anymore and don't need to avail myself of my secret antidote."

"Spike, did your dad beat you any more after that time?"

He shakes his head. "No. I guess he just gave up and didn't think it would do much good. Aside from the fight I had with him when I was thirteen, we almost never quarreled. The truth is, we hardly ever talked. After that first beating, I vowed I'd never let anybody hit me like that again without fighting back. I might lose the fight, but my opponent will know that I didn't go down easily."

He stands up. "Come on, Crabby, let's turn in. Priest, do me a favor and lock up," he says as they leave the clubhouse. As near as I can tell, Spike has kept to the last promise he made to himself.

CHAPTER 16

Neighborhood Games

Spike receives two tickets for the Friday night fights at Madison Square Garden and invites me to go along. Sean Murphy, one of the fighters on the card, gave Spike the tickets. Although, Sean is three years older than Spike, they both fought in the same Golden Gloves tournament last year. While that untimely withdrawal I detailed earlier befell Spike, Sean went on to win the middleweight crown. Sean turned professional following his Golden Gloves victory and has won his first four professional fights, all by knockouts. An Irish immigrant, the New York press takes an immediate liking to Sean and nicknames him the "Bronx Bomber."

This Friday is to be Sean's longest bout to date. It's scheduled to go eight rounds. Since none of Sean's fights have ever gone that long, Spike is worried about his stamina, should the bout go the distance. I don't know much about Sean except for what Spike has told me. Being much older, Sean doesn't hang with us. Apparently, he's originally from Northern Ireland. Why he came to America is a story that is debated in the neighborhood. One theory maintains that he was a bit of a scalawag and got into trouble fooling around with some big shot's wife.

Another rumor holds that he's a member of the Northern Ireland underground movement. According to the story, he's responsible for a car bombing that killed a couple of people. That speculation maintains there's a warrant for his arrest with Interpol. The third story asserts that he's just a petty criminal running from the law. Regardless of the conjectures, Sean showed up one day at the gym, where the gym's manager, Doogie, found him sleeping on the stairs. Having sympathy for the boy, Doogie allowed Sean to sleep on a cot inside the locker area. The gym became Sean's home, and he stored all of his possessions in a metal locker. To pay for his upkeep, Sean swept and cleaned the place and performed other menial jobs.

While working, Sean decided to try his hand at the sport. He was a natural and became the most promising young fighter in the place. It was no easy task, because there were a lot of good boxers. You can almost mistake Sean as Spike's older brother; that's how much they look alike. Although they are the same height, Sean is about fifteen pounds heavier than Spike. They both have the same fair complexion, almost milky white, with straight, jet-black hair. Except for a few freckles on Sean's nose and cheeks just below his eyes, there's little to differentiate the two. Sean combs his hair straight back, while Spike combs his to the side and back, but mostly he lets it come down naturally, hardly ever putting a brush to it. Sean's eyes are hazel while Spike's are light green.

During the Golden Gloves, Spike and Sean became good friends, and the two sparred and worked out together. Although Spike's mother has forbidden him from boxing, he still goes to the gym three times a week, and Sean and Spike are still sparring partners. Not only do we have tickets for the fights, we also have passes to go into the fighters' dressing room.

Having never been to a professional fight, I'm looking forward to the opportunity. Our seats are great, ringside, about ten rows from the action. Six fights are on the card, and Sean is number three. We arrive early and go to the back to pay him a visit. We find him sitting on a bench in a room where Doogie is bandaging his hands.

"This could have been you!" Doogie yells at Spike.

Spike just shrugs and gives no verbal response to Doogie. Instead, he directs his comments to Sean.

"Remember to pace yourself."

"It's not going the distance," Sean says confidently.

"All right, that's enough," Doogie chimes in. "Spike, you're going to have to leave."

We wish Sean well and proceed to our seats. Sean is fighting a seasoned opponent who has sixty bouts under his belt. Spike believes the match will be hard fought, and Sean is going to be tested. He hopes that Sean, who is normally cocky, isn't taking his competitor lightly. Since a lightweight championship bout is tonight's featured event, the arena is nearly filled to capacity. Sitting in my seat, I look up at the mezzanine and grandstand, and there isn't an empty seat in the place.

Even the early affairs draw a large audience, primarily due to Sean. A lot of boxing aficionados are here to see if he's the real deal. Whether he knows it or not, this is a big test for the Irishman. The first two fights are dull doings. Both go the scheduled six-round distance and are decided on judge's points. There's a break in the action, and Sean is due next.

"The fights haven't been very good," I tell Spike.

"Young boxers are too afraid to make mistakes," he replies. "They'll get better as they get more experience."

People get up to go to the restroom or to get refreshments.

"What's it feel like to box here?" I ask Spike.

"I only boxed here that one time when you saw me. My first three fights were at Saint Nick's. I don't know if you could tell that day, but I was really nervous. There's something about this place."

"No, I couldn't tell; you looked so calm," I reply. "Hey, Spike, what made you take up boxing?"

"Necessity."

"What?"

I look at him in surprise. I didn't expect that particular statement. A big grin crosses his face.

"When I first came from Italy, all the boys made fun of me. Since I didn't understand English, and not understanding what they were saying, I didn't mind their taunts. It's when I began learning the language that I started getting annoyed at their teasing. One day, Mario Farzoli tried to jump in front of me in the school line, and when I wouldn't let him in, we got into a big shoving match. Angry that I wouldn't let him in, he called me a stupid guinea wop."

"Why did he call you that? Isn't Mario Italian?"

"Yes, but he was born in this country, and I guess he doesn't feel he's a wop if he didn't come off the banana boat. Anyway, I decked him.

"When I come out of school that afternoon, every guy in my class was waiting for me and wanted to take me on. Obviously, I couldn't fight the whole class, so I told the kids to choose one to represent them. Lenny Leandro was their pick. Since Lenny wasn't much of a fighter, it didn't take a lot for me to kick his butt.

"After I beat Lenny, I reckoned the whole thing was over. The next day I was shocked to learn the opposite was true. Not only did every guy in my class want a piece of me, every boy in the fourth grade wanted in.

"That afternoon I had another fight, some kid called Billy Bones. Although Billy was a lot tougher than Lenny, I managed to kick his ass. With Billy out of the way, I hoped the kids would give up. The next day, once again, I realized I was wrong. The usual crowd of guys was waiting for me.

"This time, it was Joey Cooks. An idea came to me. I'd been winning all the fights. Maybe if I lost one, they'd stop trying. Sooner or later, I was bound to lose a fight anyway, far better I do it under my terms than to have some tough kid beat the crap out of me. The minute I got my chance I faked spraining my ankle and conceded the fight to Cooks. He was more than happy to accept my surrender and garner the easy victory, because he was more frightened than I was.

"The plan worked, and, for a while, nobody in my grade bothered with me. A year later a group of older boys began picking on me. To avoid running into them, I began coming in early, leaving late, and made sure I never traveled the same route twice.

"One day, three of the guys caught up with me outside the auditorium. I put up quite a struggle, but naturally, I got the worst of it. Then Betty came along and started pounding the guys. With her help, we made mincemeat of those bullies. From then on, she accompanied me to and from school. Nobody ever messed with me again. Still, I didn't want to rely on her help for the rest of my life, so I joined the boxing gym. Doogie allowed me to work out even though I was way underage."

"I can't believe it. Betty beat the crap out of those guys," I remark.

"She was a foot taller than any of the guys, and man can she fight," Spike reminisces. "None of the boys would take her on. There's no honor in beating a girl, and if you lost, which was extremely likely with Betty, you'd end up looking like a bozo."

"I still can't believe it," I maintain, "she doesn't stand up to anybody."

"It's hard to take on the entire world," Spike explains. "Besides, Betty has to find a way to come to terms with herself. She has to realize just how great she is. It's fine to be normal. You don't have to be perfect; all people make mistakes. As soon as she recognizes that, you'll see Betty in a brand-new light, I promise you."

"Do you really think she did that thing with Joey Cooks?" I ask. "I never believed it myself."

"Why don't you believe it?"

"Because I think Cooks is a filthy liar. Besides, Betty has never admitted she did anything."

"She's never really denied it, either," Spike points out. "The truth is, Priest, it doesn't really matter. What difference does it make? All it means is that Betty is no different than you and me and can make a mistake. Frankly, I like it better that way."

Finally, Sean makes his way to the ring. The crowd is getting restless. Sean is clearly the fan's favorite, and they cheer loudly when he's introduced. Much to Spike's dismay, his concern that Sean would take the fight too lightly comes to roost. Sean's crafty, experienced opponent is getting the best of him. By the fourth round, it's clear that Sean is in trouble and trailing badly in the match. Sensing an upset, the crowd turns on the Irishman and starts booing him. Witnessing the crowd's reaction, I can sense Spike is distraught and is worried about his friend.

The next round is a continuation of the previous four. Once again, Sean is getting beat. As the fifth round draws to a close, in a flash, Sean lands an uppercut, catching his opponent flush in the jaw. The punch stuns the old pug, and the fighter's legs buckle. Recognizing the swing in momentum, Sean starts punching wildly. We also recognize the change in fortune and hope Sean can finish off the fighter before the bell saves him. Sean must be thinking the same thing, because he's relentless in his pursuit of the flagging boxer.

Sensing the shift in the fight, the crowd gets to its feet and cheers wildly, urging Sean to finish him off. Finally, the Irishman lands a haymaker, which does the job and brings the old pug down. Drained of his strength and will, he doesn't even attempt to get up as the referee counts him out. After the match, we return to the dressing room and congratulate Sean. He tells Spike he's celebrating afterward and wants him to come along. Spike begs off the invitation, and we don't even stay for the remainder of the fights on the card, choosing to go home instead.

When we get back to the neighborhood late that night, Vinnie Beast and most of the guys are waiting for us. Apparently, something big must have happened, because there's to be a big meeting at Cicci's poolroom at two in the morning. All the gang leaders are to meet there for some type of war conference. Spike, of course, will represent the Black Knights.

Although not a gang leader, Beast is also going. Despite the late hour, nobody goes home, all of us curious to learn the news.

The meeting lasts about an hour, and when Spike and Beast return, they report there's going to be a gang fight tomorrow night at ten. Some Puerto Rican gang south of Tremont challenged the neighborhood to a fight. All the neighborhood gangs, except for the Baldies, will be involved. The Baldies can't afford any more trouble with the police. Besides, the Puerto Ricans aren't expected to put up much of a battle. Spike orders everyone to be in front of the clubhouse at nine tomorrow night, and he'll give us the final instructions. He expects everybody to be there, no excuses.

That night, lying in bed, I worry about the upcoming gang war. While there's always a lot of talk among the guys about gang fights, in reality, there hasn't been a fight since I moved to the neighborhood. Arthur Avenue has a reputation for having the toughest gangs in the Bronx. This repute actually goes beyond the Bronx and is known throughout the city. All of us share in the fame. Whenever someone asks where we're from, we proudly state, "Arthur Avenue."

This bravado is exhibited by all, even though most of us have done little to advance the notoriety. But this repute is not without a price. Like the gunslingers in the old west, some new gun is always coming around to challenge the legend. Gangs throughout the city are always testing our will. Despite my speculation as to the reason for the upcoming clash, I really don't know the cause. It won't surprise me if it's just a simple challenge to see which area is tougher.

These brawls are not harmless affairs. Guys get hurt, and at the very least, we can end up in jail for participating. I don't look forward to tomorrow's clash. I just hope my courage won't fail me. Nothing could be worse than having my friends see me turn chicken and run. After spending almost half the night tormenting myself, somehow, I fall asleep.

That Saturday morning, distracted by the upcoming fight, the guys barely pay any attention to the flirting ritual. The conversation is exclusively about the upcoming war. Spike, to his credit, barely acknowledges the event. He's either playing it close or isn't concerned. Whenever one of the guys tries to find out his plan, he dismisses him and says he'll reveal the strategy that night, before they set out. That afternoon when I tell Judy why we can't go out that night, she becomes extremely worried.

"Joey, I don't think you should go."

"How can I back out of it?" The question is more for me than for Judy. "Everybody's going! I'll be the only guy to punk out! I'll be the laughing stock of the neighborhood! I'll never be able to show my face again!"

"Listen, Joey, you know you're not the tough guy type. What will your folks think if you're hurt or arrested? Will Spike—or any of the other guys, for that matter—care if that happens? Who'll come to help you? Please don't do it!"

Judy doesn't understand the problem. There's no way out. Once the wheels are in motion, there's only one way to excuse myself, and that way gets me branded a coward. At this point, the circumstances dictate my actions; everything is out of my control.

"It's just something I have to do," I respond adamantly, not having any logical response to Judy's worries. "All the guys are counting on me."

"Will you at least promise me that you'll be careful? At the first sign of trouble, please get out of there. Don't try to be a hero; don't be afraid to run."

Agreeing to be careful, I leave Judy and wait out the remainder of the day upstairs at my place. Judy's concerns, however, start creating doubts in my mind. I'm not very brave in the first place, my courage wanes quickly as the hour nears. Of course, Judy is right. I'm not the tough guy type. I haven't been in a fight since coming to the neighborhood. Heck,

I haven't been in a fight since I was eight years old. With fear setting in, I try to devise a plan that will allow me to withdraw gracefully from the pending conflict.

That evening, at dinner, I'm so preoccupied I barely touch my food. Concerned, my mother wonders if I'm getting sick. If only that were possible. No matter how hard I plan, I can't arrive at a satisfactory strategy that will allow me to avoid the gang fight and maintain my dignity. What good will I be, anyway? Being so frightened, I'll probably run away as soon as the fighting begins, and, at that point, my reputation will be ruined. Why not dispense with the formalities and simply not show up in the first place? By the time nine o'clock arrives, I've worked myself into quite a state.

Maybe it's my imagination, but it feels like my body is shaking. Certainly, there's a chill throughout my system. Failing to arrive at an appropriately graceful alibi, when the hour nears, I head down grudgingly for the meeting. Some fifty boys, including Spike and Vito, are downstairs in front of the clubhouse. Although many of the guys aren't members of the Black Knights, they still show. No one wants to miss the action. None of the girls are around except for Betty.

Spike walks with his arm around her shoulder away from the mob of boys in front of the building. He turns and comes back to us as Betty walks away. The plan Spike devised is a good one. Five gangs from Arthur Avenue will be involved in the gang war. So as not to tip of the cops, all the gangs are to take different routes and meet up at 180th and Grote Street. From there, we'll proceed to 176th Street, just south of Tremont, where we're supposed to take on the Puerto Ricans.

Spike is worried that someone might have tipped off the police, so he divides the Knights into smaller units of five boys each, making it harder to observe our activity. He details the paths each group of boys will take. This same route is the escape path the group must use if the fuzz appears. Spike designates four reliable boys to carry the weapons:

baseball bats, stilettos, and a zip gun. The boys will walk alone and trail a block behind the larger groups.

Spike reasons the police will chase after the larger groups, and the boys traveling with the weapons can make their escape. Without weapons, the most the cops can charge us with is loitering. None of these discussions do anything to alleviate my fears. It's clear that Judy's concerns are well founded. Either I'll get hurt in the fighting or get arrested. My parents still haven't gotten over my Christmas mess. Should I get in trouble again, my dad will certainly ground me for a year. There's no talking my way out of this mess; my family will definitely brand me a juvenile delinquent.

After finishing his meticulous instructions and mapping out of the strategy, Spike concludes the meeting with the following words: "Priest, Harvey, Vito, and Casper will stay behind and guard the clubhouse in case some of the Puerto Ricans come from behind with a surprise attack!"

With that final instruction, the boys gather in their respective units and set out for their destination. Meanwhile, an incredible sensation of relief comes over me. It's a miracle! Providence has intervened and rescued me from the impending disaster. All those days of going to church have paid off. God has heeded my call and saved me from my plight. Tomorrow, I'm definitely going to church and give my thanks. Just then, Vito tears an antenna off one of the parked cars."

What are you doing?" I ask, confused as to why Vito would commit what appears to be a senseless act of vandalism.

"I'll use it as a weapon in case the Puerto Ricans raid the clubhouse," Vito answers, swinging it in the air to demonstrate its effectiveness.

A bolt of fear shoots through me. "Do you really think someone will attack the clubhouse?"

"Yeah!" Casper says. "That's been the Puerto Ricans' master plan all along. Lure all the boys out of the neighborhood using the gang fight as a ruse, and then, when the crummy clubhouse is unprotected, come around and destroy it!"

"Then why did Spike leave us behind to guard the place?" I ask.

"Because he doesn't want us four pathetic losers to get hurt or in trouble," Casper responds, exasperated that we can't comprehend Spike's reasoning. "He gave us a graceful way to avoid the fight without the other boys catching on."

When the logic of Casper's argument sinks in, Vito throws down his weapon in disgust and goes inside. Regardless of Spike's reasons for leaving us out, I'm relieved, and I'm sure Harvey and Casper are, too. Spike's premonition proves correct: The police were tipped off. The fight never does take place, as the waiting cops outnumber the participants two to one. When the guys spot the police and paddy wagons, they make a run for it. Hundreds of boys scatter throughout the Bronx. While the police manage to nab many of the kids from the other gangs, Spike's careful plans prove their worth, as none of the Black Knights are arrested, and all manage to escape.

Back in the clubhouse, the conversation centers on who tipped off the law. Speculations abound, mostly to no logical cause. Despite all the bravado the boys exhibit, if you ask me, most are relieved that the fight did not take place. Spike, however, doesn't get involved in any of the speculating, I think he's pleased that the Knights made an appearance, but didn't have to be tested.

Most of the gang activity in the neighborhood concludes similar to this affair, with the police stepping in and preventing a disaster. Still, Arthur Avenue has built its reputation winning these encounters, so some fighting does take place. One such episode soon after this particular incident turns ugly. The whole thing is kind of sketchy, but from what I'm able to gather, some of the boys in the neighborhood had a fight with some colored guys from Webster Avenue. The melee took place on

Fordham Road and the Grand Concourse, just across from Alexander's department store.

The neighborhood kids were getting the best of the brawl when one of the colored guys pulled a knife and stabbed one of the boys. They rushed the bleeding boy to Fordham Hospital. His injuries were serious, and the doctors cautioned that he might not pull through. The victim was the younger brother of a gang member from the Daggers. That Sunday night, there was another powwow of the gang leaders at Cicci's pool hall to map out the revenge strategy. The neighborhood was not going to allow some colored kid from Webster Avenue get the best in a fight. It turned out that the attacker was a freshman at Roosevelt High. The retaliation plan they devised was as follows.

All the gangs would gather at Roosevelt at two in the afternoon on Monday, just before the last period. Any kid from the neighborhood who was a student at the school would cut his last class and meet outside with the guys already waiting there. The boys would surround the building, making certain the boy inside could not escape. Anybody foolish enough to intervene would be handled instantly. When the culprit came out, they would get their revenge.

Nearly five hundred guys surrounded the school at the predetermined time. Despite the fact their archrivals, the Daggers, got hurt, the Baldies were not on the sidelines this time, but taking an active role. Police were everywhere, escorting the black students out of the building into squad cars and driving them home. Despair crept in as the neighborhood guys became concerned that the culprit might escape. Quickly, the boys devised a new plan.

They decided to create a disturbance on one side of the building to distract the police. When the cops allocated the manpower to squelch the commotion, a small group would sneak into the school through any door left uncovered. With the new plan in place, the raiding boys awaited their cue, which came when the next group of black students made their way out of the school, escorted by the police. When the signal was given, a group of boys rushed at the escorted kids.

When the police at the other locations became aware of the ruckus, they rushed to assist their fellow policemen, leaving many of the other doors unattended. That's exactly the response the boys had hoped for, and six of the guys slipped into the school undetected. They searched through the school unencumbered by the cops, and they finally found their target hiding in a stall of the boys' restroom on the second floor. They beat the boy unmercifully. When the police located the kid, he was lying on the floor of the restroom, battered and unconscious.

The young man was rushed to Fordham Hospital, and the doctors placed him on the critical list. Fortunately, both he and the boy who was stabbed survived their serious injuries without any long-term effects. With the score even, the thirst for revenge was quenched, tempers soothed, and the community calmed once more, life returning to its regular routine.

◆ ◆ ◆ ◆ ◆

Most of the neighborhood pastimes, however, are not gang related, nor do the activities involve solely the structured kind, such as the Policeman's Athletic League (PAL). Most of the time is consumed by the kids playing common street games, such as stickball, kick the can, handball, ringolevio, king-queen, hide and seek, tag, and so on. Another game is called Buck Buck, known to the rest of the country as Johnny on the Pony, one of my favorites.

Both the boys and the girls play the game. It requires two teams, usually consisting of six members. We can play with smaller squads, but we don't like playing with more. To make things even, we try to put an equal number of girls and boys on each team. Since the game is so popular, generally, more than twelve people want to play. In that event, we make additional teams. It's quite common to have five or six teams involved. Since only two teams can play at once, the other teams line up to wait their turn.

The rules of the contest are simple enough. We split the opposing teams into either the Ponies or the Johnnies. The Ponies take the following position. The first team member, usually its weakest, is called the pillow. This requires the individual to stand upright against the wall and face away from the building. The pillow has two jobs. First is to be a buffer so the team is protected from banging into the brick wall of the building. The second is to monitor that no part of the opposing players' body touches the ground. All of the remaining teammates line up, one behind the other facing the pillow, bent at the waist, arms wrapped around each other's legs for support. The entire team looks like a big caterpillar.

The Johnnies' goal is to jump on the backs of the Ponies. The leap needs to be clean, and no part of the jumper's body can touch the ground, or the team is disqualified. The best way to jump is to get a running start, place your hands on the back of the last pony, and jump with your legs open wide.

The move is similar to a leap an athlete makes on a pummel horse. All the Johnnies have to complete their jump. Should the Ponies cave under the weight and pressure of the jumps, they lose. However, if they withstand the onslaught and don't cave, they win. The losing team becomes the Ponies or, if other teams are waiting, head to the sidelines to await their turn. The winners are the Johnnies.

Two nights after the Roosevelt melee, we're playing Johnny on the Pony. Almost everybody is involved, and with so many kids participating, it becomes necessary to have six teams. I'm on Casper's squad along with Betty, Nancy, Reject, and Gaga. We're doing great and have won five games in a row.

The next team to challenge us is Judy's team. Despite having Judy on their side, the team is pretty good. It includes Beast, Hervey, Bonaparte,

Aldo, and Matilda. Casper warns us that it won't be easy to bring this line down. We're huddled across the street trying to devise a plan when Gaga notices the team has made a tremendous blunder. Judy, the weakest member of the team, refuses to be the pillow. She carries on so much that they make Matilda the pillow instead. They stick Judy in as the first link, hoping our jumps won't reach her.

Normally, the first link, the closest to the pillow, is a safe position. Other than Spike and Casper, most guys can't jump that far. For that reason, Spike and Casper are not allowed on the same side. Spike isn't playing tonight; he's over Harvey's house putting some finishing touches on a school project. As soon as Gaga notifies us of the error, our plan is sealed. One of us has to jump and land on Judy. Under no circumstance will Judy be able to withstand the force of such a leap.

Casper will be the one making the final leap that will land on Judy. Hurdling far enough to reach Judy still isn't going to be easy; the last two links in the pony's chain are Beast and Bonaparte, two massive kids. Our entire team needs to clear those two enormous guys or, at a minimum, land on their backs. Otherwise, Casper won't be able to jump over us and land on Judy. Betty goes first. Since she's the first jumper, it's absolutely vital she clear both Beast and Bonaparte for us to be successful. Realizing this, Betty runs even faster than normal to gain additional thrust. While this burst of speed allows her to negotiate Beast and Bonaparte, her aim is slightly askew, landing off kilter on Hervey's back.

She's sideways and clings to his side, hoping not to slip off and touch the ground. Recognizing Betty's predicament, the rest of us jump as fast as we can, hoping Betty can hold on until Casper makes his attempt. The process is a sloppy mess, but somehow, we all manage to complete our jumps. Except for Betty, none of the team hurdles over Beast and Bonaparte. That means Casper has to clear all of us to reach Judy. I sneak a look back at Casper, who is running at the line from across the street, heading directly at us. Without any effort, Casper clears everybody and comes crashing down on Judy's back.

The massive leap crushes Judy, dragging the entire line down on top of her. When we get up, Judy is still lying on the sidewalk motionless. For a moment, I fear Casper may have broken her back. After a moment Judy sits up, with tears pouring down her face.

"Are you okay?" Betty asks.

"The next time I argue about not wanting to be the pillow, I want you to slap me!" Judy answers as a smile appears through her tears.

"When you feel better, we'll go get an egg cream at Nat's," Casper offers. "My treat!

CHAPTER 17

Harvey's Problem

When the gang leaves for the candy store, Reject and I decide to go into the clubhouse. We're sitting on the sofa, our legs stretched onto the coffee table, when Spike barges in. Spike appears preoccupied with something. He barely acknowledges our greeting.

"What's the matter, Spike?" I ask. "Are you all right?"

"I'm fine," he shoots back, pacing around the clubhouse.

He heads for the record player. Not believing his answer, I wait a few minutes and try again using a different tack.

"Weren't you supposed to go to Harvey's house to work on a school project?"

"Yeah, there was a change in plans," he says while fumbling through the stack of records.

He places one on the phonograph and turns on the machine.

"What happened?" Reject asks.

Before Spike can answer, Harvey walks in and begins pacing, his fingers fidgeting. Spike looks at me and Reject with a wry smile. Whatever Spike was planning on telling us, it has to do with Harvey.

Harvey looks at Reject and me. "Would you guys mind leaving for a few minutes? I want to talk to Spike alone."

We see Spike shaking his head behind Harvey.

"I don't want to leave. I'm comfortable right here," Reject responds.

"Oh, come on, it's only for a few minutes," Harvey appeals.

Once again we see Spike shake his head.

"I owe a guy some money, so I can't go outside," Reject says, thinking fast. "I don't want the guy to see me."

Harvey turns and looks out the window for a moment. He walks over shuts off the phonograph and turns to Spike.

"How could you do it?" he asks. "You could have your choice of any girl in the world. Why did you pick such an innocent like Beth?"

Oh my God, I think, this is going to be fascinating.

"What can I say, Harvey? I'm very sorry. It just sort of happened," Spike replies.

"You're supposed to be my friend. How could you do that to my sister?"

"I don't know what to say; it just happened." Spike repeats, struggling for a satisfactory response. "All I can say is, I'm very sorry."

"I never realized my sister was such a tramp. I always thought she was a good kid," Harvey ponders aloud.

"Don't you think you're being a little harsh? One incident doesn't qualify your sister as a whore," Spike says.

"Then what would you call a girl who did what she did?" Harvey replies angrily.

"A normal, growing, curious teenager," Spike responds. "Harvey, maybe what I did with Beth, in light of our friendship, is wrong, but what she and I did together is not so bad. Teenagers experiment with their bodies and minds. We're all feeling our way, you know? Trying to understand how we fit into this world. Beth is no different. She's trying to understand where everything goes. Maybe, like me, she used bad judgment, but she's no tramp. Don't tell me you wouldn't have done the same thing with that girl Alice you're crazy about."

"It's different for guys," Harvey counters.

"Yes, and those attitudes aren't helping. Why can men give in to their desires and women have to suppress them? If we had a meaningful custom, explaining all these feelings, maybe teenagers wouldn't be so confused or depressed. Just maybe we could eliminate some of the anxiety suffered during our teenage years."

Harvey shakes his head. "I'm sorry, Spike, I just don't buy it. Nothing you've said explains my sister's behavior."

"Well, maybe nothing will ever allow you to view what happened today in a different light," Spike replies. "But I'll tell you this: Beth is no tramp! Maybe you can question my friendship. Had I calmly and dispassionately thought about what I was doing, my actions probably might have been different. All that proves is that I'm also human and not infallible, but I can promise you this, Harvey: I will never do it again, and neither will Beth. Please try to forgive the two of us."

"How can I ever forgive the two of you? The whole world knows what happened!" Harvey cries, more to himself than at Spike.

"So that's it?" Spike shoots back. "You're never going to forgive Beth? She's going to be an outcast? Is that what you really want? Are you disowning your sister?"

Harvey doesn't answer. He drops to the couch and sits with his hands clasping his head, shaking it back and forth. Spike sits next to him and places his arm over his shoulders.

"Listen to me, Harvey. Go back and talk to Beth. Tell her you understand and that you're there to help. Beth needs you now. She's probably embarrassed and ashamed. She's all alone and probably believes the whole world is turning on her. If you love your sister, that's what you'll do."

Harvey gets up and looks at Spike. "It's easier said than done!" he wails as he walks out.

Spike gets up and escorts him to the door and up the stairs.

"I know it's not easy, but you need to be on Beth's side," he offers as a final thought.

"Well, are you going to tell us what happened?" Reject asks when Spike comes back in.

After turning the phonograph on again, Spike turns to face us. "I'll tell you guys, but you can't tell anybody. If you do, I'll kick both of your fucking asses. Swear!"

"Swear!" Reject and I reply in unison.

With that oath, Spike agrees to reveal his secret. "I got to Harvey's place on Southern Boulevard right after work, as planned. Beth let me in, explaining that Harvey needed to run a few errands but would meet me back there when he was finished.

"She showed me into the living room, and I sat on one of the chairs waiting for Harvey. She sat across from me and tried to strike up a conversation. My responses were short, just enough to be polite. She began asking me something peculiar.

"'What's a passionate kiss feel like?'

"'Why, haven't you ever kissed someone before?' I replied.

"'No, I've never kissed a boy in a loving way. You obviously have experience, and I thought you could tell me what it feels like,' she explained.

"'What makes you think that I have so much experience?' I asked.

"'Oh, come on. Everybody knows you're popular. You dated Janice. You can't tell me you don't know what a kiss feels like?'

"'I don't know, Beth. It's hard to explain. A kiss probably feels different to each person,' I told her, trying to put an end to the awkward conversation. 'You'll just have to wait until you experience the kiss for yourself to know what it's like.'

"'I don't think I'll ever kiss anybody,' she lamented.

"'Don't say that; you're very attractive. I'm sure you'll kiss lots of boys as you get older,' I reassured her.

"'Do you really find me attractive?' she asked, delighted with my compliment.

"'Yes, I think you're very pretty,' I replied, trying to comfort her once more.

"Beth paused for a moment, and then she asked if I would kiss her. The question startled me, and it took a minute to compose myself. 'No, Beth,' I said finally. 'I don't think that's a good idea.'

"'Why not?' she asked. 'You just said I'm pretty. Don't you find me appealing? Aren't I pretty enough for you to kiss?'

"'It's not that I don't find you appealing,' I explained. 'You're Harvey's sister, and he's my friend. The whole situation is awkward.'

"'What's Harvey got to do with it?' Why does that matter?' Beth continued to argue stubbornly.

"'Look, it just does matter,' I stated, not wanting to go into a long explanation. I was trying to shut her up and put an end to the discussion. 'Wouldn't you rather wait for that special someone?'

"'I'd rather you were the first to kiss me instead of some jerky boy who doesn't know what he's doing,' she said. 'At least I'll know that it's the proper way to do it. Please, just one kiss. What harm can that do?'

"Under Beth's constant pestering, I decided to give in, hoping to get her of my back. After all, she was right, what harm could one kiss do?

"Finally getting her way, Beth smiled coyly and removed her glasses in anticipation of the kiss. I walked over and sat on the couch next to her. Since this was her first kiss, the least I could do as make it memorable for her. After all, she had gone to a lot of trouble to make sure I was the first. I also have a reputation to uphold.

"She leaned her head back, and as we embraced, I pushed her gently to the back of the sofa. Pulling her towards me, I planted a wet kiss on her. After a few moments, I forced my tongue into her mouth, her body went limp, and I was satisfied I had accomplished my mission, and she was really enjoying the kiss. Just a little longer, I thought, and I can break the embrace and bring this episode to an end. There was no feeling behind the kiss on my part.

"Suddenly, her hand slid down and started stroking my groin. Stunned, I almost jumped of the couch. I didn't know how to respond. This is Harvey's sister! I said to myself. By then, her hand was inside my pants, and her fingers were twirling my private parts. I should have stopped her and left, but I hadn't had a girl in a while."

I find this last remark from Spike unbelievable. You haven't had a girl in a while? What the heck is a while in your case, a week? How about never, like me and see how you would feel; you stupid douche! Returning from my rant, I go back to listening to Spike's story.

"Beth may not know how to kiss a boy, but she certainly knows what to do with her hands. Harvey came to mind briefly, and I felt conflicted once more. There's loyalty to my friend, but how could I ignore this gentle hand stroking my appendage so nicely? By then, I had passed the point of no return, so I said the hell with Harvey.

"Maneuvering Beth down to the couch, I began kissing her neck and nibbling on her ears—I unbuttoned her blouse and unfastened the clasps of her bra, releasing her breasts. With a little help from her, I removed both her blouse and her bra and tossed them on the floor. Diving my head into her cleavage, I stroked her beautiful, small, but firm mounds. I nibbled her pink nipples, and I sensed her purring with delight. If that really was her first affair, she was certainly enjoying it.

"From her breasts, I moved down and began kissing her stomach, twirling my tongue around her navel. Stroking her breasts with one hand, my other hand was busy unzipping her skirt. Once I got her skirt loose, I tugged at it, trying to remove it. She reached down and removed it for me.

"There she was, lying naked on the sofa except for her pink panties, and she looked quite enticing. Curious to see the rest of her, I slipped off her panties, revealing the final mystery. Excited, I dove down and start kissing her most private possession. Ever so gently, I kissed her pink honey pot and worked my tongue around her most cherished treasure. Beth moaned with delight. Realizing that the time was right, I began unbuttoning my pants to complete the affair. All of a sudden, she whimpered.

"'Please, we shouldn't. I'm a virgin.'

"'I know,' I replied, thinking, So what? I had assumed she was a virgin going in. After all, didn't she just tell me she hadn't kissed a boy before?

"'You don't understand; I want to stay a virgin,' Beth said.

"'Shouldn't you have thought of that before you started?' I was angry now.

"Tears formed in her eyes as she apologized. 'I'm sorry, please forgive me, I just can't do it.'

"Since I've known Beth from when she was a little girl, I decided not to pressure her any further. Still, she has to understand that she shouldn't lead men on so long. Some jerk might not be as sympathetic as me. At the very least, Beth needed to learn a lesson, I mean look how far she went with me before she finally turned back.

"'Listen, Beth,' I said, 'you can't slip your hands down a guy's crotch, lead him this far, and expect him to turn back. That's just not right. Guys are human, and they have desires. What do you expect from them once they've gone this far and you say no?' I asked, trying to make her see things my point of view.

"'I'm not saying no,' she explained, 'I just want to stay a virgin. Isn't there anything else we can do that will make you happy?'

"Wow, I wasn't expecting that response. Beth was full of surprises, giving me a free pass to any sexual activity except one. Now that was an offer I couldn't turn down. After calming down, I arrived at exactly what I wanted. When I told her what I wanted to do, she agreed without hesitation, but told me I'd have to show her what to do.

"I've got to admit, Beth did everything possible to make the occasion memorable. Unfortunately, just as I was depositing my fluid into her butt, her Uncle Ira walked in.

"'My God, Beth! What are you doing?' he screamed when he saw us in that position on the couch. He was so loud that the whole building probably heard him.

"I jumped up and hurried to get dressed.

"'Oh my God!' her Uncle Ira yelled. 'How could you?' Suddenly, the screaming lunatic ran out into the hallway, shouting to his wife. 'Ethel, come quick! Look what your niece is doing.'

"I was convinced the entire building was going to show up at Beth's apartment, so I tore ass out of the place, flying down the stairs three steps at a time, leaving Beth behind to face the consequences. I didn't quit running 'til I got to the clubhouse," Spike says, concluding his escapade.

Once he's finished his account, I sit there, stunned. I can't believe it! There I am, straining every ounce of my being to score, and that bastard just stumbles into it without any effort whatsoever. Life is so unfair!

That night, I sit up in bed speculating about Spike's involvement with women. I know he says he's concerned about Harvey's feelings, but I don't quite believe it. Spike doesn't really think he did anything wrong. Sex to him is no different than any other adventure. He never seems set on any goal or achievement; he simply lets the affairs run their natural courses. To Spike, it's not a conquest or a game; it's just something a couple does naturally when they're being passionate. It's not a trophy to place on a mantle, and he never brags. If he talks about it at all, it's just matter of fact like he did this evening. Eventually, Harvey forgives both Spike and Beth, and Beth never makes that mistake again. At least, if she does, her Uncle Ira never catches her.

CHAPTER 18

Spring Training

During early March, it's registration night for baseball at the PAL center. Most of the fellows have dropped out of the sport, principally because they aren't good enough to continue. The Police Athletic League runs the last amateur league before the minors. The only boys in the gang with the ability to compete at that level are Spike, Casper, Harvey, and Bonaparte. Since Bonaparte is playing for his school, Salesian, he won't be signing up. The remaining three boys, however, are planning to register again with the PAL.

Harvey and Spike are in the clubhouse waiting for Casper to arrive and walk with them to the center, some two blocks north of our clubhouse on Arthur Avenue. Beast, Aldo, and I are also there. The conversation turns naturally to baseball.

"Who do you think was the best player of all time?" Aldo asks.

"That's easy, Babe Ruth," Beast replies.

"I like Mantle," Aldo offers.

"Mantle? You've got to be kidding. How can you compare Mantle to Ruth? Ruth is the greatest hitter of all time," Beast challenges.

"Look, Beast, Mantle can hit from both sides of the plate. He's a great fielder, and I don't know anyone in baseball who can run faster. All around, you got to give it to Mickey," Aldo says, defending his man.

"All around, there's no contest. Ruth wins hands down," Beast fires back. "Ruth was a great pitcher before he became an everyday player. There isn't a position he couldn't have played."

"What about you, Spike?" Aldo asks my cousin, who, uncharacteristically, is staying out of the argument. "Who do you like?"

"Well, if you're talking about the best player, you can make an argument for a lot of guys," Spike suggests. "There's a whole list that could fit the bill. Ruth, Mantle, Mays, Cobb, Williams, Young, and so on, but the two players I admire most are Jackie Robinson and Joe DiMaggio."

"DiMaggio and Robinson? Why them?" Beast asks.

"Because not only were they great players, they were amazing human beings," Spike explains. "First of all, look at Jackie. The first black player to play in the majors. Can you imagine how difficult that must've been? Do you know the pressure Jackie faced every time he took the field or came to the plate? Jackie couldn't be just a player, he had to be an example.

"Despite the racial slurs hurled at him, from both the white payers and fans, Jackie couldn't fight back. I'm sure he wanted to punch the lights out of some of his tormentors, but that's exactly what the whites were hoping, proving that Negroes couldn't take the pressure or handle their emotions. Jackie couldn't answer back. His feats on the playing field had to do the talking. He owed it to his race to keep his emotions in check and to act dignified at all times.

"And can you name me another player who could have done a better job than Jackie? Through his excellence on the playing field and his class act off the field, he won over America and allowed millions of his people to obtain opportunities never before within their grasp. It's no coincidence that the Bums won their first championship while Jackie was on the team.

"That's the same reason I have so much admiration for DiMaggio. Joe didn't run from his heritage, changing his name to an Americanized interpretation, as many Italians are doing. The Yankee Clipper always strove to achieve excellence on and off the field. By demanding the most of himself at all times, DiMaggio not only helped his reputation, but also gave credit to his fellow countrymen. Nine championships in thirteen years, a fifty-six-game hitting streak, can anyone argue that Joe wasn't looking for perfection?"

Just as Spike finishes, we hear a knock at the door. Charla walks in. Surprised by her unexpected appearance, Spike jumps up to greet her.

"Charla, come in, please, have a seat," he says, showing her to a chair. "What brings you here?"

She reaches into her coat pocket and pulls out what appears to be a rolled cigarette. "Do you know what this is?"

Spike swallows before answering. "Yes, I think I do," he says, studying it.

"Are you guys smoking dope?" Charla gets right to the point.

I've never seen a marijuana joint before, and it takes a moment to understand what Charla is driving at. Spike, however, recognizes it immediately. Dope is making its way into the community, and not just marijuana but also the harder and more dangerous drug, heroin. Several of the older brothers of members of the Black Knights, are already hooked on smack. Many of the other boys throughout the neighborhood are also experimenting with various drugs. Drugs aren't as widespread in our community as they are in other neighborhoods around the city, but they have definitely gotten a foothold.

"Charla, I swear, it's not being done here," Spike assures her. "What's this all about?"

"I found it at the bottom of Elridge's dresser drawer," Charla discloses. "I'm concerned he may be doing drugs. I didn't think you were part of it, but still, I had to ask."

"Why don't you give the joint to me?" Spike says. "When Casper gets here, I'll find out what's going on. It might be something innocent."

"I'm having a talk with him, too," she says, handing the joint to Spike. "He's practicing with his band, after which he's supposed to meet with you to sign up for baseball. When he gets home tonight, I'm going to have a serious discussion with that young man."

"Let me talk to him first, and let's not jump to any conclusions," Spike suggests. "Sometimes it's worse if you jump down a guy's throat. Let me have a try. If I don't succeed, you can still have your chance."

Charla listens to Spike's advice and decides to wait until he has a talk with Casper. As she's leaving, she turns back. "Anthony, I'm scared. I don't want to lose my child to drugs."

"He's not lost yet," he reassures her. "Let's not jump to conclusions, let's take this one step at a time and see what Casper has to say."

There's not much talk after Charla leaves as we wait quietly for Casper to arrive. Although it feels longer, it's not more than fifteen minutes until Casper strolls in.

"I want to speak to Casper alone, guys," Spike says as Casper enters the clubhouse.

We're outside for no more than a couple of minutes when Casper storms out, followed by Spike.

"It's none of your fucking business!" Casper screams as he gets to the sidewalk. "You don't have to nursemaid me anymore! I'm old enough to make my own decisions!"

"All right, jerk off!" Spike says. "You can do whatever you like, but if you do drugs, you can't hang with us!"

"No problem, I got plenty of friends. I don't need any of you guys!"

"Plenty of junkie friends!" Spike yells and flicks the joint at Casper.

"Fuck you!" Casper snaps and heads towards the PAL hall. Realizing his ploy hasn't worked, Spike rushes after him, grabbing Casper by the arm.

"Listen, Casper, I'm sorry I snapped at you, and I know how you're feeling."

"How does a lily-white boy know how I feel?" Casper scoffs.

Spike looks like he's been hit with a thunderbolt as he releases Casper.

"You're right, Casper. There's no way I can ever know how you're really feeling deep inside. If this argument is about your color, I have no point to make. Maybe you're tired of hanging with us. Maybe you want to stay with more kids of your color. That's understandable, and while the thought of not seeing you around saddens me, I won't stand in your way.

"But what do drugs have to do with it? You're smart enough to understand this is just the beginning. You can turn your back on us, but if you continue to do drugs, eventually, you'll have to turn away from your mother. Who will you replace with her? All your life, it's just been the two of you. Are you willing to give that up? Are you willing to leave that poor woman alone, just to do drugs? Is it worth it? Please consider that before you make a decision that you might regret later.

"You know we're your real friends and are here to help. We love you, and you're welcome anytime, but not if you do drugs. Either way, do the right thing, for your mom's sake."

When Spike finishes, Casper leaves for the PAL hall. Spike watches him walk down the street for a few moments and turns to Harvey. "Let's go, we're late."

That night, we don't see Casper again, as he goes directly home after signing up. I wonder whether Casper will actually give us up. He's my best friend, and I will truly miss him. I can't believe he doesn't want to have anything to do with us any longer. After thinking it over carefully, I conclude that if Casper isn't at the usual meeting place the next morning before school, he won't hang with us anymore. Casper is not the type to change his mind once it's made up.

The next day, I'm at the appointed spot, anxious to see whether Casper will show. Spike is also present, but he pretends not to notice when Casper finally appears. Casper, for his part, doesn't acknowledge Spike either, but he smiles at me.

"Hey, Priest, how's it going?"

"Just great," I answer, casual as can be, relieved to see my friend.

That Sunday, Charla has Spike over for dinner, cooking him his favorite: fried catfish with a side of hush puppies and collard greens mixed with sausages. She also bakes an apple pie, which Spike enjoys with vanilla ice cream on top.

The following Sunday is a combination first practice and tryout for the baseball team. The tryout session is at Trojan Field, located just east of the Bronx Zoo, south of Pelham Parkway. I haven't revealed it to anybody, but I have secretly signed up to play. The only obstacle remaining is my tryout to determine whether I can make the team.

The night of the signing, when the coach learns I'm Spike's cousin, he nearly jumps up for joy. Both Spike and Vito are excellent players. Vito was selected the most valuable player in a junior league the previous year. Learning that I just moved from New Jersey and comparing me to my talented cousins, the coach concludes he has stumbled at an unexpected prospect. If I'm anywhere as good as Spike and Vito, I'll be a tremendous find.

Arriving at the field, baseball glove in hand, I notice that most of the other boys are already there. The fellows who are part of the team from the preceding year are taking fielding practice. The seven other guys who are also trying out for the team are sitting in the dugout. I go to join them. Also watching the practice session is David, Harvey's father, as well as Charla and Betty. Betty is sitting on one end of the dugout bench and I sit down next to her.

"Hi, Betty," I say as I sit down.

"Hi, Joey. What brings you out to the field this morning?" she asks.

"I'm trying out for the team."

"Really?" Betty says, somewhat surprised. "I didn't know you liked baseball? Good luck, I hope you make the team. By the way, how are you and Judy doing?"

"Just fine," I reply.

"Listen, Betty," I say after a pause. "I'm really sorry I didn't tell you about it first. I know you thought when you were ready to start dating, I'd be there for you, but Judy came along, and she's so nice."

"Oh, Joey, don't be silly. I didn't think you would wait forever for me. I just hope you and Judy are happy."

"How about you? Are things getting any better?" I ask.

"Not really. During the holidays, things began getting a lot better, but now everything is back to the way it was. I just don't know what else to do," Betty reveals as she stares at Charla, who is leaning against the fence, talking to Spike, who is playing third base on the other side of the fence.

We can't overhear their conversation, but they're both laughing lightly. I'm sure Betty must have heard the story about Charla and Spike's affair. It wasn't necessary for me to betray Spike's confidence and tell anyone. He had already done the damage when he had the fight with Casper. After that fight, everybody concluded it must have been about Charla. What other reason would Casper and Spike have for fighting? Still, if the affair bothers Betty, she isn't saying so or otherwise letting on.

◆ ◆ ◆ ◆ ◆

It was during a baseball game that Spike got his nickname. He wasn't in the country six months when he signed up to play baseball. Since there was no baseball in Italy, Spike had never played the game. Luckily for him, there were no tryouts for nine-year-olds, because he wasn't very good. At the first practice, all the other boys had a laugh when Spike showed up with a three-fingered baseball mitt. One of the old men in the social club had given it to him. The old glove was the type infielders wore some fifty years ago. It was barely larger than Spike's hand.

Since Spike wasn't much of a player, the coach relegated him to being a bench warmer. Spike didn't seem to mind, and he showed up punctually for every practice, even though he didn't play much. Things took a strange turn when most of the players on his team came down with chicken pox before the first game of the year. The coach, who never had chicken pox, worried about being infected and decided not to show up for the game either. Instead, an older brother of one of the team members took over the coaching duties. The new coach, short on players, stuck Spike on third base.

"Don't let anything get by you," he instructed Spike. "Even if you can't catch, just put your body in front of the ball and knock it down. Then pick up the ball and throw the runner out."

Spike, doing exactly as the coach instructed, knocked down any ball that came his way. He pounced on it, picked it up, and threw the runner out. He didn't catch a ball the entire day, but nothing got by him either. By the end of the game, his body was black and blue from the pounding it took.

Despite his heroic effort, Spike's team was losing eight to five when he came to bat with the bases loaded at the top of the last inning. The coach, realizing that Spike wasn't a very good hitter, had instructed Spike not to swing and to try to get a walk. Each of three previous times Spike had come to bat, Spike did exactly what the coach ordered, and each time was called out on strikes. Now with the bases loaded and his team trailing, the coach called Spike over once more.

"Anthony, we need this run badly so don't swing, just try and get a walk," he said, repeating his earlier advice.

As he walked to the batter's box, Spike overheard the opposing coach yell to his pitcher.

"Just lob it over the plate and throw strikes. He's up there to get a walk. He won't swing."

When he heard that, Spike realized he needed to swing the bat. As the pitcher heaved the first pitch, Spike disobeyed his coach's orders and swung.

"The minute I made contact," Spike said afterward, "I knew it was out of the park."

The ball few over the left field fence for a grand slam homer. His teammates went wild cheering as they took the lead in the game. Their joy, however, was short-lived. When the opposing team came to bat, at the bottom of the inning, they loaded the bases. With two outs, their best player came up to the plate. It looked as if the tables were going to be turned.

The batter hit the first pitch—a bullet heading straight for Spike. The ball hit a bad patch of infield grass and ricocheted on one hop, hitting Spike on the left cheek and knocking him to the ground. Undaunted, Spike jumped to his feet, picked up the ball, and threw it to first base, nipping the runner by half a step for the last out, sealing the victory. As the umpire made the call, Spike's coach ran out to the field, jumping up and down and waving his hands.

"You spiked them again, Anthony!"

That day, my cousin got his nickname, a starting position on the team, and a fractured cheekbone.

◆ ◆ ◆ ◆ ◆

Now Spike is next to the fence flirting with Charla. Finally, the coach, who has been shagging some balls to the outfield, hollers at him.

"Hey, Casanova, are you going to take some grounders, or did you come here just to fool around with the girls?" As Spike turns to go take his position, the coach adds, "Next time, we'll bring you a bed!"

Spike presents his middle finger to the coach.

At the conclusion of practice, the boys come off the field and gather in a circle while the coach gives them some last-minute commands. After that he turns to the new players.

"We'll take a ten-minute break, and then we'll see how good you hotshots are."

Spike comes over to me. "What are you doing here, Joey?"

"I'm trying out for the team."

"Really? I didn't know you were interested? Good for you; I hope you make it," he says before walking away to speak to Charla once more.

Casper sits down next to me while Harvey goes over to talk to his dad. It's evident Harvey's father is avoiding Spike. Harvey's dad has always been friendly with Spike, but this morning, he won't even acknowledge Spike's presence. Out of all the guys in the neighborhood, Harvey is probably Spike's oldest friend. They've known each other since they were nine. On one occasion this past summer, I accompanied Spike to the West Farms Library.

Normally, Betty went with Spike to carry his books. On that trip, however, she couldn't go. Spike, who had an image to uphold, didn't want to be seen carrying library books through the neighborhood, and since Betty couldn't make the trip, I got stuck with the job.

On the return back from the library, we passed Southern Boulevard and ran into Harvey and many of his friends hanging out. The boulevard is a wide tree-lined street with benches along the way on which pedestrians can sit. The street was swarming with people strolling on the sidewalks trying to escape the summer heat. Although most of the population along the boulevard are of the Jewish faith, Southern Boulevard is also represented by many other denominations and nationalities.

Apparently, stopping by must have been a regular routine of Spike's, as all the kids were familiar with him. The teenage group on the boulevard was even larger than our own. Spike was as at ease with that bunch as he is among his own friends. The kids, noticing the huge satchel of books, kept asking me questions about the authors or story lines. It was obvious that many of the kids had already read the tomes.

Not wanting to reveal Spike's secret, I did the best I could to respond, even though I would never think about ever reading any of the works. Later, Harvey's father stopped by to say hello and give his regards to Spike. He invited Spike to the following month's Rosh Hashanah holiday dinner at his house. Spike, I discovered that night, was a regular at Harvey's family functions. He had even attended Harvey's bar mitzvah a few years earlier. Since Spike and Harvey have been on the same team since they were nine, Harvey's dad, who almost never misses a game, developed quite a friendship with Spike.

Now Harvey's dad is standing some thirty feet from Spike, and from what I can observe, he's going out of his way to avoid him. Due to the episode with Beth, Spike won't be feasting on Jewish delicacies anytime in the near future, at least not at Harvey's home.

The break over, the coach orders the prospective players onto the field, and I run out to take my position. Everybody hollers words of encouragement for me. Betty, in particular, stops me to wish me luck once again. We all take the position we're trying out for. Mine is right field. I have determined that this outfield spot is the easiest position to play and my best chance of making the team.

Casper disclosed earlier that the team needs a right fielder, further improving my odds. After a few minutes of tossing the ball around to loosen up, the tryout begins. It doesn't take long for the coach to realize that athletic talent has skipped a family. I'm horrible. Of the twelve balls hit to me, I catch only two. My throwing is off the mark as well, and my arm is so weak I can barely reach the infield with my tosses. Needless to say, I don't make the squad.

Sweet Sixteen

Most of the girls will be celebrating their sixteenth birthday this year. Sweet sixteen is a big deal in a girl's life. I can't help but wonder why, though. Is it some rite of passage into womanhood? And why sixteen? For boys, the passage appears to be at thirteen. That's when they receive bar mitzvah, confirmation, or other religious rituals. Girls get confirmed, too, or a bat mitzvah, but it isn't as big a thing for them. I'm not sure most thirteen-year-old boys consider themselves men.

Why do they wait another three years for girls? I've always felt girls are a lot more mature than boys. Girls certainly know more about sex than guys. How else can they fight us of so successfully? Besides, most girls have been getting their period since they were ten. They certainly know what that means. I didn't even come for the first time until I was fourteen. Of course, I've been making up for lost time, jacking off every chance I get. I'm so good I can switch hands without missing a stroke.

Why the heck do they call it sweet? What's so sweet about becoming an adult? Ask any forty-year-old whether they'd rather be forty or sixteen, and what do you think they'd choose? Maybe "sweet" refers to a loss of innocence, a time when everything was pure and simple, the final year when a girl can experience youth before facing the reality of womanhood.

One April afternoon, I'm returning home from a weightlifting workout at the gym when I bump into Betty in front of my building. She's dressed as if she's going somewhere special.

"Hi, Betty. Where are you going all dolled up?" I ask, always happy to run into her.

"I'm waiting for Anthony. He's taking me out to dinner for my birthday,"

"Oh, Betty, I'm so sorry. I didn't know it was your birthday. I didn't even get you a card."

"That's all right, I didn't tell anybody. Can you believe it? I'm finally sixteen," she exclaims.

"How come you didn't have a sweet sixteen party like the other girls?"

"I don't like to make a fuss. Still, I couldn't resist having Anthony spend some of his money when he offered to take me to dinner. We're going to City Island for seafood. I'm having lobster, my favorite."

"I wish I'd known; I would've gotten you a present," I state again apologetically.

"How about giving me a birthday kiss? That will be enough of a present for me," she suggests.

A kiss? How many times have I dreamt of this moment? It doesn't last more than a few seconds, but it's still captivating. Betty's lips feel so moist and juicy. The perfume she's wearing is enchanting. To this day, I have never smelled a fragrance that's more exotic. My legs weaken from the mere touch of our lips. Unfortunately, Spike comes out right then, ruining the glorious moment.

"What's this? I pay for dinner, and Priest gets the action?" Spike proclaims as he approaches.

"I just can't resist Joey," Betty confesses.

"How about me?" Spike whines.

"You'll get yours after dinner. First, you have to pay. After all, you're not Joey," she teases.

"You're not getting away that easily. As much as this dinner is costing me, you better be prepared to give me a lot more than that peck you gave Priest."

"In that case, I'm ordering raw oysters and the bisque to go along with my lobster," Betty shoots back as she puts her arm under Spike's.

They head toward Fordham Road to get the City Island bus. As they walk away, I can't help thinking how beautiful Betty has become. She's always been nice looking, but now she's absolutely gorgeous. We have some pretty girls in our group, but Betty is in a class by herself. She's movie star material.

Why isn't Spike interested? He must have taken notice of this beautiful flower right under his nose. There's no way he can miss her. Spike takes note of any interesting young woman. Why doesn't he pay attention to Betty? If Judy's conclusions are correct, Betty would certainly welcome his advances. The status of their relationship is an enigma. If everybody has concluded that the two are right for each other, why haven't Spike and Betty?

As I watch them walk down the street, arm and arm, a weird feeling comes over me. Somehow, I feel this night will be different. Sure enough, that evening, I stumble into my answer. I spend the evening studying for an algebra exam. Despite my protests about the countless repetition of math exercises my mother demands, the work is paying off. My grade has improved from a D in the first quarter to a C+ with a B- a definite possibility.

Encouraged by my progress, instead of hanging out with the guys, I spend the entire night studying for the upcoming test. Taking a break, I flex my muscles and admire my physique in front of the mirror in my room. The bodybuilding program is beginning to show results, and I can barely fit into my clothes. I'm brushing back my brown, curly locks when my mother barges in, interrupts my lovefest and asks me to take down the garbage.

My studying finished, I tell her that after I take out the garbage, I'm going to spend a little time downstairs with my friends. The only boys still around when I get there are Aldo and Reject.

"How's it going, Priest?" Aldo says. "Where you been?"

"Studying. I have a big test tomorrow." Just then, one of the fellows, Bobby Vee, pulls up driving a beautiful white Cadillac convertible. Despite the cool weather, he has the top down. The car is magnificent. It has a red leather interior and whitewall tires with shiny chrome wheels. Bobby has the radio blasting.

"Where did you get the fancy wheels?" Reject asks, impressed with the automobile.

"It's my uncle's. He let me take it for a spin," Bobby replies.

"Do you have a driver's license?" Aldo inquires suspiciously. You need to be eighteen before you're old enough for a license in New York City, and we know Vee isn't.

"My father has a summer home upstate, and I got a junior license using that address," Vee explains.

The answer sounds believable, even though a junior driver's license is not valid in the city, and certainly not valid anywhere at night. Still, at that point, we're in no position to dispute the truthfulness of his statement, and nobody appears concerned enough to press the point.

"Why don't you guys jump in? I'll take you for a spin," Bobby offers.

"Sure," we answer, jumping into the Cadillac. Inside, the car is even more luxurious than I thought. The seats feel lush. It has bucket seats, a stick shift on the floor, and courtesy lights throughout. If I could afford a car, this Caddy will be at the top of my list. We drive around the neighborhood, having a good old time, waving to everybody.

Bobby stops for a traffic light when a police car pulls alongside us on the passenger side. The two cops inside the police cruiser turn to look at us. Unexpectedly, Bobby shifts the car into neutral, steps on the emergency break, opens his door, and makes a run for it. It doesn't take long for us to realize that Vee hasn't borrowed the Cadillac from his uncle. We hop out of the convertible and tear ass. Figuring our chances are better if we split up, we take different paths home.

I cut through a building, where the courtyard abuts the rear of mine. With a little difficulty, I climb up the wooden pole where the residents hang their clotheslines and hop over the fence, relieved as I land in my own backyard. Later, we learn that, surprised and bewildered by our escape, the cops don't even give chase. They run a check on the Cadillac, and, lucky for Bobby, it is his uncle's after all, even if he didn't have permission to borrow it. We don't see him for three weeks after that episode.

That night, however, Bobby's fate is the last thing on my mind. As I make my way through the back door of my building to go home, I notice the clubhouse lights are still on. It's the same back door I use to spy on Spike's sexual activities. Since dating Judy, however, I've cured myself of my peeping tendencies and haven't been availing myself of the familiar peephole. Not coincidentally, Spike is with some girl.

Having little interest in his activity, I proceed through the doorway to go upstairs to my place. As I'm about to enter, something catches my eye, which causes me to pause and look into the clubhouse. It's the girl, she looks familiar. Oh, my God… It's Betty! She's naked from her waist up, sitting on top of Spike. There's no mistaking what they're doing, Spike is reaching up, his hands cupping and massaging her voluptuous breasts. Betty is moving her body up and down in an unmistakable motion.

Transfixed, I can't take my eyes off her. Despite the fact I'm dating Judy, seeing Spike making love to Betty makes me envious. A huge knot forms in the pit of my stomach. I'm about to leave when the activity stops. Nobody can mistake the tranquil, climatic look that comes over Betty. Her eyes shut for a moment, and she stares out the window straight at me. She gives a conquering smile as she places her body down, lying flat on top of Spike. Happy birthday to you!

That night, I can't sleep a wink. All I can think about is Spike making love to my goddess. Don't get me wrong, I never believed I really stood a chance with her; I just didn't want anybody else to possess her. Secretly, I had already concluded that the two of them would be a couple, but for some strange reason; I never thought Spike would have her sexually. Couldn't their relationship be platonic? It's possible. After all, I still haven't scored with Judy. Had I given the matter more reasonable, unemotional scrutiny, I would have realized that it was inevitable that Spike would make love to her. Hadn't he told me that any girl he dates needs to be sexually active? Wouldn't Betty, an extremely intelligent young woman, have concluded that to have Spike would require for her to go all the way?

My mind is running rampant. I need to get some sleep; I'm facing an important algebra exam, but still, I can't control my restiveness. Someone won the girl of my fantasies, and it's not me. The best I could have ever hoped for is a tie. If I can't have her, then nobody should. Never mind that Betty would never be happy; she's for my selfish dreams only. How can I ever feel the same toward her? Somehow, I must have fallen asleep, my feelings for Betty unresolved.

It doesn't take long for the entire group to learn of Betty's new role. When I reach the usual pre-school meeting place, Betty is wearing an ankle bracelet around her left ankle, and Spike and she announce they're an item. Betty must be big. Spike has never given any girl an ankle bracelet. Upon hearing the news, most of the other hopeful girls are disappointed. All of the boys, except for me, are overjoyed. Instantly, the field has gotten significantly larger, and a whole lot of girls have become available now that Spike is out of commission. Funny, but nobody seems to mind getting Spike's leftovers.

A complete change has come over Betty; a transformation. All those years in Spike's shadow seem to have passed. She has awoken from her slumber to become his queen and to take her rightful place on the throne. All those years of teasing and that awful nickname don't seem to matter. It's as if she's saying, "See? Someone has forgiven my transgression. It doesn't matter what I did." Not just anybody, it's Spike, the dream of every girl in the neighborhood. Finally, Betty can remove that ugly label, come out of the shadows, and join the rest of the world. No longer does she need to hang her head low, ignoring the insults as if they're not being said and making believe she doesn't hear the whispers.

The metamorphosis of the caterpillar into a butterfly is complete, and the change is marvelous. No longer the meek, quiet follower, Betty becomes sociable, talkative, confident, and, most importantly, assertive. She's a proper queen to her king. Betty takes control of the girls immediately and begins dictating their activities. Surprisingly, the girls accede to her dominance without so much as a whimper. It's as if they have awaited her leadership all the while. Betty's physical appearance also takes a dramatic turn for the better. No longer content to wear jeans and drab sweaters, Betty begins exhibiting sexier, more ladylike fashion. Not that she needs any, but Betty even begins applying her makeup more liberally.

The whole community takes notice. If there was ever any doubt of her beauty, Betty dispels it. That afternoon, Betty comes out wearing these tight, pink Capri pants or pedal pushers, a rose-colored blouse, which she ties in the middle, exposing her stomach, and her hair piled on top of her head. The neighborhood guys go wild and lament that they let such a beautiful catch slip through their fingers. How in the world did they overlook this gorgeous woman? Having missed their opportunity, now she belongs to Spike.

Did anybody really stand a chance of dating Betty? Wasn't Spike the target of her affections all the time? Hadn't Judy suggested that very fact that night up at her house? Was Judy clairvoyant, or did she have a woman's perspective on Betty's silent activity? Did Betty rely on Spike for safety? Wasn't there a deeper motive all along? She didn't spend all those days in Spike's shadow in vain. Apparently, Betty knew what she was doing all the while. She waited out one girl after another until her opportunity arrived. Once the moment came, she seized her chance and reached her goal.

No longer shackled by her burdens, she does what she pleases, goes wherever she wants, and, most importantly, without Spike's escort. She also takes up an entirely new role. Arriving at this newfound happiness, she decides that the entire group should experience the same joy and become couples.

The role of matchmaker is a natural one for Betty. Staying in the background all those years, she was able to observe who would be the most suitably matched. Betty has been in a unique position. Being Spike's constant companion, she got to know the fellows well and, as one of the girls, the other girls confided their inner feelings to her. Using her guile and cunning, she proceeds to unify most of the group into couples. The Knights are moving to different dynamics. Suddenly, almost everybody has a date on Saturday night.

But is everyone's happiness Betty's real motive? Could the reason be deeper? Is it possible that having beaten every girl for Spike's affections, she has set her sights on eliminating the only final obstacle to being number one, the Black Knights? Spike's love for this ragamuffin gang is clearly evident. Why should Betty play second fiddle to them?

Although everybody else in the group is pleased with this new arrangement, it's evident that Spike is beginning to have misgivings. He's beginning to lose his grip on the group. For the first time, the guys have different priorities. No longer is the gang the most important thing in their social lives. The boys are no longer dependent on my cousin in making plans. Now they must account to their girlfriends before embarking on an activity.

The worst result of Betty's matchmaking is the impact it's having on the Knights' Saturday night poker game. It's not that the guys can't make the game, because the game doesn't start 'til one in the morning. It's that, during their dates, the fellows squander all their money, and nothing is left for poker, depriving Spike of an important source of income.

I have no sympathy for Spike's dilemma. In fact, I have to admit, his plight gives me some joy. He's made love to the two women of my dreams. Losing some of his power is his just dessert. Frankly, I don't think it's much of a price for him to pay.

The most important project Betty is tackling is getting everybody to the high school spring dance. The fellows rarely attend such affairs, especially those sponsored by the school. Judy is busy assisting Betty in this work, as they're both members of the school dance committee. Judy and Betty are very successful, and almost everybody is going. Beast, however, is a problem. The big guy doesn't have a date and isn't planning on going.

Beast is a tall, gawky kid, built like a lumberjack. A year older than most of the other boys, he's still a sophomore, having dropped out of school and then re-enrolled. Disappointed that his son quit, Beast's father asked Spike to try and use his influence over Beast and convince him to return to school. Spike agreed and succeeded in talking Beast into going back. If Betty was Spike's shadow, then Beast is his puppy dog.

There's nothing Beast won't do for Spike. Spike rewards Beast for his loyalty by making him second in command, a function that Beast takes extremely seriously. He also does all of Spike's dirty work. If somebody in the group is stepping out of line, Spike sends Beast to straighten out the culprit. In truth, the boys fear the lumbering ox more than my cousin. With a little begging or cajoling, you might be able to reason with Spike and avoid punishment. There's no negotiating with Beast.

If Spike tells him to pummel someone, he does exactly as ordered. No amount of pleading or begging can make Beast pardon the victim. Beast takes his task seriously, making absolutely certain he hurts his target, not wanting to displease Spike by doing a lousy job.

Completely trustworthy, Beast is in charge of the clubhouse treasury. One of the boys quipped that if Spike left a hundred dollars on the table in the clubhouse and Beast was responsible for its safety, when Spike returned, he would find a hundred and ten. Beast would add the additional money just to guarantee that Spike wouldn't find him short.

Now, Betty is determined that even difficult, hard-to-match Beast will have an escort and attend the dance. She really and truly likes the big guy. Through her closeness with Spike, she has gotten to know him well. It's Beast who Spike entrusted with Betty's guardianship when he wasn't around. And what a bodyguard Beast was. Guys couldn't even joke with Betty without him taking it wrong and coming after them. When Beast was her bodyguard, Betty spent all of her energy intervening and protecting innocent victims from his retribution. After the Judy incident, however, Spike, realized he may have overreacted and interfered a lot less in Betty's personal life.

The truth is, Betty has learned to protect herself pretty well and doesn't really need anybody's help. Years of teasing and taunting have hardened her, and now she can dish it out with the best of them. Being gorgeous doesn't hurt either. Something about an insult from a beautiful woman disarms most men.

After some deliberation, Betty arrives at a perfect match for Vinnie: Nancy Leandro. Nancy really is ideal. She's Vinnie in a female form. Tall, lumbering, and easygoing, all the girls like her. Having arrived at her selection, Betty approaches Beast.

"Vinnie, can I please talk to you for a minute?" she asks one afternoon.

"Sure, Betty. What's up?"

"What do you think of Nancy?"

"She's all right," Beast answers suspiciously, trying to figure out what Betty is getting at.

"I mean, do you like her? If she's willing, would you go out with her?"

Caught by surprise by this line of questioning and not trusting Betty's motives, the giant answers cautiously. "I really don't know. I'm not certain she would go out with me."

"I think she likes you," Betty reassures him.

"Really?" He grins, pleased with the disclosure.

"She wants you to ask her to the dance. I'm sure she'll go with you. All you have to do is ask. Would you like to take her?"

"Sure, I'd love to," Beast replies happily. By then, Spike has overheard the conversation and walks over.

"He doesn't want to go with that ape!" he yells at Betty. "Why are you trying to fix him up with that dog?"

"She's no dog!" Betty yells back, "Besides, he said he wants to go with her."

"That's because you're pressuring him," Spike counters. "You're meddling in everybody's business."

"I am not! I'm not twisting his arm. If he doesn't want to take Nancy to the dance, he doesn't have to ask her."

"Well, he's not going to the dance, and neither am I!" Spike shouts, finally venting all his frustrations at Betty's meddling into the lives of his beloved members of the Black Knights, even if it is a childish gesture.

"That's just fine! Nancy and I will go to the dance without the two of you," Betty storms away.

I can't believe it! Betty confronting Spike and going to an affair without him. As much as I imagined the prospect would bring me joy, it doesn't. I actually feel sorry for my cousin. Betty has come a long way, but going to the dance without him catches me totally unprepared.

Surely, she'll relent. She's worked so hard to get to this point. Will she really give it up over something so trivial? A voice deep inside of me says it won't be that easy. Betty has grown and is be the old, timid, insecure girl she was barely a month ago. Spike is in for a rude awakening.

The next morning, Betty fires the first salvo in the campaign when she doesn't show up to walk to school with Spike. This means not only that he's lost his walking companion but, almost as important, the person who lugged all of his textbooks. The duty now falls on Aldo, rightful justice for the number of times the weasel has hung onto Spike's coattails and been fixed up with some girl. Betty expands the fight further when she gives Spike the cold shoulder, refusing to have any conversation with him whatsoever. It's the first time since they were nine years old that this has occurred. As happened during Judy's banishment, the tension within the Knights begins to divide the group.

This time, Spike is not the clear-cut frontrunner. The girls side with Betty. The fellows, however, have mixed loyalties. While they would prefer to side with Spike, they're dating the girls and can't afford to show him too much favoritism. Even old faithful Beast has gone on his own, asking Nancy to the dance. For the first time, Spike is the odd man out. He appears to be alone in left field. Betty has won the first few rounds of the bout. Unfortunately, she miscalculates Spike's resolve. The counterpuncher is no quitter and bides his time for an appropriate counteroffensive. It comes on the Monday of the week of the dance.

Judy, Betty, and Nancy stay after school for a meeting of the dance committee. Since I have some affair to tend to myself, I stay after school and walk home with the girls. When we get to our hangout at the neighborhood, most of the guys are milling about. Beast is at his usual sentry position on the stairwell leading to the clubhouse. His posture means only one thing: Spike is entertaining a young lady in the clubhouse and doesn't want to be disturbed.

Judy and Nancy don't have a clue what's happening, but Betty recognizes the activity immediately. She's witnessed Beast in that watchful pose all too often. She knows exactly what it means. Betty grows silent and withdraws from the conversation. I can tell she's distraught. I hope Spike doesn't come out with the girl while Betty is here. I try to encourage Judy to take Betty home before Spike comes out of the clubhouse. However, Betty won't budge, determined to witness Spike's mystery guest. Eventually, Romeo comes strutting out with Rosa DeFavio. Betty's face turns red. Then Judy makes matters worse by blurting out one of her untimely remarks.

"I wonder what they were doing. Her blouse is buttoned backward."

The minute I hear Judy's statement, I could choke her. Judy's acid words are too much for Betty, and she scurries home in tears.

"What did you have to say that for?" I ask bitterly.

"It just slipped out; I didn't mean to hurt Betty's feelings. Should I go and apologize to her?"

"I think you should mind your own business and keep your big freaking mouth shut!"

Late that evening, the guys are in the same spot as the past afternoon when Betty appears to talk to Spike. "Talk" is a mild understatement. All they do is argue. We step aside some fifty feet to give the couple some privacy, but as loud as they are shouting, we could have been in Canarsie, Brooklyn and still have overheard their conversation.

"How could you do this to me?" Betty demands.

"Do what?" Spike asks, playing dumb.

"Make love to Rosa!"

"What makes you think I made love to her?"

"What else would you be doing with her all afternoon in the clubhouse?"

"She had a personal problem and wanted my advice."

"What personal problem?"

"I can't say. I gave her my word that I wouldn't betray her confidence,"

"Her confidence? What about us? We're going steady. We're not supposed to have any secrets from each other."

"Who made that rule? And by the way, if we're going steady, how come you haven't talked to me for a week? How come you're going to the dance without me?"

"It's you who backed out of the dance, not me. Stop changing the subject. What did you do with Rosa in the clubhouse? I want you to tell me the truth."

If Betty is hoping for a confession or a mea culpa, it's not forthcoming.

"Not that I owe you an explanation, but Rosa and I didn't do anything wrong," Spike says, maintaining his innocence.

"You're a liar!" Betty screams so loud I'm wondering if she'll burst a vein. Tears are flowing uncontrollably down her face.

"Judy noticed that Rosa had her blouse on backward when she came out! Not only did you screw her, you don't even have the guts to admit it!"

Spike grabs her in a hug, attempting to console her. "You may find this hard to believe, Betty, but I didn't do anything with Rosa."

He rubs her back gently as she buries her head in his chest.

"You're such a louse!" Betty yells, pounding his chest with her fists. She breaks the embrace and runs home.

Spike watches Betty run around the corner to her apartment and turns to me. "Hey, Priest, come here for a second."

I'm about to go over when Betty comes storming back, her tears are gone.

"If you don't care for me, why did you bother to go out with me?" she yells at Spike. "Why won't you make the slightest effort? Am I just another notch on your belt?"

I have tremendous empathy for Betty at that point. She's obviously on an emotional roller coaster. She doesn't know whether to cry, scream, or fight. Spike isn't making it any easier on her.

"You're all confused. You're the one who's decided not to talk to me. How do I know we're still a couple? Why wouldn't I think you're going to the dance with someone else? Even if I did make it with Rosa, which I did not, based on your behavior, why would I be in the wrong?" Spike knows the best defense is to go on the offense. "How do I know what you've been up to?"

"You know me better than that. I would never cheat on you!"

"And I would never cheat on you," Spike maintains.

"You're hopeless," Betty exclaims, finally giving up and starts walking toward her house.

"Are we still a couple?" Spike yells as she walks across the street. Without looking back, she raises her right arm in the air, her middle finger outstretched in an obvious gesture.

"I'll take that as a yes!" Spike taunts.

When Betty finally disappears around the corner, he turns to me. "Listen, Priest, you tell that four-eyed, big mouth bitch of a girlfriend of yours to keep her fucking mouth shut! One day she's going to open her big trap once too often, and I'm going to put my fist in it!"

When Spike rants and raves like this, I know it's better just to keep my mouth shut, and I do exactly that.

"Now go upstairs and call her! Tell her I don't care how she does it, but she better convince Betty she's mistaken about Rosa's blouse! She better convince her tonight, or not only will she be banned from hanging with us, I'll make sure she never shows her face in the neighborhood again!"

When I call Judy and relay to her what Spike said, she's terrified. She knows full well Spike means every word of the threat. She hangs up immediately and phones Betty. I don't know what Judy says to Betty during their two-hour conversation, but it must have had some effect. The next morning, Betty shows up once again in front of Spike's place, assuming her old role, carrying his books and walking to school by his side, much to Aldo's delight. The boys were beginning to refer to him as Spike's new girlfriend.

Not that everything returns completely to normal between the couple. Betty has given in, but not entirely. She's still going to the dance. There's no way Spike can stop that; she's a member of the dance committee and is required to attend. While Betty has resumed speaking to him, it's not her usual social conversation. It's more to the point dialogue. Betty hasn't really acknowledged defeat. It's merely a truce until she can resurrect the battle once again to her advantage. She has simply moved closer to Spike to keep him in sight so that he has no excuse to continue his philandering ways. There's no way she believes nothing happened between Rosa and Spike. Spike didn't go to the trouble to lure a dark Sicilian beauty into his lair just to have a casual conversation.

Giving Spike the cold shoulder for a week gave him the excuse he needed. She has to bear some of the responsibility. What's Betty really after? The argument is not so severe that they can't reach a solution. Is she unfamiliar with relationships? After all, the only other boy in her life was Joey Cooks. Sixteen years old, there had been no other until Spike. Is he too much of a leap for her? Unlike Betty, Spike is no novice. He's had an endless stream of affairs since he was thirteen. He's probably the most prolific seducer of women in the entire neighborhood. Maybe Betty has just graduated too fast. Spike is not used to losing.

To win this war requires a Herculean effort on Betty's part, fraught with peril. Betty is walking on shaky ground trying to win the upper hand with Spike. This is no soap opera on television. One misstep could cost her the man of her dreams, and she will fall by the wayside, as have the multitude of Spike's conquests. She needs to consider that possibility before venturing forth with her designs.

CHAPTER 20

The Dance

On the night of the dance, I can't believe that Spike and Betty still haven't resolved their differences. Betty must have really hit a nerve. Spike isn't usually the type to hold a grudge. He can be stubborn at first, but over time, Spike always relents. To my surprise, Betty has also maintained her position and is going to the dance unescorted. All the guys are going, with the exception of Spike and Reject, who, for some unexplained reason, is exhibiting solidarity with Spike. To his credit, Spike makes no attempt to dissuade anyone from going, keeping the squabble solely between him and Betty. The whole thing doesn't make sense to me. I can't even recall why they started fighting in the first place.

Looking down at the street from my window, although it's still early, I see that most of the boys are already gathering in front of the building, either waiting for their date to arrive or else getting ready to go pick them up. Since the plan calls for me to meet Judy and Betty in front of the building, I go downstairs to hang with the guys until they arrive. Casper is there, looking great in a gray sharkskin suit. He has his saxophone with him. His band is to play the music for tonight's affair. Casper doesn't stay long. He needs to get to the school earlier than the other kids and help his band set up.

Ten minutes pass before Judy and Betty come along. As the evening is cool, they're wearing overcoats over their gowns.

"Let's remove the coats and see your fancy gowns," Spike says when they arrive.

Judy removes her jacket quickly, but Betty protests and won't take off her coat.

"You look gorgeous," Spike says to Judy after she removes her jacket.

Spike isn't exaggerating. This is the best I've ever seen Judy. She's wearing a fantastic, low-cut crimson gown, and the color really agrees with her. Her face radiates. Under the dress, Judy is wearing a crinoline, which makes the bottom of the gown fair out somewhat and makes her waistline look even narrower. Her breasts, exposed from the cut of the dress, are accentuated further by the wired push-up bra. The whole effect leaves me speechless. Collecting myself, I quickly second Spike's opinion.

"You really do look beautiful."

Judy smiles and blushes from the attention we're lavishing on her.

"All right, Blondie. It's your turn, off with the wrap," Spike demands, tugging at Betty's overcoat.

Betty puts up a slight struggle, but finally relents to his prodding and removes her coat. She's wearing a plaid two-piece suit, and while not as showy as Judy, the outfit accentuates her lines perfectly. The suit covers Betty fully right up to her neck. There's no doubt Betty purchased the outfit with Spike in mind. The conservative style of her suit fits right in with Spike's mode of dress. Although there's nothing bold or revealing about the outfit, Betty looks fantastic. But she always looks great. A suit of armor couldn't mask her beauty.

"My God, Betty, your beauty leaves me breathless!" Spike gawks and makes believe his knees are buckling. "What was I thinking when I decided not to go to the dance."

"You can still change your mind. There's plenty of tickets still available at the door," Betty says, hopeful that he'll come to his senses and go to the dance with her.

"Now, what would poor, old Reject here do without me?" Spike counters smartly.

"Why are you so obstinate?" Betty remarks, shaking her head as she turns to start out for the high school. Judy and I rush to keep up with her.

Being members of the dance committee and responsible for the ticket counter, Judy and Betty are also scheduled to arrive early. The ticket counter, located just outside the doorway of the gymnasium, will be the girls' station until other members of the committee relieve them, some thirty minutes after the start of the shindig. With nothing to do, I leave Betty and Judy outside to tend to their jobs and go inside to check their coats.

Not much of an effort has gone into decorating the gym. On one wall are some tables draped with red paper tablecloths. Sitting atop the tables are three dishes with piles of sandwiches. Two large bowls of punch are at each table. How long will it be before someone spikes the punch with booze? Opposite that wall, at the far end of the gymnasium, is a platform where Casper and his band are assembling their equipment. The stage has long streamers above it, and a big banner saying, "Welcome to the Spring Dance." On another wall, in between the beverage tables and the stage, are some metal benches, where most of the kids will be congregating. The wall opposite the stands and to the right as people enter is bare. Except for a large ball hanging from the ceiling, which rotates and showers the dance floor with intermittent, shimmering colored light, there aren't any other decorations.

The entire student body will not be attending the dance; this event is for lower classmen only, freshmen and sophomores. The upper classes will have their own affair at a later date. After checking the girls' jackets, I walk out onto the dance floor and am surprised to discover that, despite the early hour, the place is already crowded. I search for someone recognizable, but I can't find anyone. Except for a teacher talking with some students, I don't know anyone. That teacher is Mr. D'agosto, who, along with other faculty, will be a chaperone tonight.

Although I've never had D'agosto as an instructor, I know him as one of Spike's teammates on his touch football team. Not recognizing anyone else, I mosey over to the table to get some punch. Once again, I glance at the dance floor. This time, D'agosto notices me and walks over.

"Hey, Printi, where's your troublemaking cousin and his beautiful other half?" he yells as he approaches, addressing me by my last name.

"He's not coming," I reply. "Betty is manning the ticket counter."

"Why isn't he coming?"

"He had a fight with Betty and decided not to come," I explain, not really wanting to tell a teacher all of Spike's personal business.

"Don't tell me he's letting that blonde bombshell come to the dance by herself!! Is he crazy? Every guy in the place will be putting the moves on her!" He shakes his head in disbelief and winks. "Maybe this is an opportunity for you, eh, Printi?"

"I already have a date for the night," I assure him.

"Is that right? Who'd you come with?"

"Judy Ascola."

"Ascola! Why would a smart, gorgeous girl like her go to a dance with a skank like you? She can have her pick of anybody." D'agosto shakes his head once again.

I shrug. "Temporary insanity?"

"Hey, there's Miss Sandy Moyer," D'agosto exclaims as he notices one of the other teachers. "I'll see you around, Printi," he hollers as he scampers off to talk to her.

Good thing. He was beginning to piss me off. Someone dims the lights in preparation for the dance, and I know it won't be long before the remainder of the crowd arrives. By the time Betty and Judy finish their stint at the ticket counter, the place has nearly filled. Betty looks lost without Spike. I'm so used to seeing them together that she appears out of place. This is going to be a long night for Betty. Still, I can sense she's trying to make the best of it, smiling congenially at anybody who happens by.

Already, kids are sneaking out to grab a smoke and have a drink. Many of the kids are high and feeling pretty good. Admission to the dance was supposed to be restricted to students and their guests, but many of the attendees are neither, having snuck in. Cooks and his entire mob of Disciples are here. Usually, that means trouble. Too bad Spike isn't around. One of the Disciples, a fellow named Jimmy Marzoni, has his eye on Betty.

He's a new member of the group, having moved to the neighborhood several months earlier. Marzoni is a giant, some six-foot-six, and must weigh well over two hundred and fifty pounds. It's obvious he's been drinking and feeling no pain. He keeps coming over and asking Betty to dance, but she turns him down politely each time. Betty does her best to avoid the big palooka and doesn't stray far from Judy and me. When Judy and I dance, she approaches some teachers to engage them in conversation, anything to avoid the huge monster.

The big guy makes me extremely uneasy, and whenever he comes over, I feign having to go to the restroom or other such excuse. Betty doesn't say anything, but she must be uncomfortable. What bad luck. Her first social affair, and she has to deal with this oaf. Under the circumstances, she's doing a great job. The men's room is located outside the gymnasium, directly across the doorway, which is the entrance to the dance. When the big palooka comes over once again, I make my patented exit to the bathroom. The band is playing a fast song, and Betty, just to get the guy of her back, finally relents and dances with him. As I walk through the corridor, to my surprise, I see Spike standing against the wall and talking to Mr. D'agosto and Miss Sandy Moyer.

Poor timing on Betty's part, agreeing to dance with Jimmy just as Spike makes his appearance. Although talking to the two teachers, Spike doesn't take his eyes off Betty and Marzoni going out to the dance floor. Not that Spike would mind Betty dancing with someone, but Jimmy is a member of the despised Disciples. Spike doesn't even like us to talk with that bunch, much less socialize with them.

Spike is already familiar with Marzoni. He had a quarrel with him a few days earlier, and they would have come to blows if some people hadn't intervened. Cooks was instigating the trouble. Realizing he can't whip Spike, he is trying to get Jimmy do his dirty work. If Jimmy and Spike have a fight, Cooks can't lose. If Jimmy whips Spike, then he knocks my cousin down a peg. On the other hand, should Jimmy get his ass kicked, it's no reflection on Cooks.

No sir, Spike is not pleased by the state of affairs. Outwardly, he's smiling, but inside, I know he's churning. Spike, as usual, is dressed impeccably, wearing a dark green sports jacket and a pale yellow, button-down, collared shirt with a darker yellow cardigan sweater over top. His slacks are darkish-brown, cuffed, hounds tooth, and he sports reddish-brown, wingtip oxfords.

◆ ◆ ◆ ◆ ◆

Spike is neurotic about his attire, probably the result of having to wear all those hand-me-downs years ago. His wardrobe now, however, is flawless. Although on a restricted budget, every article of his limited wardrobe is first rate. Not only does Spike take an inordinate time shopping for clothes, but he also does extensive research into the item being purchased. If he's shopping for leather gloves, for example, before he makes the purchase, he learns everything about the leather. Spike knows the difference between side and shoulder split, regular or top grain, sheepskin or cowhide.

He leaves nothing to chance—scrutinizing all the qualities of the leather. I made the mistake of accompanying him once when he wanted to buy a pair of shoes. We went to the Times Square area of mid-Manhattan. Apparently, there is an area around either 45th or 46th Street on the west side, which Spike said was filled with shoe stores. Before going, he had determined not to spend more than five dollars for the pair. If the merchant's asking price was over his budget, Spike would explain that all he has in his pocket was the predetermined amount. The shopkeeper could take it or leave it.

When we arrived at the first store, Spike noticed a pair of shoes he liked with a fifteen-dollar price tag. Knowing his budget, I thought he was insane to try them on. There was no way the owner would give Spike the shoes for one-third the price. The shoes, however, looked great. When the storekeeper asked Spike if he'd like to buy them, Spike informed him of his maximum offer. To my astonishment, the shopkeeper accepted. Thinking that our shopping excursion was at an end, I received another shock when Spike turned the man down.

"Why in the world didn't you buy the shoes?" I asked when we got outside. "They were the right price, and you obviously liked them."

"True, I did like the shoes, but the day is young, and there may be other, better bargains to be discovered."

I didn't have a clue as to what he was talking about. All I knew was he had turned down a great deal. We spent the rest of the morning visiting every shoe establishment in mid-town. Spike scrutinized each pair that suited his fancy. What type of leather did the shoes have? Did they stitch the soles as well as glue them? Were the heels made of leather, not rubber? And so on. He analyzed each pair, and in the end, he didn't buy anything! I'd sooner have all my wisdom teeth extracted, without the benefit of anesthesia, then to accompany him on another shopping trip.

In reality, Spike is the only fellow who can dress in that manner and get away with it. His mode of dress is not exactly the fashion trend.

How many teenagers wear cuffed pants and wingtip shoes for heaven's sake? There are no chinos or Ban-Lon shirts in Spike's closet. His typical preppy outfits are exactly what the faculty hopes all the students will wear. Spike's appearance does not mirror his neighborhood reputation whatsoever. His clean-cut demeanor is a big hit with the teachers. Just walking into a class in his clothes guarantees him a solid B grade. Spike is also tremendously polite and respectful, always addressing the teachers as "Sir," "Mister," or "Ma'am," a refreshing change to the treatment they receive from the remainder of the students.

Not that Spike needs any special treatment. A bright student, he always makes the dean's list. The only other person from our group who makes the list at Roosevelt is Betty. The rest of the kids don't even understand what the heck the dean's list is. They probably think it's some sort of detention roll.

One quarter, I tried to emulate Spike's behavior in the hope of improving my grades. Every day, I made sure to address the teachers as "Sir" or "Ma'am." I was always polite and courteous, all to no avail. My marks didn't improve at all. I guess you need the entire package.

◆ ◆ ◆ ◆ ◆

By now, Betty and Judy have noticed Spike and walk over to greet him.

"How long have you been here?" Betty asks, smiling broadly.

"Long enough to notice you made a new friend!" he responds harshly.

Betty gets the message, and her smile fades. "Judy, will you accompany me to the girl's room?" she asks, stone-faced but obviously upset at Spike's admonishment.

When the girls leave, I decide to continue my trip to the boys' room, thinking, *no, sir, this is not going to be a good night.* When I return,

I notice that Spike has directed his attention elsewhere. He and Reject, who also changed his mind and came to the dance, are talking to the DeFavio twins. Somehow, the Sicilian beauties had managed to convince their parents to allow them to go to the dance. Betty is on the floor dancing with Judy. Alone on the dance floor, Marzoni drifts back to his friends' side of the gymnasium.

It's Betty's turn to boil as Spike and Rosa step aside to have a private conversation. The childish antics of the love-torn duo are creating a mess. If this doesn't stop soon, somebody is going to get hurt. I just hope it won't spill over to me. The next dance is a slow song, and since I can't dance the fast tunes, I decide to take advantage of the opportunity and dance with Judy. Spike is already on the floor, locked in an embrace with Rosa.

Marzoni walks across the floor and asks Betty to dance, and she agrees. They walk out onto the dance floor, right next to Rosa and Spike. The big fellow makes sure to bump into Spike and Rosa, at one point almost knocking the couple over. Spike stares but doesn't say anything. Finally, Betty, realizing what Marzoni is trying to do, pretends to have to go to the ladies' room and ends the incident.

When the song is over, Spike walks up to Beast. "I'm taking Marzoni out tonight. Be ready in case I need you!"

That's it! Just like that, there's going to be a fight! There's no turning back now. Once Spike makes up his mind, there's no swaying him. Now what do I do?

The fight comes a short time later. Betty, Judy, and I are heading outside to get some fresh air. As we pass through the corridor, Marzoni, Cooks, and several other Disciples are coming in the opposite direction. Marzoni stops and puts his arm around Betty.

"Do you need some company outside?"

"No, it's quite all right," Betty replies and attempts to remove his hand from her shoulders. Cooks and the other Disciples egg Marzoni on.

I want to step in and rescue Betty, but fear overcomes me. Standing there frozen, I don't know how to react. Jimmy is almost twice my size. A fight with him would be disastrous for me. Marzoni grabs Betty tighter and almost pushes her out the doorway.

"Take your hands off her!" Spike's unmistakable voice orders from behind.

"This is none of your business, Spike," Marzoni fires back.

"She didn't come to the dance with you," Cooks chimes in.

"I'll deal with you later—after I finish with Jimmy," Spike promises Cooks. Spike isn't wearing his sports jacket, a sure sign he's expecting trouble.

He turns to Marzoni. "I said, let her go!"

"Get lost before I put you through the fucking lockers!" Marzoni hollers.

◆　◆　◆　◆　◆

I have always had faith in Spike's fighting ability. He's certainly fearless. On this occasion, however, I'm worried. Not only is Marzoni seven inches taller, but he also outweighs my lanky cousin by well over a hundred pounds. By now, Beast and Reject are among the onlookers. Seeing Beast around gives me a little comfort. Unlike Spike, Beast sizes up pretty well in comparison to Marzoni.

The truth is, Spike doesn't give the appearance of being much of a fighter. Some five foot ten or eleven, he weighs no more than a hundred and forty-five pounds, soaking wet. He looks like a strong gust of wind could knock him over. Despite all of his success in the Golden Gloves, it's my opinion that tonight, Spike is in way over his head.

Yes, Spike is going to the boxing gym three times a week, using those visits to spar with Sean Murphy. But how will that help him here? I've heard the stories that Spike is the only fighter in the gym who has the speed to keep up with Sean. And yes, the New York press is touting Sean as the next possible middleweight champion, but this is no boxing match in a ring, administered by a referee. This will be a wild street brawl where size matters.

Spike will need to utilize all of his fighting abilities just to avoid getting slaughtered. Winning, on the other hand, appears far out of his reach. I recall Spike telling me stories of how his boxing trainer would have him box with larger boxers who were out of his weight class, allowing Spike the practice of taking on much larger opponents. At times, the trainer let Spike spar with heavyweights in an attempt to teach him the techniques of being able to handle opponents who are taller, bigger, and much stronger. I hope Spike remembers his training; he'll need to rely on all those strengths this evening.

In boxing, Spike is a counterpuncher. Doogie was the one who advised him to go that route. When Spike signed up for the Golden Gloves, he was a last-minute entry, and the tournament wouldn't allow him to assign with a gym or an organization. That meant that throughout the tournament, Spike was without a sponsor and labeled as unassigned. Doogie feared that, in a close match, decided by the judge's points, the decision would go to an assigned or sponsored competitor. Therefore, he told Spike not to get into a boxing match or try to out-finesse his opponents, but to concentrate on knocking them out. Judges can't award a decision to a fighter who's on the mat, Doogie reasoned.

The best way to achieve a knockout was to be a counterpuncher. Basically, a counterpuncher waits for his opponent to throw a punch before he counters. Doogie related that it's at the point immediately after a boxer throws a punch that he's most vulnerable and exposed. His guard is down due to the offensive posture he requires to launch the blow. It's the optimum time for a counterpunch. With his opponent's defenses weak, a solid counterpunch can inflict the most damage.

Just as important, when a fighter is throwing an aggressive punch, he's generally stepping forward, trying to put his weight behind the blow to gain the most effectiveness. A well-timed counterpunch not only has a better chance of finding its target but also utilizes the opponent's own momentum to maximize its effect. Because the fighter is generally moving into the punch, a counterpunch is the most effective weapon in boxing, according to Doogie.

If you've ever bumped into a door while rushing out, you'll understand this principle. The door, which is stationary, does no harm. It's the force of your movement into the door that causes the damage. Now imagine heading toward that door at 100 miles per hour carrying a force of at least 150 pounds. That's how fast Spike's fists will be moving as you step towards him. Most knockouts in a boxing match occur when a fighter is moving into a punch.

Being a counterpuncher is not easy; it requires certain skills. First, it requires tremendous hand speed. The opening for the counterpunch lasts only a fraction of a second. You must strike instantly; any delay will waste the opportunity. Spike has spent hours at the gym hitting the punching bag to improve his hand speed.

It's also important to bait the opponent into being aggressive and have him miss his punches. You can't be in a position to counterattack if the aggressor is landing his blows. You need the competitor off his rhythm and out of balance. In that regard, you shouldn't waste energy attempting to block his punches. First of all, the constant pounding on your arms will take a tremendous toll on your stamina. It also has the possible repercussions of knocking your arms back into you, having almost the same effect as if the blow actually connected. Most importantly, your opponent will not be off balance and open for a counter-blow.

It's far easier and more efficient to avoid the punches by dodging, bobbing, and weaving. The main thing is to keep moving—up, down, back, and sideways, anything to keep the attacker of kilter. In this manner, even if a punch hits you, it does little damage, because your motion is away from the punch instead of toward it. Should the opponent miss, it gives you the opportunity for which you're striving: the counterattack!

◆ ◆ ◆ ◆ ◆

"A slime ball like you, wouldn't have the guts to try!" Spike challenges the Goliath.

No sooner are the words out of Spike's mouth when Marzoni hauls back and tries to hit him with a haymaker. Since Marzoni is much taller, the path of the punch heads downward toward Spike's face. Spike simply tilts his head slightly away from the blow and ducks under it. The momentum from the punch causes Marzoni to move towards Spike, which is exactly what Spike is expecting.

The next events happen so quickly I can hardly recount them accurately. I've never witnessed anything like what happened that night. In one motion, Spike explodes from his crouching position and whacks Marzoni with a left-right combination. He launches the punches so rapidly I never see his fists land on Marzoni's face. All I hear is the crack as the blows impact on Marzoni at the bridge of his nose and right between his eyes. The force of the strike halts the big goon in his tracks and whips his head backward.

His lights out, Marzoni jerks back into the metal lockers with the full weight of his massive body just as the band stops playing. The reverberation of his huge frame smashing against the metal lockers gives out such a deafening clang that everybody hears it throughout the dance hall. Marzoni slides down the lockers and comes to a peaceful rest, unconscious and in a sitting position. Blood streams out of his nose—which is flat on his face—down his chin, and onto his shirt. The bleeding is not a constant stream, but flows in rhythm with his heartbeat.

The Disciples stand there, stunned. Any notion of coming to their comrade's aid is dispelled when they see the devastation Spike has inflicted on this giant. By now, the entire dance has heard the commotion and comes running. The first teacher to reach the vicinity is Mr. D'agosto. Realizing what's occurred, he turns to Spike.

"You better get out of here." He says, it's more to protect Spike from any school disciplinary action than to caution him about retaliation.

Before leaving, Spike addresses the crowd. "You better not mess with Betty!" The admonition is not directed at anybody in particular, but he's looking directly at Cooks and the Disciples. Spike runs out, followed by Beast and Reject, who is carrying Spike's jacket. Marzoni regains consciousness, and one of the teachers drives him to the emergency room at Fordham Hospital.

Almost the entire crowd at the dance heard the warning Spike issued. For the remainder of the night, all the boys avoid Betty as if she has leprosy. Making absolutely certain that Spike will not misconstrue their words or actions, no guy comes within ten feet of her. Even the girls are uneasy around her. Every time she walks up to a group of people, they disperse. The only two who speak to her the remainder of the night are Judy and me. After the dance, we head home and find Spike standing in front of my apartment building with some of the guys.

"You had no right to interfere in my affairs tonight!" Betty says when she reaches Spike.

"You're absolutely right, Betty. I had no right to intervene," Spike concurs.

Not expecting this answer, Betty simply stares at Spike and waits for an explanation.

"I don't know what's gotten into me," Spike continues. "I've been acting like an immature jerk. Ever since we began going steady, I don't know how to behave. This whole thing has me tangled up in knots. Maybe we should take a break and not go steady. Maybe we should go our separate ways for a while until I can learn how to become more mature and deal with relationships. I can't believe how I behaved tonight. I owe you a big apology."

Betty smiles at Spike, rubbing her hand on his face gently. "Why don't we start over?" she suggests. "I haven't been easy to get along with either. Let's put this month behind us and build from here. I promise to try harder."

Spike pulls her to him and gives her a kiss, holding her tight. When he releases his hold, she looks at him. "By the way, I just got a job at Sears."

"Really?" he exclaims. "What kind of job?"

"My dad has a friend in the accounting department at the Fordham store, and they need a part-time clerk. I'll be working from six to nine Monday, Wednesday, and Friday and from nine thirty to six on Saturday. Is that all right with you?"

"Yes, of course. Why would I mind?" Spike replies. "I think it's great. Let me walk you home."

That night, lying in bed, I keep thinking about those two punches. Nothing I've ever witnessed could have forewarned me as to the damage that can be inflicted by a boxer's fists. I read somewhere that a boxer's hands are considered lethal weapons, but I never quite believed it. But if Spike, an amateur, can do such damage, I can only imagine what a pro like Sean can do.

The next day, I don't get up until late and don't get downstairs until around eleven. Spike and some seven or eight men are standing in front of Dominick's bar talking. Included in the group are Fat Augie and Mr. D'agosto, the teacher from the dance. Based on D'agosto's relaxed manner, it's obvious Spike is in no trouble with the school. Fat Augie, well dressed, as usual, and smoking a huge cigar, appears particularly pleased. And why not? His boy has just done him proud. The entire neighborhood is buzzing about the fight.

Cooks and the rest of the Disciples try to downplay Spike's victory by alleging that he hit Marzoni with a sucker punch. By definition, a sucker punch is a blow thrown when an opponent isn't looking. There were too many witnesses to the event to give any credence to the allegation. Even if you give this rumor the least bit of credibility, it still can't mask the devastation Spike did to Marzoni's face. Any person will still be impressed with the result. The big giant, roaming the neighborhood with a big white cast on his nose and two black eyes, looks hideous, like a huge goony bird. He's a walking billboard to Spike's fighting prowess, sucker punch or not.

Besides, Marzoni isn't pressing for a rematch. Had he lost because of a sucker blow, he would certainly be seeking revenge. No, this bout ended decidedly at the school gym, with Spike the undisputed winner. His reputation throughout the neighborhood soars! Later that Sunday, Sean comes by to look in on Spike, having heard of his fight with Marzoni.

"I hear you had a wee bit of trouble, Laddie."

"Nothing I couldn't handle," Spike replies smugly.

"It's always easy to get yourself out of trouble when you sucker punch your opponent," Sean digs in.

"You know damn well it was no sucker punch!" Spike retorts bitterly, the barb from Sean having some effect.

"Why don't you come to the gym and spar a few rounds with me this afternoon? I'll show you what it's like to box a real fighter," Sean taunts.

"I'll be there, but if I'm to box a real fighter, you better have somebody else take your place," Spike counters smartly.

Sean laughs. "I'm no lumbering ox, Laddie. You better be on your toes if you plan to keep up with me." They tease each other a little longer before Sean leaves.

Betty's job at Sears appears to be a godsend. It's exactly what the couple needs. With Betty so preoccupied with her work routine, she can't meddle in the Black Knights' affairs. There's still the important matter of the Saturday night poker games, but Spike resolves that problem by moving the game to Friday. A much more preferable night, as it turns out, since the guys have not yet squandered any money on their Saturday night dates with their girlfriends.

CHAPTER 21

Bad News

That spring, we receive several pieces of disturbing news. The first is that Sean has been murdered. It happened right after he won his next bout. Someone shot Sean while he was out celebrating his latest victory with some of his friends, something to do with a heroin transaction gone badly. The wound itself wasn't fatal, but while he was lying unconscious on the sidewalk, no one came to his aid, and he bled to death. The New York press gives him quite a write-up, going as far as to say he would have been the next middleweight champion, had he lived.

Spike takes Sean's death particularly hard. He hadn't suspected that Murphy was doing smack. He blames himself for being so blind. Following the funeral, all Spike does is sit on the couch in the clubhouse, his legs stretched out on the coffee table, his hands folded behind his head as he stares at the painting on the wall. He hasn't gone to work and, and he's left the building cleanup to Vito. Betty tries her best to console him, to no avail. Spike hasn't shaved, washed, or even brushed his teeth, as he grieves for his departed friend. He barely eats or drinks, nibbling on pieces of dry Italian bread. All he keeps muttering is, "What a waste."

It's nearly a week before he returns to any semblance of normalcy. On the eighth day, I walk into his house and find him sitting at the kitchen table, clean-shaven, showered, and eating a bowl of Raisin Bran with sliced bananas.

"How's it going, Priest?" He asks when he sees me.

With that greeting, I know that Spike is back to normal.

The next week, we hear the second piece of bad news. The day, strangely enough, begins on a high note. Charla comes by to see Spike, and when she finds him in front of the building, she reveals that she's just received notification that she's passed the high school equivalency test.

"I want to thank you for all your help," Charla says to Spike, who is standing alongside Betty. "I couldn't have done it without you."

"All the credit goes to you, Charla. You did all the work. All I did is point you in the right direction," Spike replies modestly. "I knew you could do it!"

"I have another favor to ask you," Charla discloses.

"Sure, anything, what do you have in mind?"

"I'm thinking of going to college on a part-time basis. I'm going to apply at Bronx Community College. Will you help me fill out the application?"

"Of course. That's really great. I'll be happy to help. It's no problem at all. I'm so happy for you. You can rely on me if you need anything."

"You're so helpful. I don't know how I could ever repay you for all you've done," she says.

"Oh, I'm sure if we put our minds together we can work something out," Spike says, smiling coyly.

Charla throws a punch at his stomach, smiling back broadly. Betty, however, doesn't look at all pleased by the remark. At that moment, Casper runs over and gives Charla some bad news. Her Aunt Bernice has called to say Charla's mother has passed away. Upon hearing the news, Charla, in tears, rushes home to call her aunt.

Later that night, Charla comes to Spike's apartment to ask my Aunt Lucy if she would mind taking in Casper for a few days. She's planning to attend the funeral services for her mother in South Carolina and doesn't want to leave Casper by himself. She says she's leaving by train on Thursday and plans to return the following Monday. Aunt Lucy agrees quickly, and when she realizes that Charla will be traveling alone, offers to have Spike accompany Charla to South Carolina. Spike seconds the suggestion. Charla is thankful, but she declines the offer, stating that, in the South, it doesn't look proper to have a black woman escorted by a white teenage boy. However, both Spike and Aunt Lucy are persistent, and under their constant prodding, Charla relents and agrees to purchase an extra ticket for Spike.

Later, when Betty comes over and Spike relates the good news of his upcoming trip, she looks anything but pleased. Spike, traveling with Charla alone, is the worst possible information she can receive. Betty knows full well the relationship between the two. She knows of the affair Spike and Charla had several months earlier. Although there's been no hint that the affair went past that one incident, the thought of them being traveling companions for four days and sharing a sleeping berth in a train makes Betty extremely nervous.

Still, she's in no position to dampen Spike's excitement of the upcoming adventure. Since coming to the United States, the farthest he's traveled is to my house in Orange. Journeying to South Carolina will be quite an experience for him.

"What's the matter?" Spike asks, realizing that Betty is not sharing his enthusiasm. "I won't be away for long, just a couple of days. I'll be home before you know it."

"I don't understand why you're going and she's not taking her son, Elridge? Doesn't that seem strange to you?"

"Charla said that she doesn't want Casper to miss any more schoolwork. He's already fallen behind. Stop being so suspicious. Charla isn't up to anything."

Betty is still not comfortable with Spike going, and when Aunt Lucy comes into the room, she says.

"It's not that. I know how you feel about the segregation policies in the South, and I'm concerned you may start trouble," Betty explains, loud enough for Aunt Lucy to hear.

Betty knows how to push the right buttons. Upon hearing Betty's concern, Aunt Lucy chimes in immediately.

"Don't be stupid, Anthony. Those people don't like Italians any more than the blacks. Don't you go down there and do anything stupid," she warns, having second thoughts about letting her son go along.

"Come on, Ma. I'm not that dumb. Charla has enough on her mind than to start being concerned about me. I'm not going to do anything that will upset her; she doesn't need me to add to her worries."

"Anthony, I want you to swear to me, that you won't get into any trouble," Aunt Lucy insists, as if an oath will make a difference.

"I swear!" Spike vows without hesitation. While this oath may have alleviated his mother's concern, it does little to lighten Betty's real doubts. He'll need to ease those trepidations later in a private conversation with her.

That Thursday, Spike and Charla, each with a suitcase in hand, board the Third Avenue El and head for Penn Station to transfer to the train that will take them to their ultimate destination, South Carolina. The schedule for Charla and Spike is extremely busy. The train will arrive on Friday, the funeral and services are on Saturday, and they will be on the return passage on Sunday, bringing them back home on Monday. Betty decides to accompany them to the El.

At my suggestion, we decide that Casper is better of sharing my room than boarding at Spike's apartment. Rooming with Casper is great. That first night, we stay up talking until three in the morning.

"Hey, Casper, who's Rudy Kazoody?" I ask him just before we're about to turn in.

"Who?" Casper is surprised by my question.

"You know, Rudy Kazoody. Who is Rudy Kazoody?"

"Sorry, Priest. I can't help you. It's a secret."

"Oh, come on, you can tell me," I beg. "Besides, what's the big secret?"

"It's no big secret. I just promised not to reveal it."

"I won't tell anyone; I swear!"

"No, I better not say."

"Oh, come on."

"Why don't you ask Betty? She thinks the whole thing is stupid anyway," Casper says finally.

"Betty knows?" I exclaim. "How does she rate?"

Just then, Mom sticks her head in. "Do you know what time it is?" she asks. Before I can answer, she adds, "It's three thirty. Go to bed!" She turns off the light and closes the door.

"Well, who is Rudy Kazoody?" I whisper after she leaves.

"Sorry, Priest. Didn't you hear your mom? Must sleep!" He turns over and goes to sleep. That weekend, I asked Beast if he knows who Rudy Kazoody is, but he is not in on the secret, which is puzzling, because Spike confides in him about almost everything.

The time passes quickly, and before long, Spike and Charla are back. It turns out Spike has jam-packed his luggage with fireworks, which he distributes evenly between Vito and me. Apparently, Hardeeville, Charla's hometown, is swarming with stores selling the explosives. Unlike New York, it's legal to sell firecrackers in the state, and although the Fourth of July is still months away, Spike couldn't resist the opportunity. Betty arrives just as Charla and Casper are about to leave. Normally, Betty's schedule requires her to work on Mondays, but she took the night off to welcome Spike home.

The minute she comes in, Spike jumps up, picks her up, and gives her a huge hug. Then he plants a big kiss, and with that warm greeting,

Betty relaxes, recognizing that all is well between them. Spike hasn't forgotten anybody. He has presents for almost everyone. How he had the time to do all that shopping amidst all the other activities is a mystery, but somehow, he got it done. He has three T-shirts with the phrase "Nothin Could be Finna than to be in Carolina" printed on them, which he gives to his two sisters and Josephine.

Betty, however, receives the most unique and interesting present of all. Evidently, Spike had gone shopping but couldn't find anything suitable for Betty. After seeing how frustrated and how important this present was to him, Charla's Aunt Bernice, who took a shine to Spike, gave him a shawl. The shawl was handed down to Bernice from her grandmother, who had stitched it to commemorate her freedom. The gray shawl features a large liberty bell at its center and smaller versions of the bell throughout the sides.

"You shouldn't have accepted such a sentimental heirloom," Betty exclaims when Spike hands her the shawl.

"Aunt Bernice insisted!" Spike explains. "She told me she didn't have any children to give the shawl to. Charla had written the woman and told her how I had befriended both her and Casper, and Aunt Bernice wanted me to have it as a gesture of appreciation for my kindness."

"Then your mother should have it. It's far too precious and important to give to me," Betty responds, handing the shawl back to him.

"Betty, I can't honestly think of anybody who would appreciate this present more than you. In honor of our friendship over the years, I want you to have it. Please take it!" Spike says, giving the wrap back to Betty once more.

With that sincere request, Betty agrees to keep the shawl.

Spike proceeds to tell us the details of his journey. The train ride was disappointing, he says. He was expecting to see the great vast expanse of America, but he didn't see much except railroad yards and run-down areas abutting the train tracks. Most of the voyage was at night, so even if there was anything interesting, it was extremely unlikely he could see the attractions anyway. The train didn't stop at Hardeeville, so they disembarked in Savannah, Georgia, where some of Charla's relations were waiting for them.

The car ride from Savannah to Hardeeville was more interesting. They crossed the Savannah River and took a road not much wider than Arthur Avenue. Parts of the route were spectacular, Spike says, especially the parts where the thoroughfare was lined with large oak trees, which are several hundred years old. Riding down the lane with the sunlight glistening through the trees gave the effect of approaching a Southern plantation in the Old South before the Civil War. Hanging from the limbs of the trees was a tumbleweed called Spanish moss, and just as lichens utilize rocks to flourish, the moss uses the trees as its host. He saw the spools of the plant everywhere. The dwellings alongside the route, however, were dilapidated.

Large families live in houses with no more than one or two bedrooms. All the homes are in a state of disrepair. They have no bathrooms; people have to use outhouses. Chickens and other farm animals roam free. It made Spike feel more like he was in war-torn Italy than the United States. The American government had been so benevolent in aiding war-ravaged Europe that their disregard for this impoverishment right in their backyard is inexplicable, Spike maintains. Despite the poverty, the people appeared content and affable.

The area is called the low country, because it hardly rises above sea level, and there are no hills or mountains anywhere. It's very flat and has marshes everywhere. Spike even caught sight of alligators, which abound in the region. The locals were doing a lot of fishing, and Spike would have liked to join them if he had more time.

Spike makes an astonishing revelation. "I found Casper's father," he reveals.

"Really, who is he?" Betty and I ask in unison.

Spike looks at us for a second, hesitating. "I guess I can tell you now. On the train ride back, Charla told me that she would finally tell Casper. Do me a favor, and don't tell anyone, including Casper. If he tells you, act surprised, like you didn't know anything about it."

With that assurance from us, Spike begins his narrative. "This young minister presided over the funeral services, and, at first, I didn't take any notice of him. After the sermon was over, he came over to express his condolences to the family. The minute he got close, there was no mistaking the resemblance. The preacher was the splitting image of Casper!

"I had wondered why Charla didn't want Casper to accompany her. The reason was clear when I laid eyes on the reverend. Everybody at the mass would have noticed the resemblance. The minute the people laid eyes on Casper, they would have known that he was the preacher's son.

"When I was alone, I asked Aunt Bernice about the minister. She must have realized by my questions that I had solved the riddle. Swearing me to secrecy, she revealed Charla's story.

"When Charla was sixteen, she and the reverend had a fling. Charla had the unfortunate luck of getting pregnant after only one episode. Terrified, she didn't tell anybody about her condition. Eventually, however, as her figure began to reveal the upcoming event, Charla had no choice but to confide in her Aunt Bernice.

"Aunt Bernice advised that under the circumstances, the best thing for her to do was to get an abortion. Bernice knew a doctor who would be willing to perform the illegal procedure. Bernice would pay for the operation, and no one would have to know Charla's secret, including Charla's mother.

"Once again, fate conspired against poor Charla. When the doctor realized how far along she was in her pregnancy, he refused to perform the surgery. He said the procedure was too risky, and he didn't want to jeopardize Charla's welfare. They then tried a midwife, who gave them the same advice as the doctor. Foiled in her attempt to abort the child, Charla had no choice but to tell her mother the truth.

"Aunt Bernice and Charla's mother decided that the best thing for Charla would be for her to go to New York City to have the baby. After the birth, Charla would give up the baby for adoption and place it in an orphanage run by some nuns.

"When she arrived in New York, Charla, who was barely sixteen, stayed in a convent with the nuns until Casper was born. Then Charla made the unfortunate—or fortunate, depending on how you look at it—decision of asking one of the sisters if she could see her son. The sister agreed and permitted Charla to hold her beautiful baby. The moment she held her newborn child in her arms, Charla determined not to give him up. She wrote to her mom and Aunt Bernice and informed them she was not returning home but was staying in New York to raise her son as best she could.

"Both Aunt Bernice and Charla's mom sent Charla whatever money they could spare from time to time. And, well, you know the rest of the story," Spike concludes. "The saddest part is that Charla never saw her mother alive again, nor did her mom ever see Casper, her grandson. By the way, Aunt Bernice promised to come to New York for a visit. And Betty, she wants you to wear the shawl when she comes."

"Of course," Betty replies. "It will be my pleasure."

Spike's mom, recognizing that her son has missed his usual Sunday pasta and meat sauce dinner, decides to prepare it for him on Monday instead. His favorite macaroni is cavatelli, a small, soft, shell-shaped pasta. Aunt Lucy, making absolutely sure that her precious boy won't miss out, makes that pasta for this dinner. Later, when we go downstairs, everybody is anxious to hear about Spike's journey, which he is glad to recite once again, all except for the part about Casper's dad.

When Spike finishes telling about his trip, Betty asks him to walk her home. "I'll try on the shawl for you and fill you in on the school assignments you missed," she says. Spike agrees to go, and we all realize we won't see him the rest of the night. His mother caught him up on one of his favorite culinary needs. Now his other most important woman will have him up catch up on the other favorite dish he's missed.

A few days later, Casper tells me that Charla told him about his dad. As I promised Spike, I play dumb.

"What are you going to do?" I ask Casper after he tells me.

"What do you mean?"

"Well, now that you know, are you going to write to him or contact him? Don't you want to know more? Aren't you the least bit curious?"

"I don't think this changes a thing," he replies. "What difference does it make? I'm sure he has his own family. Me showing up would just complicate things and cause a mess. Besides, it's always just been me and Mom. I don't ever want to change that."

CHAPTER 22

A Day in the Park

A few weeks after Spike's trip to South Carolina, we have a day off from school due to some teacher's conferences. We're playing stickball on Hughes Avenue when Judy walks by carrying a yellow picnic basket.

"Hey, Judy. Where you heading?" I ask as I stop playing and walk over to see her.

"Betty called and said that she and Spike are going on a picnic today. She asked if she could borrow my basket." Judy explains. "I'm on my way there now to bring it to her. Why don't you walk with me?"

"Sure," I reply and set out to keep her company.

"Hey, Priest, where you going?" Reject shouts.

"I'm going to take a walk with Judy. I'll be back in twenty minutes!"

"What about the game?" he says.

There were even teams of three players per side. With me gone, they won't be able to continue.

"We'll continue when I get back!"

"Screw you!" he says.

Betty answers the door wearing nothing but a man's dress shirt. It's pale blue with a button-down collar, and if Betty unfolded the cuffs, we would see my cousin's initials engraved on the sleeves. Spike loves pastel dress shirts—pale yellow, pale blue, pale green, and even light pink. Spike is probably the only guy in the neighborhood who can get away with wearing that feminine color. All of his shirts are custom-made by a Lebanese tailor in lower Manhattan. Spike haggles for hours with the shopkeeper until the man sells him six shirts for the price of four. The merchant loves bartering with Spike. It reminds him of the markets in old Beirut.

Betty greeting us with only the shirt covering her gorgeous body is an event for which I'm not prepared. However nice the shirt may look on Spike, it's nothing compared to the way it fits Betty. Somehow, I manage to maintain enough control and not drool all over the poor girl standing in the doorway.

"Come in," Betty says. "You've got perfect timing; Anthony is just cooking breakfast."

In the kitchen, Spike, shirtless, is frying some bacon and eggs. Lois is sitting at the kitchen table.

"I guess I'll get going," Lois says when we come in.

"Why don't you stay and have some breakfast?" Spike says. "It should be ready in a few minutes.

"No, I've gotta run." She hops up and gives Spike a kiss and then goes over and gives Betty a kiss.

"I'm sorry you didn't like the Village," Lois says. "I'll see you tomorrow."

"You sure you won't stay?" Betty asks.

"Sorry, I really gotta go," she says and then walks over and gives Judy a kiss.

"Bye," Lois says as she walks out the door.

Interesting, everybody got a kiss but me, I'm thinking.

"Lois is really nice," Judy remarks after she leaves.

"Yes," Betty agrees. "I'm so glad Anthony had me patch things up with her. I feel so awful at the way I treated her when she first moved to the neighborhood."

"I didn't know you could cook," Judy says to Spike, grabbing a seat at the kitchen table.

"I can't cook. Betty suckered me into doing it," Spike replies, giving Betty a dirty look.

Betty gives him an unsympathetic smile as she grabs a cup of coffee and sits alongside Judy.

"Would you like some breakfast or something to drink?" She asks the two of us.

"Just a glass of orange juice if you don't mind," I respond, sitting on Judy's other side.

"Nothing for me," Judy says.

When Betty opens the refrigerator to get my juice, the light from the fridge beams through her pale blue shirt, giving me a great view of her gorgeous breasts. She has full, firm breasts with large, rosy nipples that point straight up. If not for her panties, I'd have viewed her entire package. I turn impulsively to see if Judy has noticed my gawking and, to my surprise, Judy is ogling Spike! While his back is to us, Judy's eyes are on his butt.

As a weightlifter, I have a better physique than Spike, more pronounced, muscular, and better definition. Not that he doesn't have plenty of muscle, but it's softer and subtler. His boxing stat sheet lists him as having a thirty-seven-inch chest and a twenty-eight-inch waist. His hips are small, probably no more than thirty-four. The most striking feature of his build is his abdomen. As a result of the two hundred sit-ups he does daily, he has ridges of muscle that cut right through his stomach. It resembles a washboard. Even fully relaxed, the ridges are still visible.

Judy is getting a great eyeful of my cousin. When she notices me looking at her, she blushes. Spike once told me that he didn't think he could ever get Judy into bed. Watching her gape at him this morning, I conclude that if Spike wanted, getting Judy into the sack would be no problem at all.

"I really like your shirt; that color looks great on you," Judy says to Betty, finally taking her eyes of Spike.

"It's Anthony's. He let me put it on this morning. Normally, the fusspot doesn't allow me to wear his shirts," Betty responds, sneering at Spike.

"How come?" Judy asks."

"Because he's always whining that I put nipple marks in them," Betty replies as she gets up to get a slice of toast, squeezing Spike's ass cheeks with both hands and biting on his neck as she walks by.

"I just love the feel of cotton," Betty adds. "Don't you?"

Long, single staple, Egyptian cotton, I think, Spike's favorite, as he's told me countless times.

"Why did you let her wear the shirt now?" Judy asks as Spike places the bacon and eggs on the table and takes a seat.

"He's outgrown it," Betty answers on his behalf, sitting on his lap and munching on a slice of bacon.

"Turns out I've grown a little over an inch since last year," Spike clarifies.

I guess there's hope for me yet.

"How tall are you?" Judy asks.

"They measured me last week at the gym, and I'm five-eleven and an eighth."

"His height is not the only place he's growing, he's also getting fat," Betty says. "He's gained seven pounds, probably the result of my good loving," she adds, squeezing his sides to demonstrate the flab.

"At least I'm not beginning to sag," he counters, sliding his hand under her shirt and grabbing one of her breasts. She jumps off his lap and smacks him on his bare chest. Not a mild whack either. The sound reverberates throughout the apartment.

"Yoooooow!" he cries, clutching his chest in pain.

"Don't touch what doesn't belong to you!" she warns, sitting on the chair beside him. "And they're not sagging!" she adds for good measure, smiling coyly.

"Did you have to hit me that hard, you sadistic bitch?" he yells, still clutching his chest.

"Stop acting like a baby; I didn't hit you that hard."

"Look!" he yells, pointing to her handprint on his chest. If he's looking for sympathy, it's not forthcoming.

"Good!" She grins. "That'll teach you to say I have droopy breasts."

Spike grimaces at Betty. "You're lucky Priest and Judy are here."

"Idle threats," she replies, her grin getting even wider as she slides her tongue salaciously over her lips.

Spike and Betty's playful nature is a marvel. A few months earlier, I wouldn't have bet a nickel their relationship would have lasted a month.

One of Spike's main physical features is his expressive eyes. Most often, he doesn't have to say anything; he can make his eyes reveal his thoughts or emotions. Standing across a large room, one look from him, and he'll let you know if he's angry or happy. He also has several different grimaces. One of the looks is threatening, another is when you get the best of him, a third is when he's apologetic, and so on. While we were shooting the breeze one night last summer, the girls were talking about people's eyes. They were comparing who had the prettiest and most beautiful eyes.

The discussion began when by comparing entertainers, rock stars, and other celebrities. Eventually, they begin talking about some of the kids in the neighborhood. When the girls got to Spike, I remarked that I thought he had shifty eyes. You'd think I just knocked the Virgin Mary, the way the girls came at me. Apparently, the girls don't share my viewpoint. They feel Spike has sexy eyes. "Bedroom eyes" is the exact phrase the girls used. I don't have a clue what that phrase means.

"I don't think Lois likes me much," I reveal when I come back to the group from my drifting.

"What makes you say that?" Judy asks.

"Did you notice that everybody got a kiss goodbye but me? She didn't even acknowledge me. It was as if I didn't exist."

"Can you blame her?" Don't you remember the way you treated her when she first came to the neighborhood?" Spike reminds me.

"What about Betty?" I reply angrily. "She belted her!"

"That's just my point, you were supposed to protect Lois from morons like Betty."

Betty slaps him across his bare chest once again. This time, he doesn't protest, because he's laughing uncontrollably.

"Is your father out of town?" Judy asks, changing the subject from their childish behavior, probably wondering how Spike managed to spend the night at Betty's apartment.

"No, my father is working the night shift at the fire station," Betty replies, quite matter of fact.

"Aren't you the least bit concerned he might accidentally walk in on you?" Judy asks, her curiosity aroused.

"He knows Anthony slept over last night, if that's what you mean," she replies, very matter of fact.

"What?" I exclaim, nearly coming out of my chair.

"Anthony has been sleeping over at my house for years," Betty clarifies, understanding my reaction. "After my mother died, I was afraid to sleep at home alone whenever my father worked the night shift at the fire department. One day I asked my dad if Anthony could sleep on the couch some of the nights he wasn't around, and he agreed. He wouldn't think anything different now. Still, for good measure, we keep the safety latch on."

Here's another interesting tidbit I hadn't known about my cousin. All those times I fantasized about Betty, he was sleeping right down the corridor from her. He could have taken her anytime it suited his fancy. Still, I'm impressed with the amount of self-restraint he showed not taking advantage of her.

"How was your trip to Greenwich Village last night?" I ask.

"Horrible!" Betty answers.

"Great!" Spike replies almost at the same time.

"They have these people reciting these horrible poems, and folk singers whose voices are so flat and off key, Betty says before Spike can get a word in. "I could've done a better job. All they kept talking about was how terrible the world is. All they accomplished was to make me very depressed."

"We always mock behavior that we can't easily explain," Spike says. "The Village is one of the most unique and most interesting places in the city. It has artists, musicians, writers, poets, and others who congregate there to share their diverse ideas. They're trying to make a difference in a complex and dangerous world. You don't have to look far to see the terrible shape our world is in today. At school, we conduct civil defense drills constantly; we crawl under our desks to practice in case of a nuclear attack. As if the little wooden desks will make a difference during an atomic blast. Unless we do something about it, we're going to destroy our world. These people are out there trying to change things."

"I don't know why Anthony likes the place," Betty adds. "If you ask me, the Village is full of dirty coffee shops crowded with beatniks, misfits, and weirdoes."

"Look, those people are not all Maynard G. Krebs," Spike shoots back, referring to the work-hating television beatnik. "They're very serious about their work, art, music, and most of all, their environment. Unlike those who stay comfortable at home and never make an attempt, only later to rue lost opportunities, these people are out there, giving it their best. Most will never succeed, but at least they're giving it a shot. Those who succeed will make a difference. Of that I'm certain."

"Well, I guess I'm old fashioned," Betty says. "All I want to do is graduate from college, get a decent job, and raise a happy family."

Just then, her eyes light up with an idea. "Why don't you guys come on the picnic with us?" she asks Judy and me. "We'll have a great time. We're going to Botanical Gardens. You don't need to bring anything. I'll just make a few extra sandwiches."

It's a beautiful day, so Judy and I agree quickly, and we make plans to meet back at Betty's place in two hours.

At the eastern end of Fordham Road, on the north side, is a huge park called Botanical Gardens. It extends east almost to Pelham Parkway. Its northern limit is Moshulu Parkway. A vast park in the middle of the Bronx, it's nearly five hundred acres. The reason for the park has always been a mystery to me. It's supposed to house many exotic plants. However, except for maybe a half dozen greenhouses that contain the exotic plants, the rest of the park's immense area features only local foliage. The greenhouses are only a small part of the park.

The Bronx River cuts right through the Botanical Gardens, and the Bronx Zoo, which adjoins the place, is just south of the park. After meeting up with Betty and Spike, we set out for the huge park. The picnic basket is heavy. Betty has loaded it with enough provisions to cover three days' worth of meals. The day is turning out even more beautiful than we first thought. There's hardly a cloud in the sky, and the forecast calls for the temperature, which is already in the sixties, to reach almost eighty by the afternoon. It's going to be a great day to have a picnic.

The Botanical Gardens are located about a half mile from our clubhouse, but the entrances to the park are some five blocks away. Spike, however, knows of a hole in the fence surrounding the park that will allow us to enter without walking the extra distance. Once inside, we climb a grassy knoll and follow a path leading to a large open meadow, where we put down our blankets. Although the weather is absolutely gorgeous, the park isn't very crowded. This being a weekday, most people are probably working. We have the large meadow all to ourselves. The place is actually quite beautiful and peaceful. Since no tall buildings surround the park, it feels as if we're in the country. None of the city is visible from the spot.

Spike begins spinning some of the many adventures he's had in the park. One of the tales is when he and the guys decided to use the Botanical Gardens for a camping trip. Although the park forbids camping, this rule did nothing to deter the boys. They pitched their tents in a secluded, wooded area. Unfortunately, they picked a night that was both overcast and featured a new moon. It was so dark the happy campers could barely see their hand in front of their face once the sun went down. To compensate for the darkness, the boys built a huge campfire. Attracted by the flames, two hobos, thinking one of their own had lit the fire, walked toward the campsite.

When the guys saw the bums coming through the thicket, they were terrified and made a run for it. Because of the dark conditions, the panic-stricken boys couldn't see where they were running and kept crashing into the trees. The drifters, seeing the idiots running wild through the woods, were scared off. After some time, the guys made it to a clearing and decided to go home, leaving behind their camping gear, which, luckily, was still there the next day. Their parents, noticing the boys were badly bruised, thought they had gotten into a fight.

Spike tells us a few other stories of his escapades in the place, each one of his shenanigans funnier than the previous. After about an hour, Judy says she has to go to the bathroom.

"Just go in the bushes behind some trees," Spike suggests.

"What happens if someone comes along?" she asks.

"Joey and I will be lookouts," he assures her.

"I can't go in the woods; I'm just not comfortable," Judy protests. "Isn't there a bathroom nearby?"

"What about Fordham Hospital?" I suggest. "It's located across the street from the park."

"I've got a better idea," Spike says. "There's a bathroom across the river at a restaurant in the park. I'm sure the restaurant is closed this time of year, but the bathrooms should be open."

"How far is it?" Judy asks, "I really need to go!"

"Not far, just over the stone bridge, which you can see from here," Spike assures her. "Not more than a five-minute walk."

We fold our blankets, pick up our provisions, and head for the bridge. Right after crossing the bridge, we see the public restaurant on the left-hand side. The restaurant is closed; however, the restrooms are open, just as he predicted. We wait for Judy in the courtyard behind the restaurant. While sitting on top of the stone wall that surrounds the courtyard, Spike notices a wooden footbridge straddling the river a few hundred yards away. After Judy comes out, he convinces us to go and inspect it.

The bridge is made of a wooden board, some thirty-five feet long, two feet wide, and two inches thick. Two long boards are nailed on each side of the bottom board, rising some six inches in height but no more than an inch thick.

"Why don't we use the footbridge as a raft?" Spike suggests. "We can let the current move us down river, using our hands to paddle for direction. Once we get down river, there's a secret destination I'd like to show you."

Not being a swimmer, I'm about to protest, but Judy beats me to it. "That bridge isn't sturdy enough to hold the four of us. It will sink from our weight!" she exclaims.

"It'll hold all of us if we spread out over its length," Spike insists.

"I can't swim!" I reveal finally, terrified at the thought that such a small wooden board will be the only barrier between the river and me.

"You won't sink!" Spike assures me. "Just kneel and hold onto the sides. You won't have to do anything else. Just leave it up to me."

That's exactly what I'm afraid of, leaving it up to him. Spike has no fear. He gets himself out of trouble as easily as he gets into it. I have no such skills. Should the raft sink, I'm a goner.

"What happens if the raft capsizes?" I ask.

"The river rapids aren't that strong; it won't turn over," he says. "Should anything go wrong, hold onto the raft, and I'll swim over to get you. Besides, the river isn't that deep; you can probably walk to shore."

"I still don't believe that skinny footbridge will hold all four of us," Judy says.

"Look, let's maneuver the bridge off the riverbank. While you hold one end, I'll walk out to the other side that's floating out in the water. If it holds me, you know it will work."

Following his suggestion, we maneuver the footbridge off the far bank and let it float freely in the water. With the three of us gripping one end, Spike strolls out to the opposite end. As he predicted, the bridge holds his weight. He shouts for Betty to walk out and join him on the raft. Without hesitation, and as calmly as can be, she walks out on the raft and reaches Spike on the other side. The footbridge still holds without any problem.

"See?" he says, "if it can hold Betty's and my weight in one area, surely it will hold the four of us spread through its full length."

The demonstration convinces Judy, and, not wanting to be the only coward in the group, I decide to go along. We pull the bridge back close to the bank and load our blankets and picnic basket onto it. We take our positions, about five feet apart, with Spike as the pilot in the front and me in the rear. As the front of the footbridge drifts off, I push the rear end away from the bank, and the current begins moving us down the stream.

Immediately, I realize my genius cousin's miscalculations. Because it's early spring, the river has swelled from the melting winter snow. The water is much deeper than Spike calculated. The rapids are also more severe than he predicted. Don't get me wrong; it's not whitewater rafting, but still, to a person who can't swim, it's quite frightening. I'm convinced that the raft will capsize, and I'll be the only one to drown. It takes a while to get the knack of controlling the cumbersome bridge. We keep crashing into the riverbank or getting stuck on vegetation, which grows alongside the river. Getting caught and banging on the rocks, which crop out from the water is not my favorite, especially since Betty and Judy scream every time we hit one.

Spike works hard to set us free from the obstacles, and a few times, has to strip down to his underwear and dive into the icy spring water to free the raft, Betty handing him the blanket afterward to dry himself off. At one point when Spike is trying to disentangle the raft from the roots of a tree on a riverbank, the raft turns around completely, and I'm in the lead position. Terrified, I don't know what to do. The raft is heading down river with my back turned in the wrong direction. I'm convinced that we'll crash into a protruding boulder, and I'll go flying off. I'm so scared I dig my fingernails onto the sides of the raft and hold on for dear life.

Fortunately, the footbridge rights itself in the current, and I'm in my more comfortable position in the rear once again. After what seems like a lifetime, we arrive at the underpass that divides the Botanical Gardens from the Bronx Zoo. We notice a chain link fence hanging down from the bridge, obstructing our path. The fence almost touches the water. I'm convinced we can't get through and our journey is over. Spike notices a spot on the fence that's broken. With a little effort, he reasons, he can pull back enough of the fence to let the raft by. With this accomplished, the raft floats under the bridge, and we enter the Bronx Zoo.

The river opens into a wide, shallow bend approximately four hundred feet across. Just to the right of the expanse is Spike's secret destination, a small tree-lined island.

"There it is, ladies and gentlemen, Monkey Island!" he proclaims excitedly as the islet comes into view.

"Monkey Island?" Judy asks. "Are there monkeys there?"

"No! It's just a name the kids have given the island."

"Are you sure?" Judy asks, her concerns not completely alleviated.

"Absolutely, the place is completely desolate."

With a little hand paddling, we reach the island. We pull the raft on land and go ashore. Once we get to the interior of the small island, I understand why Spike wanted to take us there. The vegetation is so thick, even this early in the season, it's impossible for anybody on the shore to see us. We have our own private island refuge. Despite the terror, I experienced during the ride, it's worth it. The trip was like the adventure of Huckleberry Finn rafting down the mighty Mississippi. Granted, the Bronx River is not the Mississippi, but Huck knew how to swim.

"How did you know of this place?" Judy asks as we spread our blankets.

"A couple of the guys and I walked out here one winter when the river was frozen. I always wanted to come back when it was warmer," Spike replies. "When I saw the footbridge today, I knew I'd get my chance."

"This is really nice," Betty says, summing up all our sentiments.

Spike is not happy with the spot where Betty has laid their blanket. He picks it up and moves it behind some shrubs about twenty feet away. "This way we'll all have privacy," he explains.

There's no way anybody from shore can see us; the trees and the vegetation are so thick. Betty takes out the sandwiches and sodas and divides them among us. After lunch, Judy and I sit on our blanket, staring silently at the river flowing by. I glance over to where Spike and Betty have their blanket, and they're already making out. To pass the time, I start making small talk with Judy. A few moments later, I glance over at Spike and Betty, and despite the shrubs partially blocking my view, I can see Betty, her chest bare, on top of Spike. The whole thing is making me extremely horny, so I pull Judy down on the blanket, and we begin making out. It's not long when I slide my hand under her sweater and up her back. I try to unhook her bra, but I'm not having any success.

"Oh, for heaven's sake!" Judy says, exasperated by my inability to unhook her bra.

She reaches back and unfastens it with one hand. I push her sweater up in the front, and with her bra loose; her breasts are free. Judy has nice, firm breasts, not as large as Betty's but certainly nothing to be ashamed of. After fondling her two soft mounds for a few minutes, I bend down and begin kissing her nipples. This is the furthest I've ever gotten with her, and I'm waiting for the usual stop order. Since Judy says nothing, I press on and pull her sweater and bra over her head. She doesn't object! As I'm going about my business, I glance over at Spike. Betty is still on top, naked and moving in an unmistakable sexual motion.

Seeing the couple in action strengthens my will, and I begin kissing Judy's stomach, stopping to twirl my tongue in her navel. Finally, summoning up my courage, I unbutton her pants, fully expecting the no-go signal, which has always come before. She doesn't say a word! Fully excited, I pray I don't come in my pants. Once her pants are unbuttoned, I tug at them, attempting to get them off. She lifts her body up and helps me work them off.

At that point, I know this will be my day, and I'm finally going to score. All I'm thinking, don't come in your pants, fool, and you'll finally lose your virginity. She's almost completely naked, covered only by her pink panties. I rise up slightly to take it all in. She's beautiful! Sliding my hand down, I stroke her thighs and crotch, nibbling at her ears and kissing her neck as I caress her. Finally, I tug at her underwear, and again she rises up slightly and assists with their removal. Fearing that something might still go wrong and not wanting to tempt fate any longer, I unfasten my belt to remove my pants.

"Do you have protection?" she asks once my slacks are off and I'm about to get on top of her.

For an instant, panic sets in. So close, only to fail again. Then I remember the condom I stashed in my wallet on my first date with Judy those months ago. Relieved, I pull out my wallet and locate the indispensable packet. Although the wrapper shows wear, it's still intact.

"Sure!" I reply confidently, showing Judy the packet.

Fumbling for a minute, I manage to get the wrapper open. Having never seen a rubber, I hope I know how to put it on. I stare at it for a moment and then realize it's not difficult. Slipping the rubber over my penis, I concentrate on Judy.

"Joey," she whispers as I lie on top of her. "Please be gentle. This is my first time, and I don't know what to do."

"I'll be gentle," I reassure her. After a few attempts, I manage to work my way inside her. At last!

As promised, I'm tender, slow, and gentle. Her eyes close, and she doesn't make a sound. I wonder what she's thinking. How does it feel for her? For some unexplained reason, I manage to control myself and not come the minute I penetrate her. I kiss her neck as I move my body up and down in a gentle, rhythmic motion.

She picks up my tempo and starts moving in unison under me. As we progress, our pace picks up, and we thrust our bodies harder and harder. After about ten minutes of this rhythm, I can't hold out any longer, and I explode inside her. We lay there embracing tenderly for a few minutes longer, and then I pull out. As I remove my condom and put on my clothes, I look over at Judy, and she's already dressed.

"You better not tell anybody we did this!" she warns. "If I find out you told a soul, we're through."

I can't believe it, I've finally scored, and no one will know. The whole world will continue to think I'm a pathetic virgin. Don't tell a soul? Heck, I want to shout it to the entire world! What a bummer. If I talk, we're through, so nobody will ever find out. We finish dressing and are sitting in silence when Spike and Betty come over.

"We better start back," Spike says. "It's getting late, and Betty has to work at Sears tonight."

We board the footbridge once more and paddle to shore. Once on land we push the trusty raft out into the river, and the current carries it downstream. Now we're inside the Bronx Zoo. Spike points to a road that leads to an exit, and we set out on that path. Judy and Betty walk and talk some ten feet in front of us.

Spike turns to me with a wink and a smile. "Congratulations, Priest. You finally scored."

I smile back, but don't say a word. Spike witnessed the whole thing. This is the best possible scenario. I don't have to break my promise to Judy and tell anybody. Whenever the guys make fun of my virginity and Spike is around, he'll tell them I'm not a virgin, and the taunting will stop. No one will question Spike's veracity on the matter. Elated, I walk home on a cloud.

However, my joy is short lived.

"I hope you're not under the impression we're doing that again!" Judy decrees the next day.

"Why not?" I ask, confused and disappointed.

"Because I'm no tramp!"

"I don't think you're a tramp because we did it. My feelings are the same toward you as they were before."

"And I'm going to make absolutely certain it stays that way!" she replies.

"You mean we're never, ever going to do it again?" It's more of a plea than a question.

"Well, maybe not never, but not for a while."

"Didn't you enjoy it at all?"

"Enjoying has nothing to do with it!" Judy replies. "I did it to prove how much I love you. When I saw Betty and Spike doing it, I wanted to demonstrate to you that my love was equal to hers."

"Don't I have a say in this matter?"

"If you love me, you'll respect my wishes. If not, well, it's entirely up to you. Maybe we shouldn't go out anymore!"

Over the next few days, not only are we not doing it anymore, Judy barely lets me touch her. She's completely defensive, out to prove she's no slut, and nothing I can do or say will sway her from this posture. The situation is worse now than before we did it. In frustration, I spend an increasing amount of time at the gym working out. On the bright side, I'm developing quite a muscular physique. The guys are beginning to refer to me as Little Hercules.

CHAPTER 23

Betty's Story

Crabby is missing again, and Spike asks me to help look for him. It's past dinner time, and Crabby hasn't been seen since this morning. We check Crabby's usual haunts: the fish stores. Crabby usually stands in front of the store for hours until somebody gives him a crab. He gets so many crabs that his mother has to keep them in an aluminum washtub on a kitchen counter. When there's no more room, she makes a spaghetti and crab dinner. When that happens, Crabby locks himself in his room, crying inconsolably over the fate that's befallen his crustacean companions.

What's the poor woman to do? Let the stupid crabs overrun the apartment? With so many fish stores in the community, there's no end to the crabs Crabby brings home. After looking at all the usual spots, Spike decides to try Hyman's hobby shop just off Tremont.

"Hey, Hyman, how's it going? Have you seen Crabby today?" Spike asks the old man behind the counter when we get to the store.

"He's in the back room with some other boys, Spike," Hyman answers, "he's been here all day."

Hyman's back room is devoted to model trains. The place is fantastic, and many of the neighborhood kids spend hours upon hours working the switches of the trains. When we get there, two boys are at the controls as two trains make their way around the tracks. Crabby is sitting on the opposite side of the tables watching the action.

"Hey, Crabby, "What are you doing?" Spike asks when we get to him.

"I'm waiting for the boys to finish so I can have a turn running the trains."

"Just how long are you planning to wait?" Spike asks "What the hell is wrong with you? Don't you know it's past dinnertime? Your mother has been looking all over for you."

"Is my mother mad?" Crabby asks, looking worried.

"Just tell her you were playing at Hyman's and lost track of the time," Spike says. "She won't be angry. Go straight home. Don't stop off at any fish stores!"

With that, Crabby cheers up and heads home with that distinctive Crabby gait. His stride is more of a bounce or a skip than a walk. Each step ends with him rising up on his toes. His heels never touch the ground.

"Hey, Hyman, when did you start selling comic books?" Spike asks as we head out of the shop.

"Just began this month," Hyman says.

Spike picks out the latest edition of Batman.

"Spike, you can get the same comic book for five cents less at Nat's," I whisper, but my usually frugal cousin dismisses my advice.

"Who's got time to go to Nat's?" he asks as he puts fifteen cents on the counter.

"How's business?" he asks Hyman.

Hyman shakes his head. "Not good, Spike. Ever since they built that God-awful road, nothing has been the same. I thought with the new projects going up on 180th Street, things would get better, but they haven't. The new people either don't have the money or aren't interested in hobbies. My brother, Jacob, wants me to close the place and retire with him in Florida. I've resisted for years, but lately, it doesn't seem like such a bad idea."

"Oh, come on, Hyman, what are you going to do in Florida? That place is not for you," Spike says.

Hyman shrugs. "I don't have much of a choice. Business won't pick up, and I can't afford the rent. I'm sticking it out a little longer, but if things don't get better soon, I'm closing the place. Can you believe it, Spike? I've had this place for thirty-three years."

Hyman shakes his head at the thought. "When are you coming over for dinner again, Spike? Bess has been asking about you. She's anxious to cook the matzo ball soup you like so much. If you come, she'll also make the cheese blintzes. You'll do me a personal favor. She doesn't make blintzes for anybody else. I haven't had blintzes since the last time you were over."

"How about Thursday?" Spike suggests.

"Thursday is good," Hyman says. "Try to get there by six thirty."

"Can I bring Betty?"

"Of course. She's a lovely young lady, even though my wife might be disappointed. With Betty around, she won't be able to shower you with all of her attention."

"What happened to Hyman?" I ask Spike when we're outside. "I can't believe he's going out of business. He's got so many cool things!"

"He's one of the casualties of the Cross Bronx," Spike says.

"What's the Cross Bronx have to do with Hyman's store?"

"That road cuts right through the neighborhood and cuts off Hyman's store from half his customers. The people on the other side of the highway have no easy way to get there. Hyman isn't the only one. Hundreds of stores went out of business, which made matters worse. Thousands of people lost their jobs and moved out of the area.

"A lot of the buildings next to the highway are almost vacant, and the landlords can't find anybody who'll rent the apartments. I heard a rumor that one of the owners hired someone to torch his place to collect the insurance money. Now the politicians are building a city of tenement houses on some marshland near Orchard Beach. Co-op City it's called. When it's finished, it's supposed to house nearly a hundred thousand people.

Spike looks at me. "Let me tell you, Priest, when that happens, the Bronx will be ablaze."

Spike can talk about this subject for hours, and he would have if we had not passed by a social club on the way back that some gangsters frequent. Most of the mobsters are sitting around some tables out front. Fat Augie and two other guys are standing in front of the doorway. When Augie notices Spike walking by, he calls him over.

"Where's your gorgeous sidekick?" Augie asks, referring to Betty.

"She works at Sears on Saturdays until seven."

"Why are you so greedy with your beautiful girlfriend? Why don't you share her with the rest of the world?" one of the hoods asks, trying to be funny.

Spike's demeanor changes immediately as he glares at the man. Augie senses the same thing.

"What's wrong with you, you freaking moron?" Augie asks, turning to yell at the guy. "Why would you talk like that about some guy's woman? Just go in the club and leave us alone. I want to talk to Spike by myself, you fucking jerk!"

The gangster retreats into to the club, not wanting to get Augie any angrier.

"Don't mind him, Spike," Augie says. "He's uncouth; that guy has no class."

It's a good thing Augie is around. Otherwise, the whole thing could have turned ugly. Spike probably would have decked the guy. Like Spike, Augie is a great dresser. He's wearing a light blue suit, which is tailored just for him. Although his clothing is of a different fashion than his young protégée, his clothes are also first rate. Augie, however, has custom-made suits, while Spike, due to his budget constraints, is limited to of-the-rack clothes.

Still, it's Spike who turned Augie onto his Lebanese shirt maker. After Augie purchased some shirts from the Middle Eastern tailor and bragged to the other gangsters about their magnificent workmanship, the rest of the wise guys began emulating their boss and buying their shirts from the same tailor. The gangsters begin referring to a trip to the shirt maker in lower Manhattan as, "I'm going to the Arab."

Unlike Spike, who prefers subdued colors, the hoods prefer vibrant, contrasting hues. The thugs would never concede to donning a shirt that could be described using the word "pastel."

"How you been?" Augie asks, putting his arm around Spike's shoulders. "You're not doing drugs like your old Irish friend, are you?"

"You know I'm not," Spike fires back, not too pleased with the query.

"What a waste! Your pal could have been a middleweight champion," Fat Augie says. "You getting along with your girlfriend?"

"We're doing just fine, Uncle Augie," Spike responds, answering the man's questions patiently and respectfully, even though the topic appears to make him uneasy.

"She's a great kid; you do right by her," he warns, looking into Spike's eyes, obviously referring to Spikes amorous tendencies.

"I'm doing just fine," Spike assures him, knowing exactly what Augie is getting at.

"You're a good looking boy. You've got to be careful. A lot of women are going to come on to you. You got to know how to behave. Just make sure you don't hurt that girl. It's going to take a lot of willpower."

"I know, Uncle Augie. I'll behave," Spike says, keeping his responses short in the hopes of bringing the conversation to a quick end.

"How's Olga?" Augie asks shrewdly.

◆ ◆ ◆ ◆ ◆

Olga Hessmark is a gorgeous, petite brunette who lives two buildings down from us. She was born in Germany and has the loveliest German accent. She's married to a fellow who is some sort of executive at a company that makes cystoscopes on Eastchester Road. Olga is a baby-making machine. Barely twenty-nine, she has already borne four children. Having babies seems to agree with her, though, as she appears to get more beautiful every time she has one.

All the wise guys tried to get into Olga's pants, and whenever she passes the social club, they fall all over themselves trying to score. Olga does her best to lead them on. She wears the most provocative outfits. One day, Spike was sitting talking to Augie when Olga passed by. Augie turned to the wise guys.

"Let Spike have a turn at Olga. He'll show you how to put on the moves."

Usually, Spike doesn't get involved with manhood contests, but Olga looked particularly alluring that day. She was wearing tight white shorts and an even tighter navy blouse with her top buttons open, partially exposing her voluptuous breasts. Olga knew the exact reaction the outfit would have on the men, and she was not disappointed. All the guys went wild when they saw her.

Spike, trying to impress the big guy, relented and put the moves on her. He must have been just what Olga was looking for, because she fell for him immediately, much to the delight of Fat Augie, who was pleased that Spike had accomplished what none of the other hoods had been able to do. As I noted earlier, I witnessed one of Olga and Spike's lovemaking sessions in the clubhouse when he was making love to her from behind while she was on her knees.

◆ ◆ ◆ ◆ ◆

"That was over long ago. I'm not interested in her any longer." I can tell Spike is losing his patience. "Listen, Uncle Augie, you don't have to worry," he says. "I'm playing it straight with Betty!"

"Good!" Augie replies, convinced that Spike is being truthful. "Listen, I have these four box-seat tickets to tomorrow's doubleheader at Yankee Stadium." He pulls the tickets out of his jacket. "I want you to have them. Take Betty to the game, and maybe your cousin here can bring his girlfriend and go along with you."

"Thanks, Uncle Augie. I really appreciate it," Spike says as he tucks the tickets in his shirt pocket.

A trip to Yankee Stadium is something Spike would never turn down. With his arm still around Spike's shoulder, Fat Augie pulls out a fifty-dollar bill and sticks it in Spike's pocket alongside the tickets.

"Here's something to make sure you show her a good time!"

"No, Uncle Augie. That's not necessary. The tickets are more than enough." Spike takes the bill from his pocket and attempts to hand it back.

Spike always gets flustered whenever Fat Augie tries to give him money. When Spike's father abandoned the family, Augie tried to step in and provide financial support for the impoverished clan. Even in those lowly, desperate times, Spike refused to accept any charity from the big fellow. Aunt Lucy, however, was not as proud as her son, and Augie would slip her some cash, behind Spike's back.

Due to his financially strapped condition, Spike may have been tempted by criminal life if not for Augie, who made certain Spike didn't get involved with any racketeering activities. Although Augie is the head of the crime family in the area, he doesn't like his lifestyle. Having made his mistakes in his youth, Augie no longer has any options. There are no career changes or retirement plans in his profession. "You're destined for better things than this miserable life," he tells Spike.

"Just consider it payment for all the errands you've done for me," Augie counters, refusing to take back the money.

"You've already paid me for those errands, Uncle Augie. This is really too much," Spike insists.

"Don't embarrass me in front of the guys; just take the money!" Augie says, pushing the bill back in Spike's pocket. "Just make sure you give me a good table at the wedding reception when you and Betty get married."

"I'll put you on the dais with me," Spike says as he tucks the bill into his pocket alongside the tickets. As Spike and I leave, Augie turns to his men.

"Betty and Spike are the most beautiful couple I have ever seen." Even if the statement were untrue, nobody would dare argue with him.

That Sunday, with four great tickets in hand, we take the D train on the Concourse and set out for Yankee Stadium. The Yankees are playing the Cleveland Indians. The seats are great, just behind the first base dugout, some three rows back. We arrive at the top of the second inning. This is my first visit to a major league park, and it's spectacular. The most striking feature is how green the grass is on the playing field, especially in contrast with the blue stadium seats.

Sitting between Betty and Judy, I can't help but notice how much of a couple Spike and Betty have become. Betty is sitting with her legs curled under her, one arm interlocked with Spike's, her head leaning on his shoulder. They seem like they've been together forever. I can't believe I ever thought I had a chance with her. There's no way anybody but Spike had a prayer of scoring with Betty.

The Yankees win the first game and are leading in the fifth inning of the second when we decide to leave. The girls, who are just wearing shorts and a light sweater, are cold. When we get back to the neighborhood, Spike decides to separate himself from some of Fat Augie's money and treats us to pizza at the Half Moon restaurant. While the four of us are eating our pizza, who should come walking into the restaurant but the big man himself. Accompanying Augie are two of his cronies. Spotting us, he pulls up a chair between Betty and Spike.

"How did you like the game, gorgeous?"

Betty blushes at the compliment and then composes herself. "Just great Uncle Augie. Thanks for the tickets. The seats were great."

"Is that right? Well, if the game was so great, how come you were sleeping on Spike's shoulder?"

"How did you know?" she asks, mystified, because she did sleep for a portion of the game.

"Let that be a lesson to you lovebirds. I know everything you do. Don't think you can hide anything on Uncle Augie."

"We saw you on the television," one of Augie's henchmen blurts, solving the riddle. "The cameraman must have had a thing for you, because he kept showing you on TV. We saw you at least three times."

Annoyed at the man's untimely interruption and the fact he revealed his mystery, Augie turns and glowers at the two goons.

"Why don't you guys use your big mouths to get us a table and leave me here to talk to the kids?"

"What did I say?" the hood asks his buddy as they walk off.

"How could the cameraman resist photographing such a beauty?" Augie asks, squeezing Betty's cheeks.

The waiter comes over and sets down a glass of red wine for Augie.

"Will you be eating here or at the usual table?" he asks.

"No, I'll be at the usual table. I'm just going to talk to the kids for a few minutes. Make sure you put their check on my tab," he says.

"What's for dinner?" Augie never reads a menu; the cook decides what to serve him.

"He's making you tripe with linguine," the waiter replies as he walks off.

Augie nods and turns back to Betty as the waiter leaves. "How's Spike treating you?"

"Pretty good," she replies quickly.

"Because if he's not, I can take care of it for you," he says as he grabs Spike in a headlock and, making a fist, feigns punching him.

"Well, if you put it that way, Uncle Augie, there are a few things I wouldn't mind changing," Betty replies, smiling coyly, her tongue sliding over her lips in anticipation of what Augie will do next.

Augie pulls Spike tighter. "Just say the word, doll, and ba-ra-bing!" He makes believe he's about to punch Spike.

Betty bursts out laughing.

"Now that's what I mean. Listen to that beautiful laugh. It makes my whole day," Augie says, satisfied with Betty's reaction.

"Augie, your tripe is ready, and it's at your table," the waiter says.

"Well, bring it back to the kitchen, and tell him to keep it warm. But make sure it doesn't dry out! I'm not done talking with the kids."

He turns back to Betty. "Listen, sweetheart, I just want to tell you something about Spike. All his life, Spike has been a lone wolf. He doesn't know how to play as a team. He's arrogant, taking a lot of chances, always thinking his smarts will pull him out of any mess he gets himself into. Somehow, they usually do. This is the first time he's had a partner to consider. He's going to make mistakes. You need to have a lot of patience with his thick head, but eventually, he'll come around. I know you two were meant for each other."

"Oh, Uncle Augie, are we going through this again? Can you give me a break?" Spike asks.

"All right, smart guy, I'm through," Augie says. He turns to Judy and me. "Sorry I interrupted your dinner."

The big man kisses Betty goodbye. As he leaves to join his men, he taps Spike lightly and affectionately on the face.

Betty's father is working another night shift, so she invites us to her apartment after dinner. She puts an album on the phonograph and then cuddles with Spike on a chair. Judy and I are on the sofa.

"When did you guys first realize you liked each other?' Judy asks.

"I always liked Anthony, ever since I first laid eyes on him in the fourth grade," Betty says.

"I knew it!" Judy exclaims. "But why did you two wait so long to go out?"

Betty looks at Spike. "You'll have to ask slowpoke over here. If it were up to me, we would have been going steady long ago."

"First of all, in the fourth grade, I had just arrived from Italy," Spike says. "Not speaking the language nor knowing the customs, I was in no position to consider girls. I was too busy just trying to belong and feel my way. Besides, I never thought that Betty, who was a foot taller than me at the time, had any interest in me."

"If you liked Spike, how come you went out with Joey Cooks?" Judy asks.

At that moment, I'm convinced that Judy's big mouth is doing it again, bringing up things that are none of her business. I peek over at Spike to see whether or not the question has any effect on him. If it did, he's not showing it.

"Since Anthony had never given me any indication whatsoever that he had the least bit of interest in me, I thought I had no chance with him. After my mother died, I was very lonely. I had no friends, and Joey was the only one who paid any attention to me. He seemed like a nice guy, so I agreed to go out with him."

With Betty's response, I heave a sigh of relief, believing we have negotiated a minefield.

Judy ruins it. "How come you did that thing with Cooks?"

We all know exactly what Judy means, and at that point, I know she's gone too far.

"Is that really important?" I ask Judy, my eyes on Spike.

He doesn't appear to be the least bit bothered by Judy's line of questioning.

Betty looks at Spike.

"What?" he asks.

"Should I tell them?"

He shrugs. "It's your story. If you're comfortable, go ahead."

"I don't mind answering," Betty says. "After going out with him a few times, I realized Cooks was not for me. I had determined that I would break up with him. I just didn't want to hurt his feelings. One day, we were sitting in the hallway, and I had this massive migraine headache. He kept pestering me that I should… touch his private parts. With my head pounding, I finally agreed to do it and hoped that would be the end of it. He unzipped his trousers, and as I was about to reach in and touch it, he began coming in his underwear. The whole episode struck me as funny, and I burst out laughing. Embarrassed, he zipped up his pants and ran off.

"The next day, I was shocked to hear that he'd gone around and told the entire neighborhood that I had masturbated him. Nobody would believe otherwise. I know what I did was wrong, but I didn't deserve the awful name they gave me, especially since I really hadn't done anything. I never even touched him! After about a week passed and the rumors would not subside, I became extremely depressed. I even thought of committing suicide. Sinking in this deep hole, I couldn't figure any way to get out. All of the kids in the neighborhood were calling me 'Palm.'"

Betty looks at Spike. "Then one day, when I was sitting on the stoop in front of my building, feeling miserable and dejected, Anthony happened by. Seeing me so down, he sat beside me and tried to get me to reveal my problem."

She pauses for a moment. "At first, I was afraid to share my feelings, especially to admit to the boy whom I loved that I had tried to touch another boy's private parts. Eventually, with his gentle, persuasive manner, I agreed to confide in him, even disclosing that I was contemplating taking my own life.

"'That would certainly solve your problem, not the best way, but it would end your troubles. But what about your father?' he asked. 'Have you given any thought on how he'd feel if you ended your life?'

"'What would you do if you were in my place?' I yelled back, not believing that anybody could possibly know what I was going through. He told me about the time when he—"

Spike jabs Betty in the side, stopping her in her tracks.

"Oh, I'm sorry," she says to him. She pauses for a while to gather her thoughts and continues her story. "Then Anthony said to me, 'Well for starters, I wouldn't be such a coward.'

"'It's easy for you to say; you're not the one going through my problems!' I yelled back, annoyed at his smugness. 'You don't have this ugly nickname. You're not the laughing stock of the entire neighborhood.'"

"'Listen, I don't want to sugarcoat it,' he said. "What you did was wrong. But the error is not so bad that it should be punished by death. You made a mistake, the most serious of which is showing poor judgment about the boy you're dating. That's not so serious. I'm sure people will forgive you. You have to take responsibility for your actions, make amends, and start fighting back.'

"'I don't even know where to begin,' I answered pathetically.

"'The first thing you need to do is tell your father,' Anthony advised.

"'Tell my father?' I said in horror. 'Are you out of your mind? That's the last man I want to tell what I did. I can't tell him. It would break his heart. My poor dad has already suffered enough.'

"'Look, Betty,' Anthony told me, 'sooner or later, your father is going to hear somebody call you by your new nickname. He's going to wonder why they're referring to you by that name. Wouldn't it be better if he learns the real story from you first? I'm sure your father knows you're human and aren't perfect. After all, everybody makes mistakes. I don't know much about the man, but I'm sure he'll forgive you. The important thing is that he believes you learned your lesson and won't repeat the same mistake!'

"'How about the rest of the kids?' I asked. 'They're not going to be so quick to forgive. What will I do about them?'

"'That's true,' he agreed. 'The kids are going to be a much tougher problem, but if you're willing to stand up for yourself, I'll be by your side every step of the way. Together, we'll find a way to get through this mess. Someday, things will change. I promise you.'

"And, of course, Anthony was absolutely right. My father did forgive me, and, as you can see, things have changed."

"That's really a great story," Judy says.

After that, Spike and Betty go into her room. Judy and I begin necking on the couch. After about an hour or so, I can tell I'm not going to get very far. With the exception of letting me stroke her breasts outside her sweater, she puts a halt on all my other advances. While I'm up changing a record on the phonograph, Betty comes out wearing nothing but a bed sheet. She runs into the kitchen, grabs a Coke from the fridge, and rushes back into her bedroom.

Seeing Betty with only the sheet around her and realizing what they're doing in the next room, I rejoin Judy back on the sofa, more determined than ever to have my way with her. My aggressive attitude leads to a major argument, and we decide to call it a night. We knock on Betty's bedroom door and tell her and Spike we're leaving and let ourselves out.

CHAPTER 24

Goodbye, Rudy Kazoody

School is finally over, and we settle into a lazy summer routine. After adjusting to the workload at high school, my grades aren't bad at all, and my parents are pleased with my performance. While my report card is probably not as good as Spike's, I'm still proud of my accomplishment.

I while away most of my time that summer going to the beach and showing of my new muscular body. Both Betty and Judy come to the beach quite regularly with me. The beach we visit most frequently is Orchard Beach. Just one bus ride from Fordham takes us directly there. Orchard Beach is split into thirteen different sections. We prefer section eight, although most of the kids in the neighborhood like thirteen. There's a new music craze going through the rock and roll world, the surfing songs from the west coast. Due to the popularity of the new west coast beat, the beaches are more crowded than usual.

Spike rarely goes to the beach. First of all, he works longer hours at the produce market during the summer. Second, he hates lying still on the sand, baking in the sun, doing nothing. Whenever he does go, he wears a huge, embarrassing straw hat to shield his fair skin from the sun. Every time Betty asks him to go, he makes up some lame excuse. The few times he does make the trip, he sits under an umbrella with his shirt on, removing it only to go for a swim.

One of the days when he's at the beach, three members of the Daggers get into a fight with some guys from Morris Park. The Daggers are outnumbered twelve to three. When Spike notices the Daggers are in trouble, he grabs Beast and rushes over to help. Spike and Beast are enough to tilt the balance. Although still outnumbered, our side wins the fight. Our boys really cream the guys from Morris Park, going as far as to smash an empty metal trash can over the head of the one of the boys and cracking his skull.

That night, back in the neighborhood, a rumor spreads through the community that the guys from Morris Park are going to the beach the next day to get revenge. The following day, some two hundred boys from Arthur Avenue show up at Orchard Beach to confront the purported attackers from Morris Park. Spike, Beast, and the three guys from the Daggers who were involved in the initial fight aren't there. They're afraid of being recognized and getting arrested. The rumor about the impending fight turns out to be just that—a rumor. Not one guy from Morris Park shows up.

With all those guys in one spot looking for trouble, it's only a matter of time before something gets started anyway. Someone comes up with the bright idea to walk up the beach and toss people into the ocean, flinging anybody who is in the way into the water. The boys from Arthur Avenue begin with section one and work their way toward section thirteen. Not only do they toss the people in the water, but they also throw the beachgoers provisions into the ocean, including, blankets, umbrellas, radios, coolers, beach chairs, and anything else they can grab.

It's not until the guys get to section seven, almost half-way up the beach, some two hours later, that the police finally bring the riot to an end. It even makes the evening news. The melee gives Spike the perfect excuse to avoid going to the beach. Whenever Betty asks him to go, he says he can't, because he's afraid of being recognized. It's not much of an excuse when you consider Beast was also involved in the fight, and he's going again. Betty doesn't really pressure the point, though. She knows

Spike hates the place. Later that summer, Spike gets a job as an intern at a law firm in the South Bronx, and with the additional hours he's working, it's impossible for him to go.

I like going to the beach with Betty. Whenever she goes to the cafeteria, the guys behind the counter usually give her everything for free. With her looks, she can have any guy wrapped around her finger. All she has to do is give the fellow a smile. She's probably the prettiest girl on the beach. Guys are always trying to make a play for her, and I wonder why Spike lets her go unescorted. Since Betty is so recognizable by the guys from my neighborhood, whenever some fellows from other areas make a play or hassle her, somebody always comes to her side.

The fact is, Spike has nothing to worry about. I never see her stare or even glance at another guy. Betty is totally committed to him. Nor does she really need anybody else's help to get rid of the troublemakers. She's gotten quite good at putting guys in their place. One day, four guys in the cafeteria try to put the moves on Betty. As she's returning to her blanket, they continue to pursue her, unwilling to stop pestering her. One of the four is a real pain in the ass. Frustrated, Betty finally tells the stupid jerk that if he doesn't stop bothering her, she'll kick him in the balls. The fool doesn't heed her warning, and the next thing I see, the pestering imbecile is lying in the sand clutching his groin.

Other than that incident, the first fight, and the riot, the remainder of the summer is basically uneventful. Near the end of summer, our beach crowd decides to have a clam bake as a final send-off to the summer. Everybody in section eight is going. In fact, many people from the other sections will also be there.

"Can you please come?" I overhear Betty ask Spike the day before the big happening.

"I can't, Betty. There's a big deposition tomorrow, and I have to copy, collate, and reference hundreds of documents," Spike says. "There's no way for me to get out of it. Please try to understand."

"I understand," Betty says, "but you've been so busy, we haven't spent any meaningful time together. I just wanted one last summer fling with you."

The next day, our section is mobbed with beachgoers. The word has spread, and it seems like every beach regular is there. Someone has dug a pit in preparation for the bake. Betty is sitting on the blanket with Judy and me. Throughout the day, Betty barely moves from the blanket and hardly talks to anybody. She appears to be going through the motions, but doesn't really want to be there. During the late afternoon, we notice a police scooter heading our way. There's a passenger on the bike dressed in business clothes, his tie is flapping in the wind. The instant Betty recognizes him, she smiles broadly and jumps to her feet.

"Anthony!"

When Spike jumps of the scooter, Betty gives him a hug and a big kiss. "I thought you couldn't come!"

"I worked all night to get everything done," he says. "I didn't tell you, because I didn't know if I could get it finished."

The sun is setting over the horizon, the fire is blazing, and the baking of clams has begun. Someone runs an extension cord to the cafeteria and puts an LP on the phonograph. Within moments, Ben E. King and the Drifters' voices begin singing their songs, making the moment really magical. Spike and Betty walk up the beach while Judy and I sit on the blanket. The air has freshened, and Judy snuggles close. We wrap our blanket around us for warmth and gaze at the gentle waves lapping on the shore. It doesn't get any better than this.

◆ ◆ ◆ ◆ ◆

In late August, my mother is busy cooking tomatoes and jarring the tomato sauce, which we'll use throughout the following year. Cases of tomatoes are strewn everywhere, and jars are all over my room. At least four pots are on the stove, boiling the tomatoes. My father and Josephine are working the strainer. The entire family is involved in the yearly practice.

"Mom, I'm going to take a break and run downstairs for a few minutes," I say when there's a lull in the activities.

"Okay," she replies, "but don't stay down there too long; we're going to need you."

Outside my building, a car pulls up, and Spike gets out. "Hey, Spike, where've you been?" I ask.

"They just put the stone on Sean's grave today, and Satch, Doogie, and I went over to pay our respects," he says as he runs into his place.

A few minutes later, I bring my break to an end and head reluctantly back upstairs to return to the tiresome task of processing the tomatoes. Within a few hours, my mother runs out of basil and orders me out to the vegetable store to buy more. On my way back, I bump into Beast running in the opposite direction. His face is pale, and he looks scared.

"What's the matter, Beast? Are you all right?"

"Betty is on the fire escape threatening to jump!" he exclaims, breathless.

"What? Where?" I ask, still not fully understanding what he's telling me.

"At her building! Come on!" he shouts as he runs off.

I drop the basil and rush after him. We fly the three short blocks to her building. It's similar to mine: two attached buildings, each one four stories high. Steps go down into an alleyway leading to the courtyard. In front of the building are two police cars. Beast and I scamper down the steps two at a time and bolt into the courtyard, where the fire escapes are located. Inside the courtyard, a crowd is gathered and looking up at the roof. Spike and two policemen are on the roof, bent over the ledge, talking to Betty, who is on the metal ladder below them. Harvey, Rafael, and Casper are among the pack in the courtyard when we get there.

"What happened?" Beast asks.

"Cooks and the Disciples must have done something to Betty," Casper says. "One of the girls saw her running away from them in tears. The next thing anybody knows, she's standing on the ladder, threatening to jump."

Hypnotized, we continue looking up, and I pray for Betty's wellbeing. The negotiation between Spike, the cops, and Betty continues above. Spike appears to be doing most of the talking. We can't hear a word, but whatever he's saying appears to be working, as Betty begins climbing back up the ladder. One of the cops leans over to give her a hand when, to our horror, she slips. As she falls, she bounces of one of the rails of the protruding fire escapes and comes crashing down, landing on her back, face up.

I'm so horrified I turn my head and close my eyes. I can't bear to look. When I get the courage to peek out, a cop is bent over Betty. He looks up and shakes his head, signaling nothing can be done. My legs go weak, and I'm about to faint when the back door bursts open. Spike barges through. I have no idea how he got down here so fast; he must have jumped one flight of stairs at a time. He runs to Betty's lifeless body and sits on the ground next to her. Sliding his arms under her, he pulls Betty to him and embraces her, holding her tight against his chest, tears gushing down his face. And then it hits me.

This is the first time that I've ever seen Spike cry. Even when we were kids back in Italy, he never shed a tear. Those years of pent-up emotions have finally caught up with him, and they pour down his face like a deluge. He sits with Betty in his arms, rocking back and forth. The tears streaming down his cheeks are mixed with other fluids pouring out of his nostrils, passing his quivering lips, and landing on Betty. Spike is not making the usual sound of crying or sobbing, but a hollow resonance emanates from within him. It's not coming from his vocal chords, but deep down from the caverns of his soul. The reverberation of his howl echoes throughout the courtyard.

Looking around, I can see that everybody in the courtyard has joined Spike and is in tears. In shock, nobody moves to console the grieving lover, not that it will do any good, as he is inconsolable. He just sits there, rocking back and forth with Betty in his arms, tearful and making that eerie, weird sound. I've never seen anybody look more pitiful or wretched. An ambulance arrives shortly thereafter, and the attendants have quite a task prying Betty from Spike's embrace. Eventually, they loosen her from his clutches and wheel her into the ambulance. Spike jumps inside with them. Completely stunned, no one says a word as we head back to the clubhouse.

On the way, we run into Joey Cooks and some of the Disciples.

"You're a no-good, cock-sucking, motherfucker!" I yell at Cooks when we finally meet up. When he doesn't answer, I shove him. "You're a fucking punk!"

That final taunt does the trick, and he lunges for me. I'm too quick, though, and I begin hurling punches at him. I direct blow after blow at his face. I'm a madman, and he's powerless to defend himself from my furious attack. Trying to back up from my onslaught, Cooks backs into a parked car. I grab his shirt and wrestle him to the sidewalk. Pouncing on his defenseless body, I straddle him and pin his arms under my knees. With his face unprotected, I hurl punches at it unmercifully. My left hand holds his head steady while my right flings one blow after another. Finally, Beast pulls me of him.

"He's had enough! He's out cold!"

Looking down at Cooks' body on the sidewalk, I realize that Beast is right. Gasping for air, I give Cooks one final kick for good measure and walk away.

Betty's wake is at a funeral parlor two blocks north of the clubhouse. It's a one-day affair, with visiting hours from two to four in the afternoon and seven to ten in the evening. Spike and I arrive at the hall early. He's wearing a black suit. His collar is open, his black tie askew. In truth, I don't know how he got any clothes on. Spike is in his traditional grieving posture, unshaven and unkempt. He's not concerned about what he's wearing or how he looks. Aunt Lucy has Vito and me following him all over. She's convinced that Spike is going to do something to harm himself. I don't agree with her.

Spike isn't going to do anything now; the pain is the only thing tying him to Betty. Suicide is too easy. It would end his agony, and Spike wants to hurt. Even though I'm convinced Aunt Lucy is off base, I still do as I'm told and tail him everywhere. Spike sits in the front row next to Betty's dad, and the two sad souls do nothing else but stare at the beautiful girl lying in the coffin, Aunt Bernice's shawl draped around her shoulders.

The minute the parlor opens to visitors that afternoon, the hall fills to capacity. The room gets stuffy from the huge crowd, so I go out to get some fresh air. I reason it's highly unlikely that Spike will try something in the crowded room.

The spectacle that awaits me outside catches me by surprise. The people are lined four wide, and the line extends down the entire block to 186th Street and proceeds around the corner of Hughes Avenue. The procession appears never ending, as the entire two hours of the afternoon visiting session sees no letup in the crowd. Because of the throng, the funeral director keeps the parlor open right through the afternoon break. Spike and Betty's dad sit there the entire time, acknowledging all the visitors.

Moreover, it's not the usual quick salutation. Each attendee sits with them and offers their deep and sincere condolences. After returning to the hall after a brief break to have some dinner, I'm shocked to see that the crowd of visitors in front of the hall hasn't receded at all. In fact, the lines are even longer. People who had been at work are paying their respects. Thousands pass through the room. Spike is unflinching. He never wavers or moves. I never even see him get up to get a drink of water or go to the restroom.

The last person doesn't leave until one in the morning. When that person exits, the director starts locking up. Spike asks him if he can spend the night in the room with Betty. With a little prodding, the man relents and allows him to spend the night at the hall. Aunt Lucy leaves with Mrs. Maderno. When I see the spinster, Scalva's warning to Spike at the hospital comes to mind. I'm not superstitious, but recognizing what's happened makes me pause and wonder.

Still frightened by the prospects of leaving Spike alone, Aunt Lucy has me stay to keep him company. My instructions are to call immediately if Spike does anything unusual. Little good I am as a sentry, being tired from the day's activities, I doze off on one of the couches in the back of the room. It doesn't matter anyway, as the next morning I find the wretched boy, still sitting in the same position in the same seat. He hasn't moved all night.

The funeral is at Saint Raymond Cemetery, just off Tremont Avenue. Spike's mom begs him to go home and wash up before the funeral services. Spike doesn't say a word; he simply ignores her, not having the strength to argue. The procession of cars waiting outside the funeral parlor is so long it requires a huge police escort to the cemetery. Funerals of dignitaries don't get the attention that Betty's affair gets today. But as amazing as the spectacle is at the parlor, nothing prepares me for what is waiting at the cemetery.

The wall of people waiting for us is mind boggling. The entire cemetery appears filled with attendees of Betty's funeral. Two other funerals are scheduled that morning, but they can't get access to their grounds and have to await the end of our services. People have come from all over. There is seemingly no end to the people who know Betty and Spike.

The entire high school is there. So are all the neighborhood gangs, the kids from Southern Boulevard, the PAL, the boxing gym, the social clubs, the two-hand-touch football league, and Fat Augie and all his cronies, even the Disciples, sans Cooks, are there. All the shopkeepers have closed their establishments and are in attendance. Little good it would have done them to stay open anyway; all of their customers are at the funeral.

It's a bright, sunny, August day, but the weather is unseasonably cool. Although Betty is Episcopalian, the Jesuit, Father Diritto, is conducting the services. We wait for a few minutes for the priest to make his way through the massive crowd. Also in attendance is the fireman's band of bagpipers, who are going to play a song for their fellow fireman, Betty's father. When the minister finally makes his way through the large crowd, the services begin.

I look at Spike, standing next to Betty's casket. He's stone-faced, staring straight ahead. Since the time in the courtyard, Spike has not shed a tear, not even a sob or a whimper. As the reverend finishes and they lower the coffin into the ground, the bagpipers play "Amazing Grace." The tune pierces everybody's soul, and tears stream down Mr. Sargent's face. All day, I have tried to fight off the tears, but there's a point where emotions take over and the body loses control. Whether it's the bagpipers playing that sad song or the realization that Betty is really gone, I burst into tears.

I'm not alone. The sadness spreads like a virus, carried through the air by the sound of the tune from the bagpipes. Everywhere I look, people are unashamedly in tears. There isn't a dry eye anywhere. I peek over at Fat Augie and his group. Surely those thugs have to keep up appearances, but I'm wrong. The men stare at the ground, hoping nobody will notice that they're crying. Only Spike's face is dry and expressionless.

After the funeral, Spike says he's going into the clubhouse. Aunt Lucy dispatches me to continue my suicide watch. When I get in, he's reclined on the sofa, his hands clasped behind his head, his legs on the coffee table as he stares at the painting on the wall. We sit there saying nothing until Charla and Lois come in.

"Hi, Anthony," Charla says. "Can we come in?"

Spike simply nods. With Charla and Lois in the clubhouse, I decide to leave and get some fresh air.

"I'll be right outside if you need me," I tell Spike.

Spike says nothing as I walk out. Outside, no one is around. I'm leaning on a parked car when, a few minutes later, Casper happens by.

"Hey, Priest, have you seen my mother?"

"She's down in the clubhouse with Spike and Lois."

Casper nods. "How's he doing?"

"Not too good. His mother thinks he's going to do something to hurt himself."

"Not Spike. He won't take the easy way out."

"I agree. Still, I'm worried about him."

"I'm going to get my mom," Casper says and heads down the steps to the clubhouse. I follow him down. When we get there, Spike is still sitting on the couch, Charla alongside him, while Lois squats in front of him.

"I just wish there was a way to relieve the pressure," Spike says to Lois. "It never goes away."

"I think you should go see Doctor Hollingsworth again," Lois suggests.

"I already went to him months ago when you first suggested it," Spike says. "He was no help."

"You only went to him a couple of times, Sweetie," Lois says, placing her hand gently on his cheek. "A few visits are not enough. I've been under his care for three years now, and I'm only beginning to understand my problem."

"I don't think Anthony needs a doctor," Charla says. "These things take time to heal. Doctors won't make a difference."

"Anthony, you can't do this alone," Lois insists, removing her hand. "This is much harder than you think. Please consider my advice."

"All right, I'll take it into account," he says finally. "Just give me a little time."

They both give him a kiss as they leave with Casper. Alone with Spike once again, I sit directly across from him.

Spike loosens his tie. "I hear you beat the crap out of Cooks."

"Yes, I did!" I reply, thankful to be talking about something other than Betty.

"I should have beaten the shit out of him long ago," Spike says. "He's had it coming for a long time, even if this time he didn't deserve it."

"What do you mean?" I ask. "Of course, he deserved it. One of the girls saw Betty running away from Cooks in tears. He's probably the reason why Betty ran up to the roof."

"Betty was crying before she got to the Disciples. They had actually run over to see why Betty was crying and to see if they could help," Spike says. He shakes his head. "Isn't it ironic, Priest? How things changed. Her biggest tormenters coming to her aid."

"Then why was she crying?" I ask, still confused.

"Because of me!"

"What? Spike, you're not making any sense. What did you do that would make her run up on that roof?"

He pauses for a moment to clear his throat. "Let me tell you what really happened." He clears his throat once again and begins his story. "Nobody was around, and I was just standing in front of the building waiting for someone to show when who came by but Toni Boobs. She and I were talking for about fifteen minutes when she said,

'You know, I've never been in the clubhouse.'

"A warning light should have gone off, but the switch must have been malfunctioning.

"'Doesn't look like much, I'm very disappointed,' she said once inside the place. 'Is this really where you lure and seduce all the innocents? I expected more.'

"'It's not the room they come to see,' I teased.

"'Really, what do they come here to see?' she fired back.

"'The same thing you've come for,' I answered confidently.

"'And that would be?' she asked coyly, walking up and standing right in front of me, daring me to grab her in my arms.

"At that point, the warning light did go off. I knew I shouldn't go any further, but it was Toni Boobs! We've always talked about what she'd be like if we ever got our chance. Well, I was finally getting the opportunity to see if her giant breasts are real. Besides, she had just dared me, and I had a point to prove.

"So I grabbed her in my arms and pulled her to me. Bending down, I gave her the kiss she was longing for. The moment I got the chance, I began unbuttoning her blouse to get a peek and solve the mystery once and for all.

"Once her blouse was unbuttoned, I removed it and dropped it to the floor. There she was, standing in front of me in her bra, the huge mounds exposed, and, by God, they're real! Excited, I unhooked the clasps of her brassiere and freed her breasts. Despite their massive size, they stuck straight out."

At that point, he halts his story and slides his hands through his hair. "Oh God, what did I do? I can't believe I screwed up again and hurt another person that I love. Betty, I'm so sorry!"

His eyes well up from the memory. He regains his composure and continues his story. "Boobs was on top of me on the couch when the door flew open, and Betty was standing in the doorway. Tears were streaming down her face. She slammed the door and ran off.

"As quickly as I could, I got dressed and rushed after Betty, but when I got outside, she was nowhere to be found. I ran to Judy's house, hoping she'd gone there, but Judy wasn't home, and her mother told me that no one had been by. Next, I rushed to Nancy's place, but once again, nobody was around. Running out of options, I decided to try Betty's place.

"At her building, the crowd had already gathered, and Betty was on the ladder of the fire escape. I ran to the roof, three steps at a time.

"At first, the police wouldn't let me through to see her. After I explained that I was her boyfriend, they let me through to see if I could talk her off the ladder.

"'Talk to her very calmly, and whatever you do, don't argue with her,' one of the officers warned me as I got close to Betty.

"'All right,' I agreed and proceeded to the ledge above where she was standing.

"'Betty, I'm so sorry!' I told her the minute I reached her. 'Please, no matter what I did, punishing yourself is not the answer.'

"'Why did you do it?' she asked. 'Am I not enough of a woman for you? Don't I do everything you desire?'

"'This isn't your fault,' I assured her. 'I'm the butthead. You're enough woman for anybody.'

"'If that's true, why did you do it?' she asked.

"'I don't know why. I'm just an immature jerk. I'm just trying to be a big shot. I never took your feelings into account.' I rattled of a list of reasons, one after the other, hoping one would resonate. 'I made a horrible mistake, and I promise I'll never do it again.'

"'How can I ever believe you again?' she asked.

"'Look, Betty, I made a serious mistake and hurt the girl I love. I'm very sorry, and I hope you can forgive me,' I pleaded. 'Haven't you ever made a mistake before? Haven't you ever done something that needs understanding and forgiveness? Now I'm asking for the same treatment. Please forgive me.'

"When she didn't answer, I asked her to just come up the ladder so we could talk in private. 'I'm sure we can work this out. We've known each other too long not to be able to work our way through any problem. Let's just talk.'

"'All right!' she said, finally giving in to my pleas.

"She turned to come up the ladder. One of the cops reached down to give her a hand. The movement startled her, and she jumped back, slipping and falling of the ladder."

I'm stupefied, unable to say anything, simply staring at him.

"So, you see, Priest, you got the wrong guy! I'm responsible for Betty's death, not Joey Cooks!"

We're both silent for a moment. "Listen, Joey, if you don't mind, I'd like to be alone now."

I worry about what Aunt Lucy said, about not leaving him alone. He reads my thoughts.

"Don't worry, I'm not slitting my wrists. Besides, if you want, you can continue to watch over me from that backdoor peephole of yours."

I try not to betray my surprise at the revelation as I get up to leave. "Hey Spike, if you knew about the peephole all the time, how come you never said anything?"

He shrugs. "I don't know. Maybe I thought you could use a good show."

Just for good measure, I go to the back door and look in on him for a few minutes. He sits in that same position, hands clasped behind his head, staring at the painting. Watching him from that position, I realize that Fat Augie, the man for whom reading people and getting it right is a matter of life and death, had it right all along. He knew that Spike was not on the same page as Betty. The relationship needed time and nurturing. It didn't matter that Betty hadn't really gone onto the roof to commit suicide; it still led to catastrophic consequences.

Given time, Spike would have come around, and the two would have had a storybook ending. More importantly, Fat Augie understood Betty. He knew her fragile psyche, and that the minute Spike screwed up, Betty would break. That's what concerned Fat Augie the most. He knew it was only a matter of time before Spike, the lone wolf, made the inevitable misstep. Once the gaffe occurred, Augie must have worried about what the consequences would be. Now we know the answer.

However, I don't agree with Augie that Spike is a lone wolf. He loves being part of the pack. Spike just doesn't like the constraints the pack places on him. With Spike sitting alone in the clubhouse, I wonder whether I should go back in and keep him company when I notice a small crack in the window. How did that happen? The crack is in the lower left-hand corner. It's almost impossible for anything to hit the glass in that spot and cause such damage. When did that happen? Distracted by the broken glass, I forget Spike and go upstairs to my apartment.

◆ ◆ ◆ ◆ ◆

All through the fall, I go to school with a heavy heart. My grades are great, though, the best first quarter I've ever had. I even make the dean's list. While passing Spike's apartment one November morning, I notice the door slightly ajar. Hoping he's home, I let myself in. He's sitting in the kitchen, showered, clean-shaven, wearing his pajama bottoms, eating a bowl of Cheerios with sliced bananas, and reading the Mirror. Sitting alongside him are Crabby and Twitchy.

A Maryland blue crab is crawling on the table. The crab crawls to the edge and falls off. Crabby anticipates the fall and catches it before it hits the floor, placing it back on the center of the table, where the process repeats itself. Spike pays no attention to the crab and continues reading his newspaper.

"What happened, Spike? No Raisin Bran?" I ask as I sit at the table.

"It was time for a change," he replies without looking up.

"How are you doing?"

"Not bad."

"Aren't you going to school today?"

"I have an appointment to see the guidance counselor at ten," he explains as he turns the page. "She wants to talk to me for a few minutes before she gives me my new schedule. I don't have to be in school until then."

We're all silent for a few moments.

"Hey, Spike, how long have you been a sleepwalker?" I ask.

Twitchy gives me a look. "Is that really important!"

"What makes you think I'm a sleepwalker?" Spike asks as he puts down the paper.

Twitch shrugs and shakes his head at me.

"Well, that night your mother said you were sleepwalking. She said you do that a lot," I continue, ignoring Twitchy.

"I've never been a sleepwalker," he says.

"Then why would Aunt Lucy say you were?"

Twitch's glare becomes even more menacing.

"Sit down, Mister Nosy, and I'll tell you a story."

I do as I'm told and take a seat.

"I used to have this recurring dream that I was in the middle of the war, and my grandfather was wounded. Grandpa and I were on an airstrip, and on the runway, was an airplane. The plane was damaged and could only carry one person, so I decided to leave him behind and fly the plane to get help. Unfortunately, I was in a valley and needed to get over some mountains to get the help Grandpa needed.

"The plane, however, couldn't get the altitude to fly over the mountains. No matter how hard I tried, I couldn't get the plane high enough into the air to get over the mountains. The dream always ended with me crashing into the face of the rocks. The nightmare would wake me up, and I wouldn't be able to fall back to sleep. On those sleepless nights, I spent the entire time sitting in front of the house waiting for sunrise. Some neighbors saw me, and, having no explanation for my being there in the middle of the night, my mother told them I was sleepwalking."

"But she said that once you tried to hurt yourself. What was that all about?"

"You're some piece of work!" Twitch blurts, giving me another look.

Spike moves the paper to the side and glares at me. At that point, I'm thinking I may have gone too far.

"I never tried to hurt myself," he says empathically, "My mother is referring to the time I fell out of a tree after Papa Nonno died."

"You fell out of a tree? What happened? And why would your falling from a tree make your mother think you tried to commit suicide?"

"After Papa Nonno died, I felt really depressed," Spike says. "You know how much I loved that old guy. I even thought of doing myself in and went as far as writing a bunch of farewell notes to my family. Each time, however, I crumpled the notes and shoved them into one of my dresser drawers. Eventually, the sad feeling passed, and I got tired of writing the notes.

"One night, I had one of my recurring dreams. It was so bad I couldn't sleep. Luckily, there was no school the next day. Since it was almost dawn, I decided to go to the Sabariello farm and watch the sunrise. Once at the farmstead and watching the sunrise, I began feeling better. Finally, worn out, I fell asleep.

"During my sleep, I felt someone stirring me. It was Papa Nonno. 'Anthony, wake up, there's great danger,' he said. "When I woke up, I looked for him, but he was nowhere to be found. What I did see was a dog walking towards me. The dog was some distance away, but I noticed something strange about him. His head was tilting to one side, and he was wobbly and kept falling as if he was hurt. When he got a little closer, I recognized the problem. The dog had rabies.

"I climbed up a tree that was at the edge of the cliff. The dog took a position underneath and kept looking up at me. Nearly an hour passed, and the dog still wouldn't budge. He laid down, breathing hard. I was perched in the tree for hours, too scared to climb down, when, suddenly I noticed a young girl about a mile away coming in my direction.

"As she neared, I saw it was Stella, one of my classmates. She was carrying a basket filled with lunches for her father and some men who were working in a field nearby. You remember Stella, Priest. We both had a crush on her. I began yelling at Stella, trying to warn her to stay away. Stella couldn't make out what I was saying, though, and my screaming had the opposite effect. She began heading towards me.

"The dog noticed Stella and began walking toward her. Stella couldn't see the animal in the high grass. I knew if I didn't do something, it would attack her, so I decided to climb down the tree and try to distract the beast.

"As I was climbing down, a piece of my shirt got snagged on a branch, causing me to lose my balance, and I fell some two hundred feet down the cliff until some shrubs halted my fall. I couldn't move, my leg was broken.

"The minute she saw me fall, Stella dropped her basket and ran for help. That probably saved her life, because she never did see the dog.

"Stella came back with her father and some of the men who were working with him, and they rescued me from the mountainside and rushed me to the hospital at the provincial capital.

"My mother went into my dresser to bring me a change of clothes at the hospital when she discovered the crumpled suicide notes I had written months earlier. Since nobody had seen the dog, she became convinced I jumped from the tree to commit suicide."

At that moment, the crab climbs up Spike's cereal bowl, knocking it over and spilling the milk and cereal on the table. Spike jumps up and grabs a towel. He holds the crab with one hand while he cleans up the mess with the other. "In the tub," he orders, holding out the crab.

"He won't do it again, Spike," Crabby begs. "I'll hold him."

"Okay, but if he gets loose, he's crab cake!"

"So, what happened? If you weren't sleepwalking, what were you doing in the clubhouse?" I ask. "Why were you blasting the phonograph at four in the morning?"

"Why don't you just mind your own fucking business?" Twitch yells.

Spike, however, merely looks at me for a moment before answering. "The night after Betty died, I dreamed about her. It was such a beautiful dream; we were together again. That's when it occurred to me that while I may not have her in reality, I can have Betty in my dreams. Every night, I'd rush home to fall asleep and dream of Betty, and the dreams were wonderful, each one more fabulous than the one before.

"A few nights later, the old recurring dream reappeared, only this time my grandfather was not the only one hurt at the airport. Betty was also there, and she was injured, too. Now I had to get over the mountain not just to save Papa Nonno, but also to save Betty."

"So that explains it," I say. "You were upset because you couldn't make it over the mountain and save them!"

"No, that's not what happened, Priest. I made it over the mountain!"

"What?" I yelled, almost coming out of my chair.

"Yes, I made it. For the first time in any of my dreams, I made it over the mountain. As I flew over the mountain top, the airport runway on the other side was visible. There was only one more problem: the landing gear was jammed and would not engage. That forced me to make a belly landing on the airstrip.

"The plane rushed headlong down the runway and crashed against another plane. The accident knocked me unconscious, and when I came to, a shadow was standing over me.

"'Who are you?' I asked.

"'I'm Lieutenant Rudy Kazoody,' he answered.

"The spirit woke me. At that moment, I realized the meaning of that final dream. That meaning scared me more than the nightmare itself, and, at that point, I realized I'd never have that dream again."

Spike sits there, frozen, staring at nothing. Nothing comes to mind to break the silence. I'm about to leave when I decide to ask him one last thing.

"Hey, Spike, who is Rudy Kazoody?"

"Don't tell him," Crabby blurts. "He's not one of us."

Spike, however, is in no mood for any more talking. His thoughts have wandered off.

"It doesn't matter, Priest. Kazoody isn't important."

"Well, maybe I'll see you later," I tell him as I get up to leave.

"Yeah, maybe," he replies without looking up.

◆ ◆ ◆ ◆

I'm sitting on the steps in front of my building just after dinner with Aldo and Rafael when Crabby stops by.

"How's it going, Priest? Is Spike around?"

It's the same question he's asked just about every night for the past six months.

"No, Crabby, I haven't seen him." My answer is the same every time.

"Well, if you see him, will you tell him I was by to say hey?"

"Sure, Crabby." Crabby smiles and then bounces away down the street.

We aren't allowed in the clubhouse any longer. Beast was president for a while, but he wasn't any good. Some guys are just better at taking orders. Beast stops hanging with us. He's staying with some kids on Hoffman Street. I hear he has dropped out of school again, too.

Aldo and Reject take over the gang, a sort of duopoly, and for a time, they do a really good job. Then they make the fatal mistake of having a wild party in the clubhouse, and the landlord kicks us out. The Black Knights come to an end. Nothing official. Gangs just seem to die out, like fads. Harvey decides to go back and stay with his old friends on Southern Boulevard. Casper spends most of his time with his band and hardly ever comes around.

The boxing gym closes due to some sort of scandal. Apparently, one of the fighters took money to throw a fight. The New York boxing commission is investigating. Fat Augie made a bundle. Cicci sells the poolroom, and although it stays open, it isn't the same without Cicci at the helm. The girls don't hang with us anymore, but worst of all, Judy and her family decide to take one of those concrete highways Spike and Betty detested so much and move to upstate New York, a town named Pomona. Although it's only twenty miles away, it might as well be in Siberia. We swear we'll stay in touch, but after the first few phone calls, we don't. I hope she's happier in her suburban environment than I was in Orange. Aside from the one time on Monkey Island, Judy and I never made love again.

◆ ◆ ◆ ◆ ◆

I find a telescope in a trash can in the courtyard while taking out the garbage one evening. Aside from a little dirt on the lens, the telescope is in good shape. I don't know why someone would throw it out. As a result of the find, I take an interest in astronomy. I don't get many good nights to view the heavens in the Bronx unless I'm willing to get up really early, just before sunrise.

One such morning, I'm up around four. Mars is due to fly close, and I want to get a good look. The night is crisp and clear as I open the door to the roof. After setting up the tripod and scope, I sit down leaning on the chimney and staring up at the stars, waiting for Mars to appear. Because it's a clear night, the sky is full of stars.

Gazing at the universe, I reminisce about Spike and Betty. They say that time heals all wounds. I'm not sure that's true, but even if it is, sometimes a wound leaves a permanent scar. The Betty and Spike tragedy is my scar, affixed permanently deep within, a constant reminder of the pain suffered long ago.

Somewhere in a science journal, I read that some scientists believe time is relative. The past, present, and future are occurring simultaneously, just at different points of the cosmic measuring stick. They say that if you look up at the night sky, you're actually staring into the past. The stars flickering in that sky actually existed billions of years ago. Tonight, gazing at the starry night, I try to look back at that year when Betty and Spike were around.

My favorite vision comes to mind: Spike is tickling Betty's sides unmercifully as she laughs hysterically on the hood of the automobile parked in front of the clubhouse. With that beautiful thought, I doze off. The morning sun in my eyes awakens me. Mars is long gone. I get up to gather my things to go back down when I notice something scratched into the bricks of the chimney.

A closer look reveals the words "Rudy Kazoody." It's time to put an end to this character once and for all, so I pick up a rusty nail and finish the writing. If you ever visit that particular rooftop on Arthur Avenue and look for those bricks of that chimney, you will find an engraving.

It reads, *"Goodbye, Rudy Kazoody."*

www.ingramcontent.com/pod-product-compliance
Lightning Source LLC
Chambersburg PA
CBHW060858190726

48286CB00002B/288